GRAND Lies

GRAND LIES

JC HAWKE

IVY ROSE PUBLISHING LTD

Dedication

A unicorn once told me...
"People don't read for the story, they read for the way it makes
them feel."
Thank you, Tee.
Without you there'd be no Nina and Mase.

PROLOGUE

Nina
Ten years old

WHORE.

That's what they'd call her. She wasn't ever Sara, Mrs Anderson, or Mummy as she was to me.

"Whore." The word falls from his lips as if it is poison on his tongue, seeping through the paper-thin walls and into my impressionable ears. At the age of ten, I knew right from wrong. I knew not to get into strangers' cars and to look both ways when crossing the road. But still, I wouldn't allow myself to believe the rancid words he'd spit at her—even when the truth in them was easy to see.

My music plays through my headphones, and I spin, feeling weightless. I should go, leave the house and not come back until they are gone. But it's got cold out, and my leggings and cardigan are the only clean clothes I have.

My music calms me, making all the bad in the house quiet for a little while. It's when the shouting and banging starts that I turn up the volume, drowning out my mother's cries. One day I will help her, but I am just a kid. I learnt the hard way not to interfere when it comes to her houseguests. It only ends painfully for me, and the three hospital admissions have only led to social services trying to take me from her.

I don't want to go, but I don't necessarily want to stay either.

A loud thudding penetrates through my headphones, and my body goes rigid. I swallow down the fear in my throat and pinch my eyes tighter together. Don't be a hero, Nina. Don't be a hero.

I continue to dance in the small confinement of my room, ignoring the pain in my mother's voice.

I spin.

"Enough!"

Thud.

"Stop!"

Spin.

Thud.

Spin.

"STO—"

I pull the headphones from my ears, rushing out of my bedroom door on shaky legs. My heart pounds in my chest, but I don't stop, even when everything inside me tells me to leave. *Run! Go down the stairs and out the front door, Nina.*

I have to help her—nobody else will—even if it hurts me.

I've walked into my mother's bedroom twice in the years she has brought *them* here, and both times I ended up in the hospital. My broken wrist was unbearable and not something she could hide even if she tried to.

My nose was left broken for an entire week before she

allowed me back to school. Maggie, my best friend's mum, noticed the minute she saw me and drove me to the hospital. I had a broken nose and a mild concussion. It was already starting to heal, but it meant a visit from my social workers.

Both occasions were the same man. Although my mother sleeps with multiple men, she doesn't always sleep with men like him. Some of them look at me with pity in their eyes before they go to her room.

I grasp the door handle with no plan, quickly turning the knob. I open the door and let it crash into the wall.

"Get off her!" I shout, my fists clenched by my sides.

His hands are around her throat. She looks purple. Her eyes are glazed, and I can see syringes scattered next to them on the bedside table.

My eyes come back to hers, red-rimmed and wide. I need her to give me a sign to tell me what to do.

I get nothing; it's as if she has given up.

"Get off of her!" I shout again.

His hands release from her neck, and he stands. I spin away as he tucks himself into his trousers, and as soon as I hear his boots thudding on the hardwood, I run to my mother's side.

"Leave the cunt to die," he spits at me from the doorway.

My hands shake as I smooth my mother's hair. I don't dare look at him.

He will leave. He will leave.

Please leave.

"I said, leave the cunt to die!" His hand fists my hair, dragging me from the bed.

"Nina," my mother croaks.

I scream out in pain, feeling the roots of my hair clinging to my scalp.

He pulls me to the top of the stairs, hanging me over the top step by my hair. "I don't pay for a little brat to interrupt me. Fucking apologise!"

No.

He lurches my body forward, and I force my hands out to save myself, but he doesn't let me go, wrenching me back by my hair again. "Apologise!" he grunts.

I shake my head once, and then I am floating. In the seconds before my face hits the wooden steps, I pinch my eyes closed and pray it will knock me out—anything to take me away from this hell.

I hear him leave and my mother's cries. Her red dressing gown brushes my cheek as she steps over me and rushes for the door. I pull myself up and sit on the bottom step, adrenaline the only thing keeping me upright.

I did it.

I protected her.

"What were you thinking?!" my mother cries. "Are you going to pay the bills this week? Keep the house heated?!" She stands in front of me, her hair a mess and her eyes wild. I look just like her, but I hope to be everything she isn't when I grow up.

"Get up!" She pulls on my arm, and I hiss.

"Ow, Mum, that hurts."

"You know nothing about pain, little girl. One day you'll grow up and realise the real world isn't a fucking fairy tale. It's about time you started learning."

She drags me to the kitchen and over to the front door. "You think you can be big and brave?" She pushes me over the threshold, sending me tumbling to the asphalt. My knees sting as they scrape along the cold gravel. "Then you find the money for the bills. I can't feed the both of us. You forget that you need me more than I need you, Nina. It's about time you grew up!"

"Mum!" I panic.

The door slams shut, and I shake my head, wiping the stray tear from my cheek and pulling myself up off the dirty ground.

She thinks money will help us survive, but what she doesn't see is that what she is doing to earn it is slowly killing us both.

It was much later in life that I learnt to leave before she could hurt me.

1

Nina

NEVER IN MY WILDEST DREAMS COULD I HAVE COMPREHENDED how my life would turn out. I'm a firm believer that luck is the one thing between myself and some of the most unfortunate people in this world. Yet as I stand, hands on hips, chest heaving, glancing around at my studio—I know, hand on heart, that luck has absolutely nothing to do with my success.

My studio may have materialised under fortunate events —a case of being in the right place at the right time. But it was the years I spent working late nights in our local bar that allowed me to take the opportunity when it presented itself. Every penny I ever saved went into this studio, and although I might live month to month and down to the penny to keep it, I'm still damn proud of myself and what I've achieved.

It's Friday noon, and I've just finished my second class of the day. My girls are working tirelessly to nail our routine for the showcase we have coming up, and as promised, I've given them some extra time for their lunch today. It gives me a chance to be alone for a while. To gather my thoughts and let myself go in my safe haven.

It's a large open space with smooth cream wood floors. Sunlight reflects off them as it streams in through the five Victorian sash windows. A barre adorns the entire length of the mirrored wall, which stands opposite the windows, making the room look much bigger than it is. In a small rectangular bay at the back of the room sits a magnificent, sleek black grand piano. It was here when I viewed the building and was never removed. It suits the studio, so I never complained.

I feel more at home here than anywhere I've ever lived. I'd come here in the middle of the night when darkness steals the light of my existence if I didn't think I'd get caught.

I started renting the space twelve months ago when I met the owner in a café. We got chatting, and she told me about the building. She had to find a new tenant within three weeks, or she was going to have to sell. I knew I had to jump at the chance and pray I'd get the girls through the door to afford the monthly payments.

It's a two-storey building, so—after a lot of thought and deliberation and some unhelpful input from my friends—I converted the downstairs into an open gym. The memberships, along with my dance lessons, allow me to keep up the payments, and the owner, Erin, did me a deal to make it affordable until I had it up and running.

She completely changed my life that day, and I'm forever grateful to her for helping make my dreams a reality.

Dancing is my passion, it's all I know, and it's what gets me out of bed in the mornings. I'm blessed to have a career I adore so much.

I head towards the benches and pick up my phone; I have five missed calls and two texts, one from my mum and one from my best friend Lucy. I open the text from Lucy first.

Lucy: Hugh ended it. Meeting at The Pearl, 8 pm.

This doesn't shock me, and it means tonight will end up more than a little bit messy. Hugh was no good for Luce. She's gorgeous, a natural blonde bombshell and a hopeless romantic who longs for something far from reality. Hugh was only ever interested in a Monday to Thursday relationship.

Hugh was an ass.

No doubt Megan will be joining us to help drown in Lucy's sorrows. I consider calling Mum back, but I already know what she wants. It's the only reason she ever calls. Rolling my eyes, I delete her message without opening it. Chucking my phone back in my bag, I take off down the studio stairs and head for the gym, knowing I'll regret my choice to skip lunch.

"I DIDN'T LIKE that slimy bastard anyway," says Megan as she drains the last of her pinot, she waves her glass at the barman for another, earning herself a deep frown from him in return. I drop my head and chuckle. How many have they had? I'm only forty minutes late.

I screw my face up, thinking about Hugh and his less than stellar morals. "Me neither. He had all that extra body hair; I just couldn't get past it myself." I grimace apologetically at Lucy.

"Ugh, yes." Megan snaps her fingers at me. "I swear he had hairs poking out his nose when I'd speak with him, and those arms." She fakes an over-the-top shiver.

Lucy's mouth drops open, and she flicks her eyes dramatically between us. "Thanks, bitches." Her hand slaps down on the table. "You tell me this now!" We laugh into our drinks as she takes an ice cube and launches it at us. It bounces off my head and onto the bench seat, making us all break out into hysterics.

"Oh, oh, him over there with the grey tie," Megan interrupts our laughing fit excitedly.

Lucy scans the group of suits closest to our table until she spots the guy Megan is referring to.

Her eyes go wide.

"The bald one?!" Lucy openly points at the poor guy, and I drop my head in my hands. "Gee, talk about extremes, Megan."

Heads turn our way as we giggle like a bunch of schoolgirls, but I know this is precisely what Lucy needs right now. Untamed time with the girls is the best form of medicine, after all.

I get up to go to the bar—much to Megan's dismay, and she tuts, shaking her head at the barman, who is completely oblivious. Picking up her glass, I turn and give her a cheeky wink. She looks gorgeous tonight; her dark brown hair is pulled back in a sleek high ponytail, her lips painted a bright red.

I love my dear friends; I've known Lucy my entire life. I even lived with her for most of my childhood. Her parents filled a void in my life that no child should ever need filling.

Lucy moved into the city with me when we joined university eight years ago.

And *that's* where we met Megan. She was loud and silly and the missing piece of a trio we never knew we needed. She moved into our dorm room four weeks later, and the rest is history—sacred. Misdemeanours we'll take to the grave.

We managed to score one of the oval booths in the centre of The Pearl tonight. We have the perfect view of the whole place from it. The bar sits along the back wall lined with padded stools; pendant lights hang above the entire bar top setting a glow over the marble counter.

I manage to squeeze in next to a woman who's waiting for her drinks. The ratio of women to men in this place is lower than a ho's standards.

"What can I get you?" the cute barman asks.

"Three glasses of pinot grigio, please."

I slide onto one of the stools and look around the club. It's abuzz with music, the steady beat pumping through the speakers and creating the perfect Friday night vibe. My eyes drift to the four large pillars that encase the marble dance floor. It sits on a platform to the left of the bar, like a stage for men to watch upon. It's currently full of women moving their bodies with the music, probably hoping to bag one of the asshole suits for the night.

We're so off them.

As if sensing my thoughts, I catch someone from the corner of my eye sliding onto the stool that the woman has just left.

"Hey, Nina!"

"Joey, hi." I give a polite smile and then eye the barman. *Hurry up, please.*

I know this guy; he is everywhere we go on a night out, and it's getting a little bit annoying.

I look over at the girls for help. Lucy is giving me the thumbs up while Megan stands, pretending to slowly grind herself on Lucy's chair. My eyes go wide before I close them and look back to Joey.

For fuck's sake.

"I've not seen you out in a while. How's the dancing going?" Joey asks, staring far too intently into my eyes. I flick my eyes around the club, uncomfortable and not knowing where to look.

"Really great, actually. We have a show in six weeks," I mutter back.

Joey is gorgeous; I can appreciate a good-looking man when he's standing in front of my face, but there is something about him that doesn't do it for me. Many times, I've found myself stuck chatting to him about something completely mundane. Like now, he doesn't even acknowledge my mood. I'm clearly not interested and have hardly muttered a word, yet he is chattering on about God knows what.

My gaze flicks to the side as I see two men approach the bar, slipping in behind me. The barman places my order on the cool marble and takes my card. I use the opportunity to turn my body towards the bar and away from Joey. His lips are moving, but I'm lost in the divine smell emanating from the males to my right to understand a word he is saying.

"Two blue label scotches, please," a deep voice asks at my back. "Did you clock the blonde in the centre booth?"

My ears perk up at the mention of the girls. Okay, I need to get rid of Joey, so I can fully listen in on their conversation.

"No," replies the other man. He sounds bored, maybe a little bit pissy. "Don't be that man, El."

"Me, you mean, don't be me," the first guy *'El'* shoots back. "Come on, Charles, you know if you're out with me, you're my wingman for the night. I know you noticed them too." I can hear the smile in his voice as he teases his friend.

I nod to Joey, pretending to listen, not having a damn clue what he's saying.

"You'll be disappointed with that one El, she's heartbroken."

My frown is instant; I wasn't expecting that. My head snaps around, eager to put a face to the man as Joey shouts in my ear.

"It's on Netflix. You've got to watch it." I instantly lean away, head butting straight into a solid bicep.

I look up and into a pair of beautiful blue eyes. Oh god, he's flipping gorgeous. Blond hair shaved neatly at the sides and slightly longer on top. He's tall—really tall and physically fit. His muscles strain against the smooth fabric of his pale blue shirt.

"I'm so sorry," I mutter, jerking away.

My eyes find the other man and instantly betray me, widening in shock at the sheer maleness before me. Oh my fuck, they are both flipping hot! Dark hair, blue eyes, equally as fit, the two of them look like they belong on the front of a magazine.

I turn my attention to Joey and find him glaring at the side of my head.

Oh, please piss off.

"Do you want to get out of here?" Joey asks, hopefully.

I wince. He's not a bad bloke, and I feel for the guy I do, but I'm just not interested.

"No. Not tonight, Joey, sorry. I'm here with the girls."

"What about tomorrow? Do you have rehearsals?"

I would lie if I thought he'd believe me, but I'm the worst liar. I fidget and curl my fingers into my collarbone. My mum used to call me out as a kid. It was something I started doing from a young age, and even now, I don't even realise I'm doing it.

So, I tell the truth. I mean, Joey won't know I plan to sleep the weekend away. It's been a busy week in the studio, and I'm exhausted. "No, I don't work the weekend, but I am busy. Sorry."

"Ahh, that's okay, maybe another time?"

I smile and thank god that the conversation is over. Feeling uncomfortable, I look to my right again and find the two hotties listening in on our conversation. The dark-haired guy raises his brows as if in warning. Confused, I turn my head back around to find Joey still staring at me, waiting for an answer.

Oh, for Christ's sake, take a hint! I feel two hands take hold of my chair possessively, and then I'm being spun around.

"Look, mate, she isn't interested, fuck off."

Oh my god, I'm now staring at the blond's chest. He's glaring over my head. My cheeks heat with embarrassment.

"Fuck you!" Joey sneers, sounding fuming mad. What is happening? "I'm her friend, you rude prick!"

"No, you're not. You're trying your luck to get laid, soft cock. Now leave!" The last bit comes out as a growl, and I shrink down farther in my seat. I should stop this, Joey is harmless, and I've never set him straight. This is a shamble.

"Nina?"

"It's fine, Joey, you go. I'm going to get my drinks and head back to the girls." I turn my head to see him standing at my back, his face bright red with rage. My eyes plead with him.

Please don't cause a scene.

He downs the last of his pint then slams his glass down onto the bar. I eye my drinks like they are a ticket to Hogwarts and start to pick up the tray. Joey looks at me one last time before he shakes his head, turning for the exit.

"You okay?" This comes from the tall, dark-haired guy. He has a soft look in his eyes as if he feels bad for what his friend has just done.

"Yes, I'm fine, sorry. He's alright, just hasn't taken the hint yet." I drop my head, completely mortified.

"I'm Charlie."

My eyes lift and I smile. There's something about this man. He's got an air about him that instantly makes me feel safe. My hand finds his outstretched one, and he returns my smile.

My gaze moves to the blond. He is staring down his nose at me, and I squirm under his glare. What's his problem? I can see his mind ticking over as he assesses me.

This one, I'm not getting quite the same feels from. He's hot. I mean, hot doesn't even come close to this guy. He oozes power. His tailored suit tells me that alone, but that look he's giving me tells me he's the boss. Like, the boss's, boss's boss. I force my chin up and don't back down. His brows rise, then he breaks out into a chuckle.

My brows draw in. "Okay, crazy." Time to go.

I spin with my tray, ready to hotfoot it back to my girls. Where are those bitches anyway? They saw I needed an out with Joey.

"Hey, wait a second, Pixie."

I stop, slowly spinning on my heel. Pixie. Is this guy serious?

"Excuse me?" I jolt my head to the side for effect, but I have a feeling the wine has already made me tipsy, and I look like a fool.

He grins at me, and I can't help it; the wall I put up ten seconds ago crumbles with his playful manner.

"That's your friends over there, the blonde and brunette?" He smiles cheekily.

Oh, I'm so on to you, mister.

"Who?" I crane my neck, pretending to look around for said beauties. The pair of idiots are standing. Why are they standing? I screw my face up every which way. *Come and help me!* They stare at me, open-mouthed.

I roll my eyes. "Nope, I don't know them." I catch Charlie's eyes. The corner of his mouth tipping up into a smile.

"Ah, okay, no worries." The blond one gives me a wink, turning back to the bar to down his drink.

I make a dash away, finally, after what feels like an eternity since I left to go to the bar. I do my best to shimmy my way back to the girls without spilling a drop of wine, taking the long way around and heading past the dance floor to throw the boys off.

"What the hell was that?" Lucy shouts when I'm a few feet from the table. I sit down, grab my drink and down it in one, wincing from the sweetness that sets my cheeks tingling.

"Who were those guys, and what did you say to Joey? He was so angry when he left."

"Me? I didn't say anything. It was him." I search the bar for the blond guy and Charlie, but I can't see them anywhere.

"Oh, don't you worry," she scoffs, taking her drink from the tray. "We saw them, babe." She salutes me with her glass.

I roll my eyes, laughing with them.

"Did you get numbers? Please tell me you got numbers!" Megan begs.

"No! The blond guy was intense and had the attitude of an eighteen-year-old boy."

Lucy's mouth drops open again, and Megan breaks out into a face splitting grin. She has a glint in her eye that she only gets when she's on a manhunt.

I look to my empty drink and pray it will actually take me to Hogwarts. *The blond asshole is behind me.* I turn slowly, confirming my suspicions when I find him towering above me with a tray of shots, eyebrows raised high as he tries to look offended. Charlie looks at me sympathetically with a grin on his face. His head turned to the side, looking all adorable. I slide into the seat deeper, sighing as I make room for them.

"Pixie, I see you made some new friends. Want to introduce me?" His facade slips, and he cracks a smile. I elbow him in the ribs, my own smile splitting my face.

"Megan, Lucy, this is Charlie and..." I look to the blond in question. I don't remember his name. Did he even tell me? I smile. "Ken."

He throws his head back, laughing, as does Charlie.

"Tequila, girls?"

Oh god. As I said, it's going to get messy.

IT'S eleven p.m. and the club is completely packed. There isn't a spare seat in sight—every square foot filled with men and women fawning over each other.

The night has been better than I'd expected. The boys, Charlie and Ken—or Elliot as I now know him to be—have been hilarious. I have danced, sang and laughed more than I have in a long time. I feel good. I feel drunk. I'm so drunk.

Lucy is tucked under Charlie's arm, having a deep 'I won't remember this in the morning' talk. She's all tequila'd out. Is that even a word? I frown into my glass of water. We need to get her home.

Megan comes back from the dance floor with a guy on her arm, and I nod my head to where Lucy is sitting and mouth, *We are going*. She turns, giving her man an all tongue and teeth kiss as he grabs her behind, grinding into her as she whispers in his ear. I look at Elliot, sitting next to me, only to find he has the same horrified expression on his face. We both erupt with laughter.

But then he stops and stares at me, his face growing somewhat serious in his drunken state. His eyes pinch in at the corners, his lips twisting up in thought. Maybe it's the tequila, but I can't control my features, and I continue to laugh in his face. Elliot shakes his head as he looks down into his glass, his face morphing back to that megawatt smile.

Mase

I ROLL my car into my apartment building's underground car park, heading for my space at the farthest end along the back wall. My dash reads 22:34, but it feels a whole lot later.

A layer of sweat still sits on my skin from my late-night workout. It's been a shit week. The same old shit in the office topped off with a call from my father tonight.

My phone alerts me of a new message just as I'm reversing in. I put my car in park and pick it up.

Elliot: I have something for you (Pixie emoji)
Pick me up @ The Pearl

The life of Elliot Montgomery. It must be nice having all the girls, money, and power, but no burden of the empire we've built. I love my best friend. He's one of the smartest, loyalist men I know, but he's a lazy bastard. Our parents were best friends growing up, which meant by default, we became best friends. It wasn't ever a choice, but he's the family I choose now.

Clicking back on the screen, I read the message again, shaking my head in annoyance. I needed that idiot tonight, and he was out? Chasing fucking pixies. I shake my head and laugh. "Not tonight, my friend," I mutter to no one.

Climbing from my car on aching legs, I round the bonnet, grabbing my gym bag from the back seat. I walk to the elevator and hit the button for the penthouse, leaning back and running my hands over my face. The steel doors jolt open, and I flick on the lights. It doesn't feel like a home anymore, it's cold and serves the only purpose of a hole to rest my head. Its charm's lost on me. Dimming the lights and blanketing the place in darkness, my feet hit the stairs, and I leave the shadows of the apartment behind me.

Ten minutes later, I emerge from my en suite fresh from a shower. A towel wrapped low around my waist. Dropping down to the bed, I run my hands over my face and hair. I contemplate having a drink to take the edge off, but I already know nothing will be strong enough.

My mind goes back to Elliot's text and that little pixie emoji. It's been years. Blowing out a breath, I sit up in a rush, making a rash decision based on the warmth that spreads through my chest.

The streets are full and bustling with the Friday night crowd as I weave in and out of London traffic with one thing on my mind.

My Pixie.

I feel childish, even thinking about it. I'm a thirty-two-year-old man, for fuck's sake. What if Elliot is just taking the piss anyway? I've never known him to be a serious man.

I rest my elbow on the window, running my pointer finger over my bottom lip. All I know is I couldn't turn my car around, even if I wanted to.

The club comes into view, and I manage to find a space on the next road. A rarity on a Friday night in London, and the reason I barely drive myself anymore. Sliding out my phone, I shoot Elliot a text telling him I'm here, then step from my Bentley and hit lock on my key fob. Adrenaline is the only thing propelling my body in the direction of the club.

2

Nina

I HOLD A STRAW TO LUCY'S MOUTH, TRYING TO GET SOME WATER in her. She looks up at me with loving eyes slapping her dainty hand to my cheek.

"Nunnia, Ninnia," she slurs drunkenly, her brows dipping as she processes her own words. "I love you," she whispers, dropping her head to my chest. I feel my body sway from the weight of hers—maybe the tequila too. Thankfully, Charlie notices, he sweeps Lucy up into his arms, holding her like you would a bride.

"Elliot's sorted a ride for us," he says as he looks down at Lucy.

"I wouldn't normally let her get like this." I smile sheepishly up at him as guilt fills me. "She needed a good blowout tonight." I tip my head to the side and try to suppress my laugh.

She's fucked.

"Lowell's out front." Elliot smiles as he pops his brows at

Charlie. "Megan thinks she's going with that fuckface." He thumbs over his shoulder.

Megan sits on the lap of Sam, her go-to hookup. She's been dancing with him all night, and by dancing, I mean dry humping. Megan is very private on the details of her sex life but has never been afraid of PDA. The girl baffles me.

"She's okay. We know Sam." I wave my hand on a hiccup.

"Right." Elliot stands with his hands on his hips and nods to the door. "Let's go."

I go to Megan, pulling her head back from Sam's with a handful of hair gentle enough not to hurt her. I kiss her forehead, giving her 'the look'. She smiles up at me, her eyes telling me what I need to know. She's okay.

We exit the club, and the cool air hits me like a freight train. Instantly I feel more, more of everything, my body hypersensitive to the world around me. Everything blurs as I spin, looking for the guys. My eyes take a second to find focus amongst the sea of people. But they are there, right behind me, Lucy safely locked in Charlie's arms.

Thank god we met them tonight.

Mase

As I round the corner of the club, I instantly spot my two best friends already outside. Charlie has a blonde in his arms, and she looks like she's out for the count.

Poor fucker.

I see Elliot in my periphery, but my eyes don't reach him. They are drawn to the woman who stands in front of him.

She looks around in searching, visibly relaxing when she spots the boys.

Do they know this girl?

I use my concealed spot to take her in. Long brown hair hangs loose and full to her small waist. I can see the swell of her breast from her side profile. Full round hips encase the most perfect ass I think I've ever seen. Her body looks toned and tight in all the right places. I imagine my hands running over those hips.

Shit.

Elliot spots me in the crowd, a mischievous smile lighting up his face. He starts towards me, but I quickly turn and head back to my car before the brunette can spot me.

I shouldn't have come tonight.

This was a stupid idea.

Nina

ELLIOT TAKES off across the street, long strides putting distance between us. I run to keep up, looking back to find Charlie matching my silly little jog with his walk. God, I hate these heels.

"Hey Elliot, wait up, will you? You're going to get us run over in a minute, you..."

"Oh, wow. Who are you?" I ask out loud in my drunken state.

Elliot turns and smiles in triumph.

There's a man. He's lent on the top of his open car door, his dark eyes blazing all over me. My skin pebbles, but I'm like a raging inferno inside. I feel my cheeks flush with the heat. Never in my life have I been in the presence of such a man. He has dark brown hair cut shorter at the sides, subtly getting longer on the top, soft tousled strands lie in a perfect mess on his head like he's been running his fingers through it. His brows sit naturally low, making his eyes look darker than they are. They are unnerving, his gaze searing up through them and into me. He's wearing a form-fitting sweater that shows off every inch of his chiselled torso. His nose has a slight crook to it, but it only adds to his appeal.

I regret the tequila; I wish I was sober for this. Lucy is going to freak.

"Nina, Mason, Mason, Nina," Elliot introduces, his face knowing and cocky. "So, I'm going for drinks by the river with Sullivan. You good with these guys?" Elliot smirks, looking at his watch as he backs away.

My eyes drift to the fine specimen propped up against the car. His eyes haven't left me. Am I good with these guys? Who's Sullivan?

Be cool, Nina.

"Sure, fine, yeah. Yeah!" Oh, fuck off! What is wrong with me?

The gorgeous son of a bitch can't help himself, his lip tipping up on one side as he drops his head.

"Get the door, will you, Lowell?" Charlie still has Lucy in his arms, and I rush to help. She grumbles as Charlie slides in behind the passenger seat, leaving the front seat, the only one left to sit in.

I can feel him behind me, and I turn to see him looking up the road after Elliot's retreating back. He shakes his head, bringing his attention back to me. We stand closer now. He looks down at me.

"Mason Lowell." He holds his large hand out to me, my eyes falling to the Rolex watch on his wrist, and suddenly a thought comes to me.

"Oh! Are you *his* boss?" I ask, pointing in the direction Elliot went in.

He considers what I've said for a moment, then throws his head back in laughter, and it's the most incredible sound. I feel a knot form in my stomach.

My hand gets lost in his as it cradles mine. He loosens the grip slightly but doesn't let go. Traces of humour still line his face as he bites into his bottom lip, running his thumb aimlessly over my knuckles.

He's so intense. I've only just met this guy, and already I'm a puddle on the ground. I smile as I drop down into the seat, not taking my eyes off him as he shuts the door and rounds the car.

I whip my head around to Charlie. "Do you have any friends that aren't fucking hot?"

Mason slides into the driver's seat then, and I get the giggles as he starts up the engine. He cuts his gaze to Charlie in the rearview mirror. I can hear him chuckling behind me.

Lowering my window, I will myself to sober up. "Why were you not out with your friends tonight?" I ask, leaning in and fiddling with the buttons on the centre console.

"I had a meeting that ran late," he replies flatly, his eyes flicking between me and the road and then to where my hands are currently exploring.

"This car is super flashy. It's not like an average car with simple buttons!" I manage to change the clock from twenty-four to twelve hours. It now reads 11:23.

Oops!

"There we go." I grin up at the deity beside me, pretending it was intentional.

He pops a thick brow at me, a devilish smirk on his face.

He's so fucking hot.

"Can we drop Luce to her parents' house?" I ask. "I don't want her alone tonight, and her sofa is stupidly lumpy."

"Sure, what's the address?" He starts tapping the screen, and a box pops up to enter the postcode. It's outside the city, so I feel bad, but Megan will probably end up at Sam's, and I can't have Luce alone tonight. She drank far more than me, and I want to wake up in my own bed in the morning.

I shoot a text to Maggie—my stand-in surrogate mum, and let her know we are on the way.

WE PULL up to Lucy's parents' home twenty minutes later. Childhood memories flash through my mind, and I climb from the car with a smile. Both boys follow, standing off to the side of the pavement.

I lean in to wake up the sleeping beauty. "Luce, babe, we are home."

She comes around slowly, smiling up at me for a moment before realisation hits. She looks out the window with a groan. "You called my mum? Nina!" She ambles out of the car, her body swaying as I throw her arm over my shoulder and hug her close.

Maggie greets us at the door and takes Lucy from me,

pulling her into a warm embrace. I envy their beautiful relationship. Even though I know that she loves me like a daughter, I still wish I had what they did.

She looks over the top of Lucy's head, slowly opening her other arm out for me. "Come here, you," she whispers into my hair as I step into her. I'll never grow tired of that sound. I've fallen asleep on this woman as her voice has vibrated through her chest. Every child deserves to know that feeling. It's the most grounding sound of earth.

I remember we have company and turn, smiling at the gods behind me.

"Maggie, these are our friends, Mason and Charlie."

Charlie dips his head, muttering a polite hello, while Mason steps up and holds out his hand. Maggie looks more than a little flustered as she takes it.

Not just me, then.

"Nice to meet you," Mason says, flashing his beautiful smile.

I kiss Maggie's cheek and hug her waist, then promise to be there for lunch on Sunday. Just as I step away, I feel her hand squeeze my shoulder, a tentative look on her face.

"I'll be careful," I tell her.

"I know, and I'll still worry." She smiles softly. "You'll message me when you get home, okay?"

I nod.

We make our way back through the city, the boys both quiet and reserved in their seats. Although, I can feel Mason's eyes lingering on me every now and again.

Unfortunately for the two of them, I'm drunk, and I have no way of controlling my mouth.

"Who's Sullivan?" I ask, turning in my seat so I can see both of them.

"Lance?" Mason asks with a frown, his features hardening. "Why do you want to know?"

"Elliot said he was off to meet him tonight." My gaze drops to the smooth skin of Mason's hand as he fists the gear stick... hmm. "Is he pretty too?"

They both chuckle, deep rumbling sounds that only the rarest of species seem to be able to make. "Lance Sullivan and pretty isn't something that goes together in a sentence," Mason tells me, looking over at me with a warm glint in his eye. He wets his bottom lip and looks back to the road. "Think Tom Hardy, with dark hair and tattoos."

"Ohhhh, so Sullivan is the bad boy of the group? I thought that was Elliot."

"What?" Charlie questions from the back seat. "How could you think Elliot?"

"Only in the beginning when he chased off Joey." He was so in control. So possessive and—

"Who's Joey?" Mason interrupts my thoughts, adjusting his legs as he looks between me and the road.

"Just some guy at the bar. How do you guys all know each other? Are you actually Elliot's boss?" I ask Mason.

"Something like that. I've known Elliot my whole life— unfortunately. Charles here." He flicks his head back. "I met at college, and Lance runs our accounts department."

"Our?"

He gives me a panty-melting smile. "Mine and Elliot's company."

"Hmmm. So, you're both the boss."

"Uh-huh. Charlie lives just up here. You okay if I drop him off first?" he asks, a boyish look on his face.

Sober Nina would say no. I shouldn't even be in the car with two men I've just met, especially with how drunk I am. God, what was I thinking? "Well, I don't exactly know either of you, but I have more chance of taking one of you than both at the same time."

His brows rise in surprise.

"Oh, no! I don't mean—Jesus, fuck. I mean, if you were to kidnap me or try anything, not that I wouldn't have sex with you, like I wouldn't fight you if..."

Oh, my god. Shut up, Nina. Just stop talking now!

"It's fine. You can drop him off first." I roll my lips and look out the window.

"Wow," Charlie remarks at my back.

I don't dare look at Mason for the rest of the journey, but at least my embarrassment has sobered me up a little.

"CHEERS, Mase. We still on for tomorrow?" Charlie asks, climbing from the back seat and shutting the door.

Mason lowers his window farther so he can answer him. "Definitely. It's fucking needed after the week I've had."

Charlie gives a grim smile in return, then leans his head through the window so he can see me. "I'm sure I will see you again, little Pixie." He gives a soft wink before disappearing into his building.

Why Pixie? They've been calling me that all night.

Mason looks over at me again, his eyes darkening. I

squeeze my legs together, trying to ease the ache that's forming there. It's been too long.

He pulls out onto the road, thankfully not saying another word. I sit, trying to process the effect he has on me.

"Are you okay?" he asks after a few seconds of awkward silence.

"Umm, yeah. Why?" I feel my palms start to sweat.

"I couldn't shut you up twenty minutes ago." He smiles. "You've gone quiet on me, and you're fidgeting." His eyes drop to my bare legs.

"Just look where you're driving, Bossman."

His smirk does nothing to ease the fluster I've gotten myself in.

Oh god, why can't I be normal? He seems so unaffected by me, yet I can't sit still in my seat.

I turn my head a little to look up at him, taking in his broad chest... that thick neck. My clit throbs against the lace of my underwear.

First job when I get home is to fix that problem.

"You seem close to your friend's mum? Lucy, wasn't it?"

My smile is instant, and I welcome the distraction. "Maggie's the best. One of the most beautiful women I know."

"Have you known her long?"

"Pretty much my entire life. I met Lucy in nursery school, and we've been best friends ever since."

He nods in understanding. "Me and Elliot have known each other since birth. We are more like brothers than friends."

We turn onto my street, and I direct Mason to my building. As much as I want to get inside and shower off the remnants of the night, something pulls at my gut, telling me to stay exactly where I am.

Mason taps his finger on the steering wheel, a deep frown in place.

I turn to face him, rolling my lips as I think of ways to delay his departure. "Sorry about your clock." I laugh, nerves taking flight in my stomach.

"It's fine. Easy fix." He winks, and then I sit, needing to leave but unable to open the door.

"Thanks for the ri—" I cut myself off when I notice a shadowy figure at the entrance of my building. I gaze past Mason's head, trying to make out who it is.

Then he turns, giving me a perfect view of his face.

Joey.

Fuck.

I try to school my features but clearly fail. Mason watches me for a moment with a questioning stare, then frowns, turning to look behind him.

"Who's that?" he asks. I can see his jaw clenching.

"Joey. He's a friend."

"Do all your friends wait outside your building late at night?" He raises his brow as he pulls open the handle.

Shit!

"Looks like we are getting out of the car. Okay," I mutter, cringing as I pull open my door and round the car.

Joey spots me and starts walking toward us. "Nina." He looks to me and then to Mason with a look of pure disdain. "Who's this?"

"Mason," he answers for himself. It comes out a deep growl, and I quickly step in front of him.

"Right." Joey looks over my shoulder, his eyes narrowing

into a glare as he puts his weight on one foot then the other. "Nina, can I speak to you a minute, please?"

"Now isn't a good time, Joey, maybe tomorrow? You have my number, right? You can call me." I will do anything to get rid of him right now.

I feel Mason's hand take hold of my hip, bringing my body back flush against his.

My heart seems to skip a beat at the contact.

"Really, Nina? Do you even know this guy?" he spits.

"Joey, that's *really* none of your business!" I can tell he is drunk; he has never spoken to me like this. He is probably still hurt from the bar fiasco earlier.

"What happened to the blond? Or have you already fucked him, bored already?" he asks, tipping his chin.

Mason's grip on my hip tightens. "Watch your mouth," he warns, and the air crackles at the tone of his voice.

"Fuck you! You're better off giving up on this one." He looks me up and down, and my heart blisters a little. "She's a prick tease."

"I said watch your fucking mouth!"

"This has nothing to do with you!" Joey shouts.

Mason grips my arm, pushing me to the side just as Joey comes at us. He swings, catching Mason clean in the mouth. His head goes back, and I'm left standing in utter shock.

Mason recovers quickly, spinning and gripping Joey at the throat, then pins him to the car. Joey's eyes go wide as the air is squeezed from his body.

"Apologise!" Mason roars.

Joey gasps for air. I'm unsure he could speak even if he wanted to. His eyes dart to me, pleading for me to help.

Slowly, I approach Mason and gently curl my hand

around his elbow. "Mason, he can't breathe." I can feel his rage radiating off him.

His eyes meet mine, softening some before he loosens his grip around Joey's throat.

"I'm sorry," Joey splutters at me.

Mason releases him. "Good boy. Not so hard is it? Have some respect."

Joey falls to the car, trying to breathe air back into his lungs, but just as he finds his feet, Mason rears his fist back and punches him in the face. Blood pours from Joey's nose.

"Nina, get in the car," Mason tells me without taking his eyes from Joey.

"You get in first. Please," I plead on a shaky breath.

He looks around at me, regret instantly taking over his face. Reaching for my hand, he walks me to his car, opening the door and helping me inside.

He crouches down beside me, his eyes searching my face. I sit frozen as he clasps my jaw in his open palm. My head involuntarily leans into it—his thumb brushes over my bottom lip.

Why does that feel like the most natural thing in the world?

His voice drops dangerously low as he asks, "Do you trust me, Nina?"

"Yes," I answer far too quickly. Mason shuts my door, muttering something to Joey before he slides into the driver's seat. He puts the car into drive, pulling back out onto the road.

"Mason, you're bleeding," I tell him, my eyes zeroed in on his lip as blood oozes from the wound.

"Have you slept with him?" he asks unapologetically.

My head recoils at his words. "What? No!"

"Would you have let him in tonight? If I wasn't here?" His jaw tics, his annoyance blatant.

"Ummm, no. I barely know Joey."

"You barely know me," he shoots back.

I start to clutch at straws. "I know that you have a Bentley... and a best friend called Elliot," I tease, my argument weak even to my ears. "I'm here with you, aren't I? Trust me, sober Nina would not be in this car right now." I blow out a breath, running my hand through my hair in frustration. "What is it with you men anyway? You're like a bunch of testosterone-charged teenage boys."

He drops his head back to the seat, giving me a swoon-worthy smile. "Testosterone-charged teenage boys?" he teases.

I shake my head, my lips twisting up into a reluctant smile.

WE ARRIVE at Mason's a little after one a.m. and I try to act unaffected by the level of wealth in front of me. The building sits back from the tree-lined road—sleek but timeless in its structure. I manage to count maybe twenty apartments in the large building. Each one spaced out, clearly offering a substantial living space.

We park in the underground car park and quickly walk to the elevator. Mason matches my every step with his hand sat low on my back. A flare of panic rushes through me as the steel doors begin to close.

What the hell am I doing?

Maybe I should get a taxi home.

As if sensing my unease, Mason grabs me at the waist, his thumb innocently brushing along the underside of my breast. "I won't touch you while you've been drinking." His jaw clenches as if it pains him even to say it.

"You can touch me." I blink up at him, snapping out of it when he laughs and brings his nose to mine.

I swallow, anticipation stirring in my stomach.

"I brought you here so I'd know you'd be safe." My eyes search his, and I hope mine don't reflect the disappointment that he doesn't want me.

"Am I? Safe here?"

"That depends," he deliberates, playfully weighing up the options.

I choose to humour him, wanting—needing to know. "On what?"

"If you are going to continue to look at me like that."

I frown, rolling my eyes. "Like what?" I'm aware I am playing directly into his hands.

He has me right where he wants me. Our faces are only millimetres apart, and with each passing second, I can see him starting to relent. His fingers clench around my waist, then instantly smooth over the fabric. I sway on the spot, my eyes fluttering closed as he inches in closer.

"Drunk," he breathes out across my lips. He pauses, taking a deep breath. "Come on, out."

He nods his head in the direction of the apartment that stands before me. Only it's not an apartment like I first thought. No, we are standing in the foyer of the penthouse. It's enormous, rich... It's so *him*.

Stepping out after Mason, my eyes are immediately captivated by the floor-to-ceiling windows that give way to the most incredible view of the city. Like a moth drawn to a flame, my feet carry me on their own accord, lost in the visual sensation before me.

"It looks different from up here. Lit up in its slumber." I speak my mind, forgetting where I am and the man at my back. I spin, seeking him out, only to find him watching me with an intense fascination. "It's like I'm seeing it for the first time."

"Yeah," he says, his throat working on a swallow as his brows pull in farther.

My eyes scan the rest of the room, only confirming my thoughts that Mason is a lot richer than I first thought, and judging by the look in his eye, maybe—for some reason—he doesn't see the beauty in the world that surrounds him.

Large, grey sectional sofas surround the television, which is mounted on the wall. Magazines litter a rectangular padded footstool that sits on a rug in the centre.

A dining table is on the opposite side of the room, a large open space laying bare between the two areas. It would be the most beautiful spot to dance in as the city looked on.

"It's beautiful, Mason," I tell him.

"Thank you," he says in earnest as he approaches me. "Would you like a drink?"

"Not of alcohol." I waggle my eyebrows at him.

"Ah, of course. Wouldn't want you intoxicated now, would we?"

I smile wide, feeling my dimple pop in my cheek. "Absolutely not. Water. Lots of water, please."

He laughs as he leaves me, and I follow after him through to the state-of-the-art kitchen. He busies himself in the cupboards as I hop up onto the kitchen island, the cool marble teasing my bare thighs.

Handing me my water, he uses his hips to widen my legs, stepping between them and giving me a look that dares me to challenge him on the move. I lick my lips slowly, giving him the best come-fuck-me look I can muster.

I hardly know this man, yet he's making me act more brazen than I have in years—maybe even ever. I don't know what it is, but I'm drawn to him.

Reaching up, I run my finger across his split lip. He winces slightly, darting his tongue out across my finger.

"I'm sorry about Joey. Elliot already chased him off tonight," I admit.

"He did?" Mason looks surprised but wears a knowing smirk.

"Yup, testosterone-filled teenage boys," I say, shaking my head.

He smiles up at me, his hands sliding up my thighs to grasp my hips. "What is it you do for a living?"

"I'm a dancer. I own my own studio and gym."

"In the city?"

"Yeah, in the city." I smile as his brows rise in surprise. I love being able to tell people that at the age of twenty-eight, I own my own business. Pride spreads through me.

"How long have you been in London?" he asks with genuine interest.

"Since university. I moved here with Lucy in my first year. I lived with the girls for a while after that, but when I eventually opened the studio, I found myself a little place on my own so that I could be closer."

"The girls?" he asks, circling his thumbs over my hip bones.

"Lucy, you met her tonight and Megan, my two best friends. We shared a two-bed for four years whilst we studied and then found our feet after. Took turns on the futon." I grin as the memories of our uni days flash in my mind.

"They didn't want to move with you?"

"What? To my one bed, one bathroom." I laugh, pushing back on his chest as I look around at the dark grey units. "This place is beautiful, although I'd say my apartment is a little cosier."

He studies the room around him as if trying to see it from my eyes.

"What do you do for a living?" I ask. "Where does all of this come from?"

"Once upon a time. My parents. We've tripled our fathers' empire in the last five years," he declares, his own pride shining through.

"You're close with your parents?"

His beautiful face drops, making me regret my question. "I used to be with my dad. My mum died when I was four years old." His reply comes out robotic, expressionless, like he's already zoned out.

I run my fingers through the hair at the base of his neck, sensing he needs the physical touch.

"I'm so sorry, Mason."

"Please. Don't." His eyes bore into mine, adrenaline coursing through my veins as he pins me with his stare. Slowly, he lowers his mouth to mine, coaxing my lips into a kiss so urgent it sets my body aflame.

Grasping the backs of my knees, he pulls me, so I'm

sitting on the edge of the worktop, our bodies perfectly aligned. I feel his hard cock against my centre. He rolls his hips, and a shudder runs through me. His groan vibrates against my lips, and I feel it, all the way down there.

Our kiss turns desperate.

He pulls back as he bites my lip, making me moan out loud. I don't let him go, though, my lips finding their way instinctively back to his, but he quickly forces us apart again.

"Fuck!" he yells, running his hands through his hair.

I smile up at him as he tries to compose himself. Annoyance at his lack of control evident in his stance.

"Bed. Now. You need to sleep," he stresses.

"*You* need me to sleep more like... You just want me sober, don't you, Bossman."

He shakes his head, hands on hips.

"Where am I to sleep, Mr. Mason?" I ask cheekily, hopping down from the kitchen island.

"Where the fuck do you think, Pixie?"

"Pixie?" I frown. Mason is in on this too?

His face grows serious as if he has just realised what he's said. Not wanting to kill the mood, I take off on a run from the kitchen, searching for the stairs. I can hear him close behind me, and I flick my head around as I hit the first step, spotting him rounding the corner. My breath catches with the excitement that lives in his eyes. I see him smile, and then everything goes dark.

I pause mid-step, my heart hammering in my chest. Hands dust my waist as warm lips find my ear. If I didn't already know, the sheer strength and dominance in the body at my back would tell me it's Mason.

I can smell him, feel him, taste him on my lips.

"Too late now, angel." He uses his body to move mine forward, and as we reach the top step, he bends, lifting me over his shoulder.

"Wait!" I squeal.

We enter the bedroom, and I try to take in my surroundings, but all I can seem to focus on is the feel of his fingers as they dig into the tops of my thighs. The room is lit up in a soft glow from the city lights beyond the windows. Being upside down makes it impossible to make out anything else, though. "Bossman, put me down!"

I feel myself floating through the air before my back meets the soft sheets of a mattress. He hesitates only a second before lowering himself over me.

"You're fucking beautiful," he hums, his lips dropping into the crook of my neck.

I try to get closer, but he holds his body off of me, supporting his weight on his arms and not letting our bodies touch.

"Promise me when I'm sober—"

His head swoops down, cutting me off with a searing kiss. "I promise when you're sober." He smiles down at me, and my stomach flips again.

Slowly, he rises off me and leaves the room through one of the doors. I sit up quickly and look around at my surroundings, my hands fisting the silky-smooth sheets.

The bed is huge. Its plush navy headboard sits high against the white wall. There's an ottoman at the base of the bed, a large shaggy rug covering the floor beneath it. The corner of the room is made up of floor-to-ceiling windows with double doors that give way to a wraparound balcony.

It's beyond anything I've ever seen.

Mason comes back into the room from one of the two adjoining doors. He drops a T-shirt on the ottoman.

"Bed," he demands.

Usually—like any other time in my life—I'd tell him to piss off. I mean, who does this man think he is?

But, the way he can look at me and make me feel so many things... I shut the hell up and go to the en suite to change.

I remove my dress and quickly pull the T-shirt over my head, fluffing my hair in the mirror then flattening it out again. I take a deep breath and open the door, only to be caught completely off guard when I find Mason in nothing but a pair of white boxer briefs. He has his back to me, his muscles flexing as he pulls back the bedsheet.

He turns, sensing my presence, his eyes dropping down the length of my body. "Come lay with me."

And I do just that. I climb into his bed, lying on my side as his body mirrors mine. I feel the exhaustion of the past week take over my body, and my eyes grow heavy as I relax into the plush bedding.

The last thing I see as I drift off to sleep is the promise of more in the dark eyes of the beautiful man lying next to me.

I wake disoriented and confused in my surroundings. Sitting up, I look around the room until my eyes fall on the Adonis beside me.

Well, shit.

He lies on his back with one arm thrown up over his eyes, the sheet wrapped around his legs. The rest of his body is on full display.

He is magnificent.

I'm not sure I've ever seen a man in the flesh with such an incredible physique. Reaching out, I use my pointer finger to follow a large vein that runs the length of his forearm.

He groans but doesn't wake, his hand coming down to rest on the comforter.

His torso is ripped with solid muscles, his chest taut. He has a light smattering of hair leading down into his boxers.

My eyes go wide when I spot his erection.

I promise when you're sober.

I don't know what comes over me, but I kneel beside him, slowly reaching my hand out to palm him through the thin fabric. His cock twitches at my touch, growing harder.

Oh, god! What am I doing?

I freeze, looking up into his eyes in a panic. He stares down at me with a raised brow. Reaching out, he slides a strand of hair behind my ear as if challenging me to continue.

Without a second thought, I slide his boxers from his hips and free him.

Precum glistens on the head, and I bend, my eyes locked on his as I lick the entire underside of him, then flick my tongue across the tip, tasting him.

He groans, grabbing hold of my head as I smile around him. I hollow my cheeks and draw him into my mouth, swirling my tongue across his silky-smooth skin with every bob of my head. My eyes are locked on him, unable to look away as I watch him fight for his control.

His body tenses as I take him to the back of my throat, making his abs ripple under my free hand.

Sensing him losing control, I take him deeper, suck harder, until he is pumping into my mouth relentlessly, his hands holding me where he wants me with an almost painful grip on my hair, and all I can do is take him.

"I'm going to come," he warns.

I swallow around him, and he comes in a rush down my throat. I pull back, struggling to take all of him.

He breathes heavily, throwing his arm back over his eyes before breaking out in a deep chuckle.

I slowly pull back, my cheeks on fire from my arousal.

"Fuck. Is this a wind-up? Did Elliot pay you to do this to me?" He smiles.

I sit back in shock, my stomach turning. "You think I'm a prostitute?"

"What? No!" He reaches for me, trying to run his thumb over my chin, but I snap my head away and wipe it with my forearm.

My eyes burn as I look down at the sticky spot.

I think I'm going to be sick.

"I've got to go." I start to scramble for my things.

"Wait! What? Nina, hold on a second." He tries to untwist from the sheets, but I'm faster and make it out of the room and down the stairs before he can stop me. I rush to the elevator with my shoes and bag in hand, shimming my dress up my legs and discarding the T-shirt on the floor.

The elevator doors slide open, and I'm met with myself. I look into the mirror, tears burning behind my eyes.

All I see is *her*.

Just as the doors begin to close, Mason rushes forward, putting his body between them and forcing them back open.

He grabs me in a desperate hold.

"Get off me!" I yell, hiding my face from him.

"What the fuck is wrong with you?" he demands. "Did Elliot fucking pay you last night?"

I snap my head up, looking straight through him. My chest feels like it's cracking into two.

Does he honestly think that?

He can't think that.

The first tear breaks the dam, and he releases me as if I've slapped him.

"Shit. Nina, I'm sorry, I didn't mean to upset you." He runs his hands through his hair, his eyes wild.

I slam my palms against his chest with everything inside me, pushing him back and clear of the doors.

"Leave me alone, Mason."

3

Nina

I SIT IN THE BACK OF THE TAXI WITH MY LEGS PULLED UP UNDER me, my head lolling to the side as it thuds against the window in regret. I've never felt so dirty—the need to scrub at every inch of my body is overwhelming.

Is this how she felt?

My eyes grow heavy, and I blink them closed before they can fill with tears. I refuse to feel sorry for my mother. It's the last thing she deserves.

Rain falls fiercely on the windshield, the pelting so savage and unrelenting it demands my focus, but does nothing to deter my thoughts from the internal storm that's raging inside me. I stare straight ahead, feeling completely lost.

I'm not angry at Mason (lie). I'm angry at myself. Mad that I put myself in such a degrading situation. I've had one-night stands before, most of them whilst in university, but I have never been left feeling so cheap in my life. Puffing out a breath, I pull out my phone and call Lucy.

"Nina, where the hell are you? You're missing pancakes," she whines.

"Luce, I—" My voice cracks and I try to swallow the lump that's lodged in my throat.

"Where are you? Are you okay?" she asks, her words laced with concern.

A tear rolls down my cheek and I swipe it away quickly, hoping the driver doesn't notice. "I'm in a taxi on my way home."

"I'm on my way babe. I will get Dad to drop me home. Give me half an hour, okay?"

The line goes dead, leaving me alone with my thoughts again and shame gutting me from the inside out.

I notice I have a new voicemail and two missed calls from my mum. How ironic. I hit play, my scalp prickling as her voice drifts into my ears.

"Nina! For goodness sake, call me back. I am your mother! You should show me more respect. You move to the big city, get your fancy studio and think you can snub me. Never forget where you came from, little girl."

Any other day I would fight her words; it's what she wants. If we had a functional mother-daughter relationship, she'd be forced to acknowledge the guilt that I pray festers inside of her. And she is guilty. Guilty of destroying my childhood.

The taxi rolls to a stop outside my building, and I lean in to pay the driver. I catch my reflection in the mirror, instantly cringing. Dark circles surround my eyes from last night's makeup. I look pale, like I've not had enough sleep, and my hair is a matted mess.

I walk up the stairs of my building unhurried, glad to be

home and away from the outside world. My tiny apartment sits on the fourth floor, and its open-plan living makes it seem bigger than it actually is. I have a small U-shaped kitchen along the far wall with a wraparound island. My little kidney-shaped sofa sits against it. The coffee table is currently littered with paperwork, and yesterday's coffee—only half finished—sits cold beside it.

My gaze scans the corner to my left. Where most would have a place to dine, I have a place to dance. A huge free-standing mirror decorates the back wall, with cushioned mats lining the floor beneath it. Fairy lights drape from the ceiling above, illuminating the small nook. It's where I find myself when the world demands more than I'm willing to give.

I throw my bag down on the sofa on the way to my room, digging out a pair of pyjamas from my chest of drawers before heading for the shower.

I stand under the spray for what feels like forever, washing my body repeatedly until I start to feel more like myself again. The devastation I felt only hours ago washed down the drain along with all thoughts of Mason Lowell.

LUCY IS LAYING on my bed by the time I finish showering. She pulls back the duvet for me to slide in, spooning me from behind as she throws an arm around my waist. "We dropped Megan at The Elm. She's getting you breakfast," she tells me.

We lie in silence for a while until Megan arrives fifteen minutes later. She drops down onto the bed, lying sprawled out at our feet.

"Fucking hell, girls, I'm never drinking again," she groans.

I smile into my fist. I can always rely on my girls to be here when I need them, even hungover to shit they show up.

"Nina took me home to my parents. I was sick until four a.m.," Lucy whines at the back of my head.

"Exactly why I took you to your parents, stupid." I hesitate before adding, "I got a lift home with Elliot and Charlie's friend, Mason. I ended up going back to his place."

Megan sits up in a rush, instantly turning pale from the movement. "You did what?"

"I didn't sleep with him. He told me he wouldn't touch me because I'd been drinking." Megan's features relax a little. "But we kissed. A lot." Lucy giggles at my back. "And then this morning, I woke up in his bed, and he was laying there looking all incredible and hot and I... I started to touch him."

I think I've rendered them speechless, neither of them uttering a word.

"He woke up, so I kept going. I ended up giving him head."

"Nina!" Lucy proclaims, clearly not expecting it.

"That's not the worst of it." I close my eyes, memories of the look on his face too much to bear as it plays out in my mind.

"Oh god, you weren't sick, were you? I've totally choked on dick before."

Both me and Lucy lift our heads, grim expressions on both our faces. "What the fuck, Megs?!" I ask as we all fall into silent chuckles.

My face grows solemn as I admit, "He thought Elliot paid me to take him home." I pause. "He thought I was a prostitute."

"Oh, Nina, what an ass!" Lucy croons, pulling me tighter to her.

"Oh, as if! He actually thinks he could afford *you*!" Megan snaps.

"Megan!" Lucy scolds.

"Shit, sorry, Nina. I didn't think," she says apologetically.

I give her a small smile, letting her know it's okay. "I've never felt more like my mother in my life," I mutter.

Lucy sits up, looking down at me as she rests on her arm. "Well, we all know that's a load of rubbish. You couldn't be any more the opposite of that woman. Come on, dry your hair. We are going out."

"Out? Where?" I protest.

"Shopping. And the salon." She smiles.

"Can you drop me home on the way?" Megan asks, looking moments away from sleep.

Lucy gets up, pulling the towel off my body and whipping Megan with it as she heads in the direction of the kitchen. "Nope! Get up. Both of you! It's girls' day."

"Yay, girls' day." Megan quips, lifting her head and observing my state of nakedness, then flopping back to the bed.

IT HAS GONE four when we arrive back at my apartment, our arms full of shopping. We laugh our way up the stairs until we reach my door.

Lucy bends, picking something up from the floor, then spins around, her lips rolling and her eyes popping wide as she stands with a massive bouquet of flowers grasped in her already overfilled hands.

I roll my eyes as I unlock my door, yearning to lean in and smell them.

Inside I stare down at my nails, now a beautiful pale pink —my toes matching. I can tell Lucy is waiting for me to turn around, so I go to the kitchen and flick on the kettle.

"You can chuck those in the bin." I wave the teaspoon at the flowers.

She dips her head to her shoulder, looking all cute as she holds up the arrangement. "Come on, Nina. Maybe you should see what he has to say." She waves an envelope at me. "There's a note."

"I'm going to put all this shopping away, and when I come back, I want them gone. Keep them for yourself for all I care. I want nothing to do with the man or the way he makes me feel." I stomp off to my room, slamming the door like a brat as I go.

I lie on my bed, feeling stupid. I shouldn't be feeling like this over a man I have only known for only a matter of hours. Seeing the flowers only makes me feel weak, and I don't want to know that he's sorry.

I don't want to have to explain myself to him.

A few minutes later, there's a knock at the door, and Megan's head pops around the threshold. "Come on, drama queen, Luce is ordering in Chinese." She winks at me, then disappears again.

We lounge on my sofa, eating takeout from the containers. Greys Anatomy reruns playing on the television, reminding me of our uni days.

"I need a McDreamy," Lucy sighs as she stares longingly at the TV.

"You don't go from Hugh straight to a McDreamy, Luce." I shake my head at her, chuckling under my breath.

"I'll just take a night with McSteamy," Megan says, making us all laugh out loud.

I look to Megan, wondering what she would share if I asked. "Megs, how was Sam last night?" I pop my brow at her.

"Fine. We went back to his." She shrugs her shoulders. "Messed around."

This is all we ever get from her. She doesn't share the dirty escapades of her sex life with us. Sometimes we may get snippets, but rarely any details. We don't care, but it's odd. She's one of the most open people we know—especially with us. Nothing comes out filtered. It's why we love her.

I drop it, not wanting to make her uncomfortable.

"So... I ran into Joey again last night," I say into my food container.

"When?" Lucy looks confused as if trying to work it out.

"When Mason dropped me home—or tried to. I didn't get out of the car right away, and Joey was waiting for me outside."

"Fucking creeper," Megan states.

"He hit Mason, but then Mason pinned him to the car and made him apologise for almost hitting me."

The girls' mouths drop open.

"No flipping way," Lucy says, astonished, a slight smile pulling at the corner of her lip.

"I think he broke his nose." I wince, remembering the awful sound.

"Who, Mason's?" Megan asks.

"No, Joey's. Mason punched him back." The girls look at one another, smirking in unison. "I need to check that Joey is okay on Monday. It was bad, girls."

"Nina, screw him! Go check on Mason!" Lucy gets up on her knees excitedly and I frown.

"What? No! Did you forget about the part when he called me a prostitute?" I retort.

"Well, did he actually use the word prostitute?" she argues back.

I glower at her as she checks her phone that's just pinged with a text.

"Uber's about to arrive." She jumps up, the two of them going to the kitchen to clear up before saying goodbye.

"Thanks, girls, I needed this today." I hug them both close.

"Always," Megan says with a smile.

They are halfway out the door when Luce turns. "Don't forget lunch at Mum's tomorrow. It's your turn to make dessert."

I wrap my arms around myself, feeling grateful to have them both as my best friends. "Bye, girls."

IT's AROUND nine when I hear my phone ringing in my bedroom. I rush to grab it, pulling it from the charger and answering it without looking.

"Nina?!" My mother's shrill voice comes through the line. "Nice of you to finally answer. I've been trying to reach you all week. I need some help this month, I can't manage this place financially on my own."

I close my eyes as she gives me the same old bullshit excuses. "Hi, Mum. I'm fine, thanks for asking," I mutter.

"Oh please, if you'd had answered my call before now, I wouldn't be so stressed out. You can be so selfish sometimes." Ah, there we go with the blame game. It's my fault she is stressed. It's my fault the power got cut off. It's my fault she had to sell her body to pay for new school shoes.

I was just eight when she first started bringing men into our home, sleeping with them for money. She never hid it from me, never apologised or wiped my tears after a night spent hiding in my room, trying to block out the noises.

I puff out a breath, scrubbing a hand down my face and not wanting to remember. "How much this time?"

I shouldn't give it to her. It only gets spent on cigarettes, drugs and alcohol. But I know once I do, I won't hear from her for a while. It's bittersweet, really. How you can long to be held by someone just as fiercely as you fight to keep them at bay; how you can crave a person who has never given you a reason to love them.

And I love her, despite it all.

"Five hundred. I need to cover the electric. I'm two months behind." She tries to justify it, but I've heard it a thousand times before.

I think about my savings account—or the bank of Nina to my mum. I just want her gone; it's been a long week. "I'll transfer it now. Please stop calling me constantly, Mum. Text me, and I will call when I am free. I teach all day."

"Thank you," she tells me, her voice lacking all sincerity before she quickly hangs up. And as always after speaking to her I'm left feeling disappointed. What I would give to be able to speak to my mum, open up about my crappy night and have her tell me I'm being silly and it's just a boy.

I log into my banking app and transfer the money before she starts hounding me as to where it is.

Throwing my phone down on the coffee table, I round the kitchen island to get a much-needed glass of wine. I'm just about to pour it when I spot an envelope on the worktop.

Those damn girls don't listen.

I pick it up and contemplate opening it. Thoughts of Mason as he lay sprawled out on his bed flash through my mind. The feel of his hands as they roamed my torso. The way his scent engulfed me as he buried his face into my neck.

I tear open the envelope, not being able to ignore the nagging feeling in my gut.

NINA, I'M SO SORRY ABOUT LAST NIGHT.
CALL ME. JOEY

Joey?

Pain splinters through me. I toss the card into the bin and ram my hand down on top of the flowers, crushing them the best I can. The disappointment I feel at the realisation that Mason hasn't bothered to contact me is more than I care to admit, which is stupid. Why would he contact me? It was one night—who am I kidding? It wasn't even that. It was a couple hours of drunken stupidity on my part.

I ditch the wine glass and take the bottle back to the sofa instead, feeling foolish to think he would care.

Mase

I PACE my living area for the one hundredth time today, trying to work out what went wrong this morning and how I can fix it. I completely screwed things up with her, but I wish she'd given me a chance to explain.

She thought I was serious about the Elliot paying her thing. I wasn't, and I shouldn't fucking care this much.

Why do I care this much?

Why did I let her leave?

I run my hands through my hair as the elevator doors ping. Elliot strolls into my penthouse without a care in the world. "Where have you been all day, dickhead? I called you earlier."

"Mase." He smiles, walking to me and clasping my back. "It was a late one. I was sleeping when you called. You ready?" His eyes drop down my body, taking in my T-shirt and sweats. "Charlie will be here in a minute."

"I'm not coming out. I've been calling you. Do you have Nina's number? The woman from the bar. She was here last night and—"

"The Pixie? Pixie was here?" he interrupts me in shock.

"She's not called fucking Pixie," I say, pissed off that he's carrying this on.

He breaks out into a stupid, wide grin. "Look at you. You have yourself all worked up over this chick. This is totally like your Pixie," he teases.

My fists clench at my sides as I fight the urge to punch my best friend in the face.

I continue to pace. "I was going to drop her home, but some asshole was waiting outside her building. He almost hit her. I wasn't going to leave her with him lurking around, you know."

"So, you thought you'd bring her here to show off your tower." He laughs, clearly enjoying this.

"I didn't touch her. She was drunk. But she made me promise that I would when she was sober." I shake my head at the memory, knowing it sounds stupid even to my own ears. I've been over this in my head all day. "I woke up to my cock in her mouth."

His eyes pop wide and he jolts his head back. He wasn't expecting that. "Okay, tell me again the reason she isn't your Pixie?"

I ignore his question, rolling my lip before telling him, "I asked her if you paid her."

"You fucking idiot," Charlie snaps as he walks into the foyer. "For a smart bloke, you really are a stupid son of a bitch sometimes." He walks towards us with Lance Sullivan, our head of finance and close friend.

"Fuck off, Charles. I don't want your opinion on this," I tell him, knowing his advice will be the most valuable to me. Charlie is the most headstrong of the group. He knows how to handle the shit life throws at him—and the women. But I refuse to be made vulnerable to this woman.

"Sure, take that dickhead's advice," he snaps.

"Hey, what have I done?" Elliot throws his arms out at his sides smiling.

Sullivan steps forward, a bored look on his face. "If you girls are finished? Maybe we could grab a drink."

My gaze flicks between them all as I contemplate whether I should sit here all night worrying about her, or if I should go get pissed with the lads.

I head upstairs to change.

WE END up in the nearest bar to my building and a favourite of ours, The Rensley Arms. I didn't even want to come out tonight, so there was no way I was going to a club.

Elliot sits back in his seat as he sets four beers down in front of us. "Cheer up, mate," he jibes.

I run my hands through my hair in frustration. "Do you guys think I should reach out to her? She was nearly crying when she left."

I get the image of her in my foyer with her shoes clutched in her hands. God, she was so upset. That look on her face. It's all I'm able to think about.

"Why don't you go to her building and apologise?" Charlie suggests.

"I don't know what number her flat is. We didn't even make it inside." I shake my head, thinking about the way I reacted to her dickhead friend. He deserved the broken nose. He would've hit Nina if I hadn't moved her out of the way.

"Hasn't ever stopped you before." Elliot raises his brow suggestively. "Just get Vinny on it."

I've already thought about this. Vinny is my driver and is ex-special forces. He knows the right people and would get me everything I need on her within the hour.

It just doesn't feel right.

"I don't want to invade her privacy. It's not how I want to do this."

Charlie makes a point of looking at me, nodding his head as if he is impressed. I roll my eyes, taking a sip of beer.

"Shit, Mase, you really have it bad for this girl?" Sullivan's staring at me like I have grown two heads. They aren't used to me giving a shit.

Why do I give a shit?

"I barely know her! These pair of idiots wanted to play matchmaker, I all but called her a prostitute, and now I've managed to get on her shit list."

Elliot raises his glass in a toast. "To Pixies, Prostitutes and getting on their shit lists."

I glare at him. I might kill him.

Feeling defeated—knowing I have to speak with her and see that she is okay—I look to Charlie, seeking his approval. "I can't look her up, can I?" I ask.

He shrugs, a grim expression on his face as he squeezes my shoulder. "I don't know what other option you've got, mate."

I scrub my hands over my face before pulling out my phone, and then I send Vinny a text with all the details I have.

My phone rings instantly.

"I'm out," I tell him.

"You haven't given me a lot to go on here, Mase. How much do you want to know?"

I look to the boys, all of them watching me with intense looks on their faces, and I know I shouldn't ask for it, I know it's wrong, but a mixture of relief and excitement settles in my gut as I say, "Everything."

4

Nina

I GROAN AS I PUSH OPEN THE DOOR TO THE GYM, NAUSEA crawling up my throat as my stomach turns from the sheer weight of it. And probably the wine I drank last night. I came home from lunch at Maggie and John's with a bottle of wine and the other half of the banoffee pie I'd made. Rarely am I late for work, but today, I feel horrific.

Water bottle in hand, I start to weave through the throngs of people and equipment. I chose a shit time to come in today. The gym is packed with everyone rushing to get their workout done in their lunch hour. I catch Logan's eye as I'm passing the treadmills, and he gestures for me to wait a minute while he finishes up with his client.

Oh, not today, please.

I trudge to the main desk, sinking into the chair as a layer of sweat forms on my hairline.

God, I feel awful.

Logan is Lucy's cousin and has worked in the gym since I

opened it. He shares the shifts with Henry, my only other employee. I'm lucky to have them both, and I know I can trust them to have free rein on the gym.

"Anderson, you're looking rough today." Logan rounds the desk and stands behind me, checking the computer in front of me.

"Well, thanks, asshole. That better not be why you stopped me." I squint up at him, the fluorescent lights making my head spin.

"One of the reasons," He winks. "Henry can't work this afternoon. He didn't say why, but it's not like him. Do you have any classes?"

I consider lying. The only thing I want to do this afternoon is sleep. My hand lifts, my fingers running aimlessly over my collarbone.

"Don't try lying to me, Anderson. I already checked your sheet. I have a date, and I'm not cancelling." He gives me a lopsided grin that I can't help but return.

Logan is a total gym freak, his arms the same size as my thighs—maybe. But under all that hardness, he is the softest son of a bitch I've ever met.

"How the hell did *you* get a date?" I roll my eyes, teasing him.

Man, I do not want to cover the gym. I planned to leave right after my second class. Logan knows I won't say no.

"Funny, I will be leaving at four." He ruffles my hair then goes back to his client.

I make my way up the studio stairs, a calmness settling over me once I'm inside. A feeling I've not felt since I left on Friday.

This really is my sanctuary.

I give the floors a quick brush before setting out the mats for the girls' warm-up. I'm just laying down the last one when I hear their giggles as they climb the stairs. Funnily enough, they never use the back door. Something about the muscle show downstairs that they can't miss.

I smile as they come into view, brushing myself off and putting my game face on.

"GIRLS, that's the best I've seen it! We are nearly there!" I say excitedly, and they all start to jump around, high-fiving one another. I make them stretch before they leave for the day, some of them staying on to work out downstairs.

With no more classes scheduled for the rest of the day, I start cleaning the studio mirrors. Logan is here for another hour, and I need to kill some time.

I am midway through when I hear my phone ringing in my bag. Certain it won't be my mum, I go to check who it is.

Erin O'Conner's name lights up the screen, and I smile as I answer.

"Hey, you! It's been months!"

"Nina! I know, I'm sorry. I've been so busy. How are you?" I can hear her smile through the phone.

I knew the moment I met Erin that she was a beautiful person inside and out, a natural redhead, smart and stunning.

I haven't seen her since I first started renting the space, but she has stayed in touch, making sure everything is always okay with the building.

"Ah, you know how it is. Work, men, mothers." I laugh,

pulling myself up to sit on the piano, the phone tucked in the crook of my neck.

She laughs along with me. "That sounds an awful lot like my life right now."

"Well, that makes me feel better, thank you," I say with a smile. "How is your mum?" I ask, feeling bad for moaning about my mum whilst hers is sick.

"Hmmm, she is getting there. It's going to be a long road to recovery," she says sadly.

I try to lift her spirits. "Well, I feel like I'll be needing a trip after this showcase. Maybe I could visit with Luce and Megs. I'm desperate to meet some of these Australian men you've been telling me about."

"Actually, you might see me a little sooner than that. I have some documents that need to be signed and have to come home. I was hoping you'd be okay with me working out of the studio office for a couple of weeks? I know you said you don't use it, so it's totally fine if you don't want me to."

"Erin, of course, it's your office! I don't even use it. When will you be home? I will make sure the girls are free, and we can get drinks." I start to plan in my head.

"Yeah, that would be good! I've missed London so much."

My heart breaks for her a little. "It won't be long, and you'll be back here living the dream," I say, tracing the initials engraved on the back of the piano.

"I wish that were the case, Nina," she says solemnly. " So I plan to fly in on the twenty-fifth. I already booked my flight, hoping you'd be okay with me getting under your feet at the studio." She laughs.

"Well, how presumptuous of you." I smile. "Honestly,

Erin, I don't even know where the key is. I never use it. I won't even know you're here."

"Right, that's set then. I can't wait to see you. Thank you, Nina."

"Of course, take care, lovely. See you soon."

I SPOTTED the Bentley parked up on the other side of the road about an hour ago and have no idea how long Mason has been sitting there. Thankfully, he hasn't come inside—yet. It's why I plan to make a dash out the back once everyone has left the gym.

I still feel mortified about Saturday morning, although why I let my mother's mistakes define my life is beyond me. Lucy was right when she said I am nothing like my mother. Apart from our appearance, we *are* the complete opposite of each other. But sometimes, I find myself judging my morals, fearing that they are a by-product of her.

I wish I'd been more prepared for him to turn up here. I would have made more of an effort, making him feel like an idiot for chasing me away with that mouth.

Now I'm thinking about his mouth, his full soft lips...

"Shit."

Chancing a glance in the gym mirrors, I grimace. My hair is roughly pulled up on my head, my face bare of any makeup, and I'm wearing my yoga pants and a tank top. Yeah, I am definitely going out the back door tonight.

I'm just about to shut down the computer when I hear the door open and close. I know the last few members have not long left, so I sit with my head down, hoping it's just them and they have forgotten something.

Wishful thinking.

The first tell is his smell. It smothers me, taking me straight back to Friday night. Memories of his lips on my neck as he whispered sweet promises in my ear—the feel of him between my legs as I practically begged him to touch me.

God, I'm such a loser.

"Nina," his deep voice purrs from the other side of the desk.

I start to flick through the blank pieces of paper in front of me, double time, as if I am doing something important: anything to keep my hands busy and my eyes off *him*.

Why does he smell so damn good?

"Nina," he says impatiently after a beat.

He doesn't seem like the type of man who likes to be ignored. I quirk a brow at the thought. I'm going to enjoy this. He says nothing, but I can feel his eyes burning into my head.

"I came to apologise for the other morning. I'm sorry if I offended you."

I roll my eyes.

Do better, asshole.

"You left so fast I didn't get a chance to explain. I didn't think Elliot paid you—"

My head snaps up, ready to fight as anger rips through me at his blatant lie, but my words die on my lips when I catch sight of him.

He looks fucking hot. Even hotter than Friday night. He is wearing a three-piece navy suit, his muscular shoulders filling it impeccably, and his hair sits in a perfect tousled mess on his stupidly handsome head.

He looks divine.

He smiles a cocky 'I know I'm beautiful' smile, and I avert my eyes again, composing myself.

"We are closed." I push out from behind the desk, hoping he will take the hint and leave.

He watches me with amusement as I get my bag from the staff room and move to stand at the entrance, waiting for him to leave. He eventually follows, stopping when he is in front of me.

"Let me drive you home," he murmurs, his hand coming up to tuck a strand of hair behind my ear. "Please?"

I want to lean into his touch; he has a hold over me that makes me feel weak. I jerk back, slapping his hand away. "Are you mad? As if I'd go anywhere with you. Leave now! I need to lock up."

"I'm not letting you walk home alone. It's getting dark out." His eyes keep dropping to my lips, and I decide to play with him a bit. I dart my tongue out, wetting them.

Nice. And. Slowly.

"You didn't have an issue with me walking home on Saturday morning," I remind him, folding my arms in front of me.

He steps in closer, his nostrils flaring as his solid chest bumps against my arms. "No, I didn't get a chance to. You ran off like a child before I could even get dressed." He stares down at me, accusing, intense.

"That's a shame, isn't it? Leave." I shoulder past him out onto the street.

He follows behind, his annoyance at my brush-off blatant as he mutters profanity's under his breath.

I'm sure he planned to come here tonight, apologise, and

expected me to drop down at his feet. I mean, I can't imagine he is used to rejection. The mans a stud. An annoyingly handsome, rude stud.

I lock the door and turn, not expecting him to be standing directly behind me. He leans forward, caging me in with his arms on either side of my head. He looks down his perfectly imperfect nose at me, and my resistance wilts under his stare.

"I'm driving you home," he tells me in a no nonsense 'you will do as I tell you' tone.

But he has seriously underestimated me if he thinks he can make demands and expect me to bow down to them.

"What makes you think I'd do what you want?" I whisper, close enough to his lips that I can see the golden flecks in his eyes but not so close that they touch.

Inside, I tell myself it's to see how far I can push him, but I also wonder what I'd do if he closed the distance between us. Just an inch closer, and we'd touch.

My heart thumps against my chest as his eyes dart all over my face, his lips parting.

I turn my head away before he can close the distance between us, and he quickly dips his head, finding my eyes. Our gazes lock, sending a jolt of adrenaline through my entire body. His eyes are almost black now, his brows drawn low, making him look almost troubled. He might be the most handsome man I've ever met.

"I have good word from a *solid* source that you are likely to fulfil my wants and needs." He pops a brow, and I drop my head back to the door, needing the distance it creates.

"Oh, really, and who is this solid source?" I mutter, lost in his eyes.

He smirks, and I curse myself for taking the bait. "My cock."

Shaking my head, I smile sweetly up at him. "I'm afraid that's a rather unimpressive source, Mr Lowell."

Before he can see it coming, I duck under his arm, flinging my bag onto my back as I take off on a run, knowing he isn't wearing the footwear to chase me.

I make it a couple hundred yards down the street before I see his Bentley out the corner of my eye.

"Get in the car," he growls through the open window.

I look at him, frowning. What kind of fool thinks that attitude will work? I up my pace.

"You're acting like a child. Let me drive you home, and I won't bother you again."

"You promise? Although, you aren't all that good at keeping those," I tease, continuing to make him mad.

Running was my escape growing up. I could keep this up all night.

"Last chance," he warns, a white-knuckle grip on his steering wheel.

"I like my chances Bossman, I wouldn't be so sure of yours." I sass before darting off down a side street. I hear his tyres screech to a halt, then his car door being thrown open. I sprint down the cobbled path as car horns blare from the road.

I turn my head back to look at him, but he isn't chasing me. He's at a standstill, staring after me with a perplexed look on his face and absolutely no regard for the traffic jam he is causing.

A laugh escapes me as I reach the end of the path, feeling

like victory is mine. I give him a wink before turning to continue my commute home, only to crash into a solid body.

Strong hands land on my shoulders to steady me, and I look up promptly, ready to apologise. The man is in his late forties early fifties judging by his black hair that's turning silver around the edges, and wearing a black suit and tie. He removes his hands from my shoulders as quickly as he put them there but doesn't move to allow me to pass. I look back to Mason. He is smiling at us, and it's knowing, cocky, victorious. My gaze swings back to the man blocking my exit, instantly narrowing when I catch him giving Mason a nod.

The man looks down at me with amusement in his eyes. "Hello, I'm Vinny." He offers me his hand. "I'll be driving you home today."

"That won't be necessary," I tell him, annoyed at his statement. "I'm happy walking. Thank you."

I try to remember my manners and reluctantly shake his hand whilst it's still outstretched. This isn't his fault, after all.

"Nina, please, it's either I drive you home or him." He raises a bushy brow, tipping his head over my shoulder, but I refuse to look back at him. "It really isn't safe for you to be out on your own at night," he says with genuine concern.

I huff as I feel my resolve starting to slip. "It's not safe for me to be out alone this late, but it's safe to get into a car with a man I've never met, who somehow knows my name?" I question, ever defensive.

"As I said, it's either me or him," he states, horns blaring in the distance. The sound vibrates off the alleyway's walls. It's like the angry motorists are screaming at me to get into the car. It makes it hard to think.

"Well, I'm definitely not going with that asshole." I sulk, crossing my arms as I give in.

He turns and opens the door to the Audi that's sat at the curb. "I wouldn't either." He winks, giving me a warm smile.

Okay, maybe I like this guy.

I slide into the car and fasten my belt, refusing to look to my right, knowing Mason will likely be watching me.

Thankfully, Vinny doesn't say a word on the way home. We arrive at my building without me having to direct him, which only frustrates me more. Who is this man, and why does he know so much about me? Mason knew where I worked, too, although I think I mentioned it to Charlie and Elliot on Friday night. Maybe he asked them.

I lean over to open the door, but Vinny stops me, his voice commanding that I listen. "He means well, love. He's not a bad bloke."

Our eyes lock in the rearview mirror, my hand frozen on the handle. Maybe Mason isn't a bad bloke. Perhaps it was an unfortunate choice of words on his part—that I can believe. But it doesn't take back the hurt those words caused.

"Thank you for the lift home," I say as I push open the door. Vinny nods his head, not saying any more as I exit the car.

It's easier to forget *him* than the words he spoke to me. They seemed to penetrate me deeper—stuck quicker.

THE GIRLS ARE ALREADY SEATED at The Elm when I arrive. It's a quirky little café on Oxford Street. We try to meet when our lunch breaks allow it, but with our ever-changing schedules, it's hard. Lucy is a fashion designer, and Megan is a columnist for a women's magazine.

Sliding into the bench seat, I grin as I watch the girls speak animatedly between one another. I only catch the tail end of what Megan is saying, but her words have my eyes bugging out in surprise. "A picture of his damn cock!" she exclaims as she stares super close to the phone in her hand.

"Oh, Jesus, what now?" I groan, my shoulder dropping. "I don't know if I can deal with any more penis this week."

"Hugh thinks he's huge," Megan roars with laughter, thrusting the phone out at me. Stupidly, I take it, peeking down at the screen.

I lean my shoulder into Lucy, a hand grasping my chest. "He did not send you a dick picture!" I can't control the laughter that leaves me.

"Uh-huh, he thinks what? That I will be sad I'm missing out on." She screws her face up in disgust at the phone. "That?!"

Megan wipes the corner of her eyes with a napkin, trying to recover from her laughing fit, as she asks, "Why is he even messaging you? He ended it."

"He's been messaging since Sunday evening. He says he wants to meet."

"You're not considering it, are you?"

She looks at me as if I'm crazy, but I already know she will give him every opportunity to be 'Mr Right'.

"No! Of course not. He can do one. I'm so over him!" she states, resolute.

"Good, you're too good for the likes of Hugh," I tell her, plucking the menu from between the salt and pepper pots.

Megan stands to get the coffees when the barista signals

they're ready, and I'm thankful that the girls have already ordered for me. Flattening my hands to the steaming mug, I bring my hot chocolate to my lips and take a sip of the sugary liquid.

"So, Erin called today. She is coming home in a few weeks," I tell them, licking my lips.

"I didn't think she could leave her mum?" Lucy questions, her brows drawing downward in a frown.

Hmm, I didn't think about that. "Yeah, I'm presuming she has someone to help her whilst she is here." I shrug. "She wants to use the studio office. I thought we could plan a night out whilst she is here."

"Do you even need to ask?" Megan grins.

"Will she be up for it? She didn't seem like the type to hit the clubs when we met her," Lucy asks.

"She said she wanted to. And she had just found out about her mum when we met her. Having to leave everything behind here to go look after her can't have been easy."

"Yeah, I didn't think about that. It will be nice to see her! I bet she could use the break," Lucy says into her coffee.

I hear my phone ringing in my bag and lean down to dig around for it, pushing all the crap inside about to find it.

Shit.

I cringe at the screen when I see who it is. "It's Joey," I tell the girls. I stupidly gave him my number the first night I met him. He seemed like a cute guy at the time, and I didn't know he would be a clinger.

I let it ring out, missing the call.

"The note that managed to crawl out of the bin," I pin them both with a pointed glare. "it was from Joey. The flowers, they weren't from Mason."

"What? Ugh, damn Joey." Megan waves her hand dismissively.

"But then Mason turned up at the gym last night. I was covering Henry and didn't have anyone for backup."

"No?!" Lucy places her hand on her chest dramatically, hanging off my every word. "How did he know where you work?"

"I'm presuming Elliot and Charlie told him."

"Really? I don't think they would have remembered. I can barely remember anything past the second round of tequila," she says, wincing at the memory.

"Well, he knew. He apologised for Saturday and then wanted to drive me home. I refused."

"Why? I thought you said this guy is hot," Megan asks.

"He is. Trust me, girls. He is beyond hot! But he *demanded* that he was driving me home, and he called me a child for running out on him on Saturday morning."

"Oh, dickhead comment." Megan shakes her head, dropping back to the seat as Lucy's face drops in disappointment.

"Yep," I mutter, staring into my cup. "I'm not going to fall at his feet. Again. I need to put aside his looks and keep my wits about me. He needs to understand who's in charge here." I smirk. "Also, I think he made his driver come for me so I wouldn't walk home alone when I refused to go with him."

"You went with his driver?" Lucy asks.

"Yeah, Mason must have called him. I thought he was a better option than Mason's car."

"You're an idiot," Megan sighs.

"What? Why?"

My phone starts to dance across the table again. Joey. I go to pick up the phone.

"Don't answer that." Megan smacks my hand in a rush, sending the phone to the ground and causing her coffee to spill over the table.

I bend to snatch it up off the floor before someone stands on it. My accusing eyes meet hers. The screen has smashed into a million pieces. "What did you do that for, you tit!"

"Sorry!" She shrinks in the seat. "I will replace it, but you cannot seriously be willing to talk to Joey when you have Mason actively seeking you out, following you home, making sure you're safe," she points out, and Lucy all but swoons in her seat.

"I was only going to check if he is okay." I look down at my phone. "You've completely killed it," I sigh.

Lucy tries to hold in her hopeful smile. "I'm with Megs. Sorry. Team Mase all the way."

They high-five as I look back and forth at the pair of idiots, trying to hold back my own smile.

I am not team Mase.

I don't want to be team Mase.

I am so fucking screwed.

5

Mase

It has been four days since Nina ran out on me, and I can't seem to shake her off. Nothing works. Not my work. Not the gym. She's stirred something deep inside me that I don't recognise, and I have no idea why.

The fact that she doesn't listen to a fucking word I say turns me on just as much as it pisses me off.

Like her running from me yesterday, I enjoy the chase as much as the next man, but fuck, is it worth it?

I haven't felt this off-centre since Cara. Just thinking about that woman gives me chills—a perfect example of why I don't bring women into my home. You'd have thought I would have learnt after past mistakes.

It's why I know it shouldn't have felt so right having Nina in my home and in my bed. It's stupid, but I can't help but want to let the light back in again, and she seems to shine brighter than the dazzling lights of London. Maybe I should have kept my mouth shut and slept with her when I had the chance.

The image of her knelt beside me on the bed invades me, her warm mouth wrapped around my cock as she took me to the back of her throat.

My thighs strain in my trousers, and I—

"Lowell, you massive prick!" Elliot throws open my office doors, interrupting my dirty thoughts.

I quickly roll my chair under the desk, effectively hiding my semi under the hardwood—pun not intended.

"Can you fucking knock?" I snap, pretending to look at something on my monitor.

He stops short, halfway to my desk. "You're not watching porn, are you?" His face morphs into a knowing smirk. "You are, aren't you!"

"Fuck off Elliot. What do you want?"

"Why did you fire my PA?" His face turns serious as he places his hands on his hips.

Emma, Elliot's personal assistant, decided she'd had enough of his reluctance to do anything more than sleep with her. I found his office completely trashed on Friday morning, and the words 'whore' sprayed in red on the entire glass wall for the rest of the office to see. If Elliot turned up to work more than three days a week, he would have known this. I've fired all five of his previous PAs after they've either ended up going batshit crazy on him or damaged property that doesn't belong to them.

"What was her name?" I question, as I look at the same spreadsheet I've been staring at for the last two hours.

"What does that matter? I've got a shit ton of emails to get through, and my computer isn't letting me log in." He frowns. "Did you hire someone else?"

"No, do it yourself," I tell him, bored.

He doesn't say anything. We both know he doesn't have a clue where to start when looking for staff.

I huff out a long breath as I pick up the phone, and I dial Sal in HR. "I need a personal assistant for Montgomery."

She tsks, then I hear her tapping on her keyboard. "I will see what I can do, Mr Lowell, but we struggle to find anyone from the agency nowadays with Mr Montgomery's track record."

"Up the salary five-k a year, I want a male." My eyes flick to Elliot. "If it's a female, she needs to be over fifty." I hang up.

Elliot stands, smirking at me. "You know I'm not afraid of a cougar."

"Sleep with your next assistant, and I will fucking fire *you*."

"What's crawled up your ass, you miserable prick. You have slept with more than your fair share, your receptionist for starters." He gestures towards the reception desk that's hidden beyond the frosted glass windows.

"*Our* receptionist is called Alice, Elliot," I mutter deadpan. And Alice knows how this works. I don't *date* any of my employees, and I never take them to my home. There are no promises of more, and I make sure they are well aware of that before I stick my dick in them.

Elliot, on the other hand, took his last assistant to his parents for a weekend away and then wonders why she thinks she's different.

That one just ended up batshit crazy. She didn't even

cause any fuss. Thankfully, we can pay people to deal with crazy.

"Whatever. I need someone from IT to come fix my computer." He lays himself down on my office sofa, his feet hanging over the armrest.

"It's a new computer, dumbass. That's why you can't log in. The password and set-up details are in your top drawer." I open my own drawer, retrieving a key and chucking it at him.

"Where is my old computer? And why do you have my key?" He frowns in confusion but doesn't move from the sofa.

I pinch the bridge of my nose, fed up with this conversation. "It's a new desk, Elliot. Your assistant, Emma, bashed the shit out of yours with her stilettos. Your computer suffered a similar fate."

He sits up, smiling. "I knew she was a feisty little minx." He laughs.

"Your father turned up at the same time as the cleaners." I scowl at him, not finding this at all funny.

"Well shit, that's what Dad was going on about. Fuck! Sorry, Mase. Are you coming out on Friday, yeah? You completely bailed on us last weekend." He comes to stand in front of my desk, glancing around at the screen.

"I'm not watching fucking porn, Elliot." I shoot him a look of disbelief. "And I would have been out, but after I dealt with your latest victim, your father, and then had to deal with *my* father," I remind him, my rage only building with the memory. "I wasn't exactly in the mood."

"But you still showed up." He tilts his head, looking at me pointedly. "Even after dealing with your dad." He's still smirking as if this is all funny to him. Then he goes deeper.

"Why was that Mase? Wasn't anything to do with a certain Pixie?"

I clench my jaw so tight I'm surprised I don't crack a tooth. "We're not six years old anymore, Elliot. Grow up!"

"She was smoking hot though, wasn't she, and a dancer. I knew you'd like her. It's a good job I didn't have her for myself."

Rage seeps through me, and I slam my fist down on the desk. "Don't fucking talk about her," I growl.

He grins. Prick. "Calm down, Lowell. I'm winding you up. Did Vin get what you needed?"

I run my hand through my hair, trying to calm down and gather my thoughts. "When doesn't he?"

"You've been to see her, I presume?" he asks.

"What do you think?" I mutter.

"I think she's your Pixie, mate, that's what I think." He chuckles. "I don't think I've seen you this put out over a girl ever."

"Mason, your eleven o'clock is on his way up," Alice says through the intercom.

"Off you fuck, Montgomery." I stand, dismissing him as I button up my suit jacket, thankful for the interruption.

"Drinks. Friday night," he says, pointing at me as he backs out of my office.

Nina

"Why won't you open!" I yell, my hand smacking against the solid wood of Erin's office door. I searched all day for the key, finally finding it in the gym's staff room, but now I have spent the last twenty minutes trying to get inside. It will not flipping open!

"Alright, crazy, out the way before you hurt yourself." Logan comes up behind me, probably fed up with my banging.

He lifts me off my feet, moving me out of the way as if I don't weigh a thing. "Are you sure this is the right key?" He pulls it from the lock, examining it.

"Yes, I'm sure. It wouldn't be the key to anything else in this place." I look up at him, unsure. "Would it?"

"I'm not sure, Nina. This key looks new, and the lock is ancient." He shrugs, trying the door again before bending and looking through the keyhole.

I pout, crossing my arms over my chest. "I've been looking all afternoon! I'm giving up. If it doesn't turn up by next week, I'm going to need you to put those muscles to good use and break the door down." I squeeze his solid bicep.

"I've got some time now, so I'll see if I can find it. The staff room is desperate for a tidy up anyway," he offers.

"Thanks, Logan, you're a lifesaver." I push up on my tiptoes to peck his cheek before I turn and disappear into the studio to get my bag.

"Hey! There's a guy asking for you downstairs. Said his name is Mason, got riled up when I told him he couldn't come up here," he calls from the doorway.

"Mason? He's downstairs?" A flare of panic spreads through me.

"Sure is. Got a right chip on his shoulder that one. Want me to get rid of him?" he says, puffing out his chest.

God no, which is exactly why I should say yes.

I didn't sleep a wink last night, thoughts of Mason Lowell in his suit consuming me, hmmm delicious, then, sans the suit. Yep, even more delicious. I never knew I had such a fantastic imagination until now.

"No. It's fine, thanks, Logan. I'll see you Friday. Henry's in tomorrow, isn't he?"

"Yeah, if I find the key, I'll leave it in the safe," he calls out as I make my way around the studio, tidying up in a rush.

I stop at the mirror to make sure I look semi-presentable —not that I care—and my face screws up instantly. I mean, it's not great, but it isn't bad either. My hair is letting me down massively, sitting in a heap high on my head, tuffs poking out all over the place. I can't dance with it in my face, and there is just so much of it.

I pull my hairband out, fluffing it over my shoulders, trying to flatten it down and resolving to the fact that it will have to do. Then I grab my bag and take off down the stairs.

In my head, I'd walk down the stairs, take a moment to seek him out—find him first. The studio is my territory, after all. Unfortunately, I don't get that luxury, and I'm caught completely off guard by him, which is ridiculous because I knew he was here.

He stands at the bottom of the steps, waiting for me. His jaw taut, and lips pressed together. His brows pulled low. I want this man angry all the time. I mean, I have seen his smile. It's breathtaking.

But angry Mase is fucking fire. I want to douse myself in petrol and climb him like a tree.

I pull my top lip between my teeth to try and stop my smile, my walls slowly crumbling.

How am I supposed to resist this man?

"Mr Lowell, to what do I owe the pleasure?" I can't hold it in any longer, a smile splitting my face.

He seems taken aback by my mood. "Uh, I just wanted to see if you needed a lift home," he stutters.

"Oh, yes, please," I say sweetly.

He looks at me completely and utterly confused. "You do? You want a lift home? With me?" He frowns, his pointer finger nestled between his solid pecs.

I think I've broken him.

"Is Vinny here?" I ask.

"Yes, he's around the back," he admits.

"Around the back." I nod, surprised that he went to so much trouble to scope the place out. And why around the back? Was he preparing for me to run?

I take the last step, standing tall as I look up at him through my lashes. "I think I will go with Vinny today. If you don't mind?"

His jaw tightens. He doesn't argue, but I can tell he doesn't like my answer. "I'll walk you out," he grumbles, letting me go first as he follows closely behind as I walk down the narrow hall.

I'm almost at the door when I feel his hands snake around my waist, his warm fingers flexing against the exposed flesh between my leggings and crop top. He turns me, pinning me against the door, his knee pressing roughly at the apex of my thighs. My clit throbs as he looks down at me, gently bringing his forehead to rest against mine.

His hands skim me, waist to hips, holding me in place, and all I can think is how good he feels pushed up against me.

"Keep this up, Nina. I have nothing." He rolls his hips, his erection prodding my stomach. "Fucking nothing, better to do," he grits out, brushing his lips from my ear to my neck. He plants one soft kiss on the smooth skin, his nose trailing over the spot before he pulls away from me.

I stand flustered, chest heaving, and desperately craving his touch as he pulls open the door and leaves me without looking back. I let my head drop back to the wall, trying to ease the arousal coursing through me.

Taking a deep breath, I pull open the door; Vinny is waiting right outside, the Audi parked and ready for me.

I give him half a smile, mortified that he could have seen us but knowing it's impossible. "Hi, Vinny."

"Nina, nice to see you again so soon," he says as I skirt past him and climb into the car.

I wait for him to get seated in the driver's seat then say, "I'm sorry, you must have far more important things to do than drive me around the city."

"I don't do what's important to me; I do what's important to Mr Lowell." He winks.

"You're his driver?" I ask with a frown.

He has a funny look on his face as if what I am saying is amusing. "Yes. I'm his driver," he confirms.

"How long have you worked for him?" I decide to get as much out of him as I can whilst I have the chance.

"Sixteen years now," he says proudly, eyeing me in the mirror again. I want to ask so many questions.

I need to pick the right ones.

"Sixteen years? That's a long time." I study him as he drives. I wouldn't have put Vinny at much past fifty, so he had to be young when he started.

"I was thirty-eight, straight out of the forces when his father hired me," he says, confirming my suspicions.

"Do you always drive his—" I pause, looking for the right word. "Female friends."

I definitely wouldn't call Mase my friend.

"No, you're the only 'female friend' I've been asked to drive." He says with a grin.

Hmm, interesting. Does Mason feel bad about calling me a prostitute, so now he is palming me off on his driver?

Or is he actually interested?

"He normally drives them himself?" I ask, and god, I sound pathetic.

"Maybe you should ask him yourself?" he says. I take the hint, not asking any more questions for the rest of the journey.

Vinny turns in his seat once we arrive at my building, passing me a card. "My number if you need a lift ever. Mr Lowell would be grateful if you'd call me when travelling alone."

I roll my eyes, slipping the card into my bag with the rest of my junk. I don't need my own personal taxi! Who even has that much money that they can just send a driver on demand? "Thank you again for the lift," I say, climbing from the car and then waving him off.

I'M HALFWAY down Oxford street, admiring my shining new phone screen, which I haven't been able to use since Megan smashed it, and I'm shocked at how much I've missed it.

Scrolling through my messages on the lock screen, I close my eyes, cursing my friends under my breath.

The messages are mostly from Lucy and Megan. They knew I was picking it up, and they've sent me a load of dirty messages. The latest one reading, 'You left your vibrator in the shower again'. It's the first message on the list, and there's no way the repair guy wouldn't have seen it.

I scroll down the list.

'Ben called, he's got the Syph! Better get checked hun' I laugh out loud, unable to control myself. Those bitches! I will kill them!

Swiping across the screen, I see I have six missed calls, all from Joey. I really should check he is okay. I decide to call him back, and he answers on the second ring.

"Nina! Hi, I've been calling. Are you okay?" he rushes out, sounding genuinely worried.

My step falters with his tone, his concern throwing me off. "Hi Joey, I'm fine. I smashed my phone screen, and I've just picked it up from the repair shop."

"Ah, yeah. That makes sense. Do you want to meet for a coffee? I am working just up the road from your studio today."

"I'm actually heading home, Joey. Sorry," I lie and instantly feel bad. I start to backpedal. "Maybe tomorrow?" Oh god, stop talking, Nina. I put my hand on my head as I try and worm my way through the conversation. I might as well have met him today. Get it over and done with.

"Yes! Tomorrow is fine. I will meet you at the studio. What time?"

"That's okay. I'll meet you at the café. Is The Elm okay? Let's say, at twelve o'clock?"

It's close for me to get back after and I'd rather go somewhere I know, in case I need to make a quick exit.

"Sounds good Nina, I'm looking forward to seeing you."

"You too, Joey. See you tomorrow!" I hang up, regretting calling him in the first place. He is obviously okay.

I want to launch my phone at the ground because of my inability to say no. I refrain myself, though, glaring down at my reflection in my shiny new screen.

IT'S LATE when I finish my last lesson. Henry left an hour ago, locking up the gym behind him. I had one of my under fourteens in for a one-to-one session this evening. It's a great little money booster for me with bills to pay, but more importantly, it shows me their passion for dancing.

The studio lights illuminate the room as darkness blankets the vast world outside. It's my favourite time of day to be here and the only time I allow myself to switch off fully.

Making my way over to the speaker, I plug in my phone and find the song I want. Alessia Cara pours from the speakers moments later, singing about being beautiful just the way you are. I close my eyes and let the music take over my soul, dancing around the studio as I get lost in the only form of therapy my body knows.

IT'S NINE P.M. when I finally flick off the lights to the studio. I bolt down the stairs and across the gym to the main door like a wimp, afraid of the dark. Pulling open the door, I glance around to make sure no one is waiting in the shadows to mug me. My dramatics are warranted based on London crime rates these days.

My stomach dips when I spot the Audi waiting at the curb, the fear I felt moments ago chased away by a warmth that spreads through my chest.

Vinny gets out of the driver's seat and opens the door for me, dipping his head to the side in question.

I smile, turning to lock the door.

"I hope you haven't been waiting long?" I ask, stepping past him and sliding into the seat.

"Not long at all," he says, shutting the door and rounding the car. I know Vinny is lying. He has no idea when I'm coming or going; I don't have set times.

I am going to have to put a stop to this.

"You're too nice, Vinny. You should tell him to piss off." My lip twitches. "It's fun, you know, making him angry."

"You have no idea, Miss Anderson," he chuckles, the corner of his mouth tipping up like mine.

I relax into the seat, my body going lax as I finally allow myself to stop. It's been the longest day, and I really am glad for the lift.

"No Mason this evening?" I remark.

Vinny's brows pull in, his lips forming a thin line. "No. I'm afraid he got caught up at the office and couldn't get away."

I frown, checking the time on the dash. "It's nine o'clock. Does he always work this late?"

"When necessary," he mutters, not giving me any more than that. Clearly, he doesn't want to tell me, and that's fine.

"I appreciate you being here tonight, Vinny. I'm not sure my poor feet would've managed much more tonight."

His features soften a little, his shoulders relaxing. "It's my pleasure, Nina, although it would help me if you could call when you're nearly ready to leave. Mason will send me whether you like it or not," he says.

I roll my eyes as I smile. This is all well and good, but why? Why is he insistent on having me driven around? "Well, now I feel bad. How long were you waiting today?"

"Only a couple of hours," he chuckles.

"A couple of hours! Vinny, that is ridiculous! Why didn't you come in and check how long I'd be?"

"That's what—"

He's cut off by his ringing phone. Reaching forward, he taps the car's touchscreen, answering on the first ring.

"Anything?" Mason snaps, his voice echoing through the entire car.

I give Vinny a wink to let him know I've got this. "Hello Mr Lowell, how are you this evening?" I purr playfully. Vinny shakes his head as he looks out the window, but I can see his smile as I try to hold back my giggles.

"Good, you've got her. I'm ready when you're finished there," he responds, then hangs up.

I sit back in shock.

Is this prick for real?

"He's had quite the day, don't take it personally," Vinny tries to explain.

I unbuckle my belt, leaning forward in my seat. I tap on the screen pulling up the recent call list and then press on Mason's name.

He answers on the second ring.

"What?" he huffs.

I shake my head, blinking in surprise. "You didn't say

please," I say, looking at Vinny. His eyes are wide as he stares straight ahead.

I shrink back a little.

"Excuse me?" Mason shoots back.

Crap. I have to follow through. I can't back down now. "You didn't say please when you asked Vinny to pick you up. Some manners wouldn't hurt, you know, and if having someone drive me home is such an inconvenience to you, don't do it." I keep my voice steady, making sure I get my point across. At no point have I asked Mason to go out of his way for me.

I sit back in my seat, and the car goes dead fucking silent, no one saying a word for what feels like forever.

I'm waiting for him to flip.

Or hang up.

Vinny lifts his hand to end the call.

"I will see you soon, Vinny, thank you," he replies.

My head flicks around to Vinny in shock, his face mirroring mine.

"Mason?" I murmur with a slight teasing in my tone.

"Yes, Nina," he sighs, addressing me for the first time.

My dimple creases my cheek. "Thank you for the lift home. I didn't want to walk alone this late. I really do hope you have a better evening," I say softly.

I end the call, sitting back in the seat as I process the last few minutes in my head.

Maybe I should have sat back and said nothing, but manners are free, and he is lacking.

"Put your seat belt back on, Nina," Vinny tells me, his voice quiet.

The rest of the ride home is made in silence.

6

Nina

THE SHRILL SOUND OF MY DOORBELL HAS ME FREEZING IN THE shower mid hair wash. I'm not usually a jumpy person, but it's always in the shower that my apartment seems to come to life. I start to wash the shampoo from my hair double time, the bell ringing again, more violently than the first time. Not bothering to use any conditioner, I snatch my towel from the floor and wrap it around my body before I rush from the bathroom, my feet leaving puddles in their wake.

I pull open the door just an inch to see who it is.

A delivery man is standing with a long rectangular box in his hand. He thrusts it through the small gap in a rush, making the door bounce back into my forehead.

Ouch!

"Can you sign here?" he huffs.

I try to hold my towel, the box and the pen, but it's a task. I'm sure by the time I kick the door closed, he has probably seen my nipple. Not that the impatient jerk deserved the extra tip, he could see I was fresh from the shower.

Pulling my towel tight, I scurry to the sofa and sit down with the box. It's matte black with gold foiling decorating it in deep swirls. Sliding off the lid, I find a single white rose nestled in the silk lining. I can't help my smile. It's a goofy, all-teeth kind of smile that you hope no one ever sees.

One lone rose.

It's beautiful in its simplicity, and I know *exactly* who it's from. Slipping the note from the box, I stare at it.

It's from Mason, I'm sure of it. But something nags at my gut as I peel back the seal.

Still, excitement flares through me as I slide out the card.

YOU WANT MY MANNERS?
I WANT YOUR TASTE. ON MY TONGUE, MY COCK, EVERYWHERE.
PLEASE.

Excitement turns to shock as a wave of arousal sweeps over me, catching me off guard. I sit and stare at his words, rereading them until they don't make sense anymore.

I was expecting something sweet to go with the beautiful gift. I was not expecting this. Grasping the pillow at my side, I begin to fan myself, thoughts of Mason and *his* taste—that I've already stolen—causing my body to heat.

I am so flipping turned on it's ridiculous.

He would have known what his words would do to me, and I'm not sad about it. He's had me eating out of the palm of his hands on every encounter so far.

I take his note with me to my room. The rose long forgotten.

Lying back on my bed, I let the promise in his words and the gentle touch of my fingers find the release my body desperately craves.

Mase

Elliot: Come here

I FROWN AT MY PHONE, wondering what the hell Elliot wants. It's Friday and his day off.

Mase: Where?
Elliot: My office

What? Is he in today? I push my chair back from my desk, striding to the door. The reception area is empty, and Alice stands the second she sees me, her back ramrod straight.

"Is Montgomery in today?" I ask.

She nods. "Yes, he got in at around ten. Can I get you anything, Mason?"

"Yes, you can call me Mr Lowell," I deadpan, walking off in the direction of Elliot's office. It's at the opposite end of the floor, the mirror of my own. I don't knock.

"What the fuck are you doing here?" I ask, stepping into the room. He is standing in his office bathroom, rearranging his tie. "Actually, don't answer that." I don't want to know.

I walk to his desk and start looking through his paperwork, my brows rising in surprise when I see he has been working.

"Don't act so surprised, asshole. I've been in five days this week." He strides back into the office, looking cocky.

"I'm more concerned than surprised." I place my hand on his forehead. "Are you feeling okay?"

"Fuck off, Lowell," he snaps, batting my hand away. "My dad's been in my ear. If I don't start doing more, he will be coming out of fucking retirement," he grumbles, pushing his blond mop out of his eyes.

"Hey, I'm kidding," I say honestly. "It's good to have you here, mate." I drop down onto the chair opposite his desk. "I just spoke to Charles. He is on his way over."

"Good, I called Sullivan up as well," he says.

As he says it, Alice buzzes through the intercom. "I have Charlie and Lance here for you, Elliot, Mr Lowell."

Elliot sits back, affronted, before he leans in and speaks to Alice through the speaker. "You don't need to tell us that. They should be on the approved list. And it's Mr Montgomery, thanks," he tells her.

And rightfully so, she needed to hear it from Elliot too. The line of professionalism around here is thinning by the day. We need a good shakeup. Elliot being in the office more is a start.

Charlie and Lance stroll in and start chatting shit with Elliot whilst I order in our lunch. It's been months since we have all been in the office together. Charles Aldridge—our best friend—is a lawyer and works in an office just a few minutes up the road. We have known him since college. He opened his own firm six years ago and now has four spread out over the country. Turning over five million pounds last year, it's safe to say he is doing alright for himself.

Lance Sullivan works downstairs, running our accounts department. He is two years younger than the three of us, but it doesn't show. Not only does he fit with us, but he also keeps the company financially stable—A multimillion pound company. He may be a prick at times, but he is a savage, and I wouldn't have anyone else in his place.

"We are going out tonight, yeah?" Sullivan asks when I'm off the phone.

I stand and walk to the sofa, leaning on the back of it. "Yeah, I'm game. Where you thinking?" I ask.

"Somewhere that's got plenty of pussy." Elliot smiles, stretching back in the seat and widening his knees.

Charlie cringes, thwacking him in the gut with a cushion and making Elliot shoot forward.

"I'd start looking at the quality instead of quantity if I were you, mate," Charlie tells him.

He shrugs. "That's what my forties are for. I'm in my prime and ready to give a good ribbing."

"You're pure filth, Montgomery." Charlie chuckles.

"Sue me!" Elliot replies.

"Please, fucking sue him," Lance pipes up. "He wouldn't stand a chance in prison," he laughs.

"Fucking funny, Sullivan. Keep it up, and you can eat in your office on your own."

"Calm your tits, Elliot. He was only joking—"

My eyes snap up when Vinny walks into the room. I don't think I had any appointments today. Have I missed something? It wouldn't surprise me if I had. My mind has been preoccupied this past week.

"Alright, Vin?" I ask.

"A word," he says.

I look to the boys. "It's fine. What's up?"

His jaw locks, annoyance etching the lines of his face. "Nina Anderson. You asked me to let you know... she is currently at The Elm café with Joey Wilson."

Joey fucking Wilson. I should have known he wouldn't listen; the little prick has a death wish.

"She is having coffee, Mason," Vinny assures me. "I don't think It's necessary to—"

Charlie sits forward, cutting Vinny off as I stand. "Think before you do anything stupid, Lowell."

"Vinny, is Nina safe with Joey?" I ask, not looking at him, already knowing the answer.

"Sat in a public café, yes, I would have intervened if she wasn't."

"And if she leaves with him?" I shoot back.

"She is smarter than you think Mason, give the girl some credit." Vinny says.

Nina is smart. That isn't my worry. My concern lies with *him* and the file on my desk that tells me everything I need to know about the prick.

"No. Let's go." I leave my friends in the office, not willing to risk it and not giving a shit what anybody thinks.

Nina

MY FEET DRAG as I make my way to The Elm, annoyed that I agreed to meet Joey in the first place. I plan to have a coffee and then get out of there. Fast. I need to set him straight and tell him I'm not interested. He can't think he has a chance, making advances on nights out and sending me flowers.

I call Lucy before I turn the corner to the café.

"Hey, babe, you on lunch?" Lucy's infectious voice chimes down the line, instantly making me smile.

"Hey! Ugh, yes. I'm about to meet Joey at The Elm," I groan.

"What? Why?" She tuts into the phone. "You don't owe him anything, Nina."

"I felt bad, and I haven't ever set him straight. I need to put a stop to it for his own benefit. The poor bloke got his nose broke!"

She huffs, relenting. "Fair enough, but men need to learn not to presume that because we are nice to them, we want to sleep with them. You haven't led him on here. Not once."

"I agree." I start to laugh as I think of Mason and how I've not been nice to him, yet he still pursues me.

"What's funny?" she asks.

"I have so much to tell you girls! Can we go out tonight?"

"Yes! Where?" she says excitedly. "I will ring Megs now!"

"Hold on, that's not why I rang!" I rush out.

"I know, you want me to call in twenty with a broken arm or something. I got you, girl!"

I laugh at the fool. "Only if I text you! I will call after. Love you, Luce." I hang up.

Joey is already seated when I enter the café, and I make my way over to him.

He stands to kiss my cheek. "Nina! You made it."

"Of course, how are you?"

"I'm okay." His eyes drop to his watch, then flick back to my face.

"Good, sorry. I had a class," I explain.

I've only ever seen Joey at the gym in passing once, and then in the darkness of clubs when I've seen him on nights out, so I quickly do a scan of him from head to toe, trying to get a feel for his mood.

His hair is neatly cut on the sides but longer on top, the inky strands falling in front of deep green eyes until he pushes it back and off his face. I can see he still has some light, purple bruising under each eye but otherwise seems to have recovered. His body is lean, I wouldn't say he works out, but he naturally has definition in all the right places. If he didn't try so hard, I probably would have gone on a date with him by now.

"Sit down," he tells me. "I'll get our drinks. What do you fancy?"

I give him my order, and he goes to the counter.

I sit and scroll through my phone, wondering whether I can text Luce now to save me. The thought gives me pause, and I look up at Joey. He hasn't done anything wrong; he just doesn't understand where my head is at. And maybe that's on me.

Once he is sitting back down, I prepare myself, searching for the right words to say to him.

"So, I wanted to apologise for last week, and you should know I forgive you," he says.

What?

He forgives *me*?!

I swallow the anger bubbling up in my throat. "Sorry, you forgive me for what exactly?"

He seems surprised, his brows dropping low. "For leaving with that dickhead who hit me."

I sit back in my seat, trying to mask my annoyance. "Joey, you need to understand something, and I'm sorry for putting it so bluntly, but I'm not interested in anything other than a friendship with you. And! Who I spend time with has absolutely nothing to do with you. I certainly don't want your forgiveness."

"Oh, of course. I didn't mean it like that. I just thought… you know. You didn't know him so…"

"As I said, it's really not your business. I'm sorry for everything that happened in the club and the way things ended." I pause. "You did hit him first, though, Joey. You almost hit me."

He runs his hand over his face. "I know. I'm sorry, I don't know what came over me."

My shoulders sag, feeling better now I've been honest with him. "It's fine. It's done now. Let's just move on from it." I give a half smile, feeling awkward and wanting to wrap things up.

"Yeah, sure, and I'm sorry again." He steeples his hands, resting them against his mouth, a pensive look on his face.

My knee bounces under the table, my patience wearing thin. "What is it?"

"I have a huge favour to ask, and you don't have to do it if you don't want to. I feel like I've screwed things up to be honest, and I probably shouldn't ask, but you are kind of perfect for it." He watches me for a reaction, but I keep my face stoic. "I have a unit coming up in my course that looks at the art of dance. We are required to capture it in images. I'm hoping you will help me?"

My brows rise involuntarily, not expecting what he has said at all. I should say no. But it's dance, and it's what I know. He has me intrigued, and I can't help but want to know more.

"What are you studying?" I ask.

Joey's face drops, and I bristle in my seat. Crap! I'm presuming he has told me before, and it only makes me feel worse.

"Photography. The gallery I work at will display the prints as well, so it's great publicity for you and the company."

It does sound good. My classes are mostly full, but I have room for more. And I want more. I want to grow the business more than anything else.

I grab a pen from my bag and start to scribble my email down on the napkin. "Could you send me some more details? It sounds really—"

"Like you're trying to piss me off," Mason's voice comes out a growl at my back.

My pen falls to the floor as I spin in my seat, my eyes going wide when I find him standing behind me.

The man makes me feel unhinged.

A mixture of anger and elation that he has shown up stirs in my gut, and it's somewhat frustrating—and intriguing.

Today's suit is black pinstripe, and I momentarily allow myself to imagine the pleasure it would bring me to remove every single piece of it, right down to his tie pin. My eyes move to his beautiful face. His jaw is locked tight, his lips mashed in a thin line. "Out now," he barks, and although it's meant for me, his eyes are fixed on Joey.

If looks could kill, Joey would be in a box on the way to the morgue. To his credit, he doesn't cower down to Mason. He stands tall.

A laugh bubbles in my throat, and I try to find the right words as I sit bamboozled by Mason's balls. I mean, they must be pretty freaking huge at this point. "Who do you thin—"

"Don't speak to her like that! You can't tell her what to do!" Joey's voice rises, shaking with anger.

"Nina. Out. Now," Mason snarls over my head.

I recoil at his words once again. "No! Both of you stop. This is getting ridiculous." They will be brawling in the damn coffee shop in a minute.

I stand, picking up my bag. "Look, Joey, here is my email, just send me—"

Mason snatches the napkin from my hand, balling it up before claiming my wrist in his grip. He pulls me through the coffee shop and out the door.

"Mason!" I fume. "Let go of me!" I fight against him, but his hold is too strong.

"You'll damn well listen to me," he spits.

"No. I won't! Mase, let go of my arm now," I warn.

He pulls open the door to the Audi, then looks down at where I stand beside him. His forehead creases as his eyes search my face. "Please," he asks, closing his eyes briefly and pulling in a breath before loosening his hold on me. "Get in the car."

Ripping my arm away, I turn to and stand toe to toe with him. "I'm getting in the car because I deserve an explanation, not because I want to spend another second with you—and you should be thankful that I am even giving you the opportunity."

I duck down and step into the car, the door slamming shut as I turn to look at Vinny in the driver's seat. Whipping my head around, I see Mason striding back across the street and towards the café.

Shit! I go to open the door, and the lock clicks.

"Vinny! No! You didn't see him in there. He is fucking

wild," I cry, adrenaline making my hand tremble on the handle.

"Mason is only acting out of concern for you, and keeping you out of harm's way. You need to trust him," Vinny replies flatly.

I widen my eyes at him. He has gone mad. "Vinny, Please. You go, and I will wait here." I try to reason with him. "But please do something. One of them is going to get hurt."

He doesn't budge, doesn't answer me, doesn't even acknowledge I'm in the car. I sit staring in the direction Mase went, waiting for him to reappear.

It's only a few minutes later that he emerges from the café, his face like stone and muscles taut as he strides towards me, looking every bit of the god that he is. I scoot across the seat as he yanks open the door and squeeze's in next to me.

He doesn't say a word, his knee brushing mine as he widens his legs, sinking deeper into the leather. His tongue runs across the front of his teeth, and he sits, staring straight ahead.

"What the fuck was that!" I yell as Vinny pulls out into traffic.

"Don't." Mason raises his finger in the air, nodding towards Vinny.

"Vinny doesn't give a shit! He clearly knows what a head-case you are!" I proclaim, my anger getting the better of me.

His nostrils flare as he continues to try and calm himself. I don't think I'm helping the situation, but I'm not about to roll over and take his bullshit. He runs his hand back and forth across his mouth, his silence only heightening my annoyance.

"I only met up with him to apologise and make sure he

was okay. Why did you have to make such a big deal about it, and why do you even care?" I ask.

His glare turns on me. "You went to apologise? For what?"

"Everything that happened on Friday night. Your friend Elliot made a fool of him at the bar, and then you ended up choking him and—"

"He almost hit you! You..." His hands ball into fists as he pauses, shaking his head. "You don't know him, Nina. You need to be more careful."

"I don't fucking know you, Mason! But you seem to think I should obey your every word."

"You're right. You don't know me," he scoffs. "You've just confirmed my point exactly."

"What's that supposed to mean?" I squint at him.

"Well, it didn't take a lot to get you to go home with me, did it?"

Did he just say that?

I hear Vinny tut in the front seat, obviously a lot fucking smarter than his boss. "Vinny, take me back to the studio, please."

Mason's head snaps between us. "What now?"

I stare out the window, not wanting to speak or look at him when he can so easily cut me with his words. He came to me last Friday at the club, not the other way around. He came to me at the studio this week, and he came to the café today. For him to sit and judge me on my actions is infuriating.

Wait.

I whip my head around to face him. "How did you know where I was?"

He averts his eyes to the front of the car, it's quick, but I don't miss it. I look to Vinny, but his eyes are focused on the road.

"You followed me?" I shout.

"Vinny was in the area and saw you, then notified me," Mason says dismissively as if it isn't weird.

"Why? Why would he do that?" I frown.

Mason sighs, running his hand through his hair. "Because I asked him to," he mutters, his head dropping back against the seat.

"Unbelievable! Do you have any idea how fucked up this is?"

"Watch your language," he scolds me.

"Fuck yo—"

Before I can finish, he unbuckles my seat belt and tugs me across the seat to straddle him. One hand finds my hip while the other glides up my neck.

"I do what I do so that I know you are safe. I have an overwhelming need to protect you, Nina, and I won't apologise for it," he whispers, quiet enough that Vinny can't hear. His eyes skim every inch of my face as if he can't pick a feature to settle on.

"I want to take you out." His features soften, his thumb stretching up to brush across my cheek. "Please, don't fight me on this. This isn't me." He shakes his head, his eyes resolute. "You make me fucking crazy." The feel of his fingers flexing against my hips makes me shudder. "Give me a chance to show you." He licks at his bottom lip, his mouth so close I can almost taste him. "One more night. If you still hate me after that, then I'll leave you alone."

I sit back on his lap. "Like a date?"

"You can call it whatever you want."

I bite my lip to hide my smile. "I don't hate you, Mason."

He smirks, all cocky, and although I love the way he is looking at me, the way he feels beneath me, I know I need to make this harder for him.

"Say please," I taunt softly into his ear.

"Baby," he rasps, making my stomach bottom out. "You know what will happen if you demand my manners."

I ground down on him, brazenly rolling my hips over his cock as if I have every right in the world to do it. As if he is *mine*. "Say. Please."

He tips his chin up at me, dropping his dark eyes to my lips. "Please."

Leaning in, I brush my mouth over his. "I'll think about it, Bossman." I smile, climbing from his lap and back to my seat.

He shakes his head at me as he rearranges himself in his trousers. "Fuck," he mutters under his breath.

Glancing out the window, I notice we are nearly at the studio, and then realisation sinks in. I look to Vinny, feeling mortified that I allowed the sex maniac beside me to corrupt me. My cheeks heat.

Sensing Mason's eyes on me, I look at him.

"Vinny, give us a minute, please," he asks.

Vinny exits the car and stands at the entrance of the studio.

I should be mad at Mason. He completely violated my privacy by having me followed and then made a show of himself and me in the café. But something bigger, more powerful than my anger, wins out.

Sat twisted in my seat, I chew on my bottom lip as a smile slowly forces its way onto my face. His large hand grasps me at the back of the neck, pulling me forward onto his waiting mouth—and I let him.

His forehead creases as our lips touch, a deep sigh leaving him as if the kiss is as necessary as the air he breathes. His tongue swipes through my mouth, seeking mine out and deepening the kiss. My body goes lax as I melt into him, my hand smoothing through his hair.

We kiss for what feels like hours, neither one of us able to pull ourselves away, and it's not until my fingers inch up his thigh, reaching for him, that he finally releases my lips.

A whimper leaves me.

He drops his forehead to mine, his lips wet and swollen from our kiss, and he looks at me with so much desire in his eyes it has me paralysed in my seat.

Not being able to help himself, he gives me one more soft kiss before letting me go.

"I will pick you up at seven thirty tomorrow evening," he tells me.

I nod, too overwhelmed by the man in front of me to speak.

————

MY EYES RAKE over my reflection in the free-standing mirror as I stand trying to convince myself I'm not my mother. It's hard when we look so similar. I'm wearing one of Megan's dresses, and it's slightly on the risqué side. The white material plasters itself to my every curve.

Lucy has styled my hair in soft waves that fall to my waist. My makeup is heavier than usual, with smoky eyes and bloodred lips. I should have saved all this effort for my date with Mase.

Shit. My date with Mase.

I haven't told the girls yet, and I'm slightly nervous. No doubt they will be over the top about it, and I don't want to make the evening all about me.

I join them in the kitchen for a glass of wine.

"Ugh, I can't get an Uber for an hour. My rating is shit. Megan, it's your fault you miss them all the time!" Lucy complains.

"Oh, shush. Nina, you do it," Megan suggests.

I check my phone, my rating just as bad. *Crap!* I think about booking a taxi, but then Vinny comes to mind. *No. I can't, can I?* I go to my bag, searching for the card he gave me.

I stare at it for the longest time, contemplating calling the number but feeling bad, especially after this afternoon. Actually, no. He owes me after following me.

I dial the number, and he answers on the first ring.

"Nina, is everything alright?" he says, worried, making me feel bad.

"Hi! Sorry for calling so late. I was hoping I could get a lift. I can't get a Uber, and I just thought I would call you, but I can—"

"Nina, it's fine. Where are you?"

"I'm at my apartment. I'm with my friends."

"I will leave now," he says before hanging up.

"Got a lift, girls." I smile sheepishly over at them.

"Good! Now come help finish this bottle before it's time to go." Megan smiles, holding up the bottle.

WE ARE in a fit of giggles as we slide into the back of the Audi, choosing to squeeze in together rather than sit separately. We polished off two bottles of wine whilst getting ready, and now my body is buzzing with adrenaline.

"Good evening, ladies." Vinny smiles.

"Hello, Vinny," Lucy coos. "I've heard lots about you!"

"God, you're alright for an older bloke," Megan exclaims.

I elbow her in the ribs, the three of us chuckling together.

"Where are we off to tonight?"

"The Pearl, please," I say, sitting forward in my seat. "Did you drop Mase home this evening?" I ask.

"I did. I just dropped him off, actually."

"He's working late again? Is everything okay?" I ask.

He smiles. "No, not at home, and everything is fine. He is out with friends this evening."

"Oh, where did he go? Where did you drop him?" Lucy asks, poking her head forward.

"Sorry girls, it's not worth the headache," he chuckles.

"It's fine, Vinny. It's girls' night anyway," I say, sitting back in the seat.

"Screw girls' night! I want to meet the famous Mr Lowell," Megan whines.

Lizzo starts playing on the radio, and the girls start singing along, thankfully forgetting about Mason.

"Vinny, can you turn it up, please?" Luce sings.

Fifteen minutes later, we are pulling up at the curb. I glance out the window noticing we're not at The Pearl.

"Where are we?" I question.

"Melders. You girls have a good night." Vinny smirks, looking straight ahead.

"Yes! Thank you, Vinny!" Megan cheers, ruffling his short hair before climbing out of the car.

"Vinny!" I jokingly scold as Lucy slides from the car excitedly, joining Megan on the pavement.

Vinny's eyes find mine in the rearview mirror. "You didn't see me, okay?" He winks.

7

Nina

WE SHUFFLE FORWARD IN THE LINE, HUDDLED TOGETHER AS WE try to keep warm. Melders Bar is overflowing at the seams tonight. Bodies spill out onto the street as the queue wraps around the side of the building. Thankfully, it's moving quickly, and we are nearly at the entrance.

"He better be as hot as I remember, Nina. It's flipping freezing out here tonight," Lucy complains.

"Umm, I didn't want to come here tonight. This is all on you, girls. I was happy going to The Pearl."

A large group of men step from the club, and relief fills me when the bouncer allows us and the couple in front to step inside. The warmth of the club blankets me the moment we cross the threshold, instantly calming my body.

"Drinks first," Lucy says. "And keep an eye out for Mase! We need to find him first."

I link arms with my two best friends, rolling my eyes. "Screw him. Let's have some fun instead!"

We haven't been to Melders Bar before, always being put off by the wait even to contemplate entertaining the fifty-pound admission charge. It's one of the hottest places in the city to party—but it's just a club, and I will now be living off of noodles for the remainder of the week.

"So this is where all the classy girls go," Megan says with a smirk, well aware that we aren't that.

The bar is set out on two levels, and we have entered the club from the top one. A bar runs around the room in a U shape, with plush velvet seats and tables scattered throughout the area. There is a large opening at the centre, and we walk over to the railings, looking down at the crowd of people dancing below.

"This place is incredible. Let's get a drink and hit the dance floor," Lucy shouts over the music.

My gaze involuntarily scans the entire top floor, trying to seek out Mason, but it's such an immense space, and I doubt I could find him amongst all these people. We see a spot at the bar and slide in, ordering nine shots and a vodka cranberry chaser to take with us.

"Cheers, bitches," Megan smiles.

We down our shots one after another, all of us struggling by the third. Tiesto - "Wasted" starts to blare through the speakers, and the girls squeal as they slam down their shot glasses. I grab their hands, pulling them to the top of the steps that lead to the dance floor.

I'm about to take the first step when my eyes lift, locking on Charlie's. He stands at the opposite side of the opening— close to where we stood at the bar moments ago. His fore-arms rest against the railings with his glass hung leisurely from the tips of his fingers.

Holy shit. I forgot how hot they all are.

Mason and Elliot stand off to the side, engaged in a conversation with a man I haven't seen before. I quickly lift my finger to my lips and plead with my eyes at Charlie.

He shakes his head, a smile tugging at his lips.

"Please," I mouth.

He dips his head in the direction the girls went, silently telling me to go. I hurry down the stairs and onto the dance floor, wondering how long it will be before he finds me.

Mase

WE ENDED up at Melders tonight—not that it was our intention. Elliot had a phone call from Cece that had him sending Vinny here. Cece is a model who Elliot met a few years back and now meets up with whenever she's in London.

The lack of privacy at Melders is one reason I hate it so much. Too many people know me here. When I finish work for the week, I want to shut off from it, not come somewhere like this, where people only want to talk to you because of the size of your wallet.

"Lowell," Charlie says with a nod, summoning me. I walk to the railing and stand beside him. He smiles, then looks down at the dance floor.

I go to ask what, but the moment I glance at the dance floor, I see her.

In a sea of people that I can barely make out, she shines like a light. *Does she have this pull on everyone, or is it just me?* I frown as I watch her. She is breathtaking to watch. I know she is a dancer, but this is different. She is so immersed with the song, her body so in tune with the music she seems at one with it.

Lance and Elliot step up beside us to see what's caught our attention.

Elliot elbows me. "Hey, isn't that Pixie?"

"Where? Which one?" Sullivan asks.

"Brunette, tight white dress. Fuck, Mase, please tell me you are on that!" Elliot says, not taking his eyes off her.

"Another money-hungry bitch attaching herself for your money?" Lance pops a brow in question and laughs, taking a swig of beer.

"Shut the fuck up," I deadpan. If he wasn't my best friend, I wouldn't be tolerating his shit.

Charlie stands looking out at the girls, not saying a word, already in protective mode. Poor fucker is warped. "I'm going to take a piss," I say, walking in the direction of the dance floor.

"Good luck, mate. Hey, if she won't hold your cock I'm sure Lancey will," Elliot says, clasping Lance on the shoulder with all the force I'd put behind the punch.

I stand off to the side of the dance floor, unable to take my eyes off her. Her delicate hands glide over her body, moving from her thighs to her hips and then to her perfectly round tits. Men and women stop to watch her—it's not just me. She has us all captivated.

She steals a moment lifting a drink to her lips, and it has my body moving forward on impulse. I slide up behind her, my hand smoothing across her stomach and sprawling out over her ribs, pulling her flush against me. My face instantly goes to her neck, which is blanketed in her thick hair. I inhale deeply as my other hand takes hold of the drink at her lips.

She doesn't flinch. She knew I was watching her, and she wanted me to see.

"I promised you when you were sober," I whisper into her ear, taking the lobe between my teeth.

She shivers, sighing heavily as her body relaxes into mine. She lets me take her drink, her head falling to my chest as she looks up over her shoulder at me. Our noses touch, our mouths only an inch apart. "I don't know how much I will be able to tolerate tonight, Nina."

"Tolerate what, Mase?" she hums, bringing her lips even closer.

"This," I say, running my hands up her waist. I bend my knees, grinding her ass onto my dick.

"Then don't." She starts to move her body to the music, my control slipping further from my grasp with every roll of her hips.

I pass her drink off to some random girl who is standing staring at us, and she takes it without question. *Fucking weirdo.* Nina notices and goes to step away from me, but I grasp her before she is out of reach, pulling her back to me; she throws her head back over my shoulder, laughing. I bet the boys are fucking loving this. "I'm here with the girls, but if you're a good boy, I will let you take me home later," she promises.

"How about I take you home right now?" I lean in, sucking on the underside of her jaw, my arms wrapped tightly around her waist.

"Later." She looks up at me. "I promise when I'm sober," she says, pulling at my arms and stepping from my hold. She grabs the hand of the girl who is still standing staring at us, and then they skirt off through the crowded dance floor.

Leaving me alone and with a raging hard-on.

Nina

I SLAM the door to the cubicle, spinning to face the girls. "I'm so getting laid tonight. Is that okay, or does it make me a slut? I hardly know the guy." I cringe, running my palms down over my dress.

"Are you kidding? You'd be a fucking idiot not to." Lucy laughs as she sits to pee.

"Nina, you have to sleep with this man. I'm hot for it just watching the two of you," Megan says, handing Luce the loo roll.

"Girls, he's intense. I don't think I could sleep with him and then just walk away. You saw how I was after last week, and I wouldn't say he's the type to settle down anytime soon."

"Then you make sure you shag his brains out!" Megan cheers, switching spots with Lucy so she can pee.

"Shag? Megs, nobody fucking says that." I laugh.

A hand raps on the cubicle door. "Hurry up in there!"

"Fuck off," we all say in unison.

"Just don't kiss him. That always works for me." Lucy shrugs. "Keep it impersonal."

"Ugh, don't. I think I could come from his kiss alone. Kissing is an absolute must."

"No," she scolds. "No kissing. You can do this. You're a strong independent woman, and you will take all the orgasms you can get from this man and then leave the motherfucker wanting more. You will not kiss him, got it?"

"I'll try?" I smile.

"You got this, girl," Megan says, standing then straightening out her dress.

We leave the toilets and head straight for the bar. "Three vodka cranberries, please," I say, holding up three fingers in case he doesn't hear me over the music.

The barman frowns, looking between the three of us. "Just a moment, please." He backs away, giving me another once-over before whispering something to the suit at the end of the bar.

He returns a few seconds later. "I'm sorry, darling, I can't serve you," he cringes.

"What! Why? I have ID," I say, riffling through my clutch.

"It's not that. We've been told to no longer serve you this evening." He shrugs apologetically, moving on to serve the next person in the queue.

What the hell?

I turn to the girls to find them both as surprised as I am. We aren't even drunk. I look past the girls towards the railings where Mason stood earlier. He is sitting in one of the tall wingback chairs, his eyes fixed firmly on me, and I just know.

I start towards him, not stopping until I'm directly in front of him. I ignore the other men sitting around the table, my focus solely on Mason. I take his glass, the golden liquid sloshing onto my hand as I rip it from his grasp.

I tip my head back and down it in one.

He smiles as I struggle to keep my eyes from watering. "That's your last one," he says, pulling me down and onto his lap.

"Pixie, it's good to see you again."

I turn to see Elliot sitting to our right. He nods his head at me in greeting.

"Why do you call me Pixie?" I frown. "Is it my ears?" I run my fingers over the tops of them consciously.

Elliot and Mason look at each other before throwing their heads back, laughing. Confused, I look to Charlie, who's sat on the bench seat opposite us with the other man I saw earlier.

"Ignore them," Charlie mutters, shaking his head.

"No, Nina, it's not your ears," Mase whispers, his lip tipping up on one side as he tries to control his laugh.

Lucy and Megan arrive at the table, setting down a tray of shots. "Nina, care to introduce us to your new friends." Lucy winks at Elliot knowingly.

"Actually, we have already met. I drove you home Friday night, but I don't expect you to remember," Mason teases.

"Of course, I remember." She fakes a smile. "Tequila?" she offers to the group, passing around the tray.

"Ladies, this is Lance," Charlie announces, introducing the man to his right. He looks like he's just come from work in his immaculate three-piece suit. He has dark hair cut short all over and a perfectly groomed beard coating his chiselled jaw. Dark ink peeks out from his collar and cuffs. The rugged look is definitely working for him.

"This is Megan and Lucy." He gestures to the girls.

"And you must be Nina?" he presumes, looking towards me.

"I'm her." I smile, leaning forward to shake his hand. His grip is solid, his large palm wrapped tightly around mine. *Alright, asshole.* I pull my hand away with a frown.

"It's lovely to meet you. I've heard a lot about you."

"Oh, really?" I say, still trying to get a gauge on him. "Mase hasn't mentioned you before."

"That's because you spend most of the time running from me," Mason says, nuzzling into my neck.

I lean back slightly to look down at him, appreciating how edible he looks tonight. He is wearing a black shirt that fits him like a glove, drawing attention to his solid shoulders. His hair is styled in a perfect mess, making me want to run my fingers through it.

His eyes crease at the corners as he looks at me just as intently, the most beautiful smile taking over his face as he realises we are both staring. He squeezes my hip, looking up at me tenderly and making my stomach dip.

I turn to find our friends deep in conversation. All but Charlie. He sits watching the two of us. His brows are drawn in as he sits deep in thought. He smiles when we lock eyes, and it's a warm, genuine smile that brings a grin to my face.

"Charlie seems like a gentle soul," I whisper to Mase.

"He hasn't always been that way," he says quickly, without thought. "He's a ruthless lawyer by day."

"Really? A lawyer! He doesn't seem like he has it in him."

"What?! You should see him in action. You wouldn't be saying that then." He smirks.

"He seems too nice." I shrug.

"What about me? What do you think I do?" he asks.

"Other than following me around the city, causing me more issues than pleasure?" I roll my eyes. "I'd say... maybe a car salesman."

His lip twitches in amusement. "Ah, you got me. How did you know?"

"Bad haircut. Cheap suit."

He laughs as his hand glides up my thigh, inching higher and higher until he brushes the lace of my underwear, then leisurely returning to my shin. "Maybe I should quit and focus more of my time on your pleasure."

"I don't know... I wouldn't want to get you into trouble with the boss." I smile.

"Nina, come on, we are dancing!" Megan grabs my hand, pulling me from Mase's lap.

I turn back to him and catch him rearranging himself in his jeans. I want more time with him. He seems different tonight, more relaxed, softer than I have seen him before. If he asked me to, I'd leave with him right now.

"Okay, you giant horn bag. No gazing deeply into his eyes either. Let's get you a drink," Megan says, dragging me downstairs with Luce not far behind.

WE STUMBLE UP THE STEPS, what feels like hours later, Lucy crawling up in slow motion with her heels in her hand. The girls have been buying my drinks all night, but to keep it hidden I have been downing them on the spot—even though we would spot either Mase or Charlie watching us from above every so often. It's like I am seventeen again, sneaking into nightclubs, trying to get served.

We're laughing our way to where the boys are seated with not a care in the world when Lucy stops short in front of us, throwing her hand out to stop me from walking any farther, her heels slapping against my chest.

"Ahh, Luce, your shoes," I whine, rubbing at the spot.

"Who are they?" she asks.

I glance over at the boys. They all sit in the same seats only now, three women decorate the area—beautiful, long-legged, perfectly groomed women.

A blonde sits on the arm of Mason's chair, another on Elliot's lap, and the third is currently rubbing Lance through his suit pants. It's clear to me that they are hanging off the girls every word, Mase included. His arm is thrown around the blonde's back, disappearing at the other side of the chair. I imagine his hand running up and down her leg, sending a rush of adrenaline coursing through me as I approach them.

Elliot spots me first, looking over at Mason with wide eyes, and it's at that moment I know I should leave.

I grasp Megan's arm just as she says, "Well, haven't you boys been busy."

I probably shouldn't have drunk so much, and I have to fight the urge to pick up their ice bucket and dump it over Mason's head, planting my feet to the floor. Embarrassing myself is the last thing I want to do.

"Nina." Mason stands, stepping up to me so he is all I can see. "Are you ready to go?" he asks, pulling at his collar as he squirms under my glare.

"Not with you."

His eyes spark with a challenge as he turns to the women at his back. Their eyes travel the length of me, Mason and the girls, judgement in their stares.

"You'll leave with me," Mason tells me, sensing the animosity.

"You're delusional." I shoulder past him, opting to sit on the bench seat next to Charlie. He is the only one who hadn't been showing any interest in anything going on around him.

I look to the woman who had been sitting with Mase. She is watching him as he watches me. Her gaze follows his, our eyes connecting.

She is beyond beautiful, and that only makes me even angrier. I don't belong here, with these people. She openly glares at me, her lip curling up into a disgusted snarl.

Well, that's not so pretty, is it.

"She isn't worth your time," Charlie speaks into my ear.

"Has Mase slept with that girl?" I ask, unsure if I even want to know the answer.

"I don't know. I won't lie to you, Nina. Chances are he has, but he wouldn't have left with her tonight, that much I'm sure of." He looks down at me with a knowing smile. "I think you know that too."

"Do I?" I question sarcastically, crossing my arms.

"You wouldn't be sitting here if you thought otherwise."

I ponder what Charlie has said. It's true, I wouldn't be sitting here if I truly believed Mason would have left with her. But I can't help think that the only reason is that he'd already secured me as a solid fuck for the night.

Little miss perfect wasn't needed.

I seek out Mase. He is leaning against the railing, looking down at his phone with his feet crossed at the ankles.

I don't notice the blonde approach me, and it's Charlie's elbow inserting itself into my ribs that has me snapping out of my angry stupor.

"Do you have a problem?" the blonde spits out.

Lucy and Megan appear out of nowhere, planting themselves behind me.

"No, I don't, but I think you might." I swipe a finger along the end of my nose, gesturing to the remnants of white powder on the underside of hers. Charlie chuckles beside me.

"Fuck you, you ugly little bitch!"

I shake my head and smile, her words not penetrating my skin. I lean into Charlie, plucking his drink from his hand and take a sip, needing the liquid courage to deal with the delight before me as she continues.

"God, which one are you fucking? I'd have guessed Mase for sure. Although you seem a bit cheap for him, I suppose you'd suit Sullivan's budget out of the lot."

Arms come around me before I can make a move to hit her, and I would have. With no thought or feeling, I would have hit the bitch. Her implication that I could be bought has rage burning through me. I have no idea who has hold of me, but my legs flail as I try to get free.

"Don't fight me!" Mason growls into my ear as he pulls me through the club in a stronghold, my arms locked at my sides.

"Put me down!" I shout, clawing at his arms.

A door is held open for him as we enter a room at the back of the club. He leans his back against the hardwood once it's shut, my breathing and the muffled thud of the music now the only sound. He lowers my feet tentatively to the floor but doesn't release my arms.

"Nina, calm down," he whispers into my ear, his breathing calm and the opposite of mine.

"No, that little cokehead bitch thinks she can judge me!"

"I already had security on the way to tell them to leave when you reacted," he tells me. "Calm down, please."

"You didn't hear what she said, Mason," I rage.

"I didn't need to. I saw how her words affected you," he

says softly. "You should know, the only woman I have any interest in fucking, is you. You've become the first thing I think about when I wake up and the last thing I think about at night."

His words are so unexpected they have my heart hammering in my chest for an entirely different reason. I stop resisting his hold, my head dropping back to his shoulder as I sigh, processing his words.

I turn my head into his neck, his earthy scent calming me instantly.

"There she is," he whispers, planting a soft kiss on my jaw.

And that's all I get before he spins me. He drops me to my feet then pushes me back against the door, sinking onto his knees in front of me. His hands bunch the material at my waist, pulling it up and exposing my lower body to his hungry gaze.

Leaning in, he rests his head against my stomach, placing soft kisses around my navel.

"You're fucking beautiful, Nina," he rasps, hooking his fingers into the top of my underwear, slowly dragging them down my legs.

Our eyes meet as he feathers his hand from my waist down to the back of my knee, lifting my left leg and placing it over his shoulder. I shudder, swallowing thickly as I stand bared to him in the most intimate way.

He licks his lips as he looks at me there, and sensing what comes next, my hands fall to his head in a pathetic effort to stop him. Once he does this, I know we cross the line. I won't come back from it. He's already under my skin, my feelings for him being so much more than I'll allow myself to admit.

He pauses, his warm breath puffing out against me as his eyes lift, losing himself in mine momentarily. "I know," he states as if sensing my thoughts.

His hand comes between us, spreading my lips open wide. He doesn't give me a chance to think, to allow my body to adjust to the rush of cold air against my wetness. His mouth comes down on me, and the warmth of his smooth tongue tracing the slick flesh between my legs has me pulling his head in deeper. He gently nips at my clit before flattening his tongue and licking up the length of my sex, sucking the little bud of nerves back into his mouth when he reaches the top.

My hands push his hair back from his face so I can watch him, and a growl vibrates through his chest as I disturb him. A knot forms in my stomach as my body begins to burn from his talented mouth. A kiss, nibble, lick, followed by long deep sucks against my slit. I throw my head back, knowing I'll come too fast and end this perfection if I continue to watch him. It's why I'm so unprepared when his first finger enters me.

I moan, grinding my hips down to meet his hand as he fills me. He removes his finger, and I whimper at the loss until he starts spreading my wetness through my folds and up over my clit. A jolt of pleasure courses through me.

"I'm so close," I breathe out, my fingers clenching tight in his hair. "Mase," I beg.

Three thick fingers harshly stretch me open, my stomach coiling tight when Mason groans against me.

"You have no idea what you do to me," he admits, his body trembling as I struggle to take him fully. He takes his time, working his fingers to find the spot he's been looking for then rubbing against it relentlessly.

The first tremor racks through my body and my cries must slash at the last of his control. I watch in pure, unmeasurable desire as he begins pumping his hand into me whilst sucking my wet flesh almost violently between his lips.

"Mase," I gasp.

My body starts to shake as the most intense orgasm I've ever experienced rushes through me. I pinch my eyes closed as I try to control my limbs because at this moment in time they don't feel like my own—I feel so deeply sated, my body giving everything to this man.

As I come down from my blissful high, I peek down at the man who kneels at my feet.

His jaw hangs slack, lips shining from my arousal as he asks, "Can I take you home now, Pixie?"

8

Nina

HE CALLED ME PIXIE. UNTIL NOW, I'VE PRESUMED ELLIOT MADE it up as a joke, but the way Mason says it, as if still testing the word on his tongue. It leaves me assuming it's for another reason.

Are they making fun of me?

My hands flatten on his shoulders as he gently lowers my leg to the ground. Tremors still rack through my body, causing me to stagger on my feet as I try to gain control of my limbs. When he told me to stop drinking, I felt collared. The thought of doing something for him because he told me to only made me want to do the opposite. Now I'm unsteady on my feet and wishing I'd listened.

The light tap of his finger on my ankle has me snapping out of my postorgasmic daze. I lift each foot so he can slide my underwear back into place, then smooth the material of my dress down over my hips myself. I lean back lazily against the door, watching him, wondering if he is even real.

His hair is a mess from my fingers—just like I wanted it. But what's better than his just fucked hair is the satisfied smile that's plastered across his face and that smile; it makes me feel fucking powerful.

"Why are you looking at me like that?" I ask.

He steps into me again, pulling my chin between his thumb and finger. "I'm thinking I should've done that on our first night together. I didn't realise how easy it is to tame you."

My jaw drops in shock. "You cheeky prick! You make me... untamed!" I push on his chest playfully, and he captures my wrist in his hand.

"Well then, it's a good job your cunt is my new favourite pastime, isn't it? Makes for a good team." He leans in, kissing me tenderly.

His phone starts to ring, and he pulls away, digging in his pocket to retrieve it.

"Fuck," he groans, his hand running through his hair as he brings it to his ear "Scar," he mutters. He sounds dejected, and my stomach knots at the tone of his voice.

He turns away from me, walking to the desk in the far corner of the room, and it gives me a chance to take in my surroundings for the first time since entering the room. We are in an office. Minimal furniture decorates the space, and the lack of windows makes it dark and a little depressing.

Mason sits on the edge of the desk, his chin dropped down to his chest as he listens on the phone. Unsure about what I should do, I push off from the door, walking toward the sofa.

His dark eyes lift immediately, burning through me as he reaches out an arm, gesturing for me to go to him.

"It's not your problem, Scar. It's neither of our problems," he says as I step up next to him. He brings his arm around my waist, pulling me to his side and places a chaste kiss on my temple.

I wonder who Scar is. It sounds like a woman's name. The voice is slightly whiny—definitely a woman.

"Alright, calm down," he huffs in annoyance. "I will leave now, give me an hour, okay?" He hangs up, angling his body to face mine.

I force a smile. "You aren't taking me home, are you?"

His warm palm encases the side of my face as his thumb brushes my lower lip. "Not tonight, angel. We still have our date tomorrow?" he questions.

"Are you going to tell me where you are going?" I answer his question with one of my own.

His face morphs into one of displeasure, his jaw clenching tight. "No. We have our date tomorrow," he tells me.

'You need to trust him' Vinny's words resonate in me.

Should I trust this man? He's going to see a woman right now that much I'm sure of. But I don't feel the jealousy I did out in the club before. His frustration with having to go tells me enough, and it only makes me worry for him.

"You want me to come with you?" I ask, running my hand up his chest.

"No, I don't. Sorry," he says before stepping away from me.

Long strides put distance between us, and the more steps he takes the farther away I feel him drift from me. The strong set of his shoulders, his fists that are now curled at his sides, all tell me that soft, tender Mason is gone.

Mr Lowell back in his place.

I hurry to catch up with him, not wanting to be left

behind in the poorly lit room. He pulls open the door in a rush but instantly comes to an abrupt halt, making me stumble and face-plant into his back.

"Jesus Christ," he groans.

I lean back, looking up into Lucy's eyes.

What the fuck?

"Luce?" I frown.

"Hey, babes!" She smiles.

"Stay right there," Elliot's voice floats in from outside.

I look around Mason to find him holding Lucy up under her armpits. She is leaning over Megan, who kneels at her feet. Megan's face is firmly inserted in Mason's crotch. I frown, looking at Elliot standing behind them, his phone poised at the ready. "I need to get a picture of this."

"You were listening in?" I accuse.

Sneaky little bitches. I giggle to myself, looking down at Megan, who still hasn't moved. I'm sure she is loving this.

Mason looks fuming mad, which makes me want to laugh harder. He's so damn serious.

Elliot steps forward, a boyish grin in place as he takes Lucy by the waist and lifts her from Mason's grip. I help Megan to her feet, giving her a cheeky wink when she smiles wide.

"I'm heading to Lowerwick," Mason tells them, detached and cold.

Elliot's face drops, a frown taking over. "You want me to come with you?"

"No. Get Vinny to take the girls home," he says firmly before stalking off in the direction of the exit.

I stare after him, watching as security opens the door, and then he disappears, gone in a flash.

"Looks like it's home time for me." I smile sheepishly at the group, feeling conscious that they may have been listening in on the two of us.

"Sorry, Pixie, you're coming with me!" Elliot tells me, grinning in amusement.

HALF AN HOUR LATER, Vinny arrives to take us home—although we aren't going home. Elliot is taking us to Mason's. Lance voiced his opinion on the idea, and if I'm honest, I'm just as uncertain.

Mason wasn't in the best of moods when he left, and I can't imagine he will be happy to find a houseful when he gets home from dealing with *Scar*.

Who is Scar?

Elliot gets in the car with me, and the girls—silly man —whilst Charlie and Lance take a taxi.

"So, what happened to *Cece,* Elliot?" Lucy jibes in a posh accent.

"Oh darling, please, she couldn't possibly be seen with the likes of us," Megan challenges with her finest snooty voice.

"Of course. How silly of one to think such thoughts. Tell me, Eli, does she suck cock as fantastic as I'd imagine one would?" Lucy laughs, losing her composure, the last part coming out on a snort. The car is filled with our drunken cackles while Elliot sits smirking at us, not giving a shit that we are ripping into his friend.

I can't see Vinny, but I'm certain he is smiling too.

My thought process was flawed when I agreed to go with Elliot because now I stand in the foyer of Mason's penthouse, and all the emotions I experienced last weekend are waking inside of me.

Megan and Lucy come up behind me, awe on their faces as they take in the expansive space.

"Holy shit, Nina!" Megan whispers. "You never said—"

"Come on, girls. Let's get a drink." Charlie drapes an arm over my shoulder, smiling down at me with pity in his eyes.

He leads us to an entertainment room. There is a minibar, pool table, sofa, and a screen the size of the entire wall.

"What you having, girls?" Lance asks as he places six glasses on the bar top.

I stand in the doorway with my arms wrapped around myself. It doesn't feel right being here without Mason. How will he feel when he comes home and finds us all here?

Finds *me* here.

"I don't want anything, thank you," I say.

Alcohol is the last thing I need right now.

"Good," Elliot whispers so only me and Charlie can hear. I turn, finding him at our backs out in the hallway. "He will need you when he gets home, Pix." He brushes past us, joining the girls at the bar and leaving me with a growing pressure in my chest.

Is that why he brought me here. To make Mason feel better? To distract him from whatever has dragged him away?

Charlie squeezes my shoulder. "He's right. It's probably the smartest idea he's ever had."

"Will he be mad?"

"Not at you."

"At Scar?"

He frowns at my question. "No. Never at Scar."

"Then who?" I ask, confused.

Seemingly not wanting to answer, he steps into the room and grabs a pool cue from the wall. "Fancy a game?"

I purse my lips, rounding the table. "You like losing?"

IT'S GONE one a.m. when we finally relent. Mason is still not home, and the thought of him not wanting me here makes me grow more and more anxious by the second.

Lucy and Megan bounce up the hallway to 'their room', Elliot loving his new role of being their tour guide.

Luckily, there is room for us all to stay with the penthouse's multiple bedrooms. It's massive. Far more space than one person needs, that's for sure.

The girls begin opening and closing all the bedrooms' adjoining doors before flopping down onto the bed in pure elation. I smile as I look at Elliot, and I get the feeling he likes having the girls around. They are gorgeous, fun and give back his banter tenfold.

"Nina hunny, remember to shag his brains out," Lucy calls from her spot on the bed, her head dropped to the side as she points at me. "And I mean completely. We don't want any cerebrum left getting in the way of us and that marriage proposal."

"This will be my room," Megan states.

I shake my head at the idiots I call my friends. What happened to 'No kissing him, Nina.'?

"Pixie," Elliot calls, summoning me as he heads back to the room at the top of the stairs.

The master bedroom.

"He won't be long. I'm sure you're familiar with this room." He pops a brow, walking backwards and then disappearing inside a bedroom farther down the hall.

My feet flush hot against the heated floor as I stand on the threshold of Mason's bedroom. I want to go inside, but I have to force my feet to move forward. My head not quite caught up with my heart.

I step inside, closing the door behind me.

Everything is as I remembered, which surprises me for the amount of alcohol I had consumed the last time I was here. His super king bed sits dominantly in the large room, dressed with fresh white sheets. Thoughts of Mason watching me as I drift off to sleep rush through me, and I quickly walk past the bed, feeling like an intruder in his private space.

I contemplate going downstairs to sleep on the sofa, but the idea of being alone in such a colossal space has me heading towards the en suite instead. I strip down quickly before stepping into his walk-in shower, the spray hitting me hard.

Spotting his body wash on the stand, I pop open the lid and inhale.

Hmm. That's the stuff.

The woodsy scent expels some of my doubt. Mason wanted to take me home tonight—that must mean something.

Yes, he wants to have sex with you, Nina, not move you in.

Ignoring my own reasoning, I squeeze a generous amount

of soap into my hand, lathering up my body and losing myself in all things Mason.

Reluctantly I step from the shower, struggling to see anything through the steam and condensation that's filled the room. Wrapped in one of the super soft towels I found in the shelving, I walk back out to the room, a cloud of mist following me as I go.

Silence settles around me as I stand in the centre of the room. I can't hear a thing, not even the girls. Looking down at myself, I wonder what I should put on.

Can I go to bed in my underwear?

I spot one of the adjoining doors slightly ajar and wonder if it's his wardrobe. Would it be rude to go through his things? I tiptoe to the door, tentatively pushing it open, and the light flickers on automatically, making me jump.

My eyes do a quick scan of the room, relief filling me when I see a discarded white shirt on a grey padded stool in the corner of the room. I walk over, pick it up and bring it to my nose. *Mase.* Will his smell ever stop having this effect on me?

I slide the shirt over my head then smile down at myself. I look ridiculous. It's huge, hanging low on my tan thighs.

Without overthinking this whole situation any more than I already am, I leave the wardrobe and get into bed, picking the side I slept in the last time I was here.

Lying on my back, I stare up at the ceiling, trying to think about anything but the fact I'm lying alone in Mason Lowell's bed.

Mase

Fucking parents.

You would think it would be the children calling up to ask for help, not the other way around. Scarlet couldn't handle our father on her own, and it's unfair to think that she could. Unfair that she feels the need to still live with him after all these years.

Since our mother died, my father has slowly been killing himself, his purpose gone with her last breath.

I rub my hands over my face harshly, the image of my dad slumped in his chair completely unresponsive, making my stomach lurch.

I need a fucking shower and my bed.

The elevator doors slide open, and the smell of liquor instantly assaults me. I lift my collar, sniffing myself, but it's not me.

Fucking Elliot.

If he has brought Cece here, I will kill him; they already caused enough problems for me tonight.

I take the stairs two at a time, desperate to shower and at least try and get some sleep. It's just gone three a.m. and my alarm is set for my morning workout in three hours.

The moment I step into my room, I feel her. My eyes seek out the silhouette of the woman in my bed—her soft, delicate curves covered by the thin fabric of my sheets. I swallow thickly. *It's not her.* It can't be her. Vinny wouldn't have brought her here. He knows better.

It's not her. I tell myself as I quietly step inside my en suite, ignoring the hope that consumes me because if anyone could erase the bullshit I've endured tonight, it's her.

Nina

MY BODY STIRS AS the bed dips behind me, awakening me from the most peaceful sleep I have had in months. His distinctive smell wraps around me moments before his arms do, his soft lips brushing across the exposed skin of my neck as he breathes me in.

"Angel," he whispers.

"Mase, you're home. What time is it?"

"You're in my bed," he rasps, leaving open-mouthed kisses along the taut lines of my throat.

His body moulds to my back as his hand runs from my bare thigh to my waist, dragging the shirt along with it.

"You want me to leave? Elliot—"

I sigh as his hand slides into the front of my underwear, cupping me with just the right amount of pressure.

He lifts his head to look down at me, his dark eyes piercing through mine in the moonlit room. "Try leaving." He smirks, dipping one finger into my heat.

My back arches away from him, pushing me farther into the hand that cups me. Farther onto the thick finger that penetrates me at a deliciously slow pace.

"Mase," I moan, turning to give him my mouth.

Our kiss is gentle at first, slow, as our mouths find a rhythm that fits, and I can't help the soft smile that finds my lips as I think about the worry I faced at him finding me in his bed.

"Why are you smiling?" he whispers against my lips.

"I was worried you'd be mad at me coming here tonight,

being in your bed when you got home," I say, gasping against his open mouth as he pumps his finger inside me.

"You have no idea what you being here does to me, Nina." He rolls his hips, his hardened cock nestling into the line of my ass as his lips find mine again, demanding and controlled in their assault.

His fingers leave me, spreading my desire through my slick flesh, then swirling around my clit before pinching it between his fingers. I moan when he pushes inside of me again, unsure how many fingers are stretching me wide.

Mason doesn't stop. Not until I'm writhing beneath him, so close to falling over the edge, I can feel the tremor about to pulsate through me. As his hand leaves me, I whimper, but he wastes no time, grabbing my hips and flipping me to my back.

A moment seems too big a word to describe how quickly he enters me. Deep, harsh, and fully to the hilt.

"Oh my god!" I cry out as he groans, falling onto me. "Mase," I breathe, feeling overwhelmed and consumed by him. "Shit." I roll my hips, trying to ease the burning sensation between my legs.

"Stop moving," he demands, bringing his forehead to mine and closing his eyes. "Just stay fucking still a minute. Please."

I smile up at the beautiful man above me, watching as he fights for control, fights to stop himself from coming.

Holy shit. "Mase, a condom!" I say in a panic.

"I. Know!" he grounds out, his body trembling above mine.

I roll my lips trying to hold back a smile.

"Angel, you need to stop fucking smiling," he moans.

Not being able to help myself, I squeeze him tight, using every muscle I can convince to help me in what I'm sure will be my vagina's very own assassination.

His cock twitches in delight as my walls contract around him. "Fuck!"

I should know better than to push the man, but it works. With every last bit of his control shredded, he gives in, starting to move inside me. He lifts one of my legs over his arm to push himself deeper, and my smile slips as his cock rubs against the spot inside me that he's seemed to have already learnt so well. Our bodies move as one, craving the release we both search for in each other.

"Shit, I can't, you're so fucking tight," he moans.

"Not. Yet. I'm nearly. There," I beg.

A growl leaves him as he drops my leg to the bed, then he is grabbing my hips in an unforgiving hold, pounding into me relentlessly as he pulls me onto him. His lips take mine in a bruising kiss as I start to convulse around him, his own orgasm causing him to jerk above me. I feel his cum fill me as his cock jolts inside my still throbbing core.

Lying completely sated beneath him, I bring my hand up to push his hair out of his face, looking into his eyes as they spark, the dark pools seeming to glow almost black. He has the most captivating eyes I've ever seen.

"Can we name him Samuel?" I ask, trying not to laugh.

"It's not funny, Nina." He smiles, capturing my lips in a soft kiss. "Please tell me you're on something."

I school my features, swallowing thickly. "No, Mase. I'm not."

9

Nina

I WINCE AS HE HASTILY PULLS OUT OF ME, WORRY ETCHING HIS beautiful face. My hands reach for him in a desperate attempt to keep him close, but he's already sat back on his knees trying to put distance between us.

I use the opportunity to take him in, lazily moving my eyes down his body. I lie on my back, legs spread wide as I shamelessly check him out, from his strong shoulders to his broad chest. Then lower, I take in the lines of his abs, each one taut and defined under his golden skin. Short, soft, brown hair lies between the perfect v set against his hips, a perfectly groomed trail that brings my eyes to my newfound favourite thing. It hangs heavy against his muscular thigh, still slick with our arousal. I dart my tongue out to wet my lips as I look up, finding his deep black pools.

Literal pools—he looks like he is about to cry.

"Mason, I was joking. I'm on the pill." I laugh, gingerly closing my legs.

"Jesus! That's not funny," he huffs, dropping to the mattress beside me. "You're on the pill?" he asks, repeating my words back to me.

"Uh-huh." I climb over him, straddling his waist daringly as I glare down at him. "Do I need to get checked?"

His frown is instant. "Do *I*?" he asks defensively, flattening his hands on my thighs.

I plant my hands on either side of his head, leaning over him. My hair creates a veil around us. "No. It's been a while."

He perks up, pinching a nipple between his fingers. "How long's a while?"

I shrug, bringing my lips to his. "A couple months."

"A couple months?" he repeats.

I shrug again, darting my tongue out to lick along the seam of his lips. "Maybe a year."

"A year!" he pulls away, shocked.

"I win, right?" I fake a smile.

He swallows thickly, pushing my hair back from my face. "Yeah, you win." He frowns, still staring intently into my eyes. "I'm clean. I get checked regularly, and I always wear a condom."

"Always?" I pop a brow.

"No, Nina, always," he stresses.

I roll my lips as I contemplate asking the question that's on the tip of my tongue.

"Out with it," he probes, squeezing my thighs.

"You get checked regularly...because you have sex..."

"Regularly?" he finishes for me, and I have to force a fractured smile to my lips.

Of course, he has lots of sex—the man screams sex. It

oozes from every inch of him, from the way he dresses to that carnal smile.

Mason rolls us, placing me on my side to face him. My legs wrap around him as his body falls flush with mine. His heavy eyes search my face as if trying to figure something out.

He looks shattered.

"What time is it?" I ask.

His hand disappears under my shirt, lazily skimming my side. "Nearly morning."

"You sort everything with your... Scar?"

His eyes bore into mine. Sharp; protective. "Yes."

I nod my head, chewing the inside of my cheek.

He doesn't want to tell me. I get it. He hardly knows me. But what he refuses to say with his words screams at me in the depths of his eyes. Pain. It lurks in the shallows of his stare, craving the unknown.

We may not know much about each other, but I'm quickly learning. Elliot knows him well—Charlie too. And they wanted me to be here for him tonight. I may not know why, but I genuinely believe that I should be here. That maybe this man needs somebody. Maybe for the first time in my life, I want to be more than Nina Anderson, the dancer, best friend to Lucy and Megan, and daughter of an alcoholic mother.

Maybe I could let just one more in.

"You need to sleep," I tell him, smoothing out the deep lines in his forehead with my thumb. He lifts his head, nuzzling my palm before gently kissing it.

His head lies heavily in my hand, our bodies intertwined as one as he smiles warmly at me, swiftly drifting into the darkness.

I envy his ability to sleep so soundly as I lie awake

watching him, waiting for sleep to carry me away from my own demons.

THE BED IS empty when I wake only a few hours later, and I allow myself to lie in the quiet confinement of the bedroom before I go in search of him.

I feel surprisingly good considering the amount of alcohol I drank last night. My head feels clear, and what I feared might happen after spending the night with Mason hasn't happened. I don't feel dirty, or shameful, or like I want to run for the hills. Mason is consuming. He enters the room, and I can barely focus on anything else, which should scare me, but it doesn't. Because once he leaves and I'm all alone again, I don't feel any less of a person. I feel valued. Seen.

Lifting my arms above my head, I stretch out my deliciously sore limbs, my body humming with arousal as I'm reminded of him sliding in behind me in the early hours of the morning.

Where are you, Mase?

Pulling back the covers, I creep to the door then poke my head out into the hallway. Silence. Satisfied I won't get caught, I take off down the stairs in only Mason's shirt, heading for the kitchen for a glass of water. My mouth waters the closer I get, the smell of bacon assaulting me. I feel famished.

"Good morning," Lance sings, bright-eyed as he stands at the hob tending to what I presume is the bacon.

"Umm, morning," I say on autopilot, immediately wishing I'd stayed up in the room.

His eyes drop down my body, and I pull at the hem of my shirt, wishing it were longer. "Breakfast?" he asks.

"Where's Mason?"

He smiles wide. All teeth. Fake. "Probably out, making a million." He winks.

"It's a Saturday?"

"Yep." He continues to turn the bacon. "Did you make sure to shag his brains out?" He eyes me, sarcasm dripping from his every word.

"Excuse me?" I ask at the same time that keys clatter in the foyer.

I stand waiting for Lance to explain, but he doesn't. His eyes skirt over my shoulder just before warm hands encase my waist.

I close my eyes as his minty breath tickles at the skin just below my ear.

"Clothes. Now, Nina." Mason says, voice scratchy and rough as he squeezes my hips.

I turn my head into him, his lips finding my temple. He stands topless at my back, his long torso ripped with muscle and wet with sweat. I drop my eyes lower, finding his shorts sitting low on his hips. *Boy oh boy.* "Come with me?" I ask.

He licks his lower lip before pulling it between his teeth. "Later, I have a houseful to kick out first."

He steps away from me, and I quickly exit the kitchen when he moves to open the fridge.

I take the stairs two at a time, heading straight for the safety of the girls' room. I push inside, finding them awake and sitting up in the large bed. Stepping up onto the ottoman, I make my way up the middle, sinking down between my two pillars of strength.

"You seem troubled, girl," Lucy says. "Hungover?"

I shake my head, my mind in overdrive. "What do you guys make of Lance?" I ask, still stuck on his comment from before.

"He's hot!" Megan chuckles. "That beard he has going on."

I smile as she drives the heaviness away. "I think he heard us last night, talking about Mase. He just mentioned it in the kitchen."

"Heard what?" Lucy frowns.

"About shagging his brains out. You mentioned a proposal too." I smirk over at her. "I don't think he likes me."

"Why, because he thinks you want to marry Mason Lowell? I mean, is he blind? I don't think there is a girl on earth who wouldn't want to marry him."

"True," I laugh. "Maybe I'm reading too much into it."

"Probably," Lucy mutters, dropping her head to rest against mine.

"I need food," Megan groans, and just as she says it, the door flies open, and Elliot saunters in.

"Good morning, beautiful girls." He stands in only a pair of white boxer briefs, holding a tray of food.

The man's godly, and he knows it.

"Thank you, Jesus." Lucy smiles up at the ceiling.

"Come here, big boy. Mumma wants some of what you got," Megan says, grabbing the tray when he gets close enough and pulling it to her lap.

Elliot steals a piece of toast before Megan can inhale it all, then leans across our legs to pass it to Luce. I snatch some for myself.

We sit in silence, devouring the buttery pieces of heaven.

"You can go again now." Megan grins up at Elliot.

"You just want to look at my arse," he laughs, stealing the last piece before turning for the door. I shake my head after the cocky bastard.

Megan's elbow shoots out and into my ribs and I look to her with a frown.

She nods over at Lucy who sits, licking her lips as she watches Elliot's retreating back.

"Good toast, huh, Luce?"

She snaps her eyes away, blinking rapidly as her cheeks turn crimson. "Piss off." She smiles. "That man is far too easy on the eye—we all know that. He should be in a museum. Mute. He's the epitome of look but don't touch."

"Amen to that sister," Megan agrees.

Everything falls quiet, and I close my eyes, enjoying the peacefulness.

"Nina, you're not holding out on us, are you?" Megan pipes up, and I can hear the smile in her voice.

I burrow into the bed, hiding beneath the covers, but they are ripped from my grip, expectant faces glaring down at me. "Later girls, we've already established how big Lance's ears are," I say with a chuckle.

"Yes, good point." Megan nods. "Another good point..." *Here we go.* "Mason is seriously packing. I had that all up in my face last night, so I'm pretty certain, but can you confirm or deny?"

I laugh as I think back to the club, the girls listening outside the door. I look between them, my smile wide. "Confirmative girls. It's an earth-shattering, toe-curling, confirmative."

We all sigh.

WE SHOWER AND DRESS, then go in search of the boys. We find them in the lounge, scattered around the sectional sofas. Lance and Charlie are dressed, but Elliot is still gloriously naked in only a pair of boxers - not a care in the world.

My eyes lock on Mason. He sits in the corner of the room fresh from a shower, dressed in a tight white T-shirt and black jeans. He takes me in, his eyes roaming my body. I do a little two-step as my stomach knots. I want to rush him, demand he takes me back to bed for the day. He raises a brow as if challenging me to voice my thoughts. He can read me too well.

I don't want to go home.

"Everyone out," he states, his eyes stuck on me.

"Fuck off, Lowell," Elliot retorts, rooting himself deeper into the sofa, clearly too comfortable to move.

"I'll call a taxi. Do you girls need one?" Charlie asks.

"Yes, please," I reply.

"No, not you. We have our date," Mason says, running his tongue along the front of his teeth. He comes to stand beside me, blocking my view from the others. I frown as I look around him, all of them standing to leave.

"Our date isn't until seven thirty. I need to go home and get some fresh clothes."

"You don't need any clothes, and it's gone seven thirty, so technically we are late." He gives me a boyish grin, and I relax a little.

"This evening, Mason. I'm going home to change first."

"No. You're not."

Lucy gives me a wave as she starts to leave the room, and I

shake my head at her. Is she really going to abandon me with this demanding ass?

"I will call you, babes!" she states, disappearing with everyone else into the elevator.

"You're infuriating," I mutter, crossing my arms over my chest.

His lip tips up at the corner, eating away at my defensiveness. *Damn it.* Why is he so hot?

"What would you have done today? If you'd have gone home?" he asks, his voice softer now.

"I don't know, got myself prepared for this evening, caught up on some sleep." I look at him as if that's his problem. "Try and find something to wear."

"Sleep first then." He nods towards the stairs. "Back to bed."

I hesitate, unsure of his motive. "I could just go home and sleep." But I want to stay. "Are you coming with me?"

"You could go home, and you can, but then I will have to come and pick you up again later and that seems pointless." He steps closer. Pulls me closer. "And no, I have things to attend to today. I will be back in time for our date."

"You're leaving me here?"

"I won't be gone long. Get some sleep." He leans in, placing a tender kiss on my forehead. It's sweet. A softer side of him that I've only had small glimpses of shining through.

Then he ruins it. I squirm as he pulls away, pinching my nipple through the white fabric of my dress. "I could see these from the other side of the room. Elliot was looking too." He scowls, and it's all sorts of adorable.

"Ouch! Elliot didn't even know we were here." I lean away, using my hands to protect my sensitive buds.

"Montgomery doesn't miss a set of tits, especially not those." He eyes my chest, walking backwards away from me.

"I totally noticed," Elliot groans, reminding me he is still buried in the sofa. He stands, grabbing his clothes and throwing me a wink as he starts dressing.

"Don't leave me here," I call out to Mason.

"You'll be fine, Pi—" His eyes tighten and he pauses. "Make yourself at home. I won't be long."

And then he is gone, with Elliot not far behind him.

Mase

Am I mad to leave her alone in my home?

I suppose this is one way to test her. Does that make me an ass? I've not let a woman sleep in my bed since Cara. I thought I could trust her, but what a piece of work she turned out to be. She was my hardest lesson learnt when it came to the dos and don'ts of casual sex. I should check in on her, make sure she is sticking to our agreement.

The thought of Nina in my home, amongst my things—it shouldn't feel so right. Something tells me I can trust her, and maybe that makes me a fool, but the primal need to protect her, to fuck her, keep her close, is overwhelming. I didn't even use a condom.

What was I thinking?

She is fast becoming my only thought, and that's a dangerous thing, and the fact I'm about to go shopping on a Saturday in central London should tell me all I need to know on the matter.

I sit in my car, considering where I should go. I know what I need. I just don't know where to start.

I hesitate as my thumb hovers over the contact. Fuck it. I hit call and put the phone to my ear.

"Mr Lowell?"

"Alice, I need your help."

Nina

I SIT on the sofa scrolling through the channels but not paying any mind to what's on the screen. It's becoming clear that I don't like being in this place alone. Maybe it's because of the first time I was here, or maybe it's because it's so big.

Does Mason feel the same way? Being here alone all the time must be awful. What does he do in his spare time? *What do you think, stupid?* God, he even told me he has sex 'regularly'. Who brings that shit up straight after sex? How embarrassing.

After getting fed up with the TV, I start to wander around the penthouse. He told me to make myself at home, but it seemed like a rude thing to do.

Boredom won out in the end, and that's on him. He shouldn't make me wait.

The rooms are all beautifully decorated, and I'm sure someone has spent hours making it look magazine-worthy. Yet there isn't anything personal—no photos on the walls. No mess. You wouldn't know it's lived in. Like the kitchen, it's equipped with top of the range appliances, but they look unused.

I come to the only door left at the end of the hall, the one that sits between the gym room and entertainment room.

The catch clicks as I test the handle, and I feel a wave of excitement rush through me. I feel like I'm doing something wrong when I'm not.

Pushing open the door, I find an office.

It's smaller than I'd expect in comparison to the other rooms. A desk sits in the centre with shelves lining the entire left wall. Some sit empty, and some are filled with books and photos.

I lift a picture frame and smile wide at the image. Charlie, Elliot, Lance and Mason. They sit on the back of a yacht, legs dangling into the infinite blue ocean that lies calm beneath them as the sun sets in the distance.

All four men are completely different in their individual styles and personalities—all equally as hot—it makes me wonder how they met. Lance, although he seems friendly, still confuses me. He's made it clear that he is just as unsure of me as I am him.

Elliot I can't even take seriously enough to figure out. And Charlie seems to be the most complex of them all. He seems so closed off yet always aware and watching, he shows a soft side towards me and the girls, and it's not forced or fake when he asks you a question, he genuinely wants to know.

My eyes find Mason in the picture, the only one I want to understand. I feel like I have so much still to learn about him. I have seen his temper, a switch that goes from a tender sweet man to a dark, brooding beast with little influence. First with his altercation with Joey, then last night when he left to see Scar, and when he came to me at the gym—always so quick on the defence.

Other than his unreasonable, possessive attitude towards me and his need to get his way in every situation so far, I'd say he hides his emotions well. He doesn't say much with his words. But those moments when we are alone, just the two of us, I see a different man. A tender man.

I drop down into the desk chair and scan the contents. Sat off to the side is another photo, this one of a family, and the resemblance of the father and son uncanny. I reach for it, smoothing my fingers across the polished frame.

This is Mason's family. His foundations.

They stand outside of a beautiful sprawling home, a tiny baby in the arms of the mother, a young boy standing at his father's feet, proud hands placed on his son's shoulders.

My heart aches as a wave of untamed jealousy floors me.

What I would give to have a dad. A sibling. A mother who loved me more than herself. Mason may have lost his mother at a young age, but if even for just this one day, the day this photo was taken, the look in the woman's eyes as she looks at her son, her hand rested on her husband's forearm, a baby in her grasp. Even if for just that one moment they were happy, then he already had more from her than I'll get in a lifetime from my mother. His father may stand proud—the man of the family—but his mother's love visibly runs through each one of them like a thread, tying them all together with a simple look, the slightest touch.

Why is this hidden? Is this where he spends all his time? If I had these memories, I'd plaster them all over my home to remind me.

A bittersweet smile comes to my face. Because I do have photos like this one, us on holiday, in the back garden, trips to the zoo. Just not with my biological family.

I put the photo back into place, shutting the office door as I slip out. I grab my phone and go to Mason's room. I pull open the balcony door and sit down on the lounger, looking out over the city.

John answers on the second ring, always there, unconditionally, no expectations.

"Hello?" his warm voice soothes me.

"Hi, it's me."

"Nina. How are you, darling? Maggie, Nina is on the phone!" he calls out to his wife.

Tears pool in my eyes as realisation sinks in. "I'm okay," I hesitate.

"That's not all that convincing. What is it, love? Do you need help with the studio this month? You know it's not an issue."

I smile through unshed tears, two words, and he knows, prepared to trample anything in my way.

"It's not the studio, John, I just... you know how grateful I am, don't you? For everything you and Maggie have done for me. I wouldn't be half the person I am without you both. You gave me everything I could have wanted in a family. You believed in my dreams—invested in them even." I pause, feeling silly for rambling. "If I had the choice at a do-over, to be born again into a different family, a different mum, I wouldn't. I'd always choose the hurt that led me to you. I'm so thankful to you both, and I'm sorry I haven't told you that before."

"Well, that's enough of that. You're going to make an old man cry," he says gruffly. "Are you sure you are okay, Nina?"

"I am. I promise."

"Nina, hunny." Maggie's voice croons, my throat

constricting as a fresh wave of tears spring to my eyes. God, what is wrong with me today. "You'll be here tomorrow for lunch, I hope?"

I smile, pushing the wetness away with the palm of my hand. "Yeah."

SOMETHING SHARP DIGS into my hip as I roll in the bed. My eyes slowly open in the dimly lit room, the sun almost lost to the horizon and out of sight for the day. I sit up, looking at the array of items spread on the bed.

I pick up the luxurious looking hamper, filled with washes, bath salts and perfumes.

What is all this?

My hand finds a sleek black stiletto buried under my side, and I sit up to find a beautiful beaded gold dress lying at my feet. It looks expensive. It all looks expensive. Pushing back the covers, I climb from the bed but stop short at the dresser when I see a note sat beside an ice bucket, champagne open and at the ready alongside a lone flute.

I take a deep breath, trying to dispel the unease that comes with the gifts.

DON'T MAKE ME WAIT, PIXIE. I'VE ALREADY WAITED LONG ENOUGH.

My head tells me to leave, that I can't be bought with gifts —money. But my treacherous heart doesn't care. It beats fearlessly in my chest, begging me to stay. To try, for once. To be more for him.

Whatever he needs me to be.

I grasp the bottle, pouring myself a glass before I grab the hamper and head for the en suite.

I need to armour up first. If that tortured look in his eyes tells me anything, it's that his demons like my own—won't fight fair.

10

Nina

HE ASKED ME NOT TO MAKE HIM WAIT, SO NATURALLY, IT MADE me want to take my time. Soaking in a cloud of bubbles, three quarters of the champagne obliterated, I pop a chocolate truffle into my mouth. Tilting my head back against the rim of the sunken bathtub, I let the silky-smooth treat melt down my throat.

I've been no more than an hour—I'm sure of it. But as the rapping of his knuckles echoes off the smooth marble suite, I jump, legs slipping from the edge and champagne spilling over my breasts.

"Shit!"

"Nina? Are you okay in there?"

"Uh, yeah, just a sec!" I climb from the bath, wrapping myself in a towel and padding over to the door.

Swinging open the door, I find him on the threshold, arms crossed over his chest and looking down his nose at me.

I shouldn't laugh, but he's mad, and mad Mase is fun to play with.

"Hello." I smile, looking up through my brows seductively.

His head lowers, his eyes creasing in the corners as he watches me. "You're late."

I lift his wrist, checking the time. I don't miss the immaculate black shirt, dark jeans and that smell. God, he smells edible. If possible, his eyebrows drop even lower.

"I have five minutes until seven thirty."

"You were still in the bath."

"Sorry, Mr Lowell." I pout, leaning into his big body. "You want to wait whilst I finish up?"

"No," he answers quickly.

I shrug. "Okay. Close the door on your way out."

Mase

SHE'S PUSHING IT. Pushing me and she knows it. She's loving this. And so am. Fucking. I.

"Nina," I warn as she turns from me, dropping her towel in the next second. "Fuck!" I groan, my fingers in a white-knuckle grip on the doorframe.

"Come on, Mase. We can go out later." She eyes me over her shoulder.

"No, get dressed. Now," I demand.

She has no idea how fucking gorgeous she is. This is the first time I've seen her fully naked, always having something between us. Yet she is everything I imagined and more. My eyes try to take in every inch of her, but they are drawn to the curve of her hips. That ass. *Do not turn the fuck around.* Worse, she bends, picking up the champagne at her feet. Her perfect pink pussy is on full display, and it's over, my control gone. I'm behind her in two strides, one hand around her throat, the other cupping her cunt.

"You changed your mind." She smiles.

I apply the slightest of pressure to her throat while squeezing her clit tight between my fingers. "You want to play, Pixie?" I say, sliding in three fingers without warning, pulling her ass back and hard onto my throbbing cock.

She gasps, her head falling to my shoulder, her body writhing against me. "Yes!"

I drop my hand before she can rub herself towards orgasm. "Bed. Now," I ground out, spinning her to face me.

It takes every bit of my strength not to pull her puckered nipple into my mouth because if I do, I won't stop, and I can't fuck her in my bathroom right now. She smiles lazily up at me, and I worry she might have drunk too much.

I bend, lifting her over my shoulder and then carry her out to my bed.

"Fucking hell, Nina," I rasp, looking down at her lying naked on my sheets. She drops her knees to the mattress, baring herself to me. My hands link together behind my neck as I fight to keep in control.

I don't want to rush this.

Dropping my hands to her spread legs, I smooth them up her thighs.

"Is this for me?" I ask, dipping my thumb inside her tight little cunt.

"Hmmm," she purrs.

162 | JC HAWKE

"Nina," I whisper, waiting for her eyes to find mine before leaning over her. I rub my thumb along her bottom lip, smearing her desire over the pouty flesh. Her tongue darts out to swipe away the saltiness, but I'm already there, licking and sucking at what's meant for me.

Only me.

"You're wearing too many clothes," she pants between kisses. "I need you bare."

Her words set something off inside me—something primal. The thought of having her again—nothing between us—has my throat working on a deep growl.

Leaning up, she grips my shirt between her fists, then she pulls at the fabric to rip it open. It doesn't budge.

I smile down at the little spitfire, knowing what she wants but can't manage herself. Slowly, I ease off of her, standing at my full height. I pop open the first two buttons, then rip the expensive as shit material straight down the middle, buttons flying off all over the room.

"Happy?" I ask, staring down at her, feeling like a caveman.

"You know I'm not," she says with a suggestive smile.

"On your knees now," I snap, making her squeal when I grab her ankle and flip her.

She goes to pull her legs up under her, but I'm already there. I drag her up by the hips, setting her on her knees.

"Don't move."

She shivers as my hands leave her. "Mase!"

"Don't. Move."

The room falls silent, and I stand watching her, slowly shedding my clothes until I'm naked. Completely bare. I drop to my knees on the floor, my mouth salivating at the need to taste her. She sucks in a breath as my index finger trails from the top of her spine to the curve of her ass.

I glide it down over her, pausing at her rear entrance.

Just, the slightest, of, pressur—

"Mase," she panics.

I chuckle, sliding lower until I am sinking into her. Deep down to my knuckle. I give her three slow pumps, watching mesmerised as she sucks me into her heat.

"So greedy."

I pull my fingers out, planting my face exactly where it belongs. I suck on her slit long and hard as she tries to pull away from me, my arm wrapping around her waist to keep her exactly where I want her.

She moans my name, soft whimpers that have my cock throbbing with the need to be inside her. I plunge my tongue relentlessly into her, not stopping until she's screaming into the sheets, body shaking and her cum is dripping to my chest.

Her body drops lax to the bed as I rise to stand above her. She twists, looking up at me, spent.

"I'm not finished with you yet," I promise, my hand moving up and down my length.

She scoots to the edge of the bed, her lips parted and eager to please.

I shake my head, smiling as I push her down to the mattress. "I won't last long in there, angel."

I settle between her legs, palming her cheek as I thrust into her heat, every solid inch, my pelvis rolling over her sensitive clit. It's enough to set her off again, her pussy clenching my cock in a death grip.

"Fuck!" I groan. "Or in there. Shit, Nina." I search her eyes, but she is completely lost to her own pleasure.

My hips start to pound against her, my hands going to the backs of her knees to guide her body to mine. She seems to regain some composure and reaches between us, grabbing my balls and rolling them between her fingers.

I pull out, flipping her to her front again and meeting her hips as they rise to meet mine.

"Oh my god!" she cries, sinking her face into the sheet again.

I don't stop, don't ease up or relent until I get a tingling in the base of my spine, my toes curling into the carpet at my feet as my muscles lock tight.

"Fuck!" I growl, throwing my head back as I empty myself inside her.

Again.

Nina

MY BODY LIES spent beneath him, struggling to take his weight but too addicted to make him move. My initial plan was to prove a point. His gifts felt too much, too over the top.

"Why so serious?" He smiles into my neck, pulling out of me and rolling me so I'm on top of him.

A wave of panic floods me. Uncontrollable emotions I won't ignore.

I can't accept his gifts.

I climb off the bed, grabbing my towel to cover myself.

"Mase, I don't want your money. I don't want you to buy me things."

He sits up on his elbows, confusion marring his beautiful face. "It was only a bit of body wash, Nina, something you could wear to dinner."

It was so much more than that, and he knows it. Who shops for a woman he's just met? "No. It kept me here for the day, gave you the control you wanted."

"And? Are you really calling me out on buying you nice things?" he questions, still lying gloriously naked. His cock sits heavy against his abdomen, already becoming hard again.

Stay strong, Nina.

"I'm calling you out on... on..." I huff, losing my train of thought.

Fuck it.

I drop my towel hoping it renders him just as stupid as he does me.

I walk to the bed and straddle him, dropping myself down onto his length until my ass hits his muscular thighs.

He growls, bringing his head to mine, but I don't let him have the connection. I push him back to the bed, towering over him.

"I'm calling you out on keeping me here all day, alone, whilst you buggered off doing God knows what." I rise to my knees, leaving only the tip left inside me.

The cords in his neck strain as he looks down at the place our bodies meet, desperate for me to take him. "You bought me that stuff so I wouldn't need to go home today, yes?"

"Yes! I stand by that decision," he argues.

I lower my knees a fraction before letting him slide out of me completely. "Wrong answer." I smile.

"Fuck! Ride me, and I won't buy you another gift ever again."

His boyish plea has me relenting, but I want to get my point across.

Feeling ungrateful, I lean over him, still keeping our pelvises apart. "I'm thankful, truly I am. This is probably what most girls dream of, but it's not what I want." I smile sadly, wishing I wasn't such a screwup.

His hand comes up, brushing a strand of hair behind my ear. "What *do* you want, angel?" he asks, his face growing serious.

Grasping his cock between us, I line him up, hesitating for just a second. "Right now? You."

He lifts his hips, entering me on one swift thrust.

THE LIGHT SMELL of smoke wakes me in the early hours, and I roll into the body beside me, not fully comprehending the smell.

He is so warm, so solid. It makes me feel safe.

But I can smell smoke, and I'm hungry. Really flipping hungry. The growl of my stomach has my legs untangling from Mason's and carrying me from the bedroom.

We got a little carried away last night, completely giving up on our date by nine. I should feel bad, but I don't. He should have let me go home and get myself ready.

Maybe I wouldn't have freaked out.

I sneak from the room and start down the curved staircase, my feet coming to an abrupt halt halfway down. My breath catches in my throat as my heart somehow slows and speeds up within the same beat.

The entire ground floor is lit in candlelight, every surface littered with a warm glow that mirrors the London skyline beyond. Slowly, I descend the final steps, trying not to think about the man lying in bed upstairs.

Instead, I try to see the room as only an observer and not the recipient of such a beautiful, thoughtful gesture. *This isn't for me.* The dining table is set for two, champagne on what would have been ice bobs in the chilled water. An extravagant bunch of white roses sits in an arrangement in the centre. I can smell them mixed with the smoke from neglected candles.

I notice a square box sitting on one of the place settings. *This isn't for me.* Then it's in my hand. The lid popped open before I can even think twice about it.

The most beautiful gold bangle sits on a cushioned ring. It's simple, with just one lone diamond sparkling at the clasp. It's stunning, personal, and something I'd buy for myself.

I glance in the direction of the stairs, unable to keep him out any longer. He consumes me in every way imaginable. My thoughts, actions, even my body. He shouldn't be the driving force behind my decisions, but he's becoming something my head cowers to and my heart craves.

I snap the box closed, placing it back on the place setting and walk to the lounge area.

Scattered pillows surround a tray of strawberries, chocolate, and roses. Regret gnaws at me. God, I was such a bitch before, moaning about him buying me gifts. It may be over the top, but he wanted to do this for me.

My stomach growls again, reminding me it needs feeding. Feeling like a child who might get caught, I sit on the cushioned floor, my back to the sofa as I inhale the plate of strawberries.

I don't hear him at first, but when I spot his feet beside me from the corner of my eye, I start to savour the strawberry in my hand—accentuating every delicious bite, letting the juice run from my lips.

Simply because I choose heart. I choose chocolate-covered strawberries. I choose the man who wants to give me his time. I choose Mason Lowell. At least for tonight.

I plant my knees in front of him as he stands gloriously naked, looking down on me. My body stirs with arousal at the dark look in his eyes.

"Were we even going to go out tonight?" I ask.

His hands cup my jaw as he bends, licking up my chin and into my mouth, sucking my lip hard before righting himself again.

I take that as a no.

My tongue darts out, finding the remnants of strawberries, and I pull my lip into my mouth, sucking all the sweetness I can from them.

His cock twitches in appreciation, precum leaking from the tip.

"I'm not sure strawberries and salt mix," I say, looking up through my lashes and his muscular body ripples under my lustful stare.

He doesn't answer me, fisting his length at the base and dragging the tip across my mouth, painting my lips with his excitement.

I roll them, resisting the urge to lick his taste from them. "Mase, speak to me."

"I am," he says, grasping my chin and pushing the head of his cock against my teeth. "I want you to open up for me."

His words stab me in the gut.

He wants me to open up for him.

I just don't know how.

Beyond Luce and Megan, I don't allow anyone to creep past the hard shell I've spent years creating. Dancing has always been my expression. I use it to let everything out without words.

So I show him the only way I know how and plead with him with my eyes to let it be enough.

Darting out my tongue, I swipe him from my lips, watching him as my mouth forms around his tip. He groans loudly, his knees dipping as he scrapes my hair from my neck and pulls it into one hand, winding the soft strands around his fist.

It's a power play, and I want it. I want him and his threat to control me, but only here. He can control every part of my pleasure—of his. But nothing else.

He lifts my chin. "Keep your eyes on me," he manages, voice gruff.

He starts to thrust his hips, hitting the back of my throat on every stroke, slowly getting deeper and deeper.

I smile around him, making his eyes darken. He shakes his head before looking away from me. "Baby, don't give me that smile."

"Mmmmm," I murmur, his cock lodged in my throat, causing my voice to vibrate around him.

"Fuck," he snaps. The hold on my hair intensifies as he winds it even tighter, his hips thrusting even faster, harder, unapologetically. His eyes find mine again, and realisation flashes across his face as I struggle to take him. I may be the one on my knees, with his hold on my hair, but he isn't in control either. It's been lost in the moment, a free-for-all as he fights my reflexes for release.

Forcing myself back, I drop to the floor, knowing he will follow, and he does. He doesn't hesitate, lining himself up and thrusting inside me.

"Dripping. Fucking. Wet," he rasps.

He starts to roll his hips into me, lifting my leg over his forearm to get to the perfect spot. "Mase! You feel so good," I moan.

His eyes find mine, softening instantly, then his lips drop to mine, and he takes my mouth in a beautiful, slow kiss.

My leg falls to the side and he stills inside me, his arm still draped under my bent leg. His hand comes around and grasps my wrist in a stronghold. Our breathing is erratic, the only other noise between our deep, sucking kisses.

My body aches to have him, wanting more and less, and for this feeling never to end. "Mase, move. Please," I beg, clenching around him.

A growl rumbles through his chest as he brings my arms up and around his shoulders, locking them behind his neck to keep him close. He gives me exactly what I want, rolling his hips perfectly until my body locks tight and pressure builds at my core. And he knows it. His hand comes down, planting itself over my clit, tipping me over the edge and letting me free fall.

The primal need that comes over me has me focusing on nothing but the rising, inexplicable wave that's coursing through my body. I feel nothing and everything all at once as my walls squeeze and relax in unison, my sex sucking him in deeper with its hungry release.

He stands, still buried deep inside me, my body wrapped around him. He sits down on the sofa, my body straddling his. "Fuck me, Pixie," he whispers.

The position has me sinking farther onto him, aftershocks still rippling through my core. "I can feel you, baby," he groans, his mouth sucking at my throat.

I begin to roll my hips. Hard. Deep. A small circle.

His head comes up and he looks at me, his hair a dishevelled mess. "I might just keep you. Don't fucking stop," he says, planting a chaste kiss on my lips.

Using all the energy I have left, I ride him, working my hips under his hold to get him to the point of ecstasy. He comes inside of me, groaning out my name as his mouth falls from my puckered nipple.

His body shakes as his face nuzzles into my chest.

I go to speak, but nothing comes out. Reaching up instead, I run my hand through his smooth hair. My eyes catch a gold glint behind his head. I pull my wrist forward, looking over the gold band that now adorns my wrist.

"I'll send everything else back," he says, looking up at me with hesitant eyes. "But keep that. Please."

"I could get used to those manners, Bossman." I smile, giving him a long, lazy kiss.

WE LIE on the cushioned floor wrapped in a soft woollen blanket, my body curled into Mason's side. My body feels lax, but there's still an ache pulsing through my entire body, reminding me of the incredible night we're leaving behind.

I lift my head from Mason's chest, stealing a piece of cheese from the platter he'd made earlier. "How long did you spend getting all this ready today?" I ask, gesturing around the room.

The majority of the candles are burnt out with wax pooling on the hardwood floors.

"Hours," he says dramatically.

I chuckle, licking the salt from my lips. "It's beautiful. No one has ever treated me like this. It could be the best date I've ever been on, you know. Definitely the best sex for a first date."

"Just the first date, huh, like you've had better?" he mutters, feigning hurt but still smiling. "How bad did you feel? Coming downstairs and seeing all my hard work?"

I bring a piece of cheese to his mouth, letting my finger linger as his tongue comes out to swipe it. "I really did feel bad. I just..."

"I know, you don't want me to buy you things," he finishes for me.

"Mase. My mum, she wasn't the best role model growing up. The thought of becoming her—"

"You're nothing like your mother, Nina!"

"Uh, no. I'm not," I say, confused by his tone and that he thinks he knows me well enough to form an opinion. "But I promised myself a long time ago that I wouldn't rely on anyone else, and I won't be bought with shiny things. I know you have money, and I appreciate the gesture. It's all so thoughtful. I just, I feel uncomfortable with you spending money on me. It's not why I'm here."

"When was the last time you saw your mother?" he asks, completely changing the subject. I just hope he is listening.

"Two years ago. She overdosed. Ended up in hospital for a week."

He shakes his head at my confession, my honesty shocking me. "You shouldn't have to deal with it alone. What you've been through..." he says, fiddling with my bangle.

What I've been through? "How do you know I was alone?"

"Were you?"

Asshole. My body locks up as I resist the urge to bolt. "Mase, what's my mother's name?" I ask, looking down at him.

"What?"

I wait, not saying a word.

He knows I know.

"Sarah Leigh Anderson," he eventually says, his eyes wild as he gauges my reaction.

I drop my head to his chest, looking away from him. His muscles relax in what I presume is relief as his arms come around me.

He thinks he knows. The arrests, hospital admissions, the tip-offs from neighbours to social services—it's only the half of it.

"Say something," I whisper.

"I'm sorry."

"What are you sorry for, Mason?"

"Everything you have been through. Everything you continue to go through."

I roll my eyes, already over this pity party. "My childhood wasn't all bad, you've just invaded the bad bits—and that's exactly what you've done so don't try to deny it. I lived with

Lucy's parents, Maggie, you met her, and John. They took me in at eight. I was between my mums and theirs until uni after that. They made sure I was sheltered from it, somewhat."

He tucks a strand of hair behind my ear, his lips in a tight line. "If she mistreated you so badly, then why do you pay her? Why not cut her off?"

I recoil at his words. "What? Jesus, Mason. How deep did you go?" I yell.

"I wasn't going to look, but I had no way of getting hold of you. Nina, you've transferred your mother nearly fourteen thousand pounds in the last four years!"

He goes to grab me, but I'm already up, the blanket wrapped around me as he tries to do what they all do. Lucy, Maggie, John they think they know best.

They don't.

"Leave it, Mase, it's none of your business!" I head for the kitchen, knowing I need to calm down and put some space between us.

It's only because he cares, Nina.

They all care. It's my biggest war, and I fight it against myself: To defend someone who doesn't care to people who only want what's best for me.

"Fair, it's not my business. But you're going to run your studio into the ground if you don't start paying more off your business loan soon, you're struggling to keep your head above water as it is."

The sharp slap of my hand against his cheek resounds off every inch of the penthouse. We stand toe to toe, his nostrils flaring as his rage seeps out of the red on his face.

"Fuck you!" I roar, tears stinging my eyes. "Mason, by all means, fuck me. Fuck every inch of me until I have nothing else left to give, but stay the fuck out of my life. My studio. My business."

He scoffs, looking up the stairs then back to me again. "So you'll give me your body, but that's it, that's all I get? I guess the apple really doesn't fall far from the tree."

He drops his head to his chest the moment the words are out. And that's the thing with words; once they are spoken, they can't be unheard, forgotten.

"My mother did that," I whisper, a tear running into the seam of my lips. "She never lay a finger on me." Not herself anyway. "But sometimes, I wish she had—it probably would have hurt less. But no, she's just like you." I tip my chin. "She used her words to break me."

"Nina, I didn't—"

"Leave me the fuck alone."

I run up the stairs, bypassing his bedroom and rush to the room Lucy and Megan had stayed in last night. Crawling under the sheets, I let the pain in my chest bleed out through old wounds—memories from my childhood at the centre of my thoughts.

I drift off to sleep hours later, the pillow wet with tears, and my heart empty.

11

Nina

I PULL MY TATTERED BLANKET UP OVER MY HEAD AND PRESS PLAY ON *my iPod. It's not mine. It's my best friend, Lucy's. She said she would be in trouble for giving it to me, but she thought it might drown out the shouting.*

I call it shouting, but I think it's something else. It sounds like a strangled cry, grunts and groans that seep through the thin walls of our damp house.

She tells me to stay in my room, not to come out until she comes to get me, but she never comes. And I never leave. Afraid that whatever is on the other side of the door will get me into trouble, or worse, take her away from me again. My mummy is all I have, and they already tried to take me once.

I squeeze my eyes shut as the banging starts. Rough groans and deep grunts flow past the music. Is she in pain? Should I help her?

A rush of cool liquid runs from my nose, pooling on the seam of my lips. I dab it with my finger finding blood.

Why is my nose bleeding...?

In a panic, I do something silly. Something I know I shouldn't. I run for my mother. "Mummy, Mummy." I push open her door, standing on the threshold unable to move, unable to look away. What is he doing to my mummy? His eyes find me first, a grim smile taking over his face as he stands behind her, hitting into her bottom.

"Get rid of the little fucker!" he shouts, making me flinch.

My mother's eyes flare wide when she sees me. "Nina! Go now. What are you doing?"

Oh no, she's mad at me.

"My nose."

I wipe my nose with the back of my hand, but it comes away clean. I frown at the paleness of my bony hand. My eyes lift back to my mother's, but before they can find hers, a strong, calloused fist connects with my face.

"Nina!" My mother's voice rings out as everything fades to black.

"Nina!"

"Nina!"

"Nina!"

Mason?

Mase

TORTURED CRIES HAVE me bolting upright in bed. I gave up on Nina letting me in after she locked me out, and her soft cries haunted me for hours after as I sat outside her door, waiting until I was sure she was asleep.

But now she is crying again, and it's not the same cries as before. It's a tormented shrill. She sounds in pain.

I jolt from the bed, my head working faster than my body, causing me to stumble to the floor in my haste. I run down the hall and try the handle, knowing it will be locked.

"Nina! Open the door!" I shout, slapping my hand on the wood. "Are you okay? Are you hurt?"

Nothing.

"Nina!" I continue to rap my knuckles on the wood.

A broken wail seeps from the room, and the fear in her cries wrap around my throat, threatening to strangle me.

"What the fuck?" I pull on the handle, trying to force it open.

"Nina. Please just open the door!" I shout, punching the plaster surround. "Fuck!"

I let my head fall to the door, feeling at a loss as she continues to cry.

I hear a thud followed by a howl, a chilling, blood-curdling sound that has me taking two steps back. Panic fills me, feeling unhinged at my lack of control. I square my shoulders, lunging into the door and taking the lock clean off the wall. The plush carpet breaks my fall, but I barely touch the ground before I'm around the bed and kneeling at her feet.

She is curled into herself, arms wrapped protectively around her knees.

"Nina," I rasp, my chest rising and falling rapidly.

"Nina, baby."

I reach out to touch her, and her eyes snap to mine. Red-rimmed and wild, pure fear etched on her beautiful face. "Nina," I frown. "It's okay. I'm here."

Her body shakes uncontrollably, dripping in sweat. I try to grasp the blanket she's holding from her hands, but she grips it tighter, flinching as I retract my hand.

What the fuck?

"The blood. So much blood," she mutters, sounding crazed.

I start to search her body but fail to find any blood.

"Nina, you're not bleeding. There is no blood. I'm here, it's me, Mase," I say softly, unsure as to what I should do.

She squeezes her eyes tight, opening and closing them until her wary eyes find me. "Mase?" she asks.

"Yes, I'm here." I grab her, seizing the opportunity whilst she lets me. "Fucking hell." My heart hammers in my chest as I sit on the floor, holding her tight. Her body is slick with sweat, her hair damp.

"Mase," she cries, fisting my T-shirt and burrowing deeper into my chest. She breaks down in my arms.

For the first time I see her distinctively. No barrier, no wall, just raw, unfiltered pain—it's what I wanted, right?

More than just her body.

"Nina, I'm going to get you in the shower. Is that okay?"

"Why? The blood?" She panics.

"No, no blood. You're just really hot."

"Okay."

She looks up at me, my chest aching with the hurt in her eyes.

God, this is all my fault.

Why did I bring that shit up with her mum?

I lift her in my arms, carrying her to the en suite. I don't put her down, walking in the shower with her locked tight in my arms. I reach in and turn on the spray, sitting with my back to the wall as the warm water runs over her.

She lies broken in my arms.

My beautiful broken Pixie.

"He hit me," she whispers after a few minutes of silence.

"Who?" I demand, fighting to keep my voice steady.

"I don't know. I never knew their names, but he hit me. At least, I think he did."

Rage flits through my every orifice, every organ, every single nerve, burning with white-hot rage. I take a deep breath, knowing I can't be mad right now, pushing it to the back of my mind until I can use it to unleash. And I will.

"Nina, it was just a nightmare. It wasn't real. I'm here now." I lift her chin, bringing her face to mine.

Her eyes lack the light that shone in them just hours ago.

"You hurt me."

I close my eyes. *Shit.* "I'm so sorry, Nina," I force out, fuming at myself. I'm such a prick. "I didn't mean what I said."

"Please leave me alone," she states, eyes lost.

"You think I'd fucking leave you alone right now?"

"You leave, or I will."

"Let me help you." I try to hug her tighter, but she climbs from my lap, crawling to the other end of the shower.

"Please," she begs. "I need to be on my own right now."

Fuck. It takes everything inside me to stand and move my feet to the door, praying it's the right thing to do.

I go back to my room, shedding my wet clothes from my body and launching them at the TV as my anger surfaces. Sitting down on the edge of my bed, I run my hands through my hair with absolutely no idea how to fix the fractured soul I can't seem to figure out.

———

Nina

CLIMBING FROM THE SHOWER FLOOR, I drag myself up and under the spray, washing my body clean, wishing I could erase the images in my head. Maybe I should have let Mason hold me, but for all the reasons I wanted him to, there were twice as many as to why I didn't. He believes that to care is to know everything, all the things I would have told him if he had just asked. He is wrong. You can care for someone and not know their secrets, exactly how I did for him.

He took what he wanted without asking, which I could have got over—I was prepared to swallow my dignity and take his controlling nature in my stride. But that was before he trampled on my pride.

His words were the beginning of the end. He doesn't get to hurt me, especially when he doesn't even know me.

No amount of digging will expose the reality that lives with me.

Once I'm dried off, I wrap myself in a towel and leave the bathroom. I find Mason sitting on his bed, his head in his hands. His hair spiked out all over the place.

'*He means well, love, he's not a bad bloke.*'

I push Vinny's voice from my head.

What I would give to go to him, to let him hold me like before, and to let him tell me it's all okay.

It's not okay.

His head comes up as I step into view, his sad eyes meeting mine, and a sick part of me silently pleads that he doesn't let me go.

Don't give up on me, Mase.

His eyes scan my towel-clad body. "Will you stay tonight? It's late. I can take you home first thing."

"I want to go home."

"I know." He drops his head again. "But I need you to stay."

My twisted heart beats for his words, his *need*. "That's not fair. Don't put that on me."

"Nina, please. I didn't mean what I said, I just wanted you to let me in."

"Let you in? Do you even hear yourself, Mason? You couldn't even tell me where you were going last night. You took what you wanted and left me alone with your friends. Are you going to let me in? Tell me? Or should I have you looked up? Just take the information without any regard or thought for your feelings?"

The razor-sharp cut of his jaw flexes at my words, and he pushes his hair off his face as he stands, quickly closing the distance between us.

My heart lurches in my chest as I hold my breath, already afraid of what he will say.

Choose your words, Mason. Don't get this wrong.

"I took what I wanted, and I make no apologies for that. You want to know where I was last night?" he asks, looking down his nose at me. "My father likes a drink. My *sister*, Scarlet, struggles to help him through what I can imagine is fucking hell. It's no big secret, Nina."

He throws his arms out wide, stepping away from me. "Anything else you want to know?"

"He's an alcoholic too?" I mutter, surprised.

His features tighten, his face contorting into a frown. "What? No. My father is nothing like your mother."

I blink slowly, dumbfounded as I step back from him. "You're really fucking bad at this."

He tips his head to the ceiling, blowing out a breath. "Nina, please. Can you just stay the night, we can talk about this tomorrow? Please, I'm fucking this up."

"I'm going home. And I wouldn't worry, there is *nothing* to fuck up." I go to his en suite and find my clothes.

He's hot on my heels, anger radiating from every inch of him. "Fucking fine! But I'm driving you."

"I will call a taxi," I shout back, searching for my dress. "Where are my things?"

He points to the door. "The wardrobe. I'm driving you home."

He follows me into the ridiculously large walk-in wardrobe. It's bigger than my entire living space. My annoyance at him has me seeing it all so differently. His money is such a turnoff.

I don't bother to correct him, reaching up on my tiptoes to get my dress from the hanger. I spin with it, clutched in hand, only to come face-to-face with him.

There's so much anger in his stare, but it's not for me. Sitting in the lines of his handsome face, I see something else. Something I can't pin down. Fear maybe? His own pain? I don't know, but it irks me, because I don't want to stay, and I don't owe him a thing.

"I don't want you to go."

"I can't stay."

"You can."

Can I?

My heart feels like a baseball that's been pummeled by so many swinging bats. My whole life I've fought to keep the stitching together, tending to the battered edges. Yet, Mason Lowell shows up, and I allow him to hit a home run straight out of the gate.

Why am I still here?

"Sleep in my bed. I refuse to leave you alone after..." His pity sears into my skin, making me want to claw at the flesh. "Sleep in my bed, please. I will stay in the spare room and will drop you home first thing. Just don't leave."

Pride is a funny thing. It's restricting, suffocating, and at times has held me back from making life choices.

Always refusing to leave myself open to any more hits. Everything inside *me* tells me to go, and it's not my pride or morals or stubbornness that stops me.

I'm at war with something else.

It's the soul-deep pride in the blacks of his eyes that bleeds out between us.

'Just don't leave.'

And I won't. My pride, my morals, my stubbornness— who knows, but I don't leave. I let *his* pride suffocate me, restrict me, hold me back from making a choice that I may or may not regret.

VINNY ARRIVES JUST after seven a.m. to pick me up. I lay awake for the last three hours, waiting for a semi-acceptable time to call him, and his expression as I climb into the front seat of the Audi is the exact reason I couldn't call a taxi. I look like a mess.

"Good morning, Nina," he says chirpily.

"I'm so sorry, Vinny. I know it's a Sunday." I do up my seat belt and settle in as he pulls out onto the deserted road.

"You can call me anytime, you know that, love."

"Thank you. I couldn't get a taxi in this." I gesture to the oversized joggers and T-shirt I stole from Mason's wardrobe.

"I've seen worse." He winks.

I smile, leaning my head back against the seat, glad to be away from the penthouse but sad to leave Mason behind.

Vinny sits quiet, tapping his finger on the steering wheel whilst listening to the radio. I try to think of anything but the doubts in my head.

"Do you have a family, Vinny? A wife?"

"No. I'm better, happier alone." He smiles, and I can tell he is being genuine. He believes his words.

"I can relate to that," I look up at him. "You don't think one day though, if you found the right person?"

"It would take a saint to put up with me, Nina."

"Because of your job? Having to rescue damsels in distress from raving lunatics at stupid hours of the day?"

"Exactly that," he chuckles. "And then some."

"Well, I think any woman would be lucky to have you. You're a catch, you know," I say, elbowing him in the arm.

His phone starts to ring throughout the car, and Mason's name lights up the screen.

"I'm presuming he doesn't know you left." He eyes me, letting it ring for the third time.

I shake my head. "You can answer it."

He accepts the call, his expression stony. "Mason."

"Vinny."

I close my eyes at the sound of his ragged breath. I picture him tearing through the penthouse, searching for me.

"I need Nina's number. She took off this morning and Scars just called, the doctor is coming out to see Dad, I need to go to the estate."

Guilt eats at me, and in the cold light of day I second-guess myself.

Did I overreact?

Is his dad okay?

I look to Vinny, swallowing hard.

I wish I didn't leave.

"I will send the number now. Mason, calm down. Do you need me to drive you out?"

"No, I'm fine. Scar's just worried; he hasn't stopped vomiting. She thinks it may be alcohol poisoning."

'He's nothing like your mother.'

I drop my head, staring at my lap. Vinny shouldn't have to lie for me, and now I'm sat absorbing information that isn't intended for me. It's just as bad as what he did, looking me up.

"Okay, let me know if you need anything. Drive safe, Mason," Vinny says calmly, then hangs up.

"I'm sorry I put this on you."

"Send him your number, Nina," he tells me, holding out the phone.

I don't question it, typing out my number and hitting send. My phone rings moments later, and I stare at it, not wanting to answer.

"I won't tell you what you should do," Vinny starts.

"But?"

"I haven't ever seen Mason act like this. He seems to care for you very much." He shrugs as if it is that simple.

"I'm damaged goods, Vinny. I prefer to be alone."

It's what I know.

He nods, smiling smugly. "You don't think one day though, if you found the right person?"

I glare at the side of his head as he throws my words right back at me.

I check my clutch for my keys, hoping I have spare clothes in the studio. I need to get lost for a while.

"Can you drop me at the studio, please, Vinny?"

———

UNEXPLAINABLE CALMNESS. It seeps into me and makes me forget about everything that exists outside of the room. I've only had my studio a little over a year, but the sense of belonging here, the sense that I'm not alone. It doesn't make sense really, but I figure to have a place I'm so proud of, something I built on my own, having people who depend on me for a place to come and express themselves.

It gives me purpose.

I don't get to dance. I didn't have a change of clothes. Instead, I climb up on the piano and lay on my side, looking out on my purpose.

I won't give up on it. On any of it.

———

LUCY PICKS me up from the studio midmorning to take me home, and I change quickly whilst she waits in the car. She knows something is up. I don't go to the studio on a Sunday—especially not in men's clothes. But she doesn't question me, doesn't ask anything until after lunch, laying on the garden swing seat we have spent many days of our childhood and teenage years chatting on.

"I think Mason's dad is an alcoholic," I eventually voice.

Lucy's hand finds mine between us. "But that's not what has you going to the studio on a Sunday morning?"

"No." I roll my eyes at her perceptiveness. "He fucked it up, Luce. He is such an idiot."

"He's a male. It's their thing." She smiles.

"He had me looked up, looked into my mum and the studio."

"What?" she asks, taken aback.

I nod my head. "I took it on the chin too. I promised myself I wouldn't leave. We had the most incredible sex. God, the sex, Luce," I groan, making her laugh. "He prepared a beautiful date, said all the right things when I freaked about the gifts he bought me, then when I needed space, and for him to shut up so I could process the whole him having me looked up, he crushed me. Told me I would run my studio into the ground if I didn't stop helping Mum and pay back my loans."

Tears well in my eyes as I prepare for what comes next.

"How did he get that much information?!"

I shrug. "I told him to stay out of my business, that he could have sex with me, but he'd get nothing more than my body." Cringing at the memory, I close my eyes.

"Oh, Nina, that's not you."

"What?"

"Babe, you've known this man a week. You're attached already, look at you. You could never have no-strings-attached sex. It's why you have broken so many hearts over the years," she explains, pulling me into a hug.

"He compared me to my mum. Told me the apple didn't fall far from the tree," I mumble into her neck.

She tuts, shaking her head. "God, Nina, he really is a dick." She sighs. "But..."

"But?" I question, not liking that but at all.

"It's not you. You're not your mother, and he shouldn't have said that. *But.* You painted the picture for him. He just hung it to dry."

"Are you kidding me? You're supposed to be on my side."

"I am." She squeezes me tight. "I promise you I am, just don't go writing him off just yet, okay?" She fingers the bangle on my wrist. "Is this Cartier?"

I roll my eyes. "I have no idea."

"As your best friend, it's my job to step in and tell you when you don't see situations in their true light, yet you've always made it so easy for me. You have a good head on your shoulders, and you always make the right decision. I envy your balls, babe. Trust your judgement, and don't ever feel bad for letting your guard down."

"You think I should give things a go with him?"

Does Mason even want to give things a go?

"It doesn't matter what I think. You'll do you anyway."

LUCY DROPS me home just after six, and I trudge up my steps feeling exhausted from the lack of sleep last night. I need sleep, and more importantly, to refocus myself on the week ahead. The showcase is coming up, and I intend to smash it with my girls.

Inside my apartment, I strip down and shower, then pull on the comfiest clothes I can find. I'm sitting on my sofa no more than twenty minutes later, eating a bowl of Coco Pops when my phone rings. My mother's name has my spoon falling into the chocolatey milk.

Why is she calling so soon? It's been what—a week?

Every emotion I've been suppressing all day seems to come bubbling to the surface, and Mason's interrogation as to why I pay my mum is at the forefront.

I have no answer as to why and as my phone continues to vibrate across my coffee table, I rage at myself, at my inability to let her go and not let anyone else in. Lucy is right, I could never hack no strings attached sex, and it's all my mother's fault.

I launch my phone at the wall watching it flash once more before the screen dies.

Mase

SELFISH, that's what I am. She doesn't want to see me, but I need to see her.

I shouldn't have left Scarlet alone on Friday night, and maybe my father wouldn't have gotten so poorly if I'd stayed, but Lowerwick brings back too many bad memories for me.

Every time I walk through the door, I think of my mother. Her open arms as I'd run for her, the smell of cookies baking in the oven, and the music she would play us.

Four years. It's all I had, yet the memories are vivid, every single one right up to the day she died.

How Scarlet continues to stay there baffles me. As I said, I'm selfish.

I park the Bentley at the curb and make my way to Nina's building, taking her steps two at a time, not bothering to think past the need to see her, to hold her.

She pulls open the door, her eyes red and blotchy. *Shit. Was that because of me?* Her shoulders drop when she sees it's me, and I worry she will push me away.

She steps into me, her arms wrapping around my waist as her head nestles into my chest. Her body visibly relaxes, growing heavier in my arms. The weight of the world settling between us.

I drop my nose to her hair, breathing her in.

Unexplainable calmness. It seeps into me, a deep sense of belonging only she seems to bring. She pulls me into her apartment, bypassing the tiny living space and walking me through to a small double bedroom. She climbs on the bed, pulling me with her, her head dipping under my arm when I lift it so she can lay herself across my chest. And just like that, with not a single word spoken we take from each other, healing the parts we aren't ready to bare.

12

Nina

THIS IS HOW EVERY MONDAY MORNING SHOULD START—cocooned in the strong arms of Mason Lowell. I smile into his chest, thankful he turned up last night, right when I needed him.

Sleep came fast and hard, the sexcapades of the weekend catching up with us both. He held me all night, and the thought of moving right now seems insane, but I made a promise to myself last night, and it starts with him.

Lucy was right. I've known Mason a week, and if I'm honest, I'm in deeper than I should be. I should be able to walk away. Our time together so far has been chaos—toxic even.

It's time I moved forward. I won't let my mother's story control my own. It may be where mine began, but it won't be how mine ends.

Strong arms squeeze me tight, making me feel safe. I smile wide as I try to move closer.

"What are you smiling at? You know what it gets you," he says, his voice deep and rough from sleep.

"What does it get me, Mase?" I hum.

He lifts my chin, planting a soft kiss on my lips. "It gets you fucked, angel," he says, moving to kiss my neck, then dipping lower, sucking down my throat until his mouth wraps around my puckered nipple through the thin cotton fabric. My back bows off the bed, demanding more, craving more.

"Mase?" I purr.

His head lifts from my chest in answer, the light streaming in through the window illuminating his face. My heart physically aches. He is so beautiful, his dark hair a tousled mess, his jaw sporting a light coating of stubble. I trace his crooked nose with my index finger, trying my best to memorise every inch of him and this tender moment between us—both sated from sleep and lost in nothing but each other.

My finger moves to the seam of his full lips, gently tracing along the dark edges.

He kisses the tip of my finger fondly, his eyes lazy and locked on mine. "Well, now I can't fuck you," he moans, rolling his eyes and completely ruining the moment.

He climbs above me, arranging my legs accordingly.

"What?" I giggle. "What are you doing?"

He settles himself between my legs, his body blanketing my own. He takes my hands in his, locking them together and lifting them above my head.

"I don't know, but I can't fuck you right now," he says, his eyes darkening.

"Mase?" I smile nervously, goosebumps coating my body.

He doesn't wait, swooping down and taking my lips in a deep kiss as he slides into me in the same moment. His mouth falls open as he stretches me, stilling inside me.

"Fuck," he groans, his nose dusting across my own. "Baby, you feel so good."

He's too much, too big, too gentle, too beautiful. He overwhelms me in every possible way, but instead of allowing the panic that threatens to push him away and break the connection, I let him in, giving him my eyes.

He begins to move inside of me, slowly, tenderly, with deep rolls of his hips.

Mason has only ever been dominant with me. Pulling and pushing me in a way I have grown to crave in such a short space of time. But instead of my head flying back to the mattress, my body fighting its way to a release, I hold his eyes.

Each thrust, each kiss, it's all an afterthought, insignificant compared to the look in our eyes. It's petrifying. He isn't a part of my outline, he's just a subplot. In the end he will be gone, barely remembered in the story.

So why is he taking the ink and seeping himself into my soul?

MASE SITS with his back against my headboard. A coffee in one hand and his phone in the other. His head pops up when I walk into the room, fresh from a shower and still in my towel.

"Come here," he demands.

I go to him, moving to sit on the edge of the bed, but he grabs me by the hips and pulls me to straddle him.

"I'm going to be late. You're going to be late," I complain, but make no move to get up.

"I promise you won't be late, Nina." He leans in, planting a soft kiss on my lips. "I need to apologise for what I said to you on Saturday night. It was a heat of the moment comment, which is no excuse. I know I hurt you."

I drop my head, sitting quietly for a moment, not knowing what to say.

He lifts my chin. "Say something."

I swallow hard, unsure what the right thing to say is. "I want to start fresh, forget about everything that's happened."

"Start fresh." He frowns. "That simple?"

I lean into him, giving him a long, deep kiss. "Nothing's ever that simple, Mase." I smile sadly. "But as far as my mum goes, I want you to forget. I can deal with her. If I need your support, I will ask for it, and I'd like to think you'd do the same with your dad. I only want to know the things you're ready to tell me." I pause, thinking about my journey home with Vinny. "I actually have a confession to make, and you aren't allowed to get mad."

He frowns, waiting.

"I was in the car with Vinny when you called him on Sunday morning, and I was the one who sent you my number. I needed a lift home and didn't know who else to call. I asked Vinny not to tell you. I'm sorry. For leaving... and about your dad." I drop my shoulders, feeling like a weight has been lifted.

He pushes a lock of hair behind my ear. "Vinny already told me."

My eyes shoot wide. "What?"

"I pay him a lot of money to tell me, Nina. He called after dropping you off at the studio."

"That bastard! So I can't trust Vinny. Great."

Vinny was my favourite.

He chuckles at my dramatics. "Vinny's a safe bet. If you ever need to trust a man, you'd be wise to pick him."

I roll my eyes. They clearly have a good relationship with the way they both seem to defend one another.

Mason seems to be lost in thought, staring at his hand on my hip.

"What is it?"

He lets out a deep breath, hesitating before speaking. "Nina, I need to tell you something, something I found when I looked you up. Purely for your flat number, I should add."

"Yeah, okay, creeper," I joke, trying to laugh off the knot forming in my stomach. "There's nothing in my past I want to talk about." I lick my lips, wanting to retreat away to my safe space again. "Please drop it."

"I don't think you know about what I found. I think it was hidden from you. I could be wrong, but—"

"What? What could you possibly know about me that I don't already? I mean, it's my flipping life after all."

"Nina, calm down, please." He cups my cheek, pulling his lip between his teeth.

Whatever it is, he doesn't want to tell me.

Dread fills me.

"Tell me, now, Mason."

He works on a swallow, rolling his lips. "Have you ever met your father?"

His hand clamps down on my waist the second I go to move. "Wait, please. You said you want to start fresh, and if I don't tell you this now, then it will come back to bite me in the ass down the line."

Down the line? Like the future?

"Have you? Ever met him?" he asks.

"No."

"Okay, do you know anything about him?"

"He was a client, someone who tried to have me erased. My mother found out about me too late." I run my tongue across the front of my teeth in contempt. The more I think about the woman, the more my blood boils.

He pulls me closer, smoothing a hand down my back. "I don't think that's true. Your mother has been receiving payments from someone since the day you were born. Every month, for the last twenty-eight years, Nina."

I lean back, finding his eyes. I think I'm in shock. No words leave me.

"I have a name, if you want it."

I shake my head, unable to find the words. "I don't understand."

"I think he's your dad, and if the payments are for child maintenance, they aren't small. It's a lot of money."

"I need to get to the studio. I have so much to prepare for the showcase."

He lets me get up, and I start to dress on autopilot. He stands and reaches for me, clasping my hand in his.

"I'll call Vinny. Get us a lift. I'm here if you need me, Nina."

I nod, swallowing the bile that threatens to come up.

It's all too much.

Fuck this.

NINETY-SEVEN. The number of water droplets I've counted on the Audi's rain-soaked glass. It's all I can think about—until it's not.

My father, the man I thought for years didn't want a thing to do with me, who I thought didn't even know about me, has been paying my mother maintenance.

He might know me. My name and definitely my age.

I never cared growing up. Why would I want a dad who was like the rest of them? The vile men who still haunt my dreams to this day. I had learnt to stop wondering, to stop hoping for him to show up, eventually latching onto John.

He was the one who took me to anything important, and when it was time for the dad race on sports day, it was always him who would go twice. Once for each of his girls.

What is my mother playing at? Is the money she has been receiving even for me? What if it's something else? It still doesn't explain why she would need more than what she gets from the government and me. The hurt is frustrating, I don't want to feel a thing for her, not anymore.

I used to hold on to the memories. A handful of good that most would deem just standard parenting. The days she would turn up to school on time, looking fresh and happy. The times I'd open the cupboards and find food. And my favourite thing became something twisted. Whenever I hurt myself, the pain would bring me an embrace. She would hold me in her arms for a while, and life always seemed to feel a little less shit.

She has been lying to me for years, that much I'm sure of, but I don't understand why? It's all I've been able to think about since Mase told me. Is she that messed up that she didn't want me to see him? Or does he just pay her to keep her away, to keep me away?

Mason's strong hand latches onto my inner thigh, pulling my attention from the window. "Nina."

I wait for him to say more, but he sits quiet, not saying a thing. He feels sorry for me. The pity is etched into the planes of his face.

"I'm fine, Mase." I turn my face away, not being able to lie to him.

"Nina."

"What?!" I snap.

He doesn't hesitate as if he expected my irritation. "I won't let you be alone in this. You need someone to talk to. Talk to me," he says, pulling my hand to rest in his lap.

"I will call the girls later."

I know he is trying, but I'm too far gone in my head right now to focus on him. I need space.

I wish I walked to work.

"I can find my own way home tonight." I decide.

He stops fiddling with the bangle on my wrist. "You said we would start afresh?" The vulnerability in his voice has my eyes gravitating to his.

Guilt fills me. Maybe he needs me just as much as I do him.

I unbuckle my belt and climb into his lap, hiding my face in his neck like a child. I breathe him in, his woodsy scent grounding me.

"I meant what I said. I want to start fresh, but this" —I gesture between us— "it's all too much. I have my showcase coming up, and you said yourself I need to get on top of the studio. So much threatens my dreams Mason, and not physically but mentally I can feel myself slipping." I shake my head. "We don't need to be one of those things. Just give me time." I pull back to look at him. "Please?"

"Can I see you tonight?" he asks, pulling me closer.

I smile softly. This beautiful man wants to spend time with me. He's known me a week and shows more worry for me than most have in my lifetime. "No. But I will call, just give me a few days."

His shoulders drop, and he lets out a heavy sigh. "I don't like this."

"I know. But..." I roll my lips, giving him an inch. "I want to be ready for us, Mase, and right now, I don't feel like I am. Just give me some time."

He smiles down at me sadly as he leans in to kiss my temple. "Alright."

VINNY FOLLOWED ME HOME. I'm not sure if he was trying to be discrete, but the Audi was always within a short distance behind me each time I looked back.

Running always allowed me time to think, so the urge to stop and get a lift was strong.

Knowing it is Mason being overprotective, I didn't stop and bitch at Vinny for following me. If I'm honest, I don't know how I would feel if the Audi wasn't outside the studio after I finished work.

Mason's thoughtfulness and need to keep me safe only makes me want him more. I've never had someone take such concern in my whereabouts. Maybe that's one of the things that is holding me back.

I bend, my hands planted on my knees as my lungs gasp for air. Tilting my head up, I stare up at my building.

"You're quick, girl!" Vinny smiles at me from the front seat.

He leans down on the passenger side and grabs a bottle of water then holds it out to me.

"Vinny, my apartment is right there. Tell your boss he needs to ease up on the plastic. He is already putting unnecessary emissions into the air by following me home."

"I'll be sure to tell him." He smirks.

I know he won't.

"See you later, Vinny. Thank you." I wink, jogging up the steps.

The moment I get to my floor, I hear them, and I close my eyes in anticipation, wondering if I should go back to the studio.

Why are they even here?

I push into the apartment and find the entire living space in smoke. "What the hell?!"

"Nina! Hey, you're home!" Lucy shouts.

I flap my hand in front of my face as I try to make them out through the smog. Lucy is on Megan's shoulders, flapping a tea towel at the smoke alarm.

I begin to cough, the smoke being drawn into my lungs. "Jesus Christ!"

I rush to the window, opening it as far as it will go, then stalk to the kitchen where I grab the oven glove and throw the smouldering baking tray into the sink.

"Seriously?!"

Megan ducks down, letting Lucy fall to her feet.

"Chinese or Indian?" Luce cringes.

———

"WHAT ARE you guys even doing here?" I ask around a mouthful of noodles. The girls sit on the sofa behind me, both with towels wrapped on top of their heads. The apartment still smells like smoke, but at least we no longer do.

"Mason messaged," Megan says casually.

"And told you what exactly?"

"That you needed us."

"That's it? That's all he said? He didn't say why?"

"Nope, he isn't a chatty man, Nina." Lucy shrugs.

"Sooo... what did he do?" Megan asks.

I face forward again and drop my head back to the sofa. "Nothing. Everything."

"That's fucking helpful," Megan mumbles, poking me in the cheek with her toe.

"Get your foot out of my face!" I slap her away, using the moment to drop the bomb, hoping it will lessen the sting. "My mum has been receiving money from a man for the past twenty-eight years. From the day I was born."

"What?" Lucy sobers, sliding down to the floor next to me, as Megan appears at my other side. "Do you think..."

"Yup."

"And she didn't tell you? *Why?*" Lucy bites out.

I shake my head, even though I'm certain of the answer. "I've been over it in my head all day. I presume he paid her to keep quiet. Mason said it was a lot of money. Maybe Mum was a dirty secret. She said he was a client."

"Nina, why are you paying your mum money when she is already receiving it elsewhere? What is she spending it all on?"

"I have no idea, but I plan to put a stop to it." I shake my head. "Mason called you?"

"Uh-huh. He called us." Megan chuckles, nudging me with her elbow. "You want to talk about it?"

"No, but it beats the hell out of talking about my mum." I sigh. "God, girls, I don't even know where to start."

"This is why we are here." A glass of wine is slipped into my hand. "Start at the beginning."

Mase

Seven days.

I knew she was stubborn, but to go a week, keeping me at a distance, and for what? How much time did she need? She calls every night, driving me nuts with her words, but still, she tells me she needs more time.

I'm just about done with waiting.

With London's skyline laid out before me, I stand and look upon the people below, wondering what *she* is doing right now.

My intercom buzzes, Alice's voice filling the room. "Mr Lowell, your father is on the phone."

The old man is sober then.

I round the sofa and drop down at my desk. Taking in a deep breath before answering. "Dad?"

"Mason, my boy. How are you?"

I snicker, his false bravado not fooling me. "Me? Shouldn't I be asking you that question?"

"I know. I promised you and your sister I'd get on top of it. And I am."

"No, Dad, we need you to get off of it. Not on top of it." I rub my hand down my face in frustration.

"Mason, I'm doing my best. I haven't been drinking. Last week was just hard, with your mother's anniversary—"

"Just stop," I cut him off, refusing to allow the words to settle in me. I don't want to be reminded of the day my mother left me.

"Your sister, she is cooking a meal for us tomorrow. She invited the Montgomerys and Charles. Did you want to ask anyone else?"

"No."

"Okay, please don't be late, Mason. Scarlet just wants some normalcy. We haven't had you here for more than five minutes in years."

I snicker into the phone. He has no idea.

"I'm trying, Mase. It's all I can do right now." I can hear him getting choked up, and it's the last thing I need.

"I will be there. Tell Scar to send me the details."

"I love you, son." I hear him say just as the phone hits the cradle.

Nina

"GIRLS!" I yell at Vienna and Sophie, who seem to be more absorbed in what's on the phone in Vienna's hand than the routine we are working on.

"Ladies, if you want to leave, then go. I'm out to win, and you may be important to that goal, but I will replace you in a millisecond if you don't get off that damn phone and nail this section." I give them a nod and leave it at that, not wanting to seem like a complete hag.

For the most part, the girls all love me. We have a tight bond that I've spent the last year working for, and I make sure we have fun, but to keep it professional I have to have rules. They know this.

"Sorry," Sophie says, moving to the back of the group. "Henry is in today, and Vee couldn't help but insta stalk him."

"Shameless! The lot of you," I tease, shaking my head. "Last time from the dip to cross over, and we are taking a break."

THE GIRLS SMASH it as always, making me more excited about the showcase. We seriously have a chance, I know it. As newcomers, I want to make waves, and these girls are my tsunami.

Skipping down the steps, I grin wide when I see Henry at the desk. The girls aren't wrong. Henry is gorgeous—too young for me, but still, I can't help but enjoy the eye candy down here.

His girlfriend Gemma is on the treadmill, and his eyes are glued to her.

"You look pervy," I say, elbowing him, then waving to Gemma when she spots me.

"Nina," he mutters in greeting, making a show of not looking away.

"You need to tone it down; you've got my girls all flustered."

"Just your girls?" He eyes me, popping a brow.

"In your dreams, baby boy." I laugh, disappearing into the staff room to get my lunch.

It's a decent size space considering we barely use it. I prefer to eat up in the studio and the boys normally inhale their food before they make it to the rickety old table that's pushed up against the wall. It's more of a storeroom for everything we don't want people to see.

Henry comes in just as I'm manoeuvring my soup out of the microwave. "There's a letter from the music license company and one from the bank. This one is addressed to a Miss C Langer though."

He nods his head to the three envelopes, grabbing my bowl and moving it closer when he sees I'm burning my fingers on the tub.

"Thanks, probably a wrong address. I'll return to sender."

"Logan found this on Friday too, said you were looking for it." A key dangles from a chain in his hand.

"Yes! My boys! What would I do without you?" I jump up, punching him in the arm, pleased I won't have to explain to Erin why she can't get into the office next week.

In my glee, my hand catches the soup container, flipping it from the counter. It coats my stomach and leg, burning into my skin.

"Oh my god!" I begin to swipe the boiling hot soup off me, but I can feel my skin already tingling underneath.

"Fuck, take off your tights. I will get the first aid kit! I think we have some burn gel."

I lift my top so that it's off my stomach but still covering my breasts, then start shimmying out of my tights as fast as I can.

My hands shake from the shock.

I'm standing in my thong when Henry comes back in, but I don't overthink it—he is like a brother to me. I take the cold cloth he hands me and plaster it to my stomach, where the burning is more intense. He squats down in front of me, ripping open the gel packet and squirting it onto my leg. It runs down my thigh, instantly melting against the heat. My hand dashes out to rub it into the skin.

"How do you fucking manage it, girl?" Henry says, shaking his head at me.

I smile down at him, feeling like a complete klutz.

"What the fuck is going on?" Mason's voice has me jumping back, my skin prickling at his tone.

Shit.

"I burnt myself. Henry was just helping me." I try to explain, but I can see the rage as it visibly builds within him.

"Who's this?" Henry asks, standing at his full six foot two height. He's big for a twenty-three-year-old. Mason only has an inch on him.

"Her boyfriend," Mason announces, completely losing his cool—and maybe his mind.

Boyfriend?

He grasps Henry by his vest, pulling him away from me.

"Get the fuck away from her." His eyes blaze over my semi-naked form.

God, this must look awful.

"Mason, calm down. And let go of him." I try to defuse the situation, but it's a task when I'm trying to hide from the prying eyes that watch on through the open door.

Gemma steps into the room, spotting Mason and Henry in a standoff as they both grasp one another's tops.

"What on earth? Henry, stop!" she demands.

Henry eyes her for a second, then reluctantly pushes Mason back with force, removing his hand from his gym vest when Mason doesn't let go.

"Stupid prick. She burnt herself," Henry spits out.

Mason looks at me and the red creeping over my thigh and stomach. It's not as bad as I first thought, but that's only thanks to Henry's quick thinking.

"Guys, can you give us a minute?" I ask.

Henry frowns, giving me a 'are you kidding me' look.

"Of course! Henry." Gemma pulls her man from the staff room by the wrist, closing the door to allow me a scrap of dignity.

"Mason, I bur—"

"Don't," he cuts me off, shaking his head. "Nina, you've kept me away all week, and then I come here and find you like this. I need a minute."

I wince, trying to tame the words before they leave me. "Uh, maybe I need a goddamn minute." I take a deep breath through my nose. "I burnt myself, Mason, you insensitive ass! What are you even doing here, anyway?"

"Nothing, it doesn't matter. Let me see." He nods to my leg.

"No."

He sniggers, running his tongue across his teeth. "I will pick you up when you're finished here."

I let him leave. If that man thinks that I will be going with him tonight after the way he just reacted, he is sorely mistaken. God, it's Henry. Does he not have any female members of staff? The thought makes me rage. Of course, he fucking does. I bet the place is crawling with women.

It gives me an idea.

I hobble to my bag and pull out the outfit I brought to wear to dinner with the girls tonight. It's casual but sexy. I pull the dark burgundy skirt up over my hips and high on my waist, my cropped white singlet moulds to my breasts.

It's been a week, and I am more than ready to take on Mason Lowell.

THANKFULLY THE GIRLS ARE UNDERSTANDING. I had to send them home after the soup disaster, so I promised to work an extra day to cover their class fee to keep them happy.

I did my research, and if my Google Maps is correct, I should be at Ellis and Frey Real Estate within twenty minutes by foot.

I glance down at my feet, knowing it will take me twice as long in my heels, and instead, I call Vinny.

"Miss Anderson, I wasn't expecting you to call. How can I help you?"

"Hey! I need a lift. If you are free, of course. And I can't tell you any more than that because I don't trust you."

"Well, I should inform you that I sided with you this afternoon. I drove Mason to the studio," he says, and I can tell he is smiling.

"What a queen, huh?"

He chuckles down the line. "What are you planning, Nina?"

"I'm on my way to his office... I was hoping for a ride."

"That's not a good idea, Nin—"

"Vinny, you can drive me, save my feet, and I will love the hell out of you for it, or you can let your boss know I'm on my way and ruin the element of surprise. Either way, I am going with or without you. I won't cause a scene, I promise."

"Just wait there. I will be five minutes." he relents.

13

Nina

THE MONTWELL BUILDING SITS PROUDLY AMONG THE skyscrapers in London's financial district; its impressive structure flouting high up in the clouds. I watch in awe as people breeze through the revolving doors, going about their business almost robotically.

Why so serious?

"Here, you will need this," Vinny interrupts my trance, handing me a plastic card. "Tell reception I sent you, you won't be on any list. I can't promise they won't call up."

I squeeze his shoulder, giving him a warm smile. "Thanks, Vinny. You don't want to come up with me, some moral support?"

He shakes his head. "I did my bit. You're on your own now, love."

I roll my eyes. "Stay close by, I might need a lift in five."

He turns in his seat, a smirk pulling at his lips. "You said you wouldn't cause a scene."

"You said you were taking us to The Pearl," I throw back at him with a shrug.

"Touché."

My confidence takes a nosedive the moment I step into The Montwell. I look down at myself, pulling at my crop top to hide the slither of exposed skin at my ribs. Determined to follow through with my vaguely thought-out plan, I pull back my shoulders and carry on forward, my heels clicking on the sparkling floor seemingly much louder than the other women's in the foyer.

Eight large pillars line the long walkway, leading to a bank of elevators, where security guards stand on each door with scanners in their hands. I take a deep breath and make my way to the large desk that sits in the centre of the room.

"Hello, can I help you?" a kind-looking woman asks.

"Yes, hi. I'm here to see Mas—Mr Lowell," I correct. "I have this." I hand over the lanyard. "Vinny sent me."

She smiles, taking the card. "Of course. Can you just sign in here, and I will call up?"

"No," I panic, and her hand freezes on the phone. "Uh, I was hoping to surprise him. I'm his girlfriend."

"I can't allow anyone up without calling through first."

"But I wanted to surprise him." I pout my lips, not enough to look bratty but enough to make her feel bad.

She chews on the side of her cheek, unsure. "Where is Vinny now?"

"In the car." I turn and look back through the foyer, trying to see if he is outside.

"I saw him pull up before," she tells me. "If you didn't have Vinny's card I wouldn't let you up." She nods to the elevators, smiling. "Go."

"Thank you so much!"

"If you get me fired." She laughs, shaking her head

"Then we'll blame Vinny." I wink, rounding the desk and walking over to the elevators.

I stop to show my card to the guard, and he gives me a nod. I step inside and wait for the doors to close, and as the doors begin to slide shut, my brain decides to backtrack. My palms feel damp, and my legs don't feel like my own. *What am I doing?*

The lift continues to rise for what feels like forever. It has me panicking that it could be broken, but once we hit the seventy-eighth floor, it slows, and the doors slide open. I pull back my shoulders and draw in a deep breath as I step out, knowing that if I stop to think about how I look or if I should even be here, then I will end up leaving.

The reception area is clinical with stark white minimalistic furniture. It's how I imagined it to be, but it also isn't. Maybe I am naive and sheltered, but this isn't the norm. Mason has a lot of money.

I move my eyes from the small seating area, and oh, what would you know, females. Two women sit behind a tall multi-levelled desk. I can only make out their heads from here, but they seem to be engrossed in something in front of them, laughing loudly with one another.

I use the opportunity to quickly scan the area, sussing out where Mason's office would be. I'm presuming it's behind the glass wall at my left, and going with my gut, I stalk towards the door.

"Excuse me!" they shout.

I turn towards the reception desk, the two women now

glaring at me. They're both beautiful and immaculately dressed—it does not surprise me one bit.

"You're not going in there."

"Oh, I'm sorry, I don't need an appointment, I will just be a minute." I smile, trying to keep them on the side. I can see them both judging me with their catty stares.

"Mr Lowell is busy, and he doesn't have any time in his schedule today. You will have to leave, or I will call security." She raises a perfectly sculpted brow, looking down her nose at me.

I walk over and show her the card Vinny gave me, and as if they planned it, they turn to each other and laugh in unison.

"Hey, nice bracelet. I did okay with that one, huh? The other things not quite to your fancy, princess? I don't get paid to run around London after you but don't sweat it; Mason makes it well worth my while." She lifts the phone to her ear. "Security."

Hurt rips through me as the realisation of her words sink in.

This woman bought this?

Was she with him on Saturday?

Bile rises in my throat, but I force it down on a deep swallow, not allowing her to see my reaction. It's what she wants.

"That won't be necessary, Amber." Elliot's voice rings out behind me, barely registering past the whirling in my ears.

He puts his arm around my shoulder and pulls me into his side.

"It's Alice," she corrects.

"It's irrelevant," he states, sounding every bit the boss he dresses to be. "Add Miss Anderson to the list. She can come up here anytime she likes."

They look at me dumbfounded, both of their eyes pinching in the corners as Alice starts tapping on her keyboard.

"You going in, Pixie?" Elliot says, directing me away from the desk. "Lowell didn't mention you were coming."

"He doesn't know. He came to my studio and started a fight with one of my staff. I thought I'd come and prove a point." I nod towards the reception desk.

"Ah, calling him out on his bullshit again. You know I think he likes it. Those gifts you had sent back." He laughs, but it just makes me even madder now that I know he didn't buy them himself.

With the fire raging in my gut, I step out from under Elliot's arm.

"I'm right behind ya," he tells me, trailing behind.

The glass double doors vibrate off of the rubber stoppers, drawing every eye in the room to me. "Gentlemen," I greet them all as I fling the bracelet from my fingers. It bounces across the carpeted floor and knocks into Mason's perfectly polished shoe.

"Nina, what are you doing here? Montgomery?" He looks to Elliot then back to me.

"What, I can't just drop in and see my *boyfriend*?" I say with as much contempt as I can muster.

I look to the other men in the room as I try to remain in control. They all sit with curious expressions on their faces—Lance and Charlie both among them.

What on earth am I doing?

This was a bad idea.

"We will give you a minute," Charlie says, standing and leaving the room with the five other suits and Elliot.

"You've slept with your receptionist?" I ask once the room is cleared.

"No," he answers far too quickly.

"Oh, it wasn't a question," I snap, walking closer to him. "I've never slept with Henry, or Logan, or anyone on the 'regular' for that matter. Yet you turn up to my studio and act like a jealous behemoth over someone I see like a brother—"

"Nina—"

"You took someone you fuck to buy gifts for the woman you're fucking?" I can see the tic in his jaw as he clenches his teeth, but he doesn't answer me. "That was a fucking question, Mason!"

He bends, picking up the bangle from the floor. I don't like to think how much it cost. "I picked this out for you, Nina, not her."

"Oh, well good job, what do you want? A gold star? Or maybe your cock sucked? I can ask your receptionist if she is free." I thumb towards the door.

"Stop!" he barks, cutting me off.

I know I've pushed him, and the stance he takes as he steps up in front of me has my shoulders dropping a fraction.

Why do I feel so stupid?

"I haven't slept with anyone since the night I met you." He puts his hands on his hips, not knowing what to do with them.

I roll my eyes, but the relief his words bring me puts out a portion of the fire in my gut. The office doors open, but neither of us turn to look at who has entered.

This entire plan of mine has backfired.

"Security is on the way. I'm so sorry."

Mason's eyes bore into mine, and the dangerous glint in them has my throat tightening. "You're fired, effective immediately."

"What?!" she shouts. "You can't fire me!"

"Mason," I warn.

"Leave. Take your stuff and go," he tells her, his eyes still trained on me.

I look at the girl, who now has tears brimming in her eyes. "Just give us a minute, okay?"

She gives me a death stare, squeaks out a sound that a three-year-old might make over a hairy lollipop, then runs from the room.

"You can't just fire people for no reason. She didn't do anything wrong."

"You said we were starting fresh, and you're right, she had to go," he says, dropping his eyes down my body.

"It's her job, her living, Mason. You can't take that away from her because you can't keep your dick in your pants."

"I just did," he says matter of fact. "Turn around."

"No."

He grabs my waist and spins me. I hear the zip of my skirt, and then it pools to the floor. "If you think you can tame me with your mouth right now, you're going to be in for a shock. You're having a mare today, Bossman."

When he turns me back around, he is on his knees, his sole focus on my leg. "It's still red." He leans in, softly running his lips across the pink flesh. "I shouldn't have left before," he mutters, and I can see he is at war with himself, his features tightening as his eyes roam.

"It doesn't even hurt now. Henry got the first aid kit pretty fast." Not being able to deny him the contact, I reach out, running my hand through his hair.

It's been over a week. I've missed him.

"It doesn't hurt?" He looks up at me.

I shake my head, smiling at his blatant worry. I didn't expect coming here to end like this. If he'd shown this concern at the gym and not caused a scene, none of this would have happened.

He is right, though, after everything from last week and the fact I really do want a fresh start, maybe the receptionist did need to go. She wasn't exactly welcoming, and how would I feel knowing she worked so closely with him every day?

"So. My boyfriend?" I question, looking down at him.

"That's what I said."

"Just like that, you're not going to ask me?"

He stands, running his hands up the backs of my thighs as he moves. He lifts me, bringing my legs around his waist as he carries me to his desk, then sits me on the edge.

He drops into the chair in front of me. "I've dreamt about having you on this desk," he mutters, running his hands up my thighs.

I look down at the desk as a thought crosses my mind, making me frown. Has he had her on this desk? I slip from the edge and stand in front of him, not liking the way that thought makes me feel.

"Have you had sex on your desk before?" I whisper, staring at his chest, too afraid to give him my eyes.

He doesn't say anything, and I'm glad I didn't see his reaction. I swallow hard as he stands, towering over me. "Nina." He cups my face, and for no reason I can explain. Tears spring to my eyes. "Nina, I've never had sex in my office."

My glassy eyes lift to his, and I hope he can't see the emotion in them.

"I may have blurred lines with my staff at the end of a day, but never here, I promise."

I lean into him, unsure as to why I feel so emotional. His woodsy smell makes me heady. "Sorry, for turning up here," I say into his crisp white shirt, probably getting my foundation all over it. "Are you actually going to fire her?"

"Yes, she isn't even that good." I frown, pulling away from him. "What? No, I mean at her job, not... Jesus, Nina." He pulls me back to him, and I let him.

"Can't you just put her in a different role? One where she isn't around you so much."

He shakes his head. "No."

I don't want to be responsible for someone losing their job. I know how hard it is to find work in the city.

But I also know that he won't back down and I have to let it go. For now.

"I'm glad you turned up." He kisses my temple. "Although you did kick out my entire financial and legal team." He chuckles into my hair.

I groan, "How embarrassing."

"I was pissed until you declared yourself as mine." He palms my ass. "My fiery, little Pixie."

"Why do you call me Pixie? Is it because I'm so short?"

"No, baby, not because you're short." He laughs then changes the subject. "My dad, he has invited me to dinner tomorrow, asked if I'd like to bring anyone."

He doesn't say any more, and I lean my head back a little to see his face, his arms still locked tight around my shoulders, keeping me held to him.

"Would you like me to come with you, Bossman?" I ask.

"Will you?"

"Of course, I'd love to meet your family."

"Really?"

"Yes, really." I smile.

Did he think I wouldn't?

"I have a few things to finish up here before I can leave. Will you wait for me, and then we can go home?"

Home. How can something sound so right after such a short space of time?

"I need one more day." As soon as I say the words, I cringe.

"No," he says resolutely.

"I'm meeting the girls. I will come to your family meal tomorrow, and we can go back to yours after."

"No. It's been a week, Nina. I need you," he declares, making my insides heat.

I step back from him and around the desk. I keep my eyes on him, bending at the waist, legs straight and pick up my skirt. "One more night. I'm sure you can manage."

He's on me before I can right myself, lifting me over his shoulder and dropping me down on one of the sofas. My skirt is ripped from my hands and thrown over his shoulder.

"You're a tease." He smirks, quickly pulling my thong down my legs.

"Not here!"

He dips his head, ignoring my pleas. Spreading me wide with his fingers, he leans in and licks up through my centre.

"Oh my god!" My back arches as I try to push my hips closer to him, but I'm met with nothing but air.

I open my eyes and lift my head. "Mase?"

He leans over me; one leg knelt on the sofa between my legs and the other on the floor.

"Up you get, angel, I have things to get on with."

He gives me a devilish smirk, then stands and walks to his desk.

"You asshole."

"To Nina." Megan raises her glass to the centre of the table in a toast. "Who managed to get two hot men to strip her from the waist down today."

We all clink our glasses, laughing.

I drop my head when we gain the attention of the nearby tables. "My leg was on fire, I had no other choice," I try to justify.

"You don't have to explain yourself, Nina. Henry has spent many summers at my aunt's pool. I totally get it," Lucy teases.

"Whatever." I wave them off. "Erin texted me today. She's flying in on Sunday. Will you girls be free? I thought we could get takeout. She will probably be jet-lagged, so better not to go out."

"Sure," Megan replies. "We could go out though?" She grins.

"Ugh, I don't know. We will have work the next day and I need a weekend off, girls. I can't afford or stomach it," Lucy voices.

"Me too!" I say, knowing my attempt at saving any money this month is already impossible.

"You said we would take her out? She hasn't been home in over a year," Megan complains.

"I know, and I feel bad for her. Why don't we just see what she wants to do when she gets here. Hopefully she will be happy staying in."

The waiter brings our mains and we settle into a comfortable silence as we indulge in a carb overload.

"So..." I hesitate, knowing they are going to freak. "Mason kind of made us official today."

"Fuck off!" Megan shouts, then immediately turns to the couple in the window seat to apologise.

"Nina, that's fast," Lucy says, shocked.

"But holy shit! Good job, girl," Megan says, saluting me.

Lucy clutches my hand. "You're happy?"

"Yeah. Yeah, I am." I shrug, knowing I won't be able to explain to them how it feels different with him. I probably look like a stupid dumb girl, falling for the rich guy after knowing him for five minutes.

"Well then go with it, babe. We are here if it goes south." She winks at me.

"Always." chirps Megan, mimicking Lucy's wink.

"Thanks, girls."

"When are you seeing him next?" Lucy asks.

"Tomorrow, we are going for dinner with his family."

"You're meeting the fucking family?"

"Megan!" I hiss. "You'll have us thrown out in a minute." I look at the waiter and smile sweetly. "And yes. It's only food. Stop making it such a big deal, you're giving me anxiety."

The girls both sit quietly as they watch me like you would an animal at the zoo. Lifting my wine I take a sip, needing the quick buzz it gives me.

I know things are moving fast, it's why I wanted the week

away from him. But seeing him again today only confirmed that although it's moving fast, it feels right.

I just hate the judgement on my friends' faces.

"It's too soon. I know."

Megan shrugs, having nothing to say for once in her life, so I look over at Lucy.

She signals to the waiter. "More wine, please!"

Mase

ICE-COLD HANDS WRAP around my body, making my muscles tense under the soft touch. It takes a second before I smell her, her sweet vanilla scent engulfing me. I turn into her, bringing us nose to nose.

"Should I be concerned that you managed to get into my apartment without me?"

"It's a penthouse," she corrects me, eyes already closed.

I dip down, biting at her puckered nipple. She is completely naked. "Ouch!"

"Don't be smart."

She giggles. "I know a man."

I shake my head, not shocked at all that Vinny let her up here. I still don't understand his behaviour towards this woman. He tried to turn it around on me today and mentioned how I have changed since meeting her, but I have the motivation of getting my dick sucked. He doesn't.

"I've missed you. I couldn't wait till tomorrow," she whispers, trying to get closer.

I wrap her tight in my arms and just hold her. Her ability to centre me is disarming. "I've missed you too."

IT'S JUST GONE six p.m. when Nina breezes out through the gym doors, looking incredible. She is wearing a pillar box red, all-in-one thing that, at first glance, looks fucking difficult for me to get her out of. But she looks good, too good. The curve of her hip juts out as she sexily walks to me, and has me shaking my head on a laugh.

She walks around to my window, bending down and tapping on the glass.

"Mr Lowell, what are you doing here? I'm waiting on my hot date," she purrs, pushing her head through the window, bringing our lips only inches apart.

"He's a lucky man," I mutter, staring at her mouth as she darts her tongue out to lick her lips.

"He is indeed. You wanna know why?"

"Enlighten me." I lean in a fraction, giving her my ear.

"I'm hungry for him, starved for his taste. I don't think I'll make it through dinner."

Fuck, I want her.

"Get in the car."

She laughs at herself all the way around the bonnet while I try to rearrange myself in my slacks to accommodate my growing erection.

"You need a hand with that?" she says, sliding into the seat next to me.

"You are going to cop it so bad when we get home tonight,

Pix. You'll be lucky if I don't take you on the damn dining table."

"I was trying to calm you down, not wind you up more."

She wanted to calm me down?

"Come here." I pull her into me, taking her mouth in a hot kiss. She reaches between us, squeezing me through my trousers. "Fuck." I pull away from her, gripping her hand in mine. "Later."

"I can't wait to meet your family," she says, leaning back in her seat and instantly killing my hard-on.

"Charlie and Elliot will be there, Elliot's parents too."

"Why Elliot's parents?"

"They are practically family. Christmas, holidays, anything family oriented was always us and the Montgomerys growing up."

"That's nice. You must feel like you have a lot of support?"

All but her. "I suppose I do."

"And your sister? Will she be there?"

I smile wide. "Yes, Scar. You'll like her."

"Do you see her often?" she asks, pushing her hair behind her ear as she turns in her seat to face me.

"Not as often as I'd like. She's with Dad a lot, and I don't tend to come out to the house much anymore."

"Why?" She frowns.

"It's not the same as it used to be, hasn't been for a long time."

"Since your mum?" she asks tentatively, sounding unsure if she should be asking.

But for some reason, I don't feel as reluctant as I normally would to share the information with her. I want her to know. I want her to understand.

I nod once. "Everything changed after she left. The house is just that now, a house. It stopped being a home the day she died."

"Sometimes things change, Mase, and it's completely out of our control, but you shouldn't cut yourself off from going out to the house, no matter how daunting it is. I was scared to lose my mother for my entire childhood, yet once I let go and allowed other people in, people like Maggie, who gave me the love, support and a home that my mother couldn't, everything seemed to get a bit easier. I'll never understand your loss, Mase. I'm not trying to compare our situation. I'm not even sure I've made a solid point there—"

I pull her hand into mine and bring it to my lips, kissing the back of it. "Thank you, Nina."

"I'm glad you invited me."

The dark sky looms over Lowerwick Estate, making it look every bit the nightmare I remember it. Thirteen years was all I could give my dad and Scarlet after she left. The minute I was able to move out for college, I left. Elliot was more than happy to have a place of our own, and our parents knew it was what I needed. It didn't take much to convince them.

I swallow the bile that rises in my throat as Nina's dainty hand slips into my palm. Her show of support.

For someone so small, she is so strong—physically and mentally. A shield she puts up against the world that she openly invites me to stand behind.

14

Nina

THE BEAUTIFUL MOONLIT SKY CASTS A SHADOW OVER THE sprawling home before me. It's magnificent. Curved granite steps lead up from the circular driveway, leading to a terrace that runs from the left and right of the double-fronted doors. Ivy creeps up and around the windows covering a third of the mansion. It must be a listed property; it's so grand. I can't imagine growing up in a place like this.

Mason stands unmoving at the bottom of the steps, his shoulders set and his jaw tight. I slip my hand into his and squeeze.

I'm here, Bossman.

"I can't wait to see inside." I swing our arms between us. "It's stunning, Mason."

"Come on," he mumbles, pulling me forward and up the steps.

I can feel him shutting down already.

He ushers me through the door, taking his time to close it.

He doesn't turn around straight away, and I watch his back as he moves the champagne he had under his arm from one side to the other, then back again.

I step forward, sliding between him and the door, then reaching up, I take his face in my hands.

"Mase, we can leave?" His eyes search mine for something I'm unsure I hold. "But I would love to meet your family."

Let me in.

He nods his head then pulls me through the house and towards the noise at the back of the property. His family is sitting out on the terrace, which must wrap around the entire house. It's tranquil and calm, with lanterns scattered throughout the area and a fire that burns in a little chimney in the corner. Beyond that lies miles and miles of uninterrupted countryside.

"Mason, you're here."

I recognise the man immediately. He is the man from the photo in Mason's home office. His dad. He has aged some since it was taken, but the sharp line of his jaw and the deep dark brown of his eyes match his son's.

"Dad," Mason says, placing me to his front. I can't help but feel like it's a shield. "This is Nina, my girlfriend."

It's unexplainable, the feeling that flits through my chest. For a second it's almost painful, jarring my entire body, but it spreads fast and ends in the tips of my fingers.

I crave it.

"Hello, Mr Lowell." I reach out my hand to him feeling unsure when he doesn't take it immediately.

"Girlfriend? Right, sorry. Hello, Nina. Please, call me Anthony." He looks to Mason in question, while taking my hand in a gentle shake. "I can't tell you how happy I am to meet you."

"You too, Mr Lowell."

He nods his head, still looking at Mason, then his glassy eyes come back to me.

Mason puts his hand on my back and steers me forward. "I'm going to introduce Nina to the others."

"Of course." Anthony smiles, stealing a moment as he walks to the edge of the patio, looking out over the rolling hills and setting sun.

He seems frail. Much smaller than he looked in the photo. John always tells us that as you get older, the weight tends to be harder to shift. It's an excuse for extra apple pie, I'm sure—but if it is true, then that's not the case here, and as Anthony leans against the flower bed, grasping the granite planter to steady himself, I wonder just how bad his addiction is.

"Frey, Glen," Mason greets the couple standing at the fire. "Nina, these are Elliot's parents, Freya and Glen Montgomery."

I shake both their hands as they smile warmly at me.

"It's lovely to meet you, Nina. Elliot has told me so much about you. And your friends Megan and Lucy? I do hope I'm not making that up." She leans into me as she laughs.

"No, that's right." I chuckle. "Elliot told you about us?" I frown, looking across the terrace at him. He is sitting in a big circular lounge chair, chatting to Charlie, who sits opposite him.

"Oh, he loves the ladies. You'll have to get used to that and never tell the boy a secret."

I smile, deciding I already like her. Frey Montgomery is

exactly how I'd expect her to be. She oozes class, her ashy blonde hair cut into a long bob that perfectly suits her petite frame, and her clothes, all white linen.

Glen, Elliot's dad, is tall, just like Elliot, but has dark brown hair speckled with grey around the sides.

"Yes, he does seem to be quite taken with the girls." I smile, my mind wandering back to the first night we met.

"Where's Scar?" Mason asks.

"Kitchen," Freya replies. "She wouldn't let me help her."

"Why does that not surprise me? Come on, I want you to meet her." Mason leads me back towards the door, but I stop when we pass the boys, needing a moment to breathe after already meeting half the people here in under a minute.

Charlie stands to hug me. "Nina, it's good to see you."

"I should apologise for yesterday," I say, my mouth pulling down on one side as I wince.

He chuckles, taking a swig of his beer. "It's fine. I was bored shitless anyway. You don't need to apologise to me, that's for sure."

"Nor me," Elliot pipes up, standing from the chair. "I've been waiting years to see this prick get put in his place."

Mason shakes his head, placing a hand on my back. "On that note. See you later, assholes."

He guides me towards the back door again, but just as we cross the threshold, we run into a petite lavender-haired woman carrying a tray of canapés.

"Fucking-great-shit-balls!" She shrieks as the canapés clatter to the floor. "MASE! Why are you storming through the door like that for? Look what you've done!"

"Me? It's not my fault; you had the damn thing in front of your face." Mason proclaims, refusing to take the blame.

The lavender-haired girl—who I presume is Scarlet—tuts. "Always my fault." She laughs, twisting her lips into a pout then pulling him in for a hug. "It's good to see you, big brother."

I look between the two siblings, suddenly feeling nervous to meet Scarlet. She is nothing like what I expected. "Hello," I say.

She turns to me, blinking rapidly as she looks back to Mason in question. "Hello, I'm sorry, who are you?"

"This is Nina," Mason replies proudly.

"This is Nina," she repeats, still smiling as she looks between us. "And Nina is..."

"My girlfriend."

"The what the what? Girlfriend? That's a first." She laughs awkwardly, clearly surprised by the information. "Well, it's lovely to meet you. I'm sorry my brother has caught me off guard. He didn't tell me you were coming."

"It's fine!" I wave her off, bending to pick up the canapés—although they are no longer edible. "Do you need a hand? I can help you with these."

"You don't have to do that, Nina," Mason tells me, pulling on my elbow.

I shrug him off. "It's fine. Two sets of hands will get it done twice as fast." I smile over at his sister, who is on her knees, scraping up the last of the mess.

"My name's Scarlet, but you can call me Scar." She puts out her hand, then cringes when she realises it's covered in a mixture of toppings.

"It's lovely to meet you," I tell her, laughing with her when I don't take her hand.

"My brother hasn't told you anything about me, though, I presume," she says, looking up at Mason.

Mason slips his arm around my waist when I stand. "I brought her to meet *you*, Scar."

Her shoulders sag, and something in the air shifts. "Dad's been struggling," she tells him.

His hand tightens on my side, and he doesn't say anything more. An awkward silence settling between the three of us.

"I'm going to get some more champagne." Scarlet's eyes lower to the floor as Mase gestures for me to walk on in front of him, but I don't want to leave his sister alone to clean up the mess.

"It's okay, you go. I'm going to help your sister."

"You don't need to," he whispers in my ear.

I turn, kissing the side of his mouth. "I want to."

Scarlet leads me into the kitchen, which sits in the middle of the house. It's modern but traditional, with a farmhouse feel to it. It's got *lots* of mess, and it's homely. It's completely different to Mason's.

"Would you like a drink?" Scarlet asks, pulling open the fridge.

"I'd love one, thank you," I say, sliding onto a stool at the island. "Your home is beautiful."

She turns, wine bottle grasped in her hand. "Thanks. As you can see, it needs some TLC. I've barely managed to scratch the surface over the years, but I'm getting there."

"You wouldn't get someone in to do the work for you? I'm sure Mase would know someone. It's real estate your family is in, right?"

"My dad and Mase, not me. I wouldn't know where to start with the '*family*' business, and have you seen Mason's place? I'd never let his minions loose in this place." She grins, and I know exactly what she means. "And I kind of love doing it myself; it's rewarding to finish a room and then pick the next."

She whirls around the kitchen, opening cupboards and draws until she has two glasses and a bottle opener in hand. I get the feeling Scarlet is a doer. She is quirky in her style and seems like a creative 'out there' kind of person. I mean, she is wearing combat boots with her pale blue midi dress and lilac hair, yet she is rocking it. With the money that I presume comes with the Lowell name, I'm shocked at how utterly normal she is.

"I love that. I'm completely awful at all things DIY." I laugh. "Would Mase not come and help you at least?"

She looks at me as if I'd grown two heads. "Oh boy, you're in for a ride. He doesn't come here. Not unless he has to."

"Like when your dad is having a bad day?" I give her a tight smile.

"Exactly." She slumps down into the chair next to me, filling both glasses with wine. "He told you about that?" she asks, her eyebrows dipping into a frown.

"Yeah, I mean, not all that willingly." I take a small sip. "but it came up."

"Mason had our parents for three years more than me, and I think he remembers a lot about Mum, whereas I only have the pictures."

"I'm so sorry, Scarlet."

"Please call me Scar." She clinks our glasses together, taking a large gulp from her glass. "How did you meet my brother?"

"Ah, through Elliot and Charlie." My lips pull up in a

smile, and I feel my cheeks redden with my next question. "Hey, do you know why Elliot would call me Pixie?"

She snorts, choking on her wine as she seemingly inhales instead of exhaling at the wrong time, and wine starts to drip from her nose.

"Oh god, are you okay?" I grab a napkin and pass it to her.

"Sorry, did you say *Pixie?*"

"Yeah, since the first night I met Elliot, he's called me Pixie."

She hesitates, but I can see her smile beneath the napkin, the glimmer in her brown eyes giving her away. "No, I'm afraid I don't know, Nina." She wipes the remnants from her chin.

"Wow, *Scar*. Are we really starting this friendship off on a lie?" I tease, reaching over to top up her glass.

"Not my story." She shrugs with a smile before changing the subject. "You know, it's nice to have a female around here. Some days I feel like saying screw it and finding myself a job. I just can't leave Dad right now."

"Have you ever worked?" I ask, hoping I don't sound rude.

"Nope, I feel like it's too late now. I'm twenty-nine tomorrow, and I feel like my time to study has run out."

"Your birthday is tomorrow? And it's not too late to study! This is the prime of your life."

"I wanted to be a doctor. Started studying medicine after college but dropped out when Dad got sick. I never really thought about going back," she says, and I know it's a lie with the sad look in her eyes.

It's not the revelation of a lost dream. It's the confession of one that's never left her.

"You should absolutely go back. Surely Mason could help

you with your dad?" I raise my brows at her over the rim of my glass. I should probably slow down. I'm starting to poke my nose in places where it's not wanted. "What're your birthday plans?"

"Nothing really. Dad has an appointment at two, and I will need to drive him to that."

"What about tomorrow evening? Will you be out with your girlfriends?"

"You mean the snooty girls who haven't reached out since I left college?"

"Did you reach out?" I question.

She tuts, shaking her head sarcastically. "Just when I was starting to like you."

"We are sooo going out," I decide, knowing my friends and my own bank account won't hack it, especially with Erin arriving Sunday and the prospect of another night out in the city. But I can't have her stuck here all day. I'm already imagining her as a hermit for the past ten years, just with a better sense of style.

"Out? Out where?" Her eyes bug out, but she bounces on her chair, excitedly.

"Wherever you want. I have a morning class, but I could be here by twelve thirty? We could go anywhere."

"What do you do?"

"I have a dance studio in London."

"That's amazing," she says excitedly, but then her shoulders drop and I can see her mind racing.

I shake my head at her, not understanding. "Scarlet, I don't want to impose."

"But you're about to anyway." She nudges me with her elbow, giggling.

I take a sip of my wine, smiling around the rim of my glass. "But if there was a way to go back to med school, would you go?"

"I couldn't. My father doesn't have his health anymore. Mase doesn't get it."

"And neither do I, so ignore me. But you shouldn't put your life on hold for anybody else. Even if that person is your family."

She eyes me behind my wine glass, a slight smirk pulling at her lips. "Okay, it's official. I like you."

Mase

I SHOULD BE happy that my father isn't drinking tonight. Our guests wouldn't know; they never noticed when he drank. At least they never seemed to. Maybe it was the elephant in the room for all the years the alcohol wasn't visibly killing him. It's too late now. Nothing can mask the damage it's done.

He's sick. I can see it in the pale of his skin. The way his body is slower, his bones protruding. It infuriates me that he has done it to himself. All the years wasted locked away in his office with a bottle of scotch that he won't get back.

"Mason." He approaches me. "How are you, son?"

I wish I could hate him. It would make this so much easier. "I'm good, Dad."

He nods. "I was hoping we could sit down for a chat this week. I have a few things I need to go through with you. Maybe you could ask Charles—"

"Just, stop. I have enough on my plate right now without

worrying about this. I need to go and find Nina." I feel like an asshole as I leave him on the patio, but I'm not ready for what he wants to say. I won't ever be ready, and he knows that. I don't catch what he says as I walk away. I only hear the word *time*.

I hear their laughter from the other side of the house, and it wraps itself around me like a warm veil. A sound I never knew I needed and now won't ever forget.

"No!" Nina shrieks.

"Yep, the whole thing is on tape. You have to see it." Scarlet laughs.

I round the corner finding them at the kitchen island, the canapés a mess and sitting in the centre untouched. There are two bottles of wine on the counter, both emptied. I shake my head and smile my first genuine smile of the night.

They both turn at the shutter sounding on my phone.

"Did you just take a picture?" Scarlet points a finger in my direction.

"Mase!" Nina chides, hopping down from her chair, and moving around to stand beside me. Leaning up on her toes, she places a kiss on my cheek. "You okay?" she asks.

I slide my arm around her waist. *I am now.*

WE SIT in the main dining room for dinner, the cool August evening too chilly for the girls. They seem to have hit it off, and I probably should've expected it with Scarlet being only a year older than Nina. With her lack of social life, I've always seen her as much younger than she is.

"So, Nina, what is it you do?" my father asks.

"I'm a dancer."

"She owns her own studio and gym in London," I correct her, squeezing her thigh beneath the table.

"She's incredible," Scarlet admires, staring like a creep across the table.

"Scarlet was telling me about her time at med school. I told her she should go back if it's something she wants to pursue." Nina says, and I watch Scarlet's face drop.

"You want to go back to med school?" I frown, looking at my baby sister in surprise. She's never mentioned going back. Not once.

She gives Nina a wide-eyed look. "Well, thanks, friend."

"Scarlet, is that true?" my father asks her.

"I don't know." She shrugs. "I haven't really thought about it."

"That's a wonderful idea, darling. It's about time you did something for yourself," Frey says.

Scarlet chews on her lip, her eyes flicking to my father. "Maybe next year I could look into it, find out what the process is."

She looks at Nina again, and I follow her gaze, catching Nina mouth '*Sorry*'.

"I can speak to Ben if you want? I'm sure with the pull your name has at the university you could get into this year's class?" Charlie offers.

Scarlet rolls her eyes, looking back at Dad again as Nina's hand slips into mine under the table. She gives me a look.

Is it weird that I know exactly what she wants?

"You should go for it, Scar. You know I'd be behind you one hundred percent. Anything you need."

"I agree," Dad voices, grasping her hand on the table.

"Thank you, Mason." She smiles softly, looking at Nina with a warm look in her eyes.

I haven't seen my sister so relaxed in years. She usually spends all her time cooking the food or fetching drinks to keep everyone happy at family meals. To see her with that spark in her eye and to hear that she actually wants to do something with her life—after years of me thinking she was wasted here—it has a warmth spreading through my chest, and I know the woman to my left is entirely responsible.

I lean in to kiss her temple, catching Elliot and Charlie smirking at me knowingly.

I'm completely fucked for this girl.

Nina

"THANK YOU FOR COMING, Nina. It was wonderful to meet you." Anthony leans down, kissing the side of my cheek.

He's a sweet man who very clearly loves his children.

If only that were enough.

"It was a lovely evening. Thank you for having me."

Mason leans in, giving his dad a quick hug, and pulling back before a second is up.

"Thank you for coming, son. Maybe I'll see you both again soon?" he asks hopefully.

"I'd love that," I mutter, even though I know my answer isn't the one he wanted.

Mase walks me to the passenger side of the car and opens the door. I slide in, taking a deep breath as I process the events of the evening.

Once inside, he picks up my hand, kissing the back of it. "They loved you."

"Was I too much? I felt like I was a little intrusive with the Scarlet thing. I should have waited to tell you."

"No, not at all. Nina, I'm serious. Thank you. I didn't know that Scar wanted to go back to med school."

"Did you ever ask her?"

He drops his head. "No, and I feel like a dick for it."

"Don't. I had to poke it out of her. She feels like she can't, with your dad being—"

"I know."

"Mase you could help her, be there when she can't."

"Nina, he is sixty-two years old. He shouldn't need babysitting."

"No. You're right. But if it's peace of mind for your sister whilst she studies, surely that's enough of a reason to do it anyway?"

He looks at me with a glare but has absolutely nothing to say. "I'm glad we agree." I smile, rolling my lips. "Thank you for bringing me tonight. I really did have a great time."

"Yeah?"

I nod, leaning in and giving him a soft kiss.

"Hmmm, just you wait till I get you home, angel."

15

Nina

MASE INSISTED WE STAY AT HIS PLACE TONIGHT SO THAT WE would have more time in the morning before we have to go to work, and I couldn't argue with his logic. And the idea of more orgasms.

That's just a bonus.

We stop off at my apartment so I can get my dance clothes for tomorrow. Again, his idea to give us more time in bed in the morning. I grab my tights, cami and trainers, and then drop down at my bedside to get some underwear. As I search for my comfy boy shorts (they are all I can dance in), my black suspender belt catches my eye.

I've never worn the set. It was something bought years ago on sale when shopping with the girls. They totally talked me into it.

A buzz of excitement rushes through me at the thought of surprising Mason.

I quickly strip down and slide on the panties and bra,

pulling the suspender belt over the top to my waist. I look in the mirror and my eyes widen.

It looks good. The lace shows just a glimpse of my tan skin beneath it—enough to drive him wild. I've never been into lingerie like some women are, but I must say I feel fantastic. I wonder if Mason has had women dress up like this before. My shoulders sag. Of course he has, stupid.

My phone starts to ring in my bag, and I grab it.

BOSSMAN

"You changed your name in my phone?" I laugh.

"What's taking you so long?"

"Have some patience."

"No, I'm coming up if you're not out that door in the next thirty seconds."

"That's unrealistic, give me two minutes." I hang up, then grab my all-in-one up off the floor.

I get dressed, stuff my clothes into my bag, and then hop to the door as I try to get my heels back on. Just as I swing open the door, Mr Impatient raps his knuckles on the wood surround.

I drop my head to the side. "I was coming."

"Not quick enough," he says, far too serious.

"You need to loosen up." I smirk, knowing exactly how I want to christen my new underwear.

Mase

OUR MOUTHS ARE LOCKED in a slow, sucking kiss the entire ride up in the elevator, neither of us able to resist one another. The doors slide shut for the second time before I'm able to pull away, her lips pinching at mine as I deny her.

"Out, I need you naked and fucked."

She lifts herself onto her tiptoes, ignoring me as she takes my lips in another desperate kiss.

"I have plans for us tonight, Bossman," she hums, pulling my shirt open.

Her brows pop in surprise when the buttons snag and I'm bared to her.

"Plans?" I ask, frowning down at her.

"Uh-huh, don't worry, it involves me naked." My cock jerks at her promise as she bends, licking up the centre of my chest. "And fucked."

"That's a given when you're here, angel."

"Go get yourself a stiff." She palms my growing bulge. "Drink. You'll need it."

I smile down at the little minx. Never did I think she would come into my life and start making demands. Never did I think I'd let her. I mean, the fact I even went to dinner this evening speaks volumes as to how integrated she has become in my life in such a short space of time. She makes me want to do shit I never do.

"Why are you looking at me like that?"

I pinch her chin between my thumb and forefinger. "Let's get that drink, and then you can tell me all about your plan."

"Nuh-uh, it's top secret," she says, walking ahead and into my kitchen.

I notice the line of her underwear that wasn't there before dinner. And I would know, my eyes were glued to her the entire evening.

Once in the kitchen, she slides onto the stool at the island.

"Do you want a drink?" I ask.

"Yes, please."

"What took you so long at yours earlier?"

"Nothing," she says, distracted on her phone.

"No? That's strange." I chuckle, filling two glasses with wine.

"Joey is calling me," she says out of the blue, sounding surprised.

"What?" I turn to face her.

"Joey."

Holding out the phone, I see that it's his name lighting up the screen. It has my muscles locking tight. "Why is he calling you?"

"I don't know." She shrugs, putting the phone to her ear. "Hello?"

I'm surprised she answered. She clearly doesn't see my annoyance; it pisses me off that he can reach out to her so easily.

"Oh, shit! Sorry, Joey. I've not seen the email, but I will have a read tomorrow and get back to you."

I slam down the wine glasses harder than intended, spilling the contents on the marble top. Nina's eyes find mine, then she rises to her feet, rounding the island and coming to stand in front of me. Her dainty hand finds the centre of my bare chest.

I'd be lying if I said it didn't calm me.

"That all sounds incredible, Joey, and I will get back to you. I'm just busy right now, and it's late. I will call in the morning, okay?" Her eyes find mine and I see the guilt in them. "Bye, Joey. Bye."

I stand, waiting, looking down at the beautiful woman I want to keep all to myself.

"Mase, this could be incredible for the studio. I will be accepting his offer to do the photos. The gallery he works at is a big deal, and it opens the doors to so many other possibilities."

Everything inside me wants to say no, to demand that she doesn't speak to him again, and cut off every male in her life. But that would be unfair, and she doesn't deserve my bullshit jealousy right now. I nod my head. "I will be there when you meet with him."

She smiles up at me, but it disappears just as quick, a frown taking over her face. "So you are aware, I wasn't asking. And what, you don't trust me?"

"I don't trust him; I won't have it any other way."

"I don't know. You will put me off. Can Vinny come instead?"

"No. Me or nobody. Send me the details and I will carve out some time." I stare down at her, daring her to argue.

I know she wants to.

"Thank you, Mase," she says, leaning in to kiss me. "Wait ten minutes, then come find me."

"Where are you going?" I grab her waist as she tries to escape the kitchen.

"I have a surprise for you." She smiles, backing out of the room.

Nina

HE IS EXACTLY where I want him when I come back down the stairs. I moved the wingback chair to the open space between the dining table and lounge, and he seemed to presume what I wanted correctly. He sits gazing out on the incredible view wearing only his boxers, looking every bit of the powerful man he is.

My heels click on the polished wood floors as I walk to the music console in the corner of the room. I find the song I want, watching him as he takes in the first few verses. It's not until the beat drops, and his head falls back to the seat in anticipation that I make my way to him, my body moving forward with the thump of the music.

The look on his face as I come into view sets my insides on fire, adrenaline rippling through me. It's the only thing that keeps me standing.

I saunter around the chair, stepping between his spread legs. Bending down, I give him one long, deep kiss.

"No touching," I whisper into his mouth.

I hear his groan as I turn and walk to the floor-to-ceiling window. Dropping down into the splits, I lean back, falling to the floor with my back arched, legs still stretched wide. My eyes lock on his as my head tilts back and I roll my upper body with the music. His eyes are focused on the dip between my breasts and nothing else. That is until I give him my legs, lifting them together, I flip myself, rolling backwards until I'm a foot closer to him and on my knees, I plant my hands on the ground letting him see me as I swing my head around in sync with the roll of my hips.

I bring my body to the ground in a slow, gentle grind, and

I swear I hear him hiss. The music is so consuming that I can barely hear him, but the tension in the room tells me everything his words don't.

He wants me.

I roll to my back, sucking my thumb into my mouth and moving it down my body until I reach the apex of my thighs, applying pressure through the lace onto my already sensitive clit. It makes me needy, hungry for him. I bring my legs out to the sides, rolling my body up so I'm back to doing the splits, but this time I give him the vantage point of my front. Pushing my legs behind me, I rise to my knees finally positioning myself between his legs, I look up at him expecting him to be looking at my semi-naked state, but instead of looking at my body, his eyes are locked with mine. A fire burning within them that has no signs of being put out.

Mase

SHE'S every man's wet dream. A dream I never thought I wanted until Elliot thrust her into my world, and now that I've got her, legs spread wide for me on my penthouse floor, I plan to do everything in my power to fucking keep her.

Her slender body rolls backwards in a move I didn't know was humanly possible. It puts her on her knees, but still, she only gives me her back. I need her eyes. She drops her hands to the floor, putting her ass in the air for me to see, the lace of her underwear encasing the most perfectly pink pussy I have ever seen.

Mine.

My head ducks down, trying to follow her body as she grinds herself into my floorboards. The hiss that leaves me has me sitting back in the chair, my pointer finger running over my mouth as I try to look in control. Because inside, I'm ready to pounce.

It would be so easy to take her like this. To slide up behind her and get lost in her heat. But the thought of missing something—it has me rooted to the spot.

Like a caged animal I want to free her, taking her to the place she will find her release, yet right now, as I watch her dance for me, she mesmerises me. It only reminds me that this is her home, her true escape. Dancing is her passion.

I work on a swallow as she flips to her back, dipping her thumb into her mouth she sucks, slowly drawing it between her lips before she trails it between her breasts and over her stomach and then lower. My cock throbs in appreciation, making me feel like a fucking teen again as precum leaks into my boxers.

Her body lifts off the floor, her legs stretched wide until her sex is brushing the floor, and I swear she leaves a fucking wet mark.

I roll my lips, the last thread of my control gone. Sitting forward as she pushes her legs out behind her, pulling herself to her knees and planting herself between my legs. My eyes lock on hers, and I swear more is said in that one look than any words have ever been spoken between us.

The connection that we have between us is charged; there is no way she doesn't feel this.

Just as I lean in, she stands, spinning into me and dropping to my lap, her back to my front. She grasps my hands and places them on her thighs as she rolls her hips to the music. It's all the control she gets before I take over, grabbing her tits and squeezing them hard. She moans, dropping her head to the side, giving me access to her neck.

She smells fucking edible.

I lick and suck down her throat as she writhes on my cock, finding the friction she needs.

"Mase," she whimpers.

I want to reach between us, free myself from my boxers and slide straight into her, but that would end this all too soon. Instead, I lift her, making her squeal.

"Shit, Mase!"

"Stand," I groan as I take hold of her calves, holding her legs strong on the arms of the chair. Once I know she has her balance, I slide down to the floor, keeping my head tilted back against the seat. "Turn around and put your knees where your feet are. Sit on my face, angel."

She does as I ask, lowering herself on shaky legs until her pussy is hovering above me. I dart my tongue out, licking my lips.

I need to taste her.

"You're fucking perfect," I say, running my nose along the lace.

"Mase, please. I..."

The sound of her underwear being torn from her hips cuts her off. I don't give her a chance to complain, burying my face in her heat.

She drops deeper onto me.

"Oh my god."

She coats my lips. My chin. Yeah, my girl is wet for me. Grabbing her hips in a tight grip, I pull her on to me, urging her to work herself on my mouth. And she doesn't shy away, rocking herself above me as I suck and fuck her with my tongue.

The second I feel her tense I pull away, lifting her as I stand. I pull her back to my front and sit us as we were before, although this time I impale her on my cock before the backs of my thighs can hit the leather.

"Fuck!" we both moan in unison.

I pull her mouth to mine, kissing her over her shoulder as she begins to ride me. I let her have a few minutes of her torturously slow pace before I take over, my mouth losing hers as I take her hips and start to work her on me, meeting her ass with my thighs on every pump of my hips.

"Ughhh, Massseee!" she shouts, dropping her head to my shoulder.

I watch as her tits bounce, begging to be sucked. Pushing down the cups of her bra, I pinch the puckered tips between my fingers, twisting as I tease them.

My vision starts to blur, and I blink rapidly, praying I can hold off. This can't end. Knowing I can't hold off, I wrap my arm around her front, cupping her at the pelvis and giving her the friction she needs. My other hand finds the back of her neck, and then I let her have it, anchoring her in place as I ruthlessly pound into her.

She comes around my cock at the same time I explode inside her, my teeth sinking into the flesh at her shoulder as my body trembles with my release.

She sits dazed on my lap, her chest rising and falling just as rapidly as my own. I pull her against my chest, sitting us back in the seat, my cock still throbbing inside her as I try to find the words.

"Nina," I mutter, kissing her temple.

"Shh." She turns into me. "Take me to bed."

"What was your mum called?" she asks, her body sprawled out over me.

We came to bed hours ago but are yet to go to sleep—hours of getting lost in each other's bodies and easy conversation.

"Ellis. Ellis Marie Lowell," I tell her, watching as goose-bumps coat her skin under my fingertips.

"She was beautiful. I saw her picture in your office when I was snooping."

I smile at her honesty. "She was, and she would have loved you."

"I would have loved to have met her."

"She's buried at Lowerwick. I could take you some time." I have no idea why I would suggest that.

I've not been to my mother's grave in years. Don't need to visit a piece of stone to be reminded that she is dead.

She lifts her head, resting her chin on her fist. "She's buried at the house?"

"Yeah, we all have plots there. Kind of morbid, huh?" I laugh, awkwardly.

"No, Mason, it's perfect. I wish I had a place so special that I could call home. A beginning and an end. You have no idea how lucky you are to have that."

I skim a lock of hair out of her eyes. "Let me be your beginning and end."

She gives me a half smile, dipping her head and biting

her lip. "I think I might reach out to my dad," she says, surprising the shit out of me.

"Yeah?"

She shrugs. "Not yet, maybe after the showcase when things aren't so crazy. Will you help me?"

Hope blooms in my chest. The thought of making her happy bringing an obsessive need to make it happen. "With anything," I promise her.

"Hmm, there is one other thing."

"If it doesn't involve my cock in your cunt I don't want to know."

She laughs, rolling off me. I follow, positioning myself above her. "You said anything," she proclaims.

"I take it back."

"It's your dad," she says just as I line myself up with her entrance.

"You're fucking with me right now?"

She pushes on my chest, rolling me off her. "He has an appointment tomorrow—I think Scarlet said it was at two—I need you to take him."

"No."

"It's your sister's birthday, and I am taking her out. Please," she begs, mounting my waist.

"Vinny can take him. I will take you girls to lunch."

"Mase." She drops her head, hesitating. "It's not my place, but I will be here next week, next month, next year. Scarlet, too. We're not going anywhere, so push me away for crossing the line, but your father doesn't have the luxury of time left in his life. He is a sick man, and it hurts to see you deny yourself something you need, something most never get. You can spend the next few years enjoying your father for what he is.

A heartbroken man who very clearly adores his children." I huff, looking away from her, but she takes my head in her hands, bringing my eyes back to hers. "Or you can deny yourself the love that you are so blessed to receive and live to regret your choices for the rest of your life. Because you will, I promise you. You'll never forgive yourself for denying yourself this time."

"Nina, it's not that simple. He did this to himself."

"It is that simple! That's my point. He doesn't have anyone to blame like you do. It's all on him. Why add to that? He lost the love of his life, and surely you can see that he needs you now." She closes her eyes briefly, tears coating her eyelids as she opens them, and it guts me. "I pray that one day I can honour these words because she probably doesn't even deserve it, but when the time comes, I will be with my mother in her final breaths. After all she put me through, I can see past it. I can see it for what it is. She did what she thought was okay, just to survive. Her choices were selfish and callous at times, but I'm still here because she allowed me to be. I will hold her in her last breath like she did for my first. Because it's the right thing to do. You have a dad who loves you. Please don't waste that."

"Come here, baby." I pull her to me, dragging us up the bed until she is straddling my hips and hugging my chest.

How can this woman be so pure?

After everything she has been through and continues to endure at the hands of her mother. I can only hope for that level of acceptance towards my own parent.

"I will go with him tomorrow," I tell her.

"Do it for you, Mase, not for me." She sighs into my chest.

I am.

16

Mase

George, my new receptionist.

I'm unsure as to whether Sal is screwing with me with this one. When I arrived this morning to find him eagerly waiting at the doors of my office, I had to do a double take. Wearing his suit and bow tie, and shoes shinier than his forehead—which shines bright in its own right—the man was glowing.

He managed to talk my ear off for the first half an hour, telling me about his mother who lives in Canterbury and his granny in the south. Jesus, I already know this one won't last long, and he's not even female.

"Mr Lowell, your coffee," he says, placing a mug on my desk. "I familiarised myself with your system, but I think we should change it. Your clients aren't even logged in alphabetical order. It's..." He makes a face, turning his head into his shoulder. "Truly offensive."

Pinching the bridge of my nose, I lean back in my chair, a

headache already forming. "Do whatever you need to do, okay? Follow me." I stand, walking around the desk and out to reception.

"This here is a button you can press to feed me all important information. I prefer my employees to use it to avoid unnecessary interruptions." I nod, hoping it reaffirms my point.

"Oh, I find that very impersonal, Mr Lowell."

"Yes, exactly." I pat his back, leaving him at the desk as I return to my office.

The intercom buzzes not thirty seconds later. "I think we are going to get along famously, Mr Lowell."

I shake my head, a small smile tugging at my lip.

"Ahh, you fucker," Lance shouts, chucking his cards at Elliot.

"Can you pricks go do that somewhere else? I'm trying to work here."

"Don't give us that bull, you were looking at hotels in Moscow just now." Charlie smiles, calling me out.

The boys got here an hour ago, and the three of them are now sitting around my office sofas playing poker on the coffee table.

"I'm trying to find somewhere to take Nina to watch the ballet," I mutter, squinting at the screen.

"In fucking Moscow?" Lance frowns, picking up the cards he threw after losing all his chips.

"Does she even do ballet?" Elliot asks.

"She told me last night that it was her dream to watch the ballet one day."

"So, take her to The Royal Opera House to see Swan Lake," Elliot suggests, coming to stand behind me.

"Oooo, I've been to The Royal Opera House. Swan Lake. Swoon. Liam took me for my birthday. So romantic."

Did he just say swoon out loud? And why the fuck is he just walking into my office without knocking?

"What is it, George?"

"I'm just leaving for lunch. Hi guys!" He waves to the others.

"Actually, before you go, George. This is your boss, Elliot Montgomery. You should run all your queries through him from now on, and these are our friends, Charlie and Lance."

He takes his time walking around the room, shaking their hands.

"Is that The Bolshoi?" George asks in surprise, moving to stand at my back. He peers down over my shoulder to get a better look at my screen.

"It is." I look up at him. "Have you been?"

"Absolutely not. It's in Russia. It's one of the most prestigious ballets in the world."

"Useful. Thank you, George."

"Are you going? To Russia?" he asks, excited.

"That's none of your business."

"Of course, but if you're trying to impress a lady. Which I presume you are judging by the roses you had me send this morning." He brazenly leans over me, typing on my keyboard. I don't miss the look Elliot gives the boys. "Then it's got to be Paris. The Palais Garnier," he says, standing. "It's not got quite the allure that The Bolshoi has from the outside, but the interior, history and atmosphere is unbeatable." He smiles triumphantly. "I will see you after lunch. Anything you need whilst I am out?"

"No, George, that will be all." I want to thank him, but then the little shit will think I'm going soft on him.

"So, Paris?" Charlie asks.

"I will be taking the jet on Friday; you won't be using it?" I ask Elliot.

"Nope, all yours, mate." He grins.

———

MY FINGER TAPS on the steering wheel as I contemplate what to say to my dad. We've barely spoken a word on the drive and we're now only a few minutes away from the hospital.

"I appreciate you taking the time today, son."

"It's Scar's birthday, she shouldn't have to go to the hospital," I say, not taking my eyes off the road and not meaning to sound so harsh.

I don't want to be angry at him.

"You're right. Although you know how she is."

I do. My sister would never allow my father to go to an appointment alone. She doesn't have a bad bone in her body.

Maybe I'm a coward, but the hospital brings back horrific memories of my mother. It's funny—some memories I fight to remember. The best ones are so vague, yet others—the worst ones—remain so vivid.

I remember the clinical smell of my mother's hospital room, the blue lid on her jug of water, and the board above her head—it had her doctor's name on it. I was four years old, but I will never forget Dr Lucas Smith.

258 | JC HAWKE

He only ever brought the worst news.

"You wait here. I won't be long," my father tells me as he climbs from the Bentley.

I sit for a moment, knowing his pride will have me wait in the car, but I also know this scan is important and if I don't go in with him, Scar will have my ass for not getting all the information.

I watch as he struggles towards the doors, and I can tell he is fighting against the pain. I'm out of the car and opening the door before he can reach for it. He rolls his eyes at me, but I also catch the relief in them—realisation that he isn't alone.

We stand at reception, side by side.

"Anthony Lowell, I have an appointment at two p.m."

"Of course, have a seat, and Dr Sarnmer will be with you shortly. Can I get you any refreshments?" the receptionist asks us.

"No, thank you," my father replies.

A nurse comes in not long after to take my father through to his appointment. I sit and scroll through my phone, checking in with Elliot at the office.

My phone pings with a message from Scarlet.

Scar- Thank you soooooo much! The girls are hilarious. I really am having an incredible day.

A photo is attached to the message, and my eyes widen when I see what they have done to my penthouse. It's a sea of purple.

"Mason." I look up from my phone to my father's ashen face. "You can come in now."

GRAND LIES | 259

I swallow the bile that rises in my throat, push my phone back into my pocket, and follow my dad into the room.

"Mason, it's good to finally meet you," the doctor says, standing to shake my hand.

"Likewise, do you have the results?" I ask, eager to get on the road and back to the office.

His chin drops, and he looks to my father.

"Dad?"

"It's as we expected, son."

"What the fuck does that mean?" I challenge.

What were we expecting?

"Mason, your father's drinking has led to his liver not working as it should. As he has continued to drink over the years despite that fact, he now has severe swelling of the liver. He has excessive nerve damage in his body, which is a common side effect and explains why he is in such a great deal of pain. The body's ability to produce enough healthy red blood cells becomes affected, meaning not enough oxygen is being pumped around the body. I'm concerned with the nosebleeds your father has been experiencing—how often have you been getting them, Anthony?" he asks, turning to my father. I sit in a daze, trying to process the information he has just given me.

"Okay, you need to come in weekly for scans and stick to the treatment plan we have in place. In the meantime, I will have you placed on the waiting list as discussed. I'm sorry it wasn't the news we wanted."

"Waiting list?" I ask, only catching the end of what he said.

"Your father will need a liver transplant, I'm afraid all

other treatments have been ineffective, and the next step would be a donor."

"Thank you, Doc. Could you give us a minute, Mason?"

I snap out of my daze and stand in a rush to exit the room. "Of course, I will wait in the car," I mutter as I leave the room, pulling at my tie as I lean my back against the closed door, trying to control my breathing.

I look around the corridor spotting a little boy on the row of five chairs. I move to sit beside him, leaning forward and running my fingers through my hair.

A liver transplant. *What the fuck!* Why didn't I know this?

"Hey, mister, you like my cwar?"

The little boy pulls on my suit jacket, drawing my attention to the car in his hand. It's blue, with oversized wheels—another insignificant piece of information that I know I'll never forget.

"Yeah, it's cool, mate."

"You want it?" he offers.

I turn towards him. "No, that's okay, it's yours, you keep it."

"My mummy said we can't always keep the things that we wove. I should give it to you," he says reluctantly.

"Is your mum sick?" I ask, giving him a sad smile.

"No, not Mummy, my big sister." He looks up at me with big, innocent, brown eyes. "She gowes to the sky soon."

Shit. "I'm sorry. That sucks."

The door opposite us opens in a rush, the woman freezing on the threshold as her face drops in relief. "Zander, in here now. You know you're not to run off," she says, her hand on her chest.

He looks back at me, rolling his eyes, and it takes me back

to the days I spent at my mother's bedside. I never knew how important those final months were, always in a rush to get to the Montgomerys to swim in the pool.

"My fault, sorry," I say, standing to apologise to the boy's mother. "Hey, thanks for showing me your car. It's super cool, mate." I put my knuckles out and he bumps his against them. "Good lad." I give him a wink and leave the hospital.

THE CAR IS silent as we pull up to the estate. It's not an uncomfortable silence like before, though; it's just two men reflecting, unable to communicate the right words out loud. Dr Sarnmer is optimistic that they will find a donor quickly, but it doesn't take away the unease that roots itself in my gut.

"Come with me, son," he says, waiting a beat before getting out of the car.

I rub my hand over my face before pulling open the door.

My mother's grave is on the east side of the property, where she has a garden filled with all of her favourite flowers. I push through the gate and trudge through the overgrown grass, keeping my eyes on my now wet Prada loafers as I lower myself to sit beside my father on the bench.

"Is it bad that I want it to take me?" he says after a minute.

I frown, surprised at his confession. "Dad, I... Fuck."

He chuckles beside me. "Come on, Mason, watch that language." He stares out at the acres of land on the estate. "She wasn't afraid of dying, you know. I didn't understand at the time, how she could be so accepting when I was petrified for her to go. She knew she had people waiting for her, her parents, grandparents. I get it now."

I sit quiet, fighting against the lump in my throat, unsure of what I should say.

"I need to get some things put into place, maybe next month we could sit down together and go through it all. So I know I won't need to worry."

"Wait until you hear more from the doctor, Dad. God, you say it like it's no big deal. Scarlet will lose her only parent," I mutter.

"So will you, Mason."

"You don't need to worry about me. Focus on getting better—for Scar."

He nods his head in agreement. "Do you remember the summer of ninety-nine? You and Scar were on the meadow—"

I frown as I cut him off. "I told her Father Christmas wasn't real, and she hit me round the head with the shovel." He drops his head back, laughing. "I remember it well." I scoff.

"Fourteen stitches," he says, shaking his head.

"How about when you watched Jaws with Elliot and then wouldn't take a bath for a week because you were too afraid a shark was going to come through the wall?"

My lip lifts on one side. "You wouldn't believe how badly I believed that would happen." I stare down at the ground, reminiscing. "What song was it? That Mum would play us on the piano?"

He looks at me, caught off guard by my question. "'Imagine' by John Lennon," he croaks out.

"Yes! How could I not remember that?"

His eyes move to her gravestone. "She would be so proud of you. I am so proud of you." He pauses for a moment, breathing in the damp English air. "I'm not afraid. She was my world, and like her, I dread leaving you and your sister, but I can accept it. I need you to as well, and I need you to be there for your sister when the time comes."

"You know I will be." My eyes begin to burn, and I clear my throat into my fist. "Stop talking like you're going to die tomorrow, they said they will find a donor."

He clasps my knee, squeezing to comfort me in the only way he knows I will allow. "Maybe, son, maybe."

Nina

FOR A LITTLE PERSON, Scarlet sure can hold her drink. I wasn't expecting to drink as much as we have, but as I watch her dance across the sofas kicking the cushions to the floor while she points to Lucy across the room, singing in unison to "Girls Just Want To Have Fun", I know she is worth the hangover.

The girls hit it off just like I knew they would. Lucy did an amazing job with planning the day. We had massages, manicures, and pedicures, followed by deliveries of gourmet food. The penthouse was transformed into a purple wonderland, balloon arches and streamers taking up every spare expanse. I hate to think how much it would have cost, and I didn't ask. I paid for my treatments and tried not to dwell on the rest.

Scarlet bounds over to me with her lavender hair in a pile on her head. Just as she steps up in front of me, the elevator pings.

"Oh, is that the stripper?" she says excitedly, running in the direction of the foyer.

Elliot stops her in her tracks, sauntering around the corner as he pulls his shirt from his slacks.

"Did someone say stripper?" Elliot teases, and Charlie and Lance stroll in a few steps behind him.

"Me! I did!" Lucy shouts, dropping herself onto the sofa. I look at her, laughing. It's very unlike her to be so forward.

Elliot beams as Scarlet slaps his arm and scolds him, "Put your damn clothes on, I do not want to see that."

He pulls her into him, tucking her under his arm. "Happy birthday, Scar."

I stand watching as the boys all greet Scarlet and wish her a happy birthday. Checking my phone, I notice it's nearly six o'clock. I expected Mason to be back hours ago.

I go to the kitchen and dial his number.

"Hey," he answers, a calm settling over me as his voice drifts through the phone.

"Sorry, I was just worried. Where are you? Is your dad okay?"

"I'm nearly home. Are the boys there?" he asks, not answering my other question.

"Yeah, I think your sister has had a great day. Although we are all slightly tipsy." I giggle into the phone.

"Good, she deserves it."

I frown at his tone. "Are you okay?"

"I'm just pulling in, angel, I'm on my way up." And then he hangs up.

WE SIT around the fire pit on Mason's balcony. The evening air has a slight chill to it, but Scarlet wanted to be outside so we found as many blankets as we could to wrap up in.

I lie between Mason's legs on the lounger, watching as our friend's drink and chat together.

"How did the appointment go?" I whisper into his neck.

His grip on my waist tightens and I lift my head so I can see his face. "Not great." His eyes find Scarlet across the fire. "But I'm glad I went with him."

I smooth my hand up his chest, a tight smile pulling at my lips. "Whatever happens, we are here for you, all of us," I say, looking around at our friends.

He kisses my head, then shifts his hips, digging around under him. "Your phone." He holds it in front of us as we both stare at the screen.

MUM.

17

Nina

MY MUM ONLY EVER CALLS WHEN SHE WANTS MONEY. I KNOW this. So why do I have such a hard time ignoring her name as it flashes on my screen?

"You'd think it would be easy to ignore her calls after what you told me." I mutter, reclining back into the safe confinement of Mason's chest.

He wraps me up in his arms, breathing me in. "You should do what you think is right. Either way, I'm here for you."

"I don't want to speak to her, but I feel bad if I ignore her. And then when I do answer her calls, I'm always left feeling shitty. You probably think I'm stupid for even entertaining her."

"She's your mother, maybe not morally, but genetically she will always be a part of you, and I accept that if it means there is a you in the world."

I dip my head back, looking at him upside down.

"Smooth, Bossman."

He chuckles, leaning forward to kiss me. "Can I kick them out yet?" He flicks his eyes towards our friends.

I follow his gaze, catching Elliot and Lucy deep in conversation. Lucy has had a skinful this evening and I should get her to bed, but I know Elliot is harmless. She seems to be herself around him, compared to the perfected Lucy she fronts to the rest of the world—not many people get that side of her.

"No, let them stay. This place is too big for the two of us, and I like them being here."

He rests his chin on my shoulder. "Me too," he admits.

I sigh and relax deeper into him, allowing my eyes to close and my mind to rest as I soak in the contentment that comes in that moment.

STRONG HANDS LIFT ME, pulling me from sleep. "Bedtime, angel."

I open my eyes and I see that everyone has gone inside. A blanket is draped around me, and I am cradled in the warmth of strong arms.

"What time is it?" I ask into his neck.

"Late. I didn't want to wake you," he says, looking adoringly down at me.

I reach up, moving his hair from his forehead, his skin cool against my warm palm. "Mase, your freezing," I scold, pulling the blanket from around me and draping it over his shoulders.

"I'm fine." He shrugs off the material.

He walks us into the penthouse and drops me to my feet. Lance, Charlie, Megan and Scarlet, all sit around the sectional sofa watching a movie. Scarlet gets up when she sees us, rounding the sofa to hug me.

"Night, guys," she says with a lopsided grin on her face.

"I hope you've had a good day, Scar, I know I have." I yawn long and hard, lifting my hand to stifle it. I have no idea how long I've been asleep, but I feel exhausted.

"Thanks to you I have." She pulls Mason in for a hug. "Big brother, you fuck this up, and I will seriously never forgive you," she tells him, throwing me a wink over his shoulder. "Is Vinny still with Dad? He's happy to stay?"

"Yeah, have a night off, Scar," Mason tells her.

"Thank you," she says, reaching out to squeeze my hand.

———

"You seem to make everyone you meet fall in love with you."

We stand at the sinks in Mason's en suite brushing our teeth, and I pause momentarily as his comment registers.

I side-eye him in the mirror, noting the panic that's written across his face. Biting down on my toothbrush, I try to contain my amusement.

I step forward and rinse, then wipe my chin. "I do?"

"Yeah. Like my sister, Vinny and the boys," he says, slightly muffled.

"Ah, your sister, Vinny and the boys." I wait a beat before asking. "Have you ever been in love, Mase?"

"Me?" He doesn't look at me, but I catch his brows raised high in the mirror, his toothbrush going a mile a minute in his hand.

"Yes, you," I ask.

"Uh, I don't think so."

"Me neither." I shrug, hooking the tips of my fingers into the crevice of my collarbone.

I wait for him to finish his teeth then step up to him, blinking slowly as I draw his lips into a deep kiss. The taste of mint and him is the perfect mix. "Although I think I could. One day. I don't think I'm completely broken." I give him a wink.

His face grows serious, not catching on to my playfulness. "You're not broken. I have every faith that you will love someone someday."

My eyes search his, my arms wrapping around his neck. "Someone?"

He smiles, looking off to the side and shaking his head.

I bite my lip, knowing he's done with tiptoeing around the conversation.

He takes me by the waist and lifts me to sit on the counter between the two sinks.

"Me. You will love me one day because I have absolutely no clue how I could ever allow you not to. I don't know what this is, Nina," He gestures between us. "but the need to know *you*, protect you, know where you are and that you are safe. That? That, I have never in my life felt before. You consume me in a way that scares me because it's new. Every decision I've made since meeting you has had you at the centre of it."

I smooth my hand down his cheek as he leans in to kiss me, nudging my legs apart as he puts himself between them.

An overwhelming need to worship this man takes over me, and it has me pushing him back. I slide off the counter and fall to my feet.

Leaning in, I kiss him slowly, then run my hand down his chest and into the top of his boxers, wrapping my hand around his growing length.

He smiles cockily, and it sends a zap of pleasure straight between my legs. "Why are you smiling at me like that? You know what it gets you." I tell him, popping my brows once.

He laughs as I give him back his own words. "Do I? I think I must have missed that one."

"Hmm, then let me show you."

His hands find my shoulders, and he pushes me to my knees as if he knows what's coming. "Fuck, yes!"

His dark eyes hold mine as I take him into my mouth, and I try to be just as sexy for him but this man is too much. I smile around him, unable to control myself. He shakes his head, dropping it back for a moment before looking down at me when I begin sucking on the very tip, and in that moment 'my Mase' is gone. He takes my ponytail, wrapping it tight around his fist as he grasps my jaw and squeezes, pushing himself to the back of my throat.

"Take me, angel," he demands.

Mase

I FIND Lance riffling through my fridge when I enter my kitchen the next morning, which isn't surprising considering it's Lance. The man is always damn hungry.

"Sullivan. Eating all my fucking food as per?" I smirk, moving for the coffee machine.

"As if. Your cupboards are bare, Lowell. It's sad." He

moves to the hob—carrying a stack of my food in one of his arms—checking the bacon in the pan. "How'd things go with your dad?" he asks at the same time that Charlie walks in.

"Shit. I should speak to Scar about it first." I lean against the counter; my arms spread wide. I tip my chin at Charlie. "You off?"

"Yeah, I've got an eight thirty. Where did you sneak out to last night?" he asks Lance.

"Nowhere?" Lance frowns back at him, sliding himself onto the kitchen island.

"Well it wasn't Elliot. Lowell?" he asks me.

"Not me, mate," I tell him, both of us looking back to Lance.

He shrugs, taking a bite out the end of the dry baguette, not a care in the world.

"Probably Montgomery. I was surprised he wasn't already in Lucy's room when I went to bed last night," I suggest.

Lance snickers, "Doubtful. She isn't giving him an inch." He chuckles to himself, smiling around his mouthful of food. "Ha. *That's what she said.*"

Charlie rolls his eyes, moving to fill a travel mug with coffee. "So, I looked into that case on Joey Wilson. It was nothing. Was dropped a couple days after the report was made."

"Do you have the case files?"

"The sheet of paper that tells me that there wasn't enough evidence to take it to court let alone trial? Yes."

"I want them."

"Well you can't have them. Vinny said he has been stable since childhood. You can't judge him based on something that might not have happened."

"Where Nina is concerned, I will."

"Does she know you had him looked up?" he questions.

"No." I glare, knowing where this is going.

"Well, I think you should tell her. Would explain why you've been such a prick the last couple weeks."

Charlie has always been the honest man out of us all. I suppose it comes with the job in some ways, but over the past four years he has become hell-bent with the need to make every situation untainted.

It's what keeps me up at night, the thought of what I have done to the man who would never contemplate something so fucked.

"Yeah, I will tell her."

His brows furrow, clearly not expecting me to agree. "Right, I'm out. I won't see you before so enjoy Paris, man." He cuffs me on the back and smiles.

I nod my head, pleased that he has turned towards the door and can't see my grimace.

Once he leaves, my eyes lift to Lance.

"Get out your head, Lowell. He'd never live with himself if you told him."

"I know."

"You did the right thing. It's buried; move on."

I pinch the bridge of my nose, thinking back to that night and what a fuckup it was.

"Has Cara been in touch?" he asks.

"No. She wouldn't fucking dare."

He nods his head. "I know you like this chick, but be fucking careful, you don't need another Cara. That's already cost you enough."

"Nina is nothing like Cara."

"Maybe. But do you really know her yet? Would she stay if she knew?" he spits.

I frown as his question settles in me.

Would she?

"I've got your back always, Mase. Just be smart."

Nina

I STARE at my reflection in the mirror, angry that I carry so much of her in my features. The irony that the one person I want to forget is forever embedded in my DNA. They say family runs deeper than blood, and that's true. But that doesn't mean you can forget the genetics that makes you who you are.

My chest heaves as sweat runs down the dip in my back. I lower my chin, trying to get my breathing under control. My mother has consumed my thoughts all morning. Normally I can immerse myself in my dancing, allowing it to take me someplace else for a while. But today isn't one of those days.

I don't know if it's everything with Mason's dad or the fact that I just know I need to speak with her about the money she receives from the man that may or may not be my dad, but nothing I do seems to ease the need to answer the phone.

I can hear it ringing in my bag right now, and it enrages me.

Why?

Why does she do this?

MY BODY SCREAMS at me to stop, the pain rippling throughout my muscles too much to ignore. I've been at the studio for hours, leaving my phone to ring out every time, not nearly ready to chance looking in case it's her.

I pull myself up on the piano—my safe spot to sit and reflect. Flipping over my phone I see I have six missed calls, all from Mase. Is it wrong that I considered it might not be my mum calling? That maybe I just needed a minute to find myself.

It's just gone five so he's probably already on his way to me.

I call him.

"Angel."

"Hey. Sorry I missed your calls, I was dancing," I tell him the half-truth.

"I know. I spoke to Logan downstairs when I couldn't get hold of you."

"You did?" I frown, lying back on the cool wood of the piano.

"Are you finished? I will come and get you."

I need him, but I also want to be alone right now.

It's funny how I spent my childhood longing for the attention of anyone who would give it to me, craving their company. Yet now I long for my quiet.

There's safety in silence.

My mind really is all over the place right now. "It's still light out; I think I will run this evening." My aching body screams at my own words.

"You're not coming to mine?"

"I need to go home at some point. I need more clothes for a start."

"You should sell it—your apartment. Move all your things here."

My eyes widen at his words. *Is he serious?* "Don't be ridiculous."

"I'm serious. Keep your apartment if you want to, but bring your things over. It's the inevitable."

"Says who?" I laugh, letting his playfulness ground me again.

"I'm on my way to get you, Pix."

"I—"

The line goes dead, and I can't help the smile that finds my face. He is impossible. I steal a few more peaceful minutes, then jump down and turn all the lights out in the studio, making my way downstairs. Logan is in the gym but otherwise it's quiet.

"Anderson, your girls left hours ago. You okay?"

"Yeah, just one of those days." I shrug.

He nods his head in understanding. "That guy from the other week," he pauses, trying to remember his name.

"Mase." I remind him.

"Yeah him! He called and asked if you were here. I came up but the door was locked," he says with a weak smile and a quizzical look.

Logan gets me. He has known me for years and knows all about my family—or lack of.

"It's just Mum."

"I figured it would be something like that," he says, tipping his chin towards the door. "Incoming."

My stomach flips when I see Mason making his way towards the gym doors. He is in sweats and a white tee which surprises me considering the time.

I smile as he steps through the door. "Hey!"

He comes straight to me, wrapping an arm around my waist and kissing me openly in front of Logan. He invades every part of me, reaching into the depths and smothering every dark part of me with his warmth.

"This is Logan. He is my manager here at the gym. I think you got off on the wrong foot the first time you met." I raise a brow at the man by my side, but he is already reaching his hand out to Logan.

"I understand why you wouldn't let me up, and I appreciate you looking out for Nina."

I blink several times, unsure if I heard him correctly.

Did he just *thank* him?

"Of course." Logan grins wide, looking at me as he shakes Mason's hand.

My phone begins to ring in my bag, and I huff out a sigh as I check the screen.

Shit! Joey!

I completely forgot to call him back.

"Just give me a sec," I say to the boys, moving to the door for privacy.

"Joey, hi. Sorry I didn't call. Things have been manic recently. How are you?"

"I'm good. No stress, but I do need to know if you will be available to do these photos. I'm running out of time, and I need to confirm a placement." He sounds stressed and it makes me feel terrible that I never read his email.

"Yes, of course. I'd love to do the photos. It sounds like a great opportunity."

"And Tuesday, you can do it that soon?"

"Tuesday?" Should have fucking read the email. "Uh, yes,

I could probably make that work." I try to remember which groups I have in when. I usually have my one-on-ones on a Tuesday. Shit, I will have to check.

"Well that's a relief. Thank you, Nina. I will send you confirmation this evening."

"I'm actually really looking forward to it," I tell him honestly. "I checked out the gallery you mentioned on Facebook. It looks incredible. You work there, right?"

"Yes, I do, and it is incredible; you'll have to come see it sometime."

I look over at Mason. He is chatting with Logan but his eyes are focused on me. "Yeah maybe some time I will. See you Tuesday, Joey," I mumble, already drawn to the man across the room, who with one look, can undo me completely.

"Yes, you will! Cheers, Nina."

I hang up and walk to him, sliding into the spot under his arm that always fits me so perfectly. "You ready?" he whispers into my hair.

MASON HAD me shower whilst he ordered us Chinese; neither one of us wanted to cook tonight. It's only Thursday, which means I still have another full day of teaching to do this week, and I'm exhausted. I feel like the stress of the showcase and the late nights I've been having are finally catching up with me. I'm due on, and I always get tired and cranky just before.

I'm rinsing the conditioner from my hair when his hands snake around my waist and cup my breasts, pulling me back into his hard body.

"Hey," I scold. "What about my food?"

"There's a forty-minute wait." He smiles into my neck, kissing the sensitive flesh there. "I have something for you if you're hungry."

"I'm starved," I say, dropping my head back to his shoulder and smiling when I look up and see the dark look on his face.

His hand skims my stomach and slides down to cup me, making my insides coil tight in anticipation. "You ready for me, baby?"

"Always." I say as two thick fingers enter me.

"Always, Pixie. Every damn time." It comes out gruff, and I feel his erection growing steel against my lower back.

"I want in." He bites down on my shoulder.

"When have you ever asked befor—"

My feet lift from the floor as he takes me to the hilt in one thrust, cutting me off. "I'm not asking, and I make no apologies for it either. This body. It's mine. I will take from it whenever I want to. And tomorrow, when you are sore because of my impatience to get you off first, I will lick you until you're begging me to take you again."

"Mase!" I moan, trying to move my hips to accommodate him.

He has no idea what his words do to me. My clit throbs, begging for attention.

"You're mine," he groans, sliding in and out of my heat.

I reach my hand above me to cup his neck, putting our bodies flush, and slowing him down. "Yours," I murmur.

He looks into my eyes, and I notice the worry that's etched into his. I don't think I've ever seen him so vulnerable.

"Fuck," he says, pulling out of me and spinning me to face him.

I already have my arms around his neck, lifting myself when he takes my legs and pulls them around his waist. He slides back into me, using the wall at my back to get himself as deep as he can.

His head finds mine, resting it there as he pauses. "Fucking perfect."

I can feel him twitch and jump inside me, but he has his eyes clenched tight.

Unmoving.

"What is it, Mase?" I ask.

His eyes snap open, the dark pools boring far beyond my soul. "Tell me again."

I frown. *Tell him?* "What?"

He rolls his hips, his pelvis brushing my clit and making me moan. "Tell me that you are mine. Tell me that nobody else gets the parts that I do."

I try to work out what would cause his possessive behaviour, and then realisation sets in.

An impish smile tugs at my lips. "Are you jealous? Because Logan really is like a brother," I tell him, running my hand through his wet hair.

He shakes his head, searching my eyes. "I'm not worried about him."

"Who then?"

"It was Joey on the phone before in the gym, wasn't it?" he says, nostrils flaring as he stills inside of me.

I know that they have bad blood between them, and I don't want to mess with Mason's emotions, but the photos are important to me. If I go back on it now, then he will always think he can pull strings and have me dance. And that won't end well.

"Yeah." I drop my arms, bringing them between us to push on his chest.

I can see the annoyance on his face that I've pulled away from him. "I told you I'm having him take my photo. You can come along like you said if you have to."

He pulls me tighter to him as he readjusts his feet on the tile, grazing that spot inside me that has my eyes rolling back in my head—and he knows it.

"I had him looked up," he says, voice strained.

"You did wha—" He rolls his hips again.

He is too damn good at this.

I dig my nails into his abs. "Mase," I whisper.

"Seven years ago he had allegations made against him, it never came to anything but I don't feel comfortable with you being alone with him. It's all I ask."

"What were the ale—"

He cuts me off with a searing kiss, causing me to swallow my words as I get lost in him. His hands find my ass, guiding my hips as he rocks into me. His lips move to my throat and I tilt my head back, smiling at the ceiling.

How is this man mine?

I lean back against the shower wall, giving him better access to my breasts. He licks and sucks between them until he can't dip down any lower without breaking our connection. He pulls a nipple into his mouth, toying it between his teeth, teasing nips and sucks that send me wild and writhing against the shower wall.

"I need more," I whimper.

"I know, baby," he groans around me.

I can tell he is close and fighting to hold off.

His hands move to my hips, and he squeezes tight, gliding them up over my waist as I lock my legs around his lower back. I can feel him twitching inside me, and I know he is at war with himself, but I'm not there yet.

Last night I gave him all the pleasure whilst on my knees on his bathroom floor, and then I fell asleep before he could return the favour. Granted, he more than made up for it this morning; he isn't the type to take without giving. He loves it too much.

"It's okay. Fuck me, Mase, and then later, once I'm fed, I will feed you," I promise, holding his eyes as I squeeze him tight.

His lips lock with mine as he takes my hands, lifting them above my head. I smile into the kiss as his control is shattered, and he starts to thrust his hips.

"Fuck!" he roars, his body shaking as I clench around him again.

He tenses, pulling out of me and coming all over my stomach.

I kiss every inch of his face as his chest heaves between us. I lean back, our eyes locking as we stand in the moment.

"I could look at you, just like this for hours," I tell him, skimming my hand over his slackened jaw.

Mason Lowell makes me feel things.

Mase

THERE'S something about her apartment that I love. She's all around me here, her stuff littered around the place in a perfect Nina mess. It just reaffirms my point that I want her to move in with me.

I didn't tell her about my father, and she didn't ask again. I have a feeling she didn't want to push me.

She promised me she'd be here no matter what, and I should be relieved, but the thought of pulling her into the 'no matter what' makes me feel physically sick. She has no idea how ill he is. I didn't. Did Scarlet?

"Mase, you coming to bed?" she calls to me from her bedroom door.

Standing from the miniature sofa, I walk the short distance to my beautiful girl, taking her in my arms and lifting her off her feet.

For the first time in a long time something feels right. Amongst all the chaos, she is good, pure—the only thing ever to breathe light on my dark.

"I owe you an orgasm, Pix," I whisper into her neck.

"You do. I wasn't going to let you forget."

I smile down at her as I lay her out on the bed, her legs following as they fall open. "You promised once you were fed you'd feed me," I say, lifting her hips off the bed until her head and shoulders are all that's left on the mattress. "I want this. Every night." I lick up her centre, starting the argument off strong. Her excitement coats my tongue and I swallow it down greedily. "Come live with me, so that every night I can come home and taste you on my lips and be reminded that there is good in the world."

"Mase," she moans as I jab my tongue inside her.

"You're the only thing that grounds me, Nina," I say,

moving to suck on her glistening bud. She writhes on my face, trying to get away and closer all at the same time. "Come and live with me."

"I can't," she pants.

I pull away from her, blowing up her centre, then drop her to the bed. I lie over her, with one question on my lips. "Why?"

"It's too soon, what will our friends think?" she whines, using her thumb to wipe herself from me. "I like my independence. It's all I have left, all I'm used to."

I slide into her, her back arching off the bed, her mouth dropping open.

"Is that all that's in my way?" I ask, rolling my hips as I suck her thumb into my mouth.

She turns her head to face me, that incredible smile pulling at her lips, her dimples on full display. "Yes, and you won't win."

"Baby, I already have." I smirk, flattening my thumb to her clit.

"Hmmmmm."

She grabs my wrist adding to the pressure I apply there, then starts to buck into me, trying to get more friction. It takes everything in me not to move inside her.

I'm too fucking close.

"You'll move in with me?" I say strained.

"No," she declares almost sadly.

I pull my hand away, pulling out of her like she knew I would. Kneeling on the bed between her legs, I wait, knowing I won't be the one to give in.

But that quirk of her brow, it fucks with me, because I know that she won't give in either. My mistake wasn't asking her to move in with me—I know she wants it. The safety and security it would bring. No, my mistake was trying to take it from her. Her independence. Her choice.

She won't give that up.

So when she pulls herself up the bed and away from me, tucking herself in as she huffs in pure frustration. I laugh, a loud chuckle that I haven't allowed in years because I know she's just aced me.

"Get the light." She sulks.

Nina

HIS BIG HAND wraps around my ankle, and I'm whipped down the bed in a flash, my legs flattened wide under his strong forearms.

"When you're ready, whether that's tomorrow, a week, or a month from now," He rolls his eyes dramatically at me, making me laugh. "I want you to move in with me. You don't have to give up this place, your independence. But you are my girlfriend, and my girlfriend would live with me. And maybe give me oral for breakfast every day." He smirks, totally sure of himself.

"What do I get?" I ask, giving him an inch. And the smile that takes over his face makes my heart physically ache.

He licks his lips as his head drops between my legs in an attempt to show me exactly what he has to offer.

I say attempt, but who am I trying to fool.

He had me at breakfast.

18

Nina

"IF YOU'RE NOT CALLING TO TELL ME WHAT HAPPENED WITH YOU and Elliot Wednesday night, then I don't wanna know." I tease, smiling down the phone as I dust my finger along the top of the computer. I'm in the studio office making sure it is somewhat tidy for Erin's arrival on Sunday.

"Uh, what? Nothing happened."

I hang up, giggling like a child.

She calls me back moments later.

"Stop that, nothing happened between me and Elliot, why would you think that?"

"You were glued to each other all evening then disappeared, so..."

"So... We chatted and then I went to bed. You're way off on this one, Nina. You know me."

"I do, and I also saw how you were with him. You were so relaxed around him Luce, you're not fooling me."

She hangs up. I frown down at the phone, shocked. I try

to call her back but it goes to answerphone. Each time it beeps telling me 'user busy' I hit call back. I'm about to try her again when my phone starts ringing, and it's a number I don't know.

"Hello?"

"Pixie, I'm not boning Luce."

"Elliot?" I grin. Did she phone him? "Have you tried?" I ask.

"Of course I have! Weeks ago, she wasn't interested."

"And Wednesday night? You disappeared."

"She's a good girl. We bounce off each other, but that's it."

I don't know if I believe him, but what if it's just me hoping for something that isn't there?

"I've got my eye on you, Montgomery."

"Hmmm, Mase not enough for you, Pixie, need me to show yo—"

"Goodbye, Elliot!" I hang up, shaking my head as I call Lucy. This time, she picks up.

"Okay, I believe you! But out of curiosity, why not Elliot?"

"I'm on my way to yours. I was hoping to borrow a top for dinner this evening. What time are you home?" she asks, completely ignoring me.

"We will discuss this later; this conversation is far from over! And not until after three. I have a one on one before I can leave. Will you still be there when I get home?"

"No, I have things to do this afternoon. Are we still meeting on Sunday? What time does Erin get in again?"

"Late afternoon I think. I might give her a call to check in later. Who are you going to dinner with?"

"Uh... Megan."

That's odd. They didn't ask me. I frown, rolling my chair back from the desk. "Megan?"

"Yeah, you're invited too. Obviously." She laughs awkwardly, and I instantly know she is acting off.

"Where are we going?"

"Not sure, I will send you the details. Bye!" She hangs up, and I narrow my eyes at the phone.

Weird.

Mase

A FLUSTERED LUCY stumbles through the doors of my office. A suitcase in one hand and a duffel bag in the other.

"You should have asked Megs instead, she is so onto me." She huffs, pushing her hair back from her face and righting herself.

"Nina knows about Paris?" I sit up in my seat, disappointed.

"No, but she thinks I'm a shit friend who didn't invite her to dinner and only wants her for her clothes." She screws up her face and smoothes her fingers across her forehead. "I had to invite her to dinner by the way. You'll have to fix that by yourself."

I smile as she drops down into the chair opposite my desk. "Thank you, Lucy. I appreciate your help."

"What time do you leave? She finishes at three."

"We take off at six. Do you think she will go?" I ask, annoyed that I don't already know. I hope she does.

"Yes. Well, she will want to. You have to be stern with her, she will fight you on it, but she absolutely needs a break."

I nod. "I booked you and Megan a table at Groulx. Seven o'clock. On me."

"Groulx?" she proclaims, sitting forward in her seat. "Fuck off!"

"Thank you would've been fine."

"Thank you! Honestly, this is so unexpected." She palms her chest, and I can tell she means it.

"It's nothing, and I agree; Nina needs the break."

"Hmm, she said her mum has been calling again." She hesitates, but I can tell she wants to say more. "How much did she get from him, exactly? The guy who sent the money, I mean. Was it enough to live off? She won't ask you, but I know that if it was enough and she allowed them to live like they did, then Nina will lose the last bit of respect she had for her mother."

I drop my chin, not knowing how much I should tell her. "It was enough, more than most get, that's for damn sure. But it was always cash withdrawals, so who knows where it went every month."

She nods her head in understanding, biting her lower lip. "She relies on us. Me, my parents, and Megan." She stands and walks toward the door. "But this past month, her world has started spinning for an entirely different reason."

I roll my lips, knowing she wants reassurance. "I won't hurt her."

"I hope not, because if anyone deserves happiness, it's Nina."

SOME WOULD SAY I took the cowards way out, although, with the way my heart pounds against my rib cage and the sweat that keeps forming on my palms, I'm pretty sure I didn't. Not when I'm standing here on the tarmac ready to give her my world—a world she will never want, nor ask for.

As Vinny pulls up to the runway with Nina safely seated in the back, I know without a shadow of a doubt that it was the right decision.

She could never say no to Vinny.

I want to get the door and help her from the car, but I already know I'm pushing it. She will hate all this, and I have a weekend planned that's full of it. Instead, I plant my feet to the ground, pushing back my shoulders and lifting my chin.

I'm ready for you, Pix.

She steps from the car in her gym tights and vest, her hair piled high on her head. And with the pink hue of the setting sun, I'm certain that she has never looked more perfect.

I struggle to gauge her mood as she walks to me, her thick hips swaying with each step she takes.

She stops short in front of me, her face emotionless.

Nina

HIS EYES PINCH in at the corners as he looks down his nose at me, his chin held high. I want to argue, tell him it's too much and that I won't go wherever it is he planned for us to go. But what I want more, isn't for me. It's for him. Because the way he looks at me with so much uncertainty, that's what makes me want to jump into his arms and tell him I'd follow him anywhere.

"Where are you taking me?" I ask.

"Can it be a surprise?" He crosses his arms over his broad chest.

"I kinda hate surprises." I lick across my bottom lip, watching as his eyes follow the movement. "Would you like it if I told you I was going to suck your cock but leave you in suspense for hours as to where and how I planned to do it?"

"I—"

"Would be excited at the prospect and would want to know more. Am I right?" I eye his crotch, raising my brows when I spot his growing erection.

"Paris, Nina. I'm taking you to Paris." He grumbles, pulling me to him by the neck and taking my lips in a bruising kiss.

"Okay, Bossman. Paris it is." I say against his mouth.

It's like a small flipping house. Far bigger than my apartment —and it flies. I'm standing beside a large round table on the far left of the plane, wondering if I will ever get used to Mason's wealth.

I watch him as he speaks with the pilot, who is wearing a polo shirt, cargo shorts and a backwards snapback—nerves flit through me.

Would it be rude to ask for his credentials?

He looks extremely casual.

An attractive blonde-haired woman approaches me,

looking at me expectantly as if waiting for me to do something, but I don't know what.

"Sorry, am I in the way?" I ask, moving to sit on the curved bench seat.

I can feel the panic crawling up my throat.

My idea of a perfect weekend isn't all of this, but I know *this* is part of the package, and if I want Mase, then I have to accept this too.

"No." She flashes her perfect white teeth at me. "Miss Anderson, I asked if I could get you a drink. A wine or something stronger if needed?"

"Oh, I'm so sorry. Uh, a glass of wine will be fine, thank you."

I count to ten in my head, reminding myself that this is okay. I can do this and not lose myself or my moral compass along the way.

"You're sweating," his soft lips whisper against my ear, and I stand, startled.

"This is all so new to me." I eye the bar at the other end of the plane. It's the same size as my kitchen.

"What happened to the woman who was outside with me ten minutes ago? The one who promised to suck my cock if I behaved?"

I look back to him, affronted. "I didn't promise to—"

The most breathtaking smile cuts me off. He is beyond handsome. He is goddamn delicious, and I know precisely what will distract me as we prepare to take to the sky.

I look around him, eyeing the doors at his back. "Are there any bedrooms?"

He sinks his teeth into his full bottom lip as he takes my

hand and leads me into a room at the other end of the plane. "My Pixie is horny."

"Why do you call me Pixie? Are you into weird Pixie porn or something?" I ask on a light laugh, finding myself funny.

He turns into me, backing me against the door and caging me with his arms. "No, baby, that's not it," he tells me, smoothing his thumb over my brow and down my cheek.

Biting my lip, I slide down the door to my knees, breaking the intense look that passes between us. I unbuckle his belt and free him, quickly sliding him to the back of my throat.

"TELL me something I don't know about you?" I say as I try to distract myself from the ridiculousness of the private plane. We were delayed when Mason went AWOL—that might have been my fault—and only took off around half an hour ago.

"What do you want to know?" he asks, resting his head back against the seat and looking over at me all hot and sexy. He smiles as if sensing my thoughts, lifting my hand to his mouth and running his lips over my knuckles.

"If I knew that then I wouldn't be asking."

"Hmmm." He looks around the plane, deep in thought. "I never wanted to go into real estate; I only did it because Scarlet didn't."

"Really? And now? How do you feel about it now?"

"It's good, I couldn't imagine doing anything else, and it's a bonus I can do it with Montgomery. The houses we sell are always next-level architecture, listed properties or have something to them. It's easy to sell something you love."

I sip my wine, smiling at his confession. I like this game. "Tell me more."

"I'm allergic to dogs," he blurts out, his words suddenly flowing from him like a broken tap. "Just being in the same room as one sets me off. My eyes get red and itchy, and my face gets puffy. It's awful." He looks at me, his face dropping. "What?"

"Dogs. You're allergic to dogs?"

"Yep. Hate the things."

"What?!"

"I'm allergic to dogs," he says, looking at me like I am crazy.

"I heard you. Crap!" He laughs at my dramatics. "Fucking plot twist! This is it. This is your thing."

"My thing?"

"Yes. The thing that makes you imperfect. You have it all, the looks, the money, the life." The heart. "All but the dog. Damn it, is it too late to turn the plane around?" I stand, stepping past him as I playfully go to leave, but his arms wrap around me, pulling me down onto his lap. It has me laughing into his chest.

"You want a dog?" he mumbles into my neck.

I pull back so I can see his face. "Well I did," I say, rolling my eyes.

His eyes flick all over my face, and I wonder what he finds so fascinating. "I haven't found it yet," he tells me.

"Found what?"

"Your imperfection. And I'm pretty sure there isn't one."

Mase

WE STUMBLE through the suite door, not bothering to look around the room before we hit the deck.

"Let me take you to the bedroom," I moan as she dips her hand past my waistband, freeing me from my trousers.

"Later," she pants.

Not needing to be told twice, I smother her lips, strip her tights from her legs and slip the thin material of her lacy underwear to the side. I glide my knuckle through her slick flesh.

"Fuck!"

"Mase," she begs, grinding her hips forward to find friction.

I line myself up and slide into her, dropping my head to her shoulder as she struggles to take me fully.

Her warmth surrounds me, pulling me in and squeezing with every tremor.

This fucking woman.

"Move! Please, move."

"Stop. Talking." I ground out, fighting to keep my control.

I should have taken her on the plane instead of being a greedy prick. Making us wait has us both riled up. I roll my hips and she cries out, but I'm too far gone to turn back.

I flip her to her knees, sinking myself back to the hilt. I squeeze the two full globes of her ass, watching as her cunt struggles to take me.

"Oh god, Mason!"

I grasp the back of her neck and push her to the ground, my other hand clenched against her hip and keeping her glued to me. My hand slips around to her throat, my teeth trailing along her ear. "Squeeze me."

She ripples around me, and I don't move, letting her do the work for me—and fuck does she work for it. Clenching herself around me relentlessly until I'm on the edge of insanity, and the grip on her throat becomes too tight. She bucks back into me and I drop her, letting her fall to the floor. Rolling her over, I bend, placing kisses up her body and over her partly exposed tits—it's all I could manage in our haste. I keep going. Up her neck, across her jaw, sliding back into her heat as I reach her lips.

"Am I too rough, baby?" I murmur, brushing her throat with the back of my hand.

Her eyes darken. "Not nearly enough, Bossman."

My cock turns to steel inside her.

She meets my every thrust, every roll of my hips, every swipe of my tongue. Each and every one met with her own need. Our bodies move as one until it's too much and we fall over the edge together, deep into the abyss.

Nina

It's dawn when I wake, and my stomach churns with the need for food. We skipped tea last night, choosing to hole up in the room—mostly naked—instead.

Mason lies on his back, one arm behind his head and the other covering the crown jewels. His powerful body laid bare for my hungry eyes.

He couldn't be gentle with me last night. As much as he would try, it always ended up the same way it started.

His need for me uncontrollable, but mine just as insatiable.

I've never had as many orgasms as I did last night, and I know I need more sleep after such a late night, but I can't sleep when I'm this hungry.

I pull back the covers and tiptoe to the door, stepping out and into the suite. We are on the seventh floor of The Four Seasons Hotel, and after our less than classy entrance, I finally get to survey the beauty that is the Eiffel Tower suite.

Naive maybe, but I expected a room—just one—a bathroom and perhaps a pokey little window that I pictured hanging out of with Mason at my back. Cute, boutiquey, Paris kind of vibes.

This isn't that.

Everything about it is luxurious with high ceilings, fresh white walls, and cream and soft beige furnishings. Everything complements something else in the room. Like the two windows that look out over the city, both wide and the size of the wall, yet dressed with thick velvet drapes, showcasing the stunning view. White flowers are placed in vases and cover nearly every surface, the smell caressing me like a fresh summer's day.

I step past the sectional sofas and towards the bow window that looks over the terrace. It extends from the room, offering panoramic views over the iconic tower.

"Wow."

This place is... incredible.

Too much? A little. But he is too much, and I only want more of him.

I search the suite for the room service menu, then fall back to the plush cream sofa. I don't know much French so it's hard to navigate what I'm reading, but I think I spot avocado, and I know crepes are pancakes, but I would be devastated right now if I didn't like what I ordered.

I'm nervous when the dial tone starts.

"Bonjour, comment puis-je vous aider?"

Shit, I should've waited for Mase. "Uh Bonjour, roomy servicce?" I say in a French accent, my hand snapping up to my forehead.

This is mortifying.

"Of course, Madam. What can I get for you?"

"Uh, du croissant?" I squirm, wondering if I have gotten that right.

"Two croissants. Would you like any coffee?" she asks.

"Oui, merci. Uh, uno sugarr." I don't know if Mason will have sugar, but I should get some just in case.

He'd probably say something cocky like, 'I have some sugar here for you, Pix.'

"There's sugar in your room, Mrs Lowell. Is there anything else I can get for you?"

"No, uh, merci." I frown, Mrs Lowell? "Wait. Are you English?"

Realisation dawns on me as I replay the conversation in my head.

She giggles into the phone. "Australian, you did great, by the way." I can hear the smile in her voice.

"Oh, wow, how embarrassing."

"Not at all, it's refreshing that you gave it a shot. We get a lot of orders in many languages, and not many take the time to give the native language a go."

"I didn't even want a croissant. I just didn't know how to ask for anything else." I laugh.

"Well, that just won't do. What is it you would like, Mrs Lowell?"

"It's Anderson. My name, it's Nina Anderson."

"Oh, I'm sorry. It must be an error. I will correct that on the system."

"It's fine, honestly. But I'd kill for some eggs, scrambled, on toast." I ask cheekily.

"Absolutely, and so you know, all of the concierges are bilingual; it's part of the job. Just let us know what you'd like, and we will happily help you."

"Thank you so much. Sorry again about my horrific French."

"You're most welcome. Breakfast will be with you shortly. Enjoy Paris, Miss Anderson."

"I will."

I am. Because of him. And scrambled eggs on toast.

AN HOUR later I crawl back into bed, my belly full and my eyes tired. Pulling at Mason's arm, I slip in under the sheets, letting him pull me back and into his warmth.

"Where have you been?" he asks, kissing my neck.

"I was hungry. I got you a croissant." I smile to myself.

"Hmm, I was going to take you out for breakfast."

"You still can, it's early yet."

"Good. We can work off that croissant and then go for round two," he says, rolling me to my back and hovering above me.

"I had eggs." I bite the inside of my cheek, trying to stop my smile.

"Eggs? And I got a measly croissant?" He nips at my ear, playfully.

"You were asleep. It would have gone cold."

"Right, let's work off those eggs, then we are going to feed me. My Pixie is an impatient little devil."

I laugh into his neck as he pins me to the mattress.

Mase

I CHUCKLE to myself as Nina bounces over to the elderly couple at the nearby benches. They smile up at her as she speaks to them, and her infectious personality has them warming to her instantly. The elderly gent stands, taking the camera from Nina just as I make it over to her.

"Come on, I want to get the whole tower in the picture," she says, pulling me in the opposite direction to where I was headed.

She hasn't stopped all day. We have been to the Louvre, the Triomphe and now the Eiffel Tower. She didn't want to stop for lunch, but I made her, promising to come back again soon so we can see more of the city.

Once she finds the perfect spot, she plants herself in front of me, beaming at the man just a few feet away who holds my camera in his wrinkled hands. I wrap my arms around her waist, hugging her to me, then direct a rare smile at the camera.

She looks up at me, a dimple forming on her cheek. It

gives me pause. So many thoughts whirl through my mind, but what I have in my pocket is at the forefront.

Nina frowns as she searches my eyes. "What is it?"

The world around us creeps into the moment, stealing her attention as the crowds of people on the green start cheering and whistling. I look up from Nina, scanning the area until I see them.

"Oh, Mase! He just proposed, how romantic. Woooo, congratulations!" she shouts, cupping her mouth with both hands.

I shake my head, laughing as I lean in to kiss her neck.

Now is definitely not the time.

"Thank you so much!" Nina exclaims, running to retrieve the camera.

She starts to snap photos of me as I approach her, and I shove my hands in my pockets, squeezing the rounded edge.

"Stop that. I will have a million photos of myself at this rate." I pull her to me by the camera strap that hangs around her neck, dropping my lips to hers. I suck her bottom lip into my mouth and then pull away.

"Where to next?"

"Notre Dame!" she squeals, grabbing my hand.

"Nina, wake up."

"No," she groans, her nose twitching.

I grin, pulling the covers from her body. "I'm taking you out tonight. Up!"

"Maaaseee." She reaches for me—or maybe the covers.

"Please, I've had the most incredible time. Let's order in; I'm so tired."

"It's already planned, table is booked and it's a big fucking favour. You want to get up, baby."

Her eyes pinch in at the sides as she glares up at me. "How long do I have to get ready?"

"An hour."

She smirks, then rolls out of bed completely naked, disappearing into the en suite.

I drop to the bed, smug, knowing I will be getting laid tonight.

19

Nina

MASON IS NOWHERE TO BE FOUND WHEN I COME OUT OF THE EN suite, but a note lies on the bed along with four bags. I bypass them and head straight for the minibar, pouring myself a glass of wine.

I pull open the terrace doors and look down on the bustling street below, trying to decipher the emotions that seem to be bubbling to the surface.

This trip has been perfect, and I know I will remember it for the rest of my life. It's only made my feelings for Mason that much clearer. But the money thing, I worry it won't ever stop being a problem for me, and with that comes doubt.

I will give him this weekend because saying no will be futile, but once we are home, he has to understand that I will pay for my own stuff. I probably sound like a broken record to him, and I want to want these things, but I can't allow him to buy me. It goes against everything I stand for as a person.

Taking in a deep breath I return to the suite, heading for

the bedroom.

I read the note.

DON'T STRESS IT, PIX. BREAKFAST IS ON YOU
MEET ME IN THE BAR
MASE

Damn him and his perfect self.

———————

MY EYES BLINK SLOWLY over and over as I take in the gown that adorns my body. Its fitted bodice is covered in black beads and scattered diamonds. Diamonds! They sparkle against the glowing light of the bathroom suite. The deep v neckline dips low, complementing my full breasts. The skirt is flowy with a high slit up each leg. It's comfortable and sexy and exactly what I would choose for myself.

I can't believe he got it so right.

I roll my lips, grasping the cool marble counter as I try to contain my smile.

What is this man doing to me?

Once I have my hair dried and curled the best I can, I open the last remaining bag. So far, I've had extremely naughty underwear, the gown and my beautiful strappy shoes.

I'm hesitant as I pull off the ribbon, sliding out the rectangular box—I already know its jewellery, but I worry it will be ostentatious and over the top.

I gasp when I open it, suddenly laughing at my presumption. I fall to the bed, grinning like a fool at the final gift.

A key to Mason's penthouse. I don't think about what it means, only him, in the bar downstairs, and the need to be in his arms.

I snap the box closed and grab my purse.

Mase

I SWALLOW THICKLY as she comes into view.

She is perfection, and she is mine. She doesn't search for me, our eyes finding each other without question. There is nothing else around us in this moment—just me and her. I stand, rearranging myself in my trousers as she makes her way over to me.

I don't go to her, lifting my chin and letting her close the distance between us, knowing that she needs to make this move.

"My man in a tux." She pops a sleek brow at me. "You sure we can't go back to bed for the night, roomie?"

I squint my eyes at her, unsure of her playful manner. "Roomie?"

She shrugs. "It's the inevitable." A smile tugs at her lips, then she dips her head.

"Hey!" I grasp her chin and lift her head, bringing her eyes up to meet mine. "Don't ever hide from me." I dart my tongue out, wetting my lips. I feel fucking nervous. "You'll move in with me?"

"Yeah, I will."

Fuck, I wasn't expecting it to be so easy.

My boyish grin can't be contained, and I lift her into the

air. "She said yes!" I shout, and everyone starts cheering and yelling congratulations at us.

"Mason, what are you doing?!" she hisses, trying to wiggle free.

"Just go with it, Mrs Lowell." I squeeze her thighs, letting her slide down my body. "Come on! We have someplace to be."

I grab her hand, pulling her out the hotel doors and into the waiting car.

IT's a short ride to our destination, and as we near, I can feel the buzz that radiates from the woman at my side. She knows.

"Mase, please tell me I'm not wrong. I mean, I'm dressed for it," she asks, full of hope as she looks from me to the window.

The car comes to a stop outside of the building, and I only have to nod my head once before she has the door thrown open and is running up the steps.

I hop out and thank the driver before joining her at the top.

"You must have thought I was a right bastard when I told you we would have to put it off until next time."

She reluctantly tears her eyes away from the magnificent building in front of us. "You have no idea what this place means to me."

"Show me." I nod my head in the direction of the main doors, and the smile she gives me as she pushes forward has my heart somersaulting in my chest.

Nina

THE PALAIS GARNIER is one of the most famous opera houses in the world, it's beauty is something I have only ever been able to dream about.

I stand at the bottom of the Grand Escalier, looking up at the magnificent thirty-metre-high vault and the double stair-case that I know leads to the multiple foyers. I close my eyes as Mason's arm wraps around my waist, his lips brushing my shoulder.

"My boy did good." I smile as I look back at him.

He too can hardly take his eyes off the impressive archi-tecture before us.

We move forward together, up the sprawling steps, and I grasp his arm, allowing me to take in every detail without needing to concentrate on where I am going.

"Everything is marble," I state, observing the multiple colours that are etched into the ground. It's unlike anything I have ever seen.

We're led through to the auditorium; it's shaped in a horseshoe and is a sea of red and gold. I marvel at the view from the seats that we are led to and suddenly feel overcome with emotion.

I blink rapidly, trying to clear the liquid pools that have gathered in my eyes. Reaching out, I run my hand over the golden pillars that I've seen so many times in photos. Nothing can explain the feeling of experiencing this monumental, iconic room in the flesh.

We are seated in one of the pods, just the two of us, with

the most spectacular view of the stage.

"You've gone quiet on me," he murmurs into my ear.

———————

Mase

HER EYES ARE GLISTENING when she turns to me, and a sharp pang shoots through me.

I smooth her hair back from her face. "Hey, what is it?"

She shakes her head as if she is lost for words. "You have no idea Mason Lowell. You have no idea."

———————

THE BALLET IS ASTOUNDING. I must admit it's held me captive the majority of the performance, but since the last interval, my eyes haven't left her. The way her body tenses up with every move they make, the jerk of her shoulders as if she knows what's coming next. She is so immersed with the ballerinas on stage; she doesn't even see anything else. It must be for her what she is for me.

Everything I never knew I needed.

She chances a look at me, tears rolling down her cheeks as the show comes to an end. She grasps my hand as the audience stands, a roar that vibrates through the entire room, setting adrenaline racing through me.

I can only imagine what she is feeling. But as she lifts my hand and pulls it to her chest, I feel her heart beating wildly under my palm. I pull her to me, placing a soft kiss on her temple.

People start to leave the auditorium, but I can tell she is reluctant to leave. I bend, taking her face between my hands. "Come with me, angel. I have something for you."

I lead her to the ground floor, weaving through the people and over to the front of the stage. Lifting the wooden panel, I slip into the orchestra pit.

"You can't go through there!" she panics, pulling on my arm.

"Do you trust me, Pix?" I ask, stepping up to her so we are nose to nose.

She smiles, her shoulders dropping. "Always."

I take her by the waist and lift her onto the stage. "You have fifteen minutes. It's all I could afford."

"What?" she mutters, her face turning pale.

I worry she may faint.

I nod my head to the lady at the curtain. "She has a list of music you can pick from. Go, dance!"

"Mase, I can't dance," she whispers down at me, looking out on the auditorium. "Nobody is here."

"I'm here. Dance for me."

Her hands grasp her face in excitement. "Oh my god!" And then she is crying, full-blown sobs.

"Nina, babe. Fifteen minutes."

"I know, I'm sorry. Oh my god. No one gets to be on this stage." She shakes her head in disbelief.

"I know. You almost didn't." I laugh.

She has no idea how much I have paid for the measly fifteen minutes I had to beg for, but the look on her face right now makes it worth every penny.

I walk a few rows down the auditorium and find a seat, spreading my legs to make myself comfortable as I wait.

My finger taps on the velvet armrest relentlessly.

I hope she can dance okay in her dress.

The lights go down, and I suddenly feel nervous, my throat growing tight and my palms sweating. I run my pointer finger over my lip, my knee bouncing.

But then my angel is lit up in a single spotlight.

The music begins, and she starts to move. Everything disappears, my eyes riveted to her, held completely captive by the pull she has on me. The lean lines of her body ripple as each muscle is pulled taut under the smooth skin. The passion and emotion that she puts into every expression and move she makes has me mesmerised.

I sit with a heavy ache in my chest, feeling not only honoured to be watching this woman dance but incredibly proud of every part of who she is.

She holds it together for the entire four minutes, hitting every step with perfect precision, but as the curtain falls, I stand. All the emotion she exerted on stage falling on my shoulders.

She will need a moment to catch her breath. I know that. But I'm unwilling to give it to her—because I need her more.

"Nina," I call, climbing onto the stage and pulling back the curtain. "Angel."

She stands in the same spot, right as she was when the curtain fell.

"That was incredible," she whispers, her eyes finding mine, brimming with unshed tears.

My world stops spinning with the look in her eyes.

On the Palais Garnier stage, I pull the box from my tux pocket, flipping the lid and taking her hand in mine.

"Before my mother died, she had this little Pixie." Nina's

eyes bore into mine, transfixed and filled with untamed adoration. "She kept it on her bedside table, and every evening I'd sneak in before bed and steal it. The day she died, she told me to go and get my Pixie. I did, but when I came back to her, she was gone." I pause, biting into my bottom lip and stealing a moment.

"Mase, you don't have to—"

"My father told me she wanted me to keep it. Her little glass Pixie." I smile at the ground as I'm taken aback. It's been so long since I've let the memories in. Her hand squeezes mine, and my gaze comes back to her.

"I took it everywhere with me, never allowing it out of my sight. It became a thing. I was slightly obsessed."

She laughs lightly, stepping into me. "You loved your mother's Pixie," she defends.

I shake my head, needing to finish. "When I was six years old, two years after my mother passed, Elliot—the big idiot that he is—broke it. He didn't mean to, but I went mad, punched him in the face and swore I'd never forgive him. So... he promised me that he would replace it, that he would find me another *Pixie*."

She shakes her head, finally understanding.

"I loved my Pixie then, Nina, and I love my Pixie now," I tell her, my heart beating strong and sure in my chest.

I lift her bangle from the box and slide it onto her wrist. "This is from *me*." I spin it around so she can see the added engraving on the back.

"I promise you forever, my Pixie," she chokes out as her tears start to fall down her cheeks.

Nina

RELUCTANTLY, I left the opera house, feeling like I'll leave behind a part of my soul forever. I curl into Mason's side as we walk back to our hotel, knowing I will never get to experience it ever again in the same way.

The memory of this evening will be engraved in my mind for a lifetime.

"Mase?"

"Hmm," he hums into my hair.

"Thank you. You have no idea how much this all means to me."

"Maybe you can show me." He smiles deviously down at me.

"You have to make *love* to me first, Bossman."

"I have a lifetime for that. Tonight, I want to fuck you."

My mouth drops open, and I slap his arm playfully. "Mase, how can you be so romantic and then that?"

"Forgive me," he murmurs, taking my lips in a heated kiss and moaning against them.

We come to a standstill on the pavement, lost in the moment.

I go to pull away but he palms my cheek, pulling my bottom lip down with the pad of his thumb. "Forgive me at my worst and I will love you at yours."

"I thought you said I was perfect," I say, biting the pad of his thumb.

"Then I watched you dance," he deadpans.

"Oh my god, Mase!" I step back in shock from his words.

His head drops back, and he laughs so freely it makes my heart soar. I've never seen him so carefree.

"Baby, I'm joking. You were unlike anything I have ever seen before. I wish the whole world could have watched you on that stage, but now it's solely my memory, and that means the world to me."

I roll my eyes, pulling him by the lapels and onto my waiting mouth.

———

I FEEL emotional as the plane starts to glide down the runway; my memories of Paris locked away in a special part of my heart. Mason is on his laptop catching up with everything he missed on Friday afternoon in the office.

I've been sat watching him for the last half an hour, unable to focus on anything but him.

Yet the farther we get from the hotel suite, and as the plane hurtles down the runway, my life back in London, the reality that will forever keep me on my toes, it screams at me.

My mother, the showcase, and my possible father situation. It's everything I allowed myself to forget this weekend, and now I have to go back and face it before it drags me down.

"Nina."

My eyes find his dark ones, and the promise they hold would be enough, but he doesn't care, choosing to slay my woes with his words. "I promised you forever. I'm here. Always—no matter what."

I nod my head, not knowing how else to express what his declaration means to me. His key sits in my purse, and for the first time in forever, I feel excited about something that I haven't earned myself.

He sees me coming and snaps his laptop closed, placing it on the seat next to him as I crawl into his lap. For the first time in my life, someone wants to shield me, protect me, and I believe it.

I believe him.

Mase

She's giddy as she exits the lift and marches into the penthouse, chucking her key into the tray as she starts to unbutton her top.

"What are you doing?" I chuckle.

She fell asleep on the flight home, and since waking up has been a ball of energy.

"House rules. No clothes are permitted between the hours of five p.m. and six a.m." She smiles triumphantly as she continues to strip down.

"Unless we have guests," I add, unbuttoning my shirt.

"Of course." She nods in agreement.

I'm in my boxer briefs and about to remove my socks when she tackles me to the ground and straddles my waist.

She rocks herself over me, my cock hard as it nestles itself in the line of her pussy. A scrap of material lies between us. "Baby."

She takes her weight on her knees, allowing me room to lower my boxers. Wrapping her hand around me, she fists me, pumping me twice before sinking onto me.

"Fuck yes!" I groan.

Her hips roll over me at a tortuously slow pace, but I give

her the time she needs, letting her take the lead. It doesn't take long before her whimpers turn into deep moans. She lifts herself up and then sinks slowly back down, rotating then rolling her hips. It drives me insane. I smooth my hands over her waist and her eyes spark, a glint that tells me she knows.

I flip us, holding my arm between her lower back and the marble. My other hand lifting her leg and placing it around my waist. I sink in deeper.

"Yes. Mase."

My mouth finds hers as I move inside of her, her core already tightening around me. I rain kisses down her neck until I'm met with her breasts. I draw her nipple into my mouth, biting down on the hard nub until she starts to convulse around me, her moans fading as she loses herself in her climax.

I squeeze my eyes tight, stars invading my vision. My head bows back, and I let loose, pounding into her.

"Mine."

Thrust.

"Mine."

Thrust.

"Mine!" I still inside her, my body rippling above her as I empty myself, twitching with every spurt she draws from me.

Her head drops to the marble with a thud, and I waste no time pulling out of her and rolling to the side, unable to hold my weight any longer.

"It's not normal is it, *this?*" She looks to me, her chest heaving.

"No, Pix. It's definitely not normal. But it's our normal now."

20

Nina

AFTER TWO NIGHTS AWAY WITH MINIMAL SLEEP, I BARELY managed to make it to four o'clock before I passed out on Mason's sofa. My sofa. Yeah, that does not sound right. Not yet.

Arching my back, I stretch out my muscles on a long yawn. I have no idea how long I have been sleeping, but I already know I'll sleep like a baby tonight.

Paris has zapped me of all my energy. We didn't stop from the moment we touched down to the moment we took off again. I'm definitely booking a girls' trip after the showcase; some R and R will be just what I need.

I can feel my body telling me to slow down, but I only have two weeks until the showcase, and I can't stop now. It's everything we have worked for this year.

I knew it wouldn't be easy.

My phone starts to vibrate under my head, and I pull it out from under me. I have three missed calls from Megan and two texts. It must have been what woke me. I slide my thumb across the screen and open the messages.

Luce – Nina what time does Erin get in? Meg can't get hold of you.
Megan – Bitch where are you?

Holy shit! I completely forgot about Erin. I check the time and jump up from the sofa. It's six thirty. I've napped for hours. I look around the penthouse, wondering where Mason could be.

Taking the stairs two at a time, I hotfoot it through the bedroom, searching for him. I pull the shirt I'm wearing over my head and start to change into my jeans and white T.

How could I forget Erin flying in?

God, I am a hot mess at the minute.

I find Mason in his office, and I'm slightly out of breath as I push through the door. I pause on the threshold.

"Angel," he murmurs, not looking up from his computer.

"I forgot my friend is flying in today, I slept all afternoon and she is probably already here, and I didn't ring her, I said I would. I'm going to go home and meet her with the girls. I completely forgot."

Mase looks up at me, a deep frown in place. "Slow down. I can take you home. I just need to finish this. You'll be back home later?" he questions, and I can sense his unease.

"Yeah, I will be home later." I bite the inside of my cheek, loving how that sounds. "I can get an Uber, though. You look busy."

"Do you drive?" he asks.

"Uh, I have a licence. I haven't driven in years."

"Take the Bentley."

"No."

"Why?" he snaps back.

"I will crash your car, Mase."

"No, you won't. It's an automatic. You can't go wrong." He stands, rounding the desk and walking me out to the foyer.

WE HAVE SPENT the time he could have driven me, teaching me all the different controls. I try to take it all in, but it's a lot. "Maybe you should drive me. I don't feel comfortable driving myself."

"I will if you want me to, but you literally cannot fuck this up. I trust you."

I stare up at him from the driver's seat. I know he is busy.

I huff, straightening in the seat. "Fine, I will drive."

"Good girl." He bends down, taking my lips in a soft kiss. "Text me when you get there, okay?"

I DID IT. I drove for the first time in over five years. My legs are shaky when I step out of the Bentley. I parked around the corner of my building, not trusting myself on the busy street that would have been closer but so much harder to park on.

I text Luce and Megs, to let them know I am home, then call Erin.

"Hello." she answers.

"Erin, hey! Where are you? You must have landed?"

"Only just, I was delayed. I'm now on my way to the hotel."

"Come over. Megan and Luce are coming to mine, and we planned to get dinner together."

"Oh, I don't know. I'm shattered, Nina."

Me too, I roll my eyes. "I did not just turn down hot sex for you to wig out on me. You know where I live still."

She giggles down the phone. "Yes, okay. Give me an hour. I need to freshen up."

I'M JUST FINISHING CLEARING the draining board when Luce and Megan come laughing through the door. I smile over at them, excited to catch them up on the last couple days.

"Girls, it's a Sunday!" I eye the four bottles of wine they carry between them.

"One each." Luce shrugs.

"I'm driving, save them for tomorrow." I roll my eyes as Megan approaches me, pulling me into a hug. Lucy joins a few seconds later, and I frown into their shoulders as they sandwich me in.

"What is going on?"

"We," Lucy looks to Megan, "had the most incredible evening Saturday night. Like out of this world."

"Luce pulled." Megan nods enthusiastically.

"You did?" I laugh. It sounds like we're back in school.

Lucy flushes red, and I become desperate for details. "Just a kiss?" I question, knowing she isn't one for a one-night stand.

"Nope, she brought him here," Megan offers.

My mouth drops open as Luce scoots around the sofa with a bottle of red. "Luce?"

"I was going to tell you."

"Tell me now," I interrupt.

"So Scarlet came out with us. She met us at Groulx for food and was going to go home straight after because of her dad, but then Vinny texted and said he was fine for a few more hours and not to rush home. So we went out."

"Scarlet was steaming. She's a crazy chick," Megan adds.

"And the guy?" I ask.

"Was just a guy."

"Bullshit." There's a knock at the door, and I squint my eyes at Lucy, wondering what is up with her.

Pulling open my apartment door, I'm met with the effortless beauty that is Erin O'Connor.

"Erin, it's so good to see you!" I smile as I pull her into a hug, her fiery red hair getting stuck on my gloss.

"It's great to see you too, sweetie. You're looking great," she tells me, her eyes scanning me from top to toe.

"Come in. The girls are here."

"Hey!" they both sing, standing to hug her.

"How was the flight?" Luce asks.

"Long, it never gets any easier."

"Damn, you look good," Megan tells her.

She's right. Erin *is* looking good; everything about her scream's health and wealth.

"Yeah, I've been working on me lately." She smooths her hair, giving us a small smile.

"It shows," I tell her, checking out her designer bag dangling on her arm.

"So, how long are you here for?" Luce asks, looking at Erin from the other side of the coffee table.

We decided to order in Chinese. The girls couldn't stay long with Lucy having an early start in the morning, and I want to get back to Mason's so I can sleep. Even after my nap I am knackered.

"Two weeks," says Erin, sucking in a noodle.

"Your mum?" I ask, "How is she? Is someone with her, or is she okay on her own now?" I give her a sad smile.

She drops her fork and I regret my question immediately.

I've made her uncomfortable. I know how much she has struggled with her mother's health—I shouldn't have brought it up.

"Uh, yeah, she is doing better, actually."

"That's good. Do you think you could come home soon?" I ask.

"No," she looks into her container. "I think I want to stay in Australia now."

I frown as I watch her, but she doesn't meet my eyes.

Why do I feel like she is lying?

"I don't blame you. Aus looks good on you," Megan says, clinking her glass with Erin's.

"Thanks," she smiles. "Hey, you!" she perks up as she turns to look at me, changing the subject and the atmosphere instantly. "Are you going to tell me about this hot sex you are missing out on tonight?"

"Oh, you have no idea," Lucy waves her fork in the air, her eyes closed and a dreamy look on her face. "He is *fit*!"

"Nuh-uh, you can go first today." I eye Lucy.

"Oh, fuck off already. It was just sex!"

"In my apartment! And it's never just sex with you."

"This time it was. I don't even know his name."

"You slut!" I shout, my mouth dropping wide as the girls all fall into a fit of giggles.

THE GIRLS HAVE NOT LONG LEFT, but Erin is still here. She's stood at my sink washing the few dishes we used, even though I told her she didn't have to.

"Thank you for this evening. It's been just what I needed," she tells me, smiling back over her shoulder.

"Of course, it's good to have you home. Where are you staying anyway?"

"The Hilton."

Shit. That's expensive. "Perfect, it will be nice to have another female around the studio for a change, that's for sure." I force a smile.

"I bet. How old are the boys again?"

"Too young for you!" I laugh, and she shakes her head, tutting. "Erin, I'm sorry for bringing up your mum before, I didn't mean to upset you."

"Don't be silly, it's fine."

"I know, but I don't believe you. I think you were lying earlier."

"What?" She freezes, her hands pausing on the glass she is washing.

"You don't want to live in Australia permanently, do you? If you could come home you would, right?"

She drops the glass onto the drainer and turns to me, a

sad smile on her face. "In a heartbeat." She looks to the ground, rolling her lips as if she wants to say more. "Sorry, Nina, I better go. I need to get some sleep before tomorrow, I have so much to get sorted over the next couple weeks."

"It must be so hard, but it will get better, I'm sure. You managed to take this trip. You will make it back here, one day." I squeeze her arm as she reaches for her fur coat.

"Yeah, maybe." Her lips thin into a tight-lipped grimace. She walks to the door but pauses when she gets to it.

Her throat works on a swallow as her eyes find mine. "Sorry, Nina. I hope you don't think I'm being rude." And then she leaves.

Her obvious discomfort leaves me feeling awful. I wish I kept my mouth shut, but I could tell she wasn't being honest, and I was right–she doesn't want to live in Australia. I think it's amazing that she has given up so much to help her mum.

I finish washing up the dishes, then send Mase a message telling him I'm on my way home.

The Bentley is a welcome distraction from the worry for Erin, and instead of overthinking all the things I wish I didn't say to her, I am forced to concentrate on the beasty machine that is Mason's car.

Mason's *very* expensive car.

The drive home is plain sailing, and I even put the radio on for the last five minutes of my drive as my confidence starts to grow. It really is an easy car to drive.

I'm about five minutes from Mason's when my phone starts to ring, and I answer without looking—too afraid of taking my eyes from the road—then switch it to speaker.

"Hello?"

"Hey, it's Scar!"

"Hey! I'm just driving." I tell her on impulse. "I'm actually in the Bentley."

"Mason let you drive the Bentley?" She's shocked.

I chuckle, wiggling my bum into the seat. "I know. I wouldn't trust me either."

Her laugh echoes through the car, making me smile. "So, I wanted to know if you would do lunch with me tomorrow? Dad has a two-hour appointment which he refuses to let me go to; he's a stubborn fool."

"Of course, I'd love to! How is he?"

I mentally try to remember what classes I have tomorrow.

"He's good. Seems upbeat about it all. I just hope they find a transplant."

"A transplant?" I frown.

"Yeah, Mason didn't tell you?"

"No." I bite my bottom lip in worry.

"Typical." She huffs, and I hear her shuffling on the other end of the phone. "Dad needs a liver transplant, he is high on the list, though, and they think it will be within the next six months."

"Wow. That's big." My shoulders drop as disappointment floods me. Why would Mase not tell me? "What's his appointment for tomorrow?"

"Blood tests, I think he said. He refused to have me sit and wait the full two hours, so I said I would drop him off and meet you. If you were free."

Two hours for blood tests? That seems like a long time.

I jolt forward in the seat, my body lurching into the steering wheel before it's thrown back into the leather.

"What? Nina? What was that noise?"

"Oh my god!" I panic, looking over the steering wheel to see the bonnet crumpled.

"Nina?"

"Scarlet."

"No... Nina. Tell me you haven't?"

"Fuck, Scarlet," I cry.

"You haven't, tell me you haven't."

"I have."

"I EXPECTED WORSE." Scarlet shrugs at me as the paramedic passes me a form.

I stare down at the front of Mason's Bentley—which is now embedded in the back of a black cab.

Luckily it was empty and the driver is fine.

"Worse? How does this get any worse?" My phone rings for the sixteenth time and I reject the call.

"I will call him," she states, pulling out her phone.

I stare at her wide-eyed, shaking my head at her. "Scar, no!"

"Mason. I'm with Nina."

I palm my forehead, wondering whether I should start running now.

MY STOMACH ROLLS as the Audi approaches, and I'm surprised I manage to stay on my feet. I can't believe I crashed his car. His Bentley.

My body shakes with adrenaline, and I know I'm only

moments away from tears. My emotions bubble to boiling point when I see him step from the car.

He doesn't say a word to anyone. He strides across the asphalt, walking past the Bentley as if it's not even there —broken.

Jesus, I crashed his car.

My feet leave the ground as he wraps his arms around me, shaking his head as it burrows deep into my neck. "What are you trying to do to me, Pix."

"I'm so sorry. Your car. I don't know wha—"

"The car doesn't matter," he says, pulling back and shaking his head. "Why didn't you call me? It's been over an hour since you texted me."

"I thought you'd be mad."

"Mad? I am fucking livid, Nina. All I ask is to know you are safe." His voice shakes as his anger rises. "Why the fuck didn't you call me before?" he bellows at Scarlet.

"Mason, calm down," Vinny says, stepping forward.

"She's fine, big brother. Just chill, okay?" Scarlet says, giving him a pointed look as her eyes dart to me.

"Chill? I would be fucking chill if one of you bothered to call me."

Mase

"MASON!" Scarlet whisper-shouts at me.

I follow her line of sight and find Nina swiping at her tear-stained cheeks.

Fuck.

"Nina," I soothe, pulling her into my arms.

"I'm so sorry." She sniffles into my chest, her body trembling.

I look up to the night sky willing myself to calm down.

She is safe.

A paramedic approaches us and takes some papers from Nina, and he checks them over then tears off the bottom piece. "So I'm happy for you to go home and rest without needing to go to the hospital, but please call 111 if you feel any of the symptoms listed within the next forty-eight hours, okay?"

"Yes, okay. Thank you," Nina tells him.

Vinny looks over at me in question, and I give him a nod. "Come on, love."

He wraps his arm around her and walks her to the Audi.

"You're sure she doesn't need to go to hospital?" I ask the paramedic as he starts to remove his gloves.

"The car took the brunt of the impact." He looks at the crumpled front bumper. "She should be fine, but as I said, call if you have any concerns. She is pretty shaken up but otherwise is fit and healthy." He nods to me before climbing into the back of the ambulance.

I start to empty the Bentley of all my belongings before it gets towed away. Scarlet stands at my side as I open the boot.

A suitcase stuffed full lies in the bed.

"She said you asked her to move in." Scarlet smiles.

"Yeah," I say, staring down at the small case. *Does she have more than this?*

"Dad has an appointment tomorrow."

"Not now, Scar, please." I look at her, running my hand down over my face. "Just not tonight."

"When then, Mase? You didn't even tell Nina!"

"Tell her what?" I frown.

"Jesus Christ. About Dad! The transplant!"

"I was going to."

She rolls her eyes, knowing I wouldn't have. "It's about time you started taking his health more seriously. Before it's too late." She stalks off towards her car, and I slam the boot.

Nina seems to have pulled herself together once I slide into the Audi. I look to Vinny in the rearview mirror, and he gives me a warm smile that tells me she's okay.

"Come here," I whisper, pulling her onto my lap and breathing her in.

Nina

WORDS AREN'T NEEDED on the elevator ride up to the penthouse. Mason's hold on me seems to soothe the adrenaline that invades me as much as my embrace diminishes his stress.

'I only ask to know that you are safe.'

Guilt eats at me for not calling him sooner.

"I need a shower," I tell him, not releasing him.

I don't want to let him go.

As if he understands, he takes my hand and leads me up the stairs. He pulls me into his en suite, leaning in to turn on the spray as I sit on the edge of the bath.

"It's late, baby. Let's get you showered and in bed. Do you feel okay, still?"

I nod and stand, my body aching as I go to lift my top, but

he's already there. He pulls my T-shirt up over my arms, then removes my bra.

Leaning forward, he kisses my forehead, pausing with his lips there. "I was so fucking scared. Petrified that something had happened. I thought the worst and then Scarlet called and for the first time in a long time, I didn't feel in control."

"I'm sorry."

"Shh," he murmurs against my head. "It's not your fault."

He reaches between us, unbuttoning my jeans and shimmying them down my legs as his lips find my neck. He moves down my body, nipping at my breasts and stomach as he lowers to his knees.

His fingers hook into my lace underwear, and I frown as his eyes widen.

"Nina, you're fucking bleeding!"

He kneels, staring at my centre, and I step back, looking down at myself. I have a small patch of blood on my underwear.

"Oh my god! Get out!" I panic, using my hands to cover myself.

"I will call an ambulance." He stands and runs out of the bathroom.

"What? No, wait, Mase! It's just my period."

"What?" He comes back into the room with his face screwed up.

"I'm fine. It's just my—"

"I heard you the first time." He grasps the back of his neck, squeezing his eyes closed. I stand watching him, not wanting to laugh but unable to control it.

"It's not fucking funny, woman."

"Imagine if you called an ambulance." I snort. "'*Excuse me can I get an ambulance my girlfriend got her period*'."

His hands find his hips, his lip tipping up on one side, and it only makes me laugh harder.

Reaching up, he grasps his T-shirt behind the neck and pulls it over his head, rendering me stupid as his solid muscles ripple with the move.

Mother nature, you are a bitch.

"What are you doing?" I ask.

"Shower. Now," he tells me, nodding towards the running water.

"Uh, I don't think so. Get out."

He ignores me, stepping into me and lifting me in his arms. He walks us into the shower with me still in my underwear, and him in his jeans.

I'm lowered to the ground, but he keeps me close, my breasts pressed against his solid chest.

"The T-shirt couldn't get wet but fuck the jeans, right?" I smile, teasing him.

"House rules. No smiling on your period." I throw my head back and laugh, then he adds, "You know what it gets you."

"Okay, Bossman. No smiling." I school my features, leaning in to kiss my beautiful man.

His hands drift over my hips, pulling my thong down my legs. I step out of it, and he bends to pick it up, discarding it to the back of the shower. Picking up the soap, he starts to lather his hands as he rounds me.

Starting at my back, he rubs his hands expertly into my muscles, using the soap suds to glide his hands over my pebbled skin. I moan as he reaches my mid-back, the muscles feeling tender there. He moves lower, spending time to massage each leg, not missing an inch of me.

His front moulds to my back, and I sigh. The feel of his erection against my back makes my body hum with want and need.

"This isn't fair," I moan.

His lips fall to my neck as his large hands capture my breasts, brushing over each nipple and pulling them between his skilled fingers. He spends the most time on my breasts, growling each time I involuntarily arch back into him.

"I love you," he tells me, tenderly kissing my temple.

21

Nina

I TRUDGE UP THE STUDIO STAIRS FEELING AWFUL. MY BACK IS sore—presumably from the crash, and my head pounds. Vinny stopped on the way here to get me water and paracetamol, and Mase made me promise to call if I felt off in the day.

As I reach the top step, I spot Erin in the office looking nothing less than perfect. Rolling my eyes, I walk into the room, feeling like I have been dragged through a bush backwards. "How do you look so fresh after your flight and then a late night?" I ask, falling into the seat opposite the desk.

"Nina, your head, what happened?" she worries, eyeing the bruise on my brow.

"Don't ask," I say, shaking my head. She doesn't need to worry about me, and I don't need to relive the guilt of crashing Mason's car.

"I love what you've done with the place. It's looking incredible. You never told me how big the gym was. I expected a couple of treadmills."

"Yeah, it's getting there. I love it here really. Sorry, I must seem like a right grumpy cow. I got my period last night, and it's hit me hard."

"Ugh, cue the car crash." She laughs. "I'm a raving bitch on my period."

I laugh at the irony in her comment. "Oh, you have no idea."

MY MORNING ONLY GETS WORSE. Both my one-on-ones were late, which now only gives me twenty minutes until my next class. I call Scarlet and tell her I can't meet, but that the girls will be free if she still wants to do lunch.

I am wiping down the mirrors when Erin pops her head around the door. "Oh, thank god you've stopped. You're one busy lady!"

"Don't, I'm starved."

"I have half a sandwich left if you want it? Cheese and pickle."

"Yes! Can I? I don't know how I will make it to five o'clock."

"Sure, hold up."

She disappears, returning seconds later with the sandwich.

"Thank you, Erin." I take it from her, biting into it immediately.

She smiles, but a frown creases her brow.

"What?" I wipe at my mouth, thinking I must have pickle there, and my cheeks heat.

"Nothing," she says. "Your mum called. I wrote down the

number, it's in the office. She said she has been trying to reach you, and the phone had like fifty-something messages on it."

"Oh, thanks, sorry about that."

How did she get the studio number? I haven't answered a call from my mum in weeks, yet she rings every other day like clockwork. I promised myself I'd wait until after the showcase to deal with both my mum and my potential dad situation.

"Don't apologise," she says, waving me off.

Her eyes roam the studio, falling on the piano. She walks over to it, gliding her petite, pale hand over the top of it. An aching primal urge wracks through me, and I want to tell her not to touch it, which is odd, considering it's hers.

She turns to me and smiles tight. "I better get back to it."

"Of course. Shout if you need me."

She leaves the studio, closing the door behind her, and I turn back to the piano and stare at it, wondering why she has it here. Leaning in, I run my pointer over the initials I've traced a hundred times before. EML.

Mase

I NEED to stop allowing my friends in my office for lunch.

And my receptionist.

Although the bastard seems to be growing on me.

"Oh, your poor girlfriend, it sounds petrifying," George mutters around a mouthful of taco.

"Fucking hell, Lowell. How much is that costing you?" Lance asks.

I lean back in my chair, perplexed. "No idea; I don't even want to know to be honest."

"And Nina, she was okay?" Charlie asks.

"Yeah, she had a small bruise on her head, and she is sore, but otherwise okay."

"Jesus, mate." Elliot shakes his head. "Good 'I can make your head feel better sex' though, am I right?" He grins, and I flip him off.

"I had an accident once, Mason. I was on my way to Alton Towers and my—"

"We don't give a shit about your accident on the way to Alton Towers, George," Lance tells him, cutting him off.

Lance can be a proper prick sometimes, but he's a solid friend. He knows more than the boys do about me, and the fact he hasn't shared that information confirms that I can trust him. The boys would be pissed if they knew I kept things from them, Elliot especially, but some things are better for everyone left unsaid.

"Don't listen to Sullivan, George. What was it you were going to say?" I tell him, shaking my head at Lance with a smirk.

"So I was on my way to Alt—"

My phone starts to ring, cutting him off again. "Sorry, Georgie." I accept the call and raise my phone to my ear. "Vin?"

"Mason. Nina just called, she isn't feeling well. Just a headache, but I'm going to go get her."

She still has a headache. Is that normal? "Where are you?"

"Downstairs, about to leave."

I pinch my lip between my fingers, contemplating

whether I can blow off my afternoon. I look to Elliot and he frowns. He's been in almost every day for the past two weeks and I don't feel as anxious about leaving with him here like I normally would.

"Give me five, Vinny. I'm coming with you."

I hang up, standing and buttoning my suit jacket. "Sorry, boys."

NINA IS WAITING at the curb when we pull up at the studio. I hop out and take her bag from her.

"Hey, baby. You look pale."

Her shoulders drop. "Great!"

I lean in and kiss her forehead. "You're still the most beautiful girl in the world, Pix."

She rolls her eyes and winces.

"We're going to the hospital, get your head checked."

"I agree, you're questionable to even myself, but I don't need my head tested," she sasses, making me relax a little with her cheek.

I round the car and stop to put her bag in the boot before slipping into the back seat next to her. Lifting her hand to my lips, I kiss her knuckles, and she leans back in the seat, clenching her eyes shut.

"Just take me home, Mase. I need to sleep off my headache, and then I will be fine," she says without opening her eyes.

I glance at Vinny in the mirror, and he shrugs at a loss.

Helpful. Thanks, Vin.

NINA HAS BEEN asleep for hours. I worked from her bedside, hoping she would wake up feeling better after an hour or so. She didn't.

After the fourth hour, I decided to go down to my gym, burning off the pent-up energy I had from being sat around. It didn't work.

I cooked us dinner, following a recipe from the cookbook Scar got me last Christmas—it was alright. I ate alone at my dining table, contemplating how long before I could wake her up without feeling bad.

On the sixth hour, I watched a documentary on *Bear Grylls* in the jungle. The guy's a savage.

On the seventh hour, I Googled head injuries, and pages of information later I was adamant she was dead or dying.

Taking the stairs two at a time, I burst through the door, finding her curled on her side, sleeping peacefully.

I can't help myself though, placing my hand on her back to check she is in fact breathing. Letting out a sigh of relief, I remind myself never to believe everything I read on Google. With nothing else left to do, I take her small hand in mine and lay with her, hoping that she will wake up soon.

Nina

WHEN I WAKE, my head is clear, and I roll to my back to find it's dark out, the moon the only lighting in the room. Mason is lying beside me in a T-shirt and shorts, his hand locked in mine.

I smile at the beautiful specimen before me, feeling lucky to have him come into my life.

"Mase," I whisper, but he doesn't answer.

His brow is creased. Even in sleep, he doesn't relax. My forever brooding beast. I trace his lips with my finger—he doesn't flinch.

"I love you too," I tell him.

I FOUND leftover chicken pie in the oven and wolfed it down in a matter of minutes. It was delicious and exactly what I needed, and I wondered while I ate it who the hell made it. Can Mason cook? *Why didn't I know this about him?*

I don't feel tired, and with the unwelcome thoughts of my mother plaguing me, I decide to do what I always do when everything gets too much. I get lost in the only other world I know.

I flick through my phone, deciding on Jesse Ware "Say You Want Me,". And the surround sound has the music blistering through me, setting me in motion.

I CAN FEEL him watching me, and as he steps towards me, I spin, knowing it will bring us toe to toe.

"You're feeling better?" He smiles, holding me.

"So much better." I brush his nose with mine, leaning back when I realise I'm all sweaty.

He pulls me back to him by the shirt. "I love you," he tells me, taking my lips in a sweet kiss.

And it's like the first time all over again. The way my heart beats almost painfully, and the ache that seeps through my veins, and to the tips of my fingers. It's only for a split second, but that zap of energy reminds me that I am alive. I've never felt more alive than when I'm in his arms.

"You like this spot?" he asks, flashing a devilishly hand-some smile.

I'd been dancing in the space between the sofas and the dining table. It's a wide-open space and looks out over the London skyline.

It's where I danced for him the first time.

"I do. I was going to suggest putting something here, being my house now as well." My lips pull up in a smile, and I wrap my arms around his neck as I tease him. "But I suppose I could keep it for dancing."

"I like you dancing in this space. Makes it feel special again," he says between kisses.

"Well then, let's keep it for dancing."

22

Mase

NINA IS STILL ASLEEP WHEN I GET IN FROM MY MORNING RUN, and although I should probably wake her, I know that once I do, she will be back to her nonstop self and, much to my annoyance, off to the studio to meet with Joey fucking Wilson.

I don't care that Charlie came up with nothing. The prick has issues, and I don't trust him around her.

Instead of waking her up, I opt for a shower.

LEANING OVER THE BED, I take her lips in a soft kiss, her eyes fluttering open moments later, followed by the most beautiful smile, showcasing her dimples

"Angel."

"Hmmm, morning," she says, stirring in my arms.

She stretches against me, and I can't help myself, dipping

my head down to take her nipple in my mouth. Her hands lift to my head, running through the damp strands, and it's the best fucking feeling. The small moments like this—just the two of us.

"Can we stay here all day?" she hums, and it goes straight to my cock.

I lift my head from her chest, smiling wide. "Fuck, yes!"

"I'm kidding." She giggles, pushing my head away. I turn, nuzzling into her hand to place a kiss on her wrist, just below her bangle.

"What time is it?" she asks.

I hide my face in her breasts. "Just gone eight thirty," I tell her, with not an ounce of guilt.

"What?! Fuck!"

I roll my eyes and sigh, taking her place in bed as she jolts out from under me. I fall to my back, watching as she tries to rush to get ready, but she only moves shit around from one spot to another, not actually doing anything.

"Why didn't you wake me?"

"You had an accident. I never should've allowed you to go to work yesterday."

She bends, picking up her sock, and I get the perfect view of her lace-clad ass. Spotting her other sock already on the bed, I snatch it up.

"Shit! I have nothing ready for Joey." She starts to pull on her bra, and as she looks down to fasten the straps, I toss the sock to the door. "I didn't even clean the studio!"

"That's a shame," I say, shrugging when she eyes me suspiciously.

"You fucking did this on purpose, didn't you?"

"I think you are more than capable of setting an alarm, angel."

She pulls on her first sock, then starts riffling through the sheets for the other.

"Fuck!"

"Over there." I nod to the door, trying to be helpful.

She rushes over, bending down and snatching it up off the floor. "I am so flipping late." I grin wide as I get another eyeful.

Fucking perfect.

"I will text Vin," I tell her.

"You know, I'm pissed with you right now. You knew I had to be up. No sex for you tonight, Bossman."

"I wouldn't have got sex tonight anyway. You have... issues." I wave my hand in the direction of her nether regions.

"Issues? My period, you mean. And it's rarely for more than two to three days. I stopped last night," she answers smartly.

My mouth drops wide, and I sit up in the bed. "And you're only fucking telling me this now?"

"You could have woken me up like you normally do." She shrugs. "You'd have at least got your dick sucked. You need to learn to pick your battles, and Joey... isn't one of them." She pops her brow as if she has it all figured out.

She slips from the room with her tank halfway over her head.

I give her thirty seconds, purely because it's all I can physically allow.

"Hey!" I call out as I jog down the stairs. She turns, her hand already on the elevator button.

I pull her to me by the waist, and she comes willingly, her

arms grasping mine as I lean down and take her pouty lips with my own. Her back arches, and I lift her from the ground, my cock jumping to attention as her body moulds to mine.

"I love you," I tell her.

Her body goes lax, her smile not faltering. "I love you too," she murmurs against my mouth.

My eyes blink closed as I absorb her words. Three words that ground me so easily, bringing me back down and rooting me to earth.

"I'll see you at eleven," I tell her.

She nods her head at me, a sweet innocent smile on my not so innocent girl's face.

Nina

RUSHING THROUGH THE GYM, I throw my hand up at Henry in greeting, knowing I have a million things to do before Joey arrives. My heart feels like it is pumping a million beats a minute as I poke my head in Erin's office door, but she isn't there. She is either late like me or already out on a meeting.

I shoot the girls a text and tell them I will meet them for lunch, but I may be late.

The studio isn't in the worst shape, but it's not immaculate either. The floor-to-ceiling mirrors are the bane of my life. I spend hours on them every week, and they never seem to stay clean.

I sweep and mop the floors, wipe the windows, the mirrors, and then dust the benches off to finish. It's the best I can do with the little time I have.

Henry finds me in the staff room as I'm putting away the mop bucket.

"Anderson, you look a hot mess."

"Henry, don't. I have a photographer coming in today."

"To take pictures of what?" he asks, frowning as he unboxes a delivery.

"Me!"

His eyes lift, scanning my body and he cringes. "It's not that bad, is it?" I ask, looking down at myself, my voice rising in panic.

"No." He shakes his head, clearly sensing I'm a donkey on the edge. "You look great."

"Fuck off, Henry," I say, storming from the room. "Asshole."

"What did I do?" he shouts after me.

IT'S TEN TO ELEVEN, and neither Mason nor Joey are here yet.

Nothing I do seems to ease my anxiety, and with Henry downstairs and Joey on his way, I am really freaking anxious. I didn't think about Henry being here. Mason has come to blows with both men, and now I'm going to have them —*together*—under one roof?

Yeah, I didn't think this through.

Sticking the last bobby pin in my hair, I check myself out in the mirror. I am wearing a plain black long-sleeved leotard, I found it at the bottom of my gym bag, and it passed the sniff test, so it was a go. It's the best I could do given this morning's sabotage by Mason.

A knock sounds on the studio doors, and I instantly know it's Joey.

Mason wouldn't knock.

Walking over, I open the door, finding Joey struggling with a handful of different shaped bags on each arm.

"Hey! Come in," I tell him, taking one of the many bags he is carrying. "Here, let me help you. God, what do you have in here?"

"Thanks, Nina, and you'd be surprised." He makes it just inside the door and drops down half the bags gently to the floor. Shaking out his arm, he looks around the studio. "Wow, this place is huge. It's all yours?"

"Yep! The gym too," I tell him proudly.

"That's mad. You're killing it; it's better than I expected, that's for sure. No offence."

"None taken." I chuckle.

"The lighting is great in here."

"Yeah, the windows are a godsend for lighting, but come summer, it's stifling in here. They open like a centimetre, and that's it."

"They normally only do that for crazy people." He laughs, dropping down the last of the bags. He stands to his full height, and I take him in.

He has on dark jeans with a long baggy vest, his lean but defined frame on display. His hair is a dark mess of perfection, although I can imagine it's annoying as hell keeping it out of his eyes. He seems to be constantly pushing it back.

"I haven't seen you and the girls at The Pearl for a while."

"Ah no, we haven't been out as much. We tend to go hard after payday and then struggle for the last two weekends."

"I get that." He nods as he grins wide.

"So, my boyfriend was going to pop in later. You have met him—Mason." I cringe.

"The guy from the café?" he questions, clearly surprised.

"I was hoping the two of you would just get on with it for the sake of the photos."

I see his nostrils flare, and my stomach drops. This was a bad idea.

"Of course. I am here for work, Nina." He says as if he's reminding himself, bending down as he starts to unpack his bags.

I THOUGHT it would be different angles and poses, but Joey had me dance instead. He said it was the best way to catch me naturally, and I have to admit, it's been kind of fun.

Some of the shots Joey showed me are unreal. He has an obvious talent for photography, and I'm surprisingly excited to see the finished prints.

I'm sitting drinking my water when he comes to sit next to me, his gaze focused on his camera.

"How long have you been studying photography?" I ask.

"Two years. I'm in my final year now."

"How old are you?" I frown.

"Twenty-eight, I didn't start straight away."

"How come?"

"I used to look after my mum when she was sick," he says, completely emotionless, his thumbs flicking through the photos on the camera.

"You used to?"

"Yeah. So can we just do one more song? Maybe in front

of the mirrors, even with me in the shot. It will add to the image we are creating."

What is it with me lately, always opening my big mouth and making everyone uncomfortable? Although Joey doesn't seem uncomfortable—more preoccupied. But still, it's none of my business.

"Of course, I really am loving this." I beam at him, trying to lighten the mood.

"I can tell. Look at that smile," he tells me, chuckling, and I drop my head embarrassed.

Cool it, Nina.

"So, when you're dancing, I want your profile in the reflection."

I nod, moving to stand in position with my head dipped, still feeling silly at my over-the-top enthusiasm.

"No, your profile," he says, walking to me and planting his hands on my waist. He turns me to face the mirror. "Profile to the mirror."

Joey's fingers flex into the silky material at my hips as the studio door clicks shut. Mason stands just inches away, his eyes wild.

"Mase," I say in surprise, watching as he stands unmoving.

He seems to have a laser focus on me. It's like he is seeing me for the first time, his eyes boring dangerously into my own, questioning.

He steps back, flicking his gaze to Joey.

"Are you okay, Mase?" I try, but my heart drops as his eyes only blaze straight through me, a hard expression masking his face.

"Nina, I have some things I need to get to. Are you okay

here?" He starts to leave, and I move for him.

"Mase?"

I jog after him, the studio door banging closed behind me, but he's already halfway down the stairs, his suit-clad back moving farther and farther away from me.

My shoulders drop as disappointment fills me.

What the hell?

I expected more.

Mase

I SLIDE into the back of the Audi, slamming the door and dropping my head between my knees.

"FUCK!" I shout, the sound vibrating off the windows.

"Mason?" Vinny mutters.

Lifting my head, I place my forearms on my knees, staring down at the note in my trembling hands.

Nina,

I had to go home to Mum.

I will call when I can.

Erin.

I'd know it fucking anywhere, and everything I thought I'd feel seeing it again is an afterthought, my only concern being Nina.

"Mase."

My mind is a cluster of thoughts, each one more confusing than the next, and each one threatening to rise up from a buried past and pull me down with them.

"The woman who owns Nina's studio, Erin. Get me all you have."

He gives me a tight nod. "Home or The Montwell?"

"Office."

Nina

"HONESTLY, Mase might as well have not shown up at all. I think I'd prefer him to cock his leg and piss on me than do nothing."

All the girls laugh, but Scarlet screws her face up at me. "That's disgusting," she says.

I smile over at her. "Sorry, Scar. But he was a complete ass. He just left. I presumed he was acting a jealous ass as usual, but he left me there with Joey. It made no sense." I frown as I go over it in my head, not understanding his reaction.

"Didn't he storm in here when you met with Joey the first time for coffee?" Megan asks.

"Yes!" I throw my hands up. "Exactly, what happened to that guy and why do I want him back?" I laugh. My phone starts ringing, and I pull it from my bag.

"It's Erin," I tell them, waving my phone at them. I've called her five times in the last hour, she was supposed to meet us for lunch but hasn't shown.

"Erin, hey! Where are you?"

"Nina, did you not get my note?"

"Note? What note?" I frown.

"I left it on my desk, I had to go home to my mum."

"No! Erin, you were here a day."

What the hell?

"She's sick again. I will be in touch, okay?"

"Erin—" I check my phone to find she has already gone.

"She went home?" Lucy asks.

"Yeah. Her mum is sick again."

"That's shit," Megan says, sipping her coffee.

"Yeah, it is." I frown.

Mase

"Where the fuck is Vinny!"

I'm about to call him when George comes barrelling through my office doors, his infuriating smile in place.

"Mason. Have you eaten today? You came back from Nina's photography session rather quick. Either way, I ordered you in, just in case." he tells me with a wink.

"I'm fine, fucking knock or use the damn intercom!" I yell, taking my frustration out on him and then feeling like a dick for it instantly.

"Of course," he says, unaffected by my words. "I put an extra sugar in." He nods, and I know he is trying to suss me out. He places the cup of tea on the edge of my desk.

"Get out. Please, George," I say, deflated, running my hands through my hair and not having the energy to deal with him.

VINNY DOESN'T ARRIVE until gone four, and he enters my office too fucking calmly, taking his time to close the door behind him.

His grim expression as he faces me has my gut twisting.

I've had too much time to think.

"What took you so long?" I hold my hand out for the file he has in his hand.

He chucks it to my desk, and I flip open the first page before it has even stopped moving. "Mason."

"What's this?" I hold up the first sheet of paper.

He lifts his chin, swallowing thickly. "A death certificate."

"Whose?"

"Erin O'Connor's. She died six weeks ago."

"What? No." I frown. "Erin O'Connor was with Nina Sunday night!"

He drops his head, and when he lifts it again, there is regret in his eyes.

"Vin."

His shoulders drop, and I know.

It's *her.*

"Fucking tell me, Vinny!"

"Cara Langer." He steps forward, pulling a sheet of paper from the file. "She bought the studio a week previous to you meeting her. She changed every detail that could trace it to her and put it in a different name. Honestly, I don't know how I missed it."

My head spins, my eyes pinching tight as I bring my hand up to my forehead.

How has this happened?

"Cara. She owns Nina's studio?"

"I'm so sorry, Mason."

Fuck! I link my hands behind my head and turn my back to Vinny.

She can't be there. I can't have her there.

I grit my teeth, closing my eyes as pain slices through me. "Sell it."

"What? You can't sell it when it doesn't belong to you."

"I can and I will. I can't have it linked back to Nina. Imagine how it would look. Have it put on the market for a quick and quiet sale."

"No."

My head snaps around, my eyes wild as I try to control my anger. "You'll fucking sell it!" My fist comes down on my desk, and he recoils. Shame fills me, but I don't stop, too far gone. Everything is too far gone. "You think you can stand there and tell me fucking no, Vin? I pay you to do a job, so prove to me you can do it," I spit.

"She would never forgive you, you know. Dancing is her life."

My heart throbs. Actual physical pain that runs deep in my chest. "What choice do I have?" I say at a loss. "I can't let her be connected to this. I won't allow it."

"You're making a huge mistake. You want to sell her studio, then you do it yourself." He shakes his head at me, placing the sheet of paper back on the desk. His fist clenches white against it, and I know there's no persuading him.

"George, get me Lance Sullivan," I say through the intercom, rolling my tongue over my teeth as my knee bounces in agitation.

"On it now, boss!" George buzz's back.

The keys to the Audi hit my desk, followed by the set of keys that belong to everything I own. "That's me, Mase. I'm done here." Vinny leans in, and my nostrils flare, my eyes burning as I stare down at the carpet, unable to hold his eyes.

My chin trembles and I clench my jaw to stop it.

"Sixteen years, and I have never been more disappointed in you." He rights himself, then leaves my office, not looking back.

"FUUCKK!" I roar, my chest rising and falling as I try to control my emotions.

Picking up the mug off my desk, I launch it across the room, shattering the glasses and jug of water laid out across the coffee table. Not satisfied or feeling remotely better, I walk over, flipping the table with my foot and smashing it to pieces.

Everything was too good, too easy.

I should have known.

"Lowell? What the fuck, man?" Lance mutters as he steps into my office, eyeing the mess. "What's going on?"

"Cara—she's here in London. Fucking find her or find me someone who can."

"What? Is she fucking stupid?"

"Turns out she isn't as stupid as we once thought."

23

Nina

THE SUN IS OUT IN FULL FORCE WHEN I LEAVE THE ELM, SO even though I am cutting it fine, I opt to walk instead of calling Vinny. I pull the straps of my vest top off my shoulders as the warmth seeps into my skin.

Mason seems to be ignoring my messages, and I refuse to ring him. I'd rather save that argument for later. I can't believe he just walked out when he said he would be there. I thought he knew that it was for my benefit just as much as his —I wanted him there. He told me that Joey had an allegation made against him in the past, but I never pressed him on it. He said it never came to anything, but somewhere in the back of my mind I wonder what happened.

I felt like I saw a completely different side to Joey today. If I'm being fair, then that's all I can judge him on. He seems harmless.

With the sun on my back, I head off in the direction of my studio, ready for my last session of the day with my girls.

Once in the studio, I set the mats up for the girls and make sure everything is ready for my class, then I go to the office to find the note Erin said she left me.

I scan the desk and move the files, but nothing shows up. I will have to ask Henry later, but there's no way he would have come up even if he found it.

———

"Girls, you do that in two weeks' time, and you will be taking home the trophy. That was insane!"

"We will, you mean," Bethany, the eldest of the group, calls over at me.

I smile, pulling her into my side. "I'm proud of you, girls. Honestly, this past year you have come so far. I'm feeling quite emotional." I start to flap my hand in front of my face as the girls all stand awkwardly watching me. "You guys head out, don't mind me. We have a session Friday now. Don't overdo it at the gym, okay?"

As always, the girls help me to put the mats away before leaving. I'm just packing up my things when my phone rings.

It's Mason.

A gut feeling tells me not to answer. I don't know if I have the energy to fight tonight. But I relent, accepting the call and bringing the phone to my ear.

"Nina?"

"Yeah, I'm here," I tell him, resting my back against the piano.

"I'm sorry about earlier. I wanted to be there, but Elliot needed me at the office, and I've been flat out ever since."

I roll my eyes even though he can't see me. Does he think

I'm stupid? "You can just say you didn't like the fact I was with Joey, you know. Not that there is any reason for you to be jealous. You knew what you were walking into, Mason. He was just positioning me, and it was the first time he touched me the whole session."

"He fucking touched you?"

I bite my tongue, my eyes zeroed in on a small mark on the floor. "Uh, yeah. You seemed pissed when you left —jealous."

"I had a shit day, Nina. I'm not jealous." I hear him blow out a breath. "Things are just a little crazy here at the minute."

Shit.

I feel bad. Maybe I read him wrong earlier. He sounds so stressed. "Do you want me to come to you? I'm finished for the day."

"No, get yourself home. I've booked you a cab, but it's not until five. I can rearrange it for earlier?"

"No, five is fine. Where is Vinny?" I ask.

"Taken a week off."

I frown, but it transforms into a surprised smile. "Surely not on holiday?"

"Yeah, I suppose. He didn't say exactly, just that he needed some time."

"Well, yes, I can get a taxi. What time will you be home?"

"I'm not sure. Hopefully not too late."

"Okay." He stills sounds off, and I wonder if he is being honest with me about Joey. "I love you," I tell him.

"I love you too."

I smile, pleased that we are okay.

With half an hour until my taxi, I plug in my phone and

make the most of my time. I press play on *Ella Eyre* "We Don't Have To Take Your Clothes Off" and let my body move around the studio. No routine or thought, just my body moving like it was made to, along with the beat of the music.

When I'm done, I lie back on the studio floor, my chest rising and falling as the music cuts out, and I'm surrounded by nothing but silence. I close my eyes, smiling between my heaving breaths, welcoming the calm and solace my little studio brings me.

I never feel quite alone here. It feels like home.

Mase

I STAND at the bottom of our bed, watching the rise and fall of her chest. How do I get into bed with her, knowing what I've done?

I couldn't come home right away. I sat in my office until every last person cleared out of the building, and then I sat some more, too afraid to come back here and look her in the eye.

She's about to lose something I know means more to her than anything else.

What if my reasoning isn't enough?

Stripping down, I pull back the sheets and climb in behind her, my gut twisting with every glance in her direction.

Why does she have to be so good?

So pure?

She stirs, and I freeze, my eyes closing as I slowly slip down under the covers, careful not to touch her.

She settles again, and I scrub at my face, feeling more confused than ever.

I stare up at the ceiling, feeling sick to my stomach.

I HAVE no idea what time it is, but something warm and wet is wrapped around me. Lifting the covers, I find her on her knees between my legs, my cock buried deep in her throat.

"Baby?" I murmur, pulling back the covers and stroking down her cheek.

It's still dark out, but I can see the soft glow of the sun on its way up. I'm surprised I slept at all with the guilt that's festering in me.

"Hmmm," she hums around me, and it has my balls drawing in tight.

Shit.

I pull out of her mouth with a pop, leaning down and lifting her at the waist to pull her up the bed, placing her under me.

My brow dips low as I look down at her, my chest feeling like it's caving in.

"You were late home," she whispers, her hand twisting into the hair at the nape of my neck.

With no idea what to say to her, I lean down, pulling her bottom lip between mine and seeking out her tongue. My hand moves between us, sliding into her pyjama shorts.

"Angel," I moan, finding her wet and ready.

Sitting back on my heels, I hook my fingers into her

shorts and pull them down her legs until they're completely off, and like the devil that she is, her legs instantly drop to the bed, baring herself to me.

"Yours," she promises.

I shake my head, feeling like a fraud. Leaning in, I give her exactly what she wants because it's all I have to give right now.

I dip my finger into her heat, brushing over the spot inside that I know drives her wild. "Mase," she whimpers.

My body moves up over hers, nipping and sucking at her stomach, then to her breasts—both getting the same amount of love and attention. Kiss, suck, bite, kiss, suck, bite.

She convulses on every bite, squeezing my finger as her core throbs. "You like that, baby?"

She rolls her hips but shakes her head.

I pull my fingers out of her, taking her face in my hand. "No? I need words, Nina."

I have a firm grip on either side of her mouth, but not enough to hurt her. I wait for her to tell me what she wants, but she doesn't.

With my fingers still wet from her pleasure, her tongue peeks out, gliding along the length of my pointer, tasting herself.

She holds my eyes, and I know she is on a different level right now. Daring me to join her.

"Make me yours," she mutters, her eyes hooded.

I frown, not understanding. A twisted smile takes over her face, and she flips, giving me her ass.

"Nina," I groan, resting my hand on her lower back. She is fucking perfect. I run my hand down over her until I'm cupping her.

"I need you."

Goddammit. How do I deny her when she is all I need, yet nothing I deserve?

I bring my middle finger to my mouth and wet it before dropping it to her ass, teasing her entrance with slow circles.

My cock strains between us.

She pushes back, trying to increase the pressure, and it sends me wild. "Nina," I hiss, needing inside.

I push the tip of my finger in, and she groans.

Fuck.

I lick my lips, looking up at the ceiling as a layer of sweat coats me.

I don't feel in control, my need for her too much.

Slowly I sink my finger the rest of the way, right down to the knuckle. She pulls away from me on a sharp intake of breath. "Oh, god!"

I give myself two long pumps; my eyes fixated on the way she tightens around me. I slowly slide my finger out of her, letting my cock fall heavy into the line of her ass.

"You want me here, Pix?" I ask her.

"Yes," she pants.

I roll my neck, stretching the muscles as they coil tight in anticipation.

"Fuck." I adjust my knees on her bed as I slide my cock into her pussy, and she contracts around me, coating me like I needed her to.

I pull out and smooth over her hips, line myself up, then push into her.

She moans, deep and throaty, dropping her head to the bed, and I freeze with only the tip inside her, my eyes squeezing tight as I start to see stars.

"Nina," I bite out.

"More! I. Am. Yours."

This fucking woman!

"Look at me," I demand, grasping her neck and angling her face towards me. "Why?"

Lust-filled eyes find mine, but I can't read her. She is someplace else right now, and I have no idea why.

Why tonight? Is this the universes way of fucking with me?

Her lips part, ready to say something, but my conscience won't allow it.

Not being able to bear her words, I push the rest of the way into her as I bend forward and take her lips with mine.

"Mase!" she cries out, dragging her mouth away from mine.

I squeeze my eyes tighter, focusing on anything but the feel of her or the delicate moans that fill the room.

My chest heaves as my arousal starts to grow.

"You feel incredible, baby." I breathe across her shoulder.

"Make it good for me," she begs.

My hand wraps around her front, the pads of my fingers teasing her clit.

"Yes!"

I feel her convulse, and I can barely stop the tremor that racks through me. I hold my breath and think of anything but where my cock is.

She's too tight.

"Nina, I'm going to come." I roll my hips, needing the friction, but knowing it will all end if I move.

"Uggghhh, no! Don't stop."

I start to move inside her whilst continuing my assault on

her clit. Her body trembles, and I flatten my finger to keep her spasming around me.

"Fuccckkkk!!" I roar, pushing myself to the hilt as her orgasm draws me in further, and it's all I can take. I grasp her hips and let her have it, unleashing everything I've held inside since walking through the penthouse doors.

She takes it all, every bit of me, right down to the remnants of my tattered soul.

I fall to her back as I release inside of her, dropping my lips to her neck as my chest heaves.

"I'm sorry," I mutter, quiet enough that she won't hear.

Nina

LAST NIGHT WAS IMPORTANT. I gave Mase something I've never given anyone before, and I hope it shows him that it's only him—he is all I see.

Joey doesn't matter, and I am his.

I thought he would be in a better mood this morning, but he was still quiet. He told me he is busy in work, but I don't know if I believe him, especially with everything that happened yesterday.

The girls called this morning and asked if I could do lunch today. Scarlet and her dad are in the city again, and I knew it would be nice to make it up to Scarlet for bailing on them the other day.

I enter The Elm and spot the girls around the sofas. Ordering a coffee, I grab some sugar and make my way over to them.

362 | JC HAWKE

"Sorry I'm late girls, it's been one of those mornings."

"Better late than never," Megan tells me, and I can tell she is in a spunky mood.

"I had to go register for the showcase. It's ridiculous the rigmarole that I had to go through, and the lady on the reception was a complete bitch. Nowhere on the damn form did it say I needed my fucking passport. Some people just have a shitty manner." I huff, dropping my bag down and falling onto the sofa, grateful for the cushion under me.

I'm a little sore.

Megan frowns at me. "Who shoved a stick up your ass?"

I choke on my coffee, spraying it out all over Luce and the table.

"Hey!" Lucy cries.

"I am so sorry," I say, taking the napkin that Scarlet holds out to me.

A bright smile washes over my face as my eyes drop down the length of her. She looks her usual vibey self today. Her lavender hair is set in perfect curls, her face lightly made up, and she is wearing ripped mom jeans with an off the shoulder tee.

"Okay! Spill it," Megan says, intrigued.

"Just not all over me." Lucy glowers as she blots at her face, trying her hardest not to ruin her makeup

I eye Scarlet, not sure she would want to hear it. I never hold out on my girls, but this is different.

"Don't hold back on my account," she tells me.

"I can't." I laugh, not being able to say it out loud.

"Don't act a queen about it, and then not tell us." Megan tuts, watching me.

I eye her, shaking my head. "It's bedroom stuff. I'm sure Scarlet doesn't want to hear it."

"Cover your ears," Megan tells her.

"Oh my god, you did anal!" Lucy shrieks. My eyes go wide, and I snap my head to her. "You literally had a stick up your ass; it's why you sprayed me."

I drop my head into my hands. This is a nightmare.

"Wow," Scarlets says in shock.

"No! Did it hurt?" Megan asks.

"Wow," Scarlet says again, her face paling.

"Nina, you are so brave," Lucy tells me, wide-eyed with a hand on my arm.

"I am so fucking brave," I agree, welcoming my friend's pity.

"Brave? Anal isn't brave, you little butt slut." Megan laughs. "I had a friend who had a slip of the dick once, literally no warning, one minute they're fuckin', the next, all the way in."

"Holy shit, accidentally is different! Imagine not expecting it, and then BAM! All at once. Poor girl." Lucy shivers.

"Wow," Scarlet mutters for the third time. I think we've broken her.

"Scarlet, I'm so sorry," I tell her, trying to hold back a smile.

"It was a Tuesday yesterday," she says, staring at the table. She lifts her eyes to me and raises a perfectly groomed eyebrow "Who does anal on a Tuesday?"

"Oh. My. Fucking. God!" Megan roars as she and Lucy bend over in the seat, laughing.

I bite my lip, unsure as to what I should say to the poor girl in front of me.

"Anal Tuesdays for the win!" Megan heaves out between her hysterics.

"We are not making this a thing. Both of you stop." I point at them.

"You already did, don't blame us. Anal Tuesdays is a thing, and it's all yours. Own it." Megan chuckles, raising her coffee cup.

My mortification only rises when Scarlet lifts her cup to the girls.

"To anal Tuesdays." She shrugs.

Fuck my life.

I LEAVE my immature friends at the coffee shop. They are corrupting Mason's poor sister, and I don't think there is anything I could do about it.

She just fits with them.

Us.

I could do with Vinny today, and it's odd not having him waiting for me. I have a one on one at two, and it's already quarter to. I weave through the busy streets fast walking and dodging passersby to try and get myself there on time. Rounding the corner to the studio, I spot a commotion at the entrance. I stop on the corner, taking in the scene, but the second Logan's fist rears back, I am catapulting myself towards him on autopilot.

"Logan!" I shout.

He stills, turning to face me. "Fucking hell, Nina! Where have you been? I've been calling all morning!"

I frown, then remember that I put my phone on silent when I was in the registration office. "Sorry, I was in a meeting. What's going on?" I frown as I notice the suit that is currently sticking a SOLD sign in the gym window.

"Umm, what the hell are you doing?" I grab his sleeve, and he shoves me off unamused.

"If one more person touches me, I'm calling the police," he warns, his face red with anger.

I can tell Logan has given him just about as much as he can take.

I step back with my hands up. "Okay. This is my studio, and it's not for sale. There must be some kind of mistake."

"Then go fix it!" he spits, turning and stomping off down the road towards his car

I turn to Logan, shaking my head in utter shock. "What the fuck?"

"I have no idea; they turned up an hour ago demanding I left the premises."

"I will call Erin, it will be a misunderstanding."

It has to be.

I go to push through the door, but it's locked, so I open my bag in search of my keys, only Logan stops me with a hand on my arm.

"They changed them, Nina. The locks. I tried to stop them, but he had all these documents. I didn't know what else to do."

I stare at the door, completely at a loss.

What the hell is going on?

Digging into my bag, I find my phone. I have a missed call from Erin, and my heart sinks.

My hand trembles as I lift the phone to my ear, pressing play on the voicemail that's waiting for me.

My nostrils flare as her emotionless voice fills the line, and tears fill my eyes.

"Nina, I've had to sell the studio. Don't contact me again. I need a fresh start and a clear break from London." She huffs down the phone, and I frown at her heartless words. They have absolutely no sincerity in them. "Thanks for everything."

"It's been sold, hasn't it?" Logan mutters, hands on his hips as he shakes his head in disbelief.

"I don't know." A tear rolls down my cheek.

"Well, either it's sold or it's not Nina? What did she say?"

Everything seems to slow, the cars on the street, the people that step around us, everything.

I struggle to find my voice as I look up at Logan.

He takes my phone and listens to the voicemail. "Bitch. What is that all about? Thanks for everything; like this is your fucking fault!"

"I'm so sorry. I will help you find another job. We can set up someplace else," I rush out. Then I think of Henry, and how this will affect him too.

My body starts to tingle, and sweat forms on my brow. My stomach rolls. Oh god.

I bend, vomiting onto the curb.

"You're sure I'm okay to leave you here?" Logan asks as we enter my apartment, his hand smoothing over my back.

"Yes, you go. I will be fine. I'm so sorry, Logan."

"Will you stop that?! We will get it sorted."

I nod my head, but the sinking feeling in my gut tells me we won't.

I can feel everything slipping away from me.

"Call the girls, yeah?" he tells me, turning and moving for the door, but looking back at the last minute with a sad look in his eyes.

He doesn't want to leave me.

"Go. I will be okay."

He slips through the door, closing it gently behind him, and as the lock clicks, my tears fall. I look around my little apartment, wondering what comes next—the loans, this place, the showcase.

My showcase.

The girls have worked so hard for this. *I* have worked so hard for this.

I go to my bag and pull out my phone.

I call Mason.

Nothing.

"Mase," my voice cracks and I try to swallow past the lump in my throat. "Can you call me back?"

I try Lucy instead.

Nothing.

My shoulders shake, no longer being able to hold back the faucet of tears. I slide down the wall to the floor. My studio is gone. Erin has sold it. I knew it was too good to be true.

My hand covers my mouth as a sob escapes me, and I do

nothing to stop it, not the pain, not the tears and not the wails that echo throughout the apartment.

"Why!" My hand hits on the ground in a feeble attempt to free my hurt. "Why couldn't I just have one thing. One safe space," I cry.

My head thuds to the floor boards as I curl into myself, my body shaking with each broken cry.

I've never felt more alone.

24

Mase

SOLD.

That's what my email told me when I checked this morning. Cara sold the studio overnight, and the locks were changed this morning.

A sick feeling fills my gut all day, knowing there is no going back.

I've sold her studio. To think last night she completely gave herself to me, and I took it.

It's early afternoon when the call comes. The call I've been waiting for, but now that it is here, and she needs me, I don't answer. Instead, I watch as it rings out and goes to voicemail.

My body is at war with itself. The need to know where she is and that she is okay is overwhelming, but the coward in me wants to stay far away.

I did what had to be done.

Fuck.

Nina

AFTER CALLING MASON, Lucy and Megan with no luck, I knew there was only one other person I had left. I breathe out a sigh of relief as Maggie passes me a cup of tea, joining me on her sofa.

As soon as I called, she left work, telling her boss she was leaving for a family emergency whilst I was still on the phone.

Family, she had said.

"What am I going to do, Mags? I barely scrape through each month as it is. I won't afford my apartment without the studio and the loans. How will I make this month's payment?"

She reaches over and takes my hand in hers, giving me a look. "Well, that's enough of that. You know me and John would never see you struggle, darling."

"I can't rely on you guys again. You've already done too much."

"We will be the judge of that. Now, where are you with the lease on the apartment? Can you ask for a month's grace until you find your feet again?"

I worry my lip. I haven't told Maggie about Mase yet. She knows I have a boyfriend but not how deep I've gotten myself involved. I drop my head, staring into my mug. "I'm living with Mason. I haven't slept in my apartment since I got back from Paris."

Her hand leaves mine, and she lowers her tea to the coffee table. "You're living together?" Her smile widens in approval. She looks happy for me.

"Kind of." I shrug.

"You didn't say anything! Nina, this is wonderful news. You're happy?" she questions.

"I'm so happy. He cares for me, maybe more than anyone ever has."

I look down at my lap as I think about his beautiful face, the way he smiles unashamedly when he's with me. I know I'm lucky; I get the Mase nobody else gets to see.

"Well, that's impossible," she whispers.

I lift my eyes to hers as her voice cracks, finding tears welling in her eyes. "Why are you crying?" I ask.

"My dear girl, you have so much love, so much ambition and drive. I have told you a million times over how proud we all are of you, and you still don't see it. You're more than we could have ever hoped you to be. To see you happy and finally letting someone in–because you sure as hell never let me in," she teases. "It just makes a mother very happy."

"Mags." I look to the ceiling trying to stop the tears.

Maggie has always been the mother I wished I had, and with that comes guilt.

"I know, I'm not helping. Get the laptop, darling. I will look up spaces for rent whilst you call the bank."

I climb to my knees and lean down, cuddling her, feeling grateful to have a woman like her in my life.

WE FOUND NOTHING. Everything was either too expensive or not suitable and would need a ton of work. There are a couple of warehouses outside the city, but I know the girls won't travel that far for rehearsals, and as of right now, I have

372 | JC HAWKE

no transport myself. We tried to find somewhere to hire on an hourly basis, but nothing is consistent—nothing that would work. Nothing that even comes close to my studio.

"I've set up an alert, so anything coming up for rent will pop up on my email. You should set it up on yours, too. In case I miss it."

"Yeah, I will." I drop my head back, defeated.

"We will find something. Don't panic."

"I'm not." I smile sadly, feeling an ache in the back of my throat.

She lies back on the sofa next to me, a comfortable silence falling over us.

"Luce mentioned your mum may have kept money from a potential…" she hesitates, not knowing how to say it.

"Father," I finish for her.

"Have you spoken to her?"

"No. I was waiting until after the showcase."

She nods, looking back to the ceiling. "How do you feel about it?"

My phone starts to vibrate on the table, and I'm glad for the interruption. As much as I love Maggie and appreciate all she does for me, there is nothing I hate more than discussing Mum.

Mason's name lights up my screen.

Finally.

"Hey!"

"Where are you?" he panics.

"I'm at Lucy's parents'. I couldn't get hold of you. Did you get my message?" My voice quivers and Maggie's hand slips into mine. "Erin sold the studio."

"Yeah, did she say why?" he asks.

"No. Maybe. I can't remember; I was in shock. They changed the locks. Can they do that? I don't even have my things from inside."

"We will get your things. Send me the address, I'm on my way to get you now."

Relief fills me, and I let out a breath.; He is all I need right now.

"I will text it over now. Thank you, Mase."

Maggie stands, pulling me up with her. "He seems like a good egg. I'm pleased for you, but you know where we are."

"Thank you. For everything." I smile, wrapping her up in a hug.

Mase

ONCE AGAIN, I underestimate Nina Anderson and her ability to remain so strong. She made it easy. Easy for me to lie to her.

Lucy and Megan have been here for the past three hours, and never have I been so grateful that she has such good friends. I'm in my office looking up potential studios for her —I know what I need to do.

Make it right.

I've narrowed it down to three, and they are all above and beyond what she had before, but it doesn't ease the weight of my guilt.

I print out the advertisements and gather up all the information.

The girls are all laughing when I enter the living area, and

I pause, the sound grating on me. This whole time I've been worried about how Nina would deal with all this. I didn't stop to think about how I would.

Can I do this?

How do I live with myself—with her, knowing I will have to keep it from her. There's no way she would stay if she knew.

She doesn't deserve this.

"Mase, take her to bed and make her forget about today. She's considering stripping as her next form of income."

I snap my eyes to Nina's in mortification, but she gives me a reassuring look. "Calm down, Bossman. You know I would never." She looks at Megan. "Why are you trying to wind him up?"

"It's too easy." They chuckle, and I plaster a forced smile on my face.

"Come on, bed," I tell her.

The girls stand to hug Nina, and Lucy whispers into her ear, but it's loud enough that I catch it. "He's so hot when he gets aggy."

"Thank god it's a Wednesday," Megan adds, and they all start to laugh again.

"Thank you, girls. I will see you tomorrow," Nina tells them.

They disappear into the elevator, and she stands in the foyer watching after them. I slide up behind her and pull her to me.

"Mase," her voice cracks.

Fuck.

"What am I going to do?"

She turns in my arms and stares intently into my eyes, searching for a hope that's impossible to find.

"It's going to be okay. I promise." I close my eyes as the words leave my mouth, knowing I've broken every promise I've made so far.

"My little studio. It's gone. It's not mine anymore. It was all I had, and the only thing I could say I did on my own. What do I do now? Who am I without it?"

Panic rises in my chest, the hurt in her eyes gutting me.

I can't lie to her.

I can't do this.

"I need to go back into the office for an hour this evening." I pull away from her, my feet faltering as I step back. "Will you be okay here until I get home?" I pick up my keys from the tray, then bend to slide on my trainers.

"What? You're leaving?" Tears stream down her cheeks, and I can't bear the look she's giving me.

"I will be an hour tops." My throat constricts, and I struggle to pull air into my lungs. I give her a tight smile as I enter the elevator and hit the button for the garage.

Her face is a mask of hurt and confusion as the doors slide closed.

What the fuck have I done?

Nina

THURSDAY MORNING HITS ME HARD. I wake with a headache, and I feel lower than I have in maybe ever. I was up most of the night going over in my head what I'll do now I've lost my studio. Everything I came up with is impossible.

Mason didn't come to bed last night, and he was already gone when I woke up. I don't know what is going on with him, but he pulled away from me last night—left me when I needed him most.

Pulling myself from the bed, I shower and dress in some comfy clothes. I have nowhere to go, and the feeling is devastating.

Tears sting my eyes as I lift the sticky note from the worktop.

CALL ME IF YOU NEED ME ANGEL

"I needed you last night, Mase," I mutter to myself.

I wrap my arms around my body and glance around the penthouse, hating how cold the space feels without him here. Switching on every light possible, I find my phone and plug it in, moving to my spot in the window and letting loose.

As always, my dancing brings me the escape I desperately crave. But after two hours of solid dancing, I have to stop. My muscles are on fire from pushing my body to the brink of collapse.

My day went downhill from there.

I decided to make a cake. Maggie told me how easy it is and to do eight ounces of everything. I called her in a fit of tears when the sloppy mixture wouldn't hold together. We soon figured out that I used eight eggs instead of eight ounces, but yeah, I cried over a cake.

I tried not to let it get me down, moving to the walk-in wardrobe where I rearranged my things, finally hanging up the few items I'd packed up, feeling like an imposter in some-body else's home, but hoping it would make Mason a little happier.

He's been stressed with work the last few days, or so he says. I know the Joey thing is still playing on his mind. And his dad. God, I'm such a bitch. I haven't even thought about his father.

I pause at the thought, dropping the T-shirt I was holding to the floor.

It's just a job.

I find myself laughing hysterically in the confinements of the wardrobe. *It's just a job.* My laugh soon turns into tears.

I wish it were just a job.

———

THE PING of the elevator has my eyes snapping open. I must have drifted off watching the television. My eyes feel heavy, and I know it will be obvious to Mason that I've been crying. I sit up and look at him over the top of the sofa. He looks tired. His eyes just as red as I expect mine are.

"Did you even come home last night?" I ask before he can greet me.

"I did. It was late and I had to be up early this morning."

I nod my head waiting for him to come to me. He doesn't. "Is everything okay, Mase?" My throat bobs, and I know I'm going to cry any second.

His brows pinch in, his fists clenched at his sides. "Yeah, sorry, are you okay? How was your day?"

"It was fine, I didn't do much. Have you heard from your

dad lately?" I ask, trying to not bother him with my own problems.

"Uh, yeah. I spoke to Scar yesterday."

"Have you spoken to him, though?"

"Not since I took him to the hospital."

I drop my head to the side. "Mase."

"Don't, Nina. Why are you bringing this up? I don't want a lecture on my dad right now," he snaps.

I sit back affronted. What on earth? "I wasn't giving you a lecture. But I think you should give him a call." I roll my lips. "Scar told me about the transplant."

He scoffs, rolling his eyes and looking to the ceiling. "You don't need to worry yourself with it. Let me deal with my own shit."

My eyebrows pinch together. "Why are you getting angry?"

"Because you think you always know best about him but you don't. You don't even know him, and I'm not interested in continuing this conversation after just getting in the door."

"Okay," I say, shocked at his outburst.

He pinches the bridge of his nose, not looking at me. "I'm going to go shower. Have you eaten?"

I sit cross-legged with my back to him, staring at the coffee table, tears staining my face and dripping onto my leggings.

"Nina."

"What?" I snap.

"Whatever." He huffs and takes off towards the stairs.

Mase

MY JAW CLENCHES tight as I lean my arms against the shower wall, the water cascading down my back.

I clench my eyes tight as I think back to everything Lance told me this afternoon. Cara is back in Australia. She sold the studio, and I seem to have more control than ever.

For nearly two years, it's all I've wanted, yet now I have it; my world feels like it is slipping through my fingers.

I stare down at the tiles, watching as the water runs down the drain.

Because the woman I love, the woman who still tries to put on a brave face for me, tries to fix me, she sits on my sofa none the wiser to who I am and what I have done.

And I have no idea how to face that.

Nina

AFTER LAST NIGHT'S ARGUMENT, I found myself waiting for Mason to come find me. He didn't. I spent the entire night in the spare room.

I need him.

Probably more than I care to admit, and he hasn't been here.

It has me questioning everything I thought he was.

Everything I thought we were.

I stare down at my bangle. *I promise you forever, my Pixie.*

My head hits the back of the seat, and I tell myself I am doing the right thing. I have to push my own problems to the back of my mind right now. Mason has a lot going on, and I want to be there for him.

It's why I'm in a taxi and on my way to Lowerwick. I want to do something, something that will take my mind off of the studio, and something that will allow me to be there for Mason's family while he can't.

After contacting the girls from the studio, I felt reassured. They all vowed to practice at home until I found a space, but I know the more days that tick by, the lesser our chances are at winning the showcase. Losing the studio couldn't have come at a worse time.

Henry picked up work with his dad on a building site for the time being. He is a chilled guy and didn't stress that he was out of a job. And Logan has been on the phone constantly worrying about me. Unlike Henry, he doesn't have a job or any idea what he's going to do, but his only concern is how I am.

I hope we can find somewhere with a similar set up for both of our sakes.

Lowerwick comes into view, cutting off my thoughts, its beauty undeniable and captivating. It baffles me that Mason can be so absent from his childhood home when it is so beautiful.

I pay the taxi and cringe at the amount. It's foolish of me to be spending so much when I am in such a financial mess.

Taking the sprawling steps, I knock on the door and wait.

After a few minutes, I try again, but no one answers. I push on the handle, and it opens.

"Hello?"

I walk into the entrance and peer into both the rooms on my left and right, but they are empty.

The entire house is silent, no life or soul, and no love. It was full of it when I was here before, the Montgomerys and Lowells as one, but looking around now I can see it as the broken home that it is.

My heart hurts for Mason, and I find myself rubbing absently at my chest.

"Hello," I call out again, moving farther into the house.

I hear a light cough, and I halt in my steps. "Anthony?"

"Who's that?"

I push open the door at the end of the corridor and find a small living room. Anthony rises from the chair, and straightaway I notice the pained look on his face.

"Oh, don't stand! Here." I grab the cushion that has fallen and prop it up against his back as he gives up and sits back in his seat.

"Nina, I'm sorry, I must have nodded off. I wasn't expecting you."

"I didn't tell anyone I was coming. Sorry, I should have called."

"No, you're always welcome here. Scarlet is here somewhere. You will have to give her a call; as you know, it's a big house—she could be anywhere."

"That's okay. Can I get you a drink?" I ask, feeling a little awkward.

"No, no. I'm grand love." He waves his hand around.

He doesn't look grand. His skin looks off colour and frail —even more so than before.

"How have you been?" I ask, unsure of my words.

I feel bad for disturbing him.

"Good, it's been beautiful weather the last couple of days. I've been out on the meadow for the most part."

"The meadow?"

"Yeah, it's on the other side of the estate. Mase has never mentioned it?" he asks, sounding slightly gutted as his brows draw in.

"No, I don't think so."

"Hmm," he sniggers. "Do you want to see it?"

His eyes light up in excitement.

"I'd love to!"

I go to help him from the chair, but he shrugs me off. It's as if speaking of the meadow has bought him a new lease of life. It makes me smile.

"I may need a new liver, but my legs still work, young lady."

"Sorry," I mutter as he chuckles.

"Come on."

I follow him out of the house and down to a garage. He lifts the door and smiles over at me.

"I thought you said your legs work fine." I laugh, climbing up into the golf-style buggy.

He doesn't say anything as he sits in the driving seat and pulls out of the garage.

It is a bumpy ride down to the meadow, but it's worth it. Sat two fields away from the estate, the most beautiful meadow lies covered in an array of wildflowers. The grass is greener than any grass I've ever seen. It's bright and vibrant, and seems full of life.

Trees line the boundary but open up at the bottom of the hillside. Anthony comes to a stop at the gate, and I jump out to open it.

He speeds in past me, his eyes sparkling in delight.

I can tell he is loving this.

"It's beautiful," I beam, slipping back into the buggy beside him.

He shakes his head, smirking at me, and I see so much of my beautiful man in that look, it makes my chest constrict.

They are so alike.

"You've not seen nothing yet. Hold on."

He takes off through the flowers, and I spin in my seat, shocked. "Anthony, the flowers!"

He laughs freely. "They will bounce back."

I look behind us to see the trail of destruction, but my eyes lift instead to the beautiful view.

We come to a stop at the top of the hill, and I sit speechless in my seat as I absorb Lowerwick in all its beauty. I can see the entire estate from here, and it seems so much bigger, grander. More.

"Wow," I mutter.

"Look at this," he says, tapping my arm.

I turn, my eyes following his finger to where he is pointing, and the view in front of me takes my breath away. At the bottom of the meadow sits a glistening lake. I see no end to it, just miles and miles of uninterrupted water.

Stepping from the buggy to get a better look, I take in the paddle boat and rope swing that lies broken on the floor.

Mason.

"He loved it out here. They both did."

I twist towards him. "They don't come here anymore?"

"Scarlet does. Nearly every day. Mase hasn't been in years."

I swallow the lump in my throat, turning fully to take in Lowerwick at my back.

"This has to be the most peaceful place on earth," I tell him.

"It is." He smiles sadly. He steps from the buggy and sits on the grass, then nods his head to the spot beside him, encouraging me to drop down next to him. "You see there—to the left of the property." He points.

I squint, trying to work out where he means—until I spot it.

The headstone stands large and proud in a garden of colourful flowers.

"Ellis. Your wife."

"When she first passed, Mason and Scarlet would play on the lake whilst I sat here. So she could watch them with me."

"It's perfect." Tears fill my eyes—there's no controlling them—and I try to blink them away.

"It is, isn't it." He picks at the grass, rolling it between his fingers then letting it go in the light breeze. "Scarlet will never leave, and that fills me with so much joy, but I always hoped Mason would end up back here one day. That maybe I'd see my grandchildren play on the lake, and I could sit on the hill and watch them with her. Like we watched our children."

I roll my lips, not knowing how to reassure him when his life seems so uncertain. "I have faith in him, faith that he will come around. Deep down he loves it here." I grasp my collarbone, closing my eyes briefly as I process that lie.

Does Mason love it here? Maybe that's something I can talk to him about.

"I wish that were true, Nina." He smiles warmly at me. "You're good for him, I can see that. Scarlet even more so. She's left me alone twice this week to do *girly lunch*." He bumps me with his shoulder, lightening the mood.

"She is incredible. They both are." I grin, feeling my dimple pop.

"What brought you out here today anyway?" he asks.

"I lost my job."

"Ah, yes. The studio."

"How do you know about that?"

He frowns. "Scarlet, she mentioned it had been sold. I'm sorry to hear that."

"Yeah, I'm gutted about it. I'm looking for somewhere new, though, and something will come up."

"Good things come to us when we are least expecting them, Nina. Believe in that, and you will be just fine."

I replay Anthony's words in my head as we sit on the meadow together for over an hour, taking in the scenery. No conversation needed—just the sun on our backs and the hope for better days.

25

Nina

I FEEL REFRESHED WHEN I LEAVE LOWERWICK. IT MADE ME SEE that there are so many more important things in life than the studio. Seeing Anthony and the poor health he has right now, it makes me realise that sitting around and wallowing over my misfortune won't make a difference. You have to get out, do something. I plan to explore all my options over the weekend so that when Monday comes I am ready to get my shit together.

I have to stay positive.

Mason's been on my mind all afternoon, and being at his childhood home made me feel closer to him. He is distant right now and it's hard to understand his headspace, but I want to make things okay between us.

Pulling out my phone, I call him, hoping he will answer.

"Angel," he says down the phone, his voice smooth and comforting.

I smile wide at the endearment. "Hey."

Silence stretches between us, and I worry I should have just waited until I got home to talk. I just missed him.

"Sorry I didn't call today. It's been busy in the office," he tells me.

"You don't need to apologise, it's me who should be sorry. I know you have a lot on right now, and I should be better. I was a little emotional last night, and I was deflecting my own problems."

"What?" he says, sounding confused.

"It's just a job," tears fill my eyes, and I fight to keep my voice steady. Do I even believe my own words? "I will find something else, and I will work at making it just as good. But I shouldn't be dragging you down into my mess, it's not your fault and you have enough going on."

He clears his throat. "Can we talk about this when I get home, babe? I'm nearly there."

"Uh, yeah, you might beat me back though." I chuckle as I think about my impromptu afternoon.

"Where are you? You've been out?"

"Yeah, I went to see your sister and dad."

"Where?"

"Lowerwick." I frown, gripping the phone tight.

Shit.

Should I have asked him first?

"The girls were both working, and I knew Scar would be home," I try to explain.

"It's fine. I will see you at home."

I already know it's not fine. The tone of his voice tells me it's not fine. I keep fucking this up.

"Okay. I'm sorry, Mase."

"Stop saying sorry. Please. There is nothing for you to be

sorry about." He exhales heavily down the phone, and my heart aches in my chest.

Why does he feel a million miles away from me right now?

"I'll see you soon," he says, hanging up.

My mood hits rock bottom, and I regret calling him. I drop my head to the taxi window and let the first tear fall.

Crying. Again.

I feel fed up.

I feel hurt.

And I feel like a fool. I can't mask the turmoil that's plaguing me, not when my only escapes are gone.

My studio and my Mase.

Mase

I MADE it back before Nina, and with my head thoroughly fried after a day trying to find the perfect studio, I decide to order in Chinese for dinner, knowing it's her favourite.

I've been in the gym every morning and evening this week, trying to work off the guilt that seems to be hanging over my head. Despite my constant workouts, my body is still wound tight, and I have no idea how to shift it.

And as for her, I struggle to even look at her, knowing what I've taken away.

"Mase?" she calls, making her way through the penthouse.

"In here," I call back.

"Hey!" She smiles as she steps into the kitchen, and my heart sinks when I see her red-rimmed eyes.

I go to her, taking her in my arms and holding her close. "I can't stand to see you cry."

"I'm okay." She sniffles as more tears fall to my shirt.

I take her chin and lift her face so I can see her. I haven't given her this connection in days. Our eyes blaze, and I can't look away, something passing between us that's deeper than anything I've ever experienced before.

A carnal need to take what we both crave.

I shake my head as my mouth comes down on hers, and the world seems to tilt just an inch back into place.

Nina

I'M HUNGRY FOR HIM. Starved. If you told me ten minutes ago this is how my evening would go, I would have laughed in your face. But this is us, and it's what we know. It's what we are good at.

Mase pulls at his tie, loosening it enough to pull it over his head. His shirt follows moments later. And this isn't a romantic undressing of one another, we shed our clothes ourselves as we rush to have the connection.

I only manage to get my jeans off of one leg when he lifts me, pushing me back hard into the fridge. My legs wrap around his body as he pulls my trousers down over my foot.

His strong, powerful body ripples under me and I squeeze my legs around him, urging him to come closer.

The lace of my underwear tears as he rips my thong from my hips, and in the next second, he fills me. He drops his head on a deep groan, resting it against my breast bone. He takes a second—unmoving—his breath fanning my heated skin.

"Mase."

When his head comes up and his gaze meets mine, I see the darkness lurking there.

His brows dip low as I smile down at him, and it seems to break his trance. He begins to move inside me. Hard and fast, not giving me a moment to catch my breath.

His hand lifts my leg, putting it flush to the fridge. My other leg drops an inch from his waist, and the move has him rubbing perfectly against the spot inside me.

"Fuck!" he bites out. "Don't come yet."

I close my eyes and try to think of anything but the feel of him.

His movements are uncontrolled and unlike him; a hyper wave of adrenaline as he thrusts into me relentlessly. I grit my teeth as his hand grips my thigh tight enough to mark.

He is wild. Unleashing everything he has.

My eyes flash open as a tortured cry leaves his throat. His sad eyes are locked on my face, and for a moment, he looks utterly broken.

Dropping his head, he hides from me, picking up the pace until my toes are curling and I can't hold off any longer. My body coils tight around him, and I jerk forward as my orgasm takes me. He follows behind me, pumping three more times inside me before he stills, gripping my shoulder hard as he rains open-mouthed kisses against my throat.

What the fuck was that?

"Mase?"

His head rests heavily on my shoulder as we stand connected as one, but he doesn't answer me. My leg begins to cramp, and I push from his grip, letting it fall to the ground. My tired eyes meet his, and the smile he gives me soothes some of the worry.

"Go shower, angel, and I will set up the table for dinner."

I YAWN AND STRETCH, feeling incredible, my body the perfect kind of sore. Mason couldn't get enough last night. Every time I thought he was done, he would be desperate for more and I know I will pay for it today; I feel exhausted.

Slipping from the sheets, I reach for my phone and see Maggie has texted me.

Maggie: No news this end. Have you had any luck?

I exit the message and chuck my phone to the bottom of the bed.

Shower first, then I'm fixing this mess.

Mason isn't in bed, so I head for the stairs to look for him. I'm not surprised when I find him in his home office. It's where he spends all his time recently.

"Hey." I smile, moving around the desk and climbing into his lap. He buries his nose into my hair, kissing my neck. "You're up early, Bossman. Even for you."

"Hmm, I had to get some things sorted for the day. I have something to show you."

"Yeah?"

He reaches forward and picks up a folder from the desk. I

frown, stilling on his lap as he flips over the page and hands me the top sheet. "You can have your pick, but I think this one is perfect," he whispers into my shoulder.

My heart rate begins to pick up. "I don't understand; this is for sale and won't be in my budget—*ever.*"

"The price is because of location, it puts you close to my office." He squeezes my hip, watching me for a reaction.

I think he is trying to suggest this as a new studio, but that would be ridiculous because I could never afford it. "I need to find someplace for rent, Mase. This is ridiculously big, and completely out of my budget." I laugh nervously.

"I know. Which is why *I* placed an offer."

"You what?" I utter, standing and staring down at the sheet of paper in my hands.

"I've been looking for days. I viewed a couple, but none of them were right. Then this one came up just yesterday. Do you like it?"

I've been looking for days.

"Yeah, but I don't want it." I drop it to the desk and leave the office, making my way to the kitchen. I stand at the coffee machine on autopilot and switch it on.

I've been here alone the past two days, and he has been out looking at new studios?

"What do you mean you don't want it?" he fumes, following in after me. "It's ten times better than your old studio."

My eyes lift to look at him.

I don't want to argue.

I don't want to yell.

I want to run because I know what comes next.

"I don't want you buying me things," I tell him, my hand

shaking as I pour the coffee. "I've told you this so many times."

"Fucking this again. I thought we were past this? Nina, you won't be able to afford the start-ups on a new studio now. Let me help you."

"No. Drop it, please. I will figure it out. I always do."

"So, what? You're going to mope around here all day until a studio miraculously lands in your lap?"

"I'm not moping, thank you, asshole!" You'd know if you'd been here. "Leave me alone, I'm not doing this now."

His anger is pissing me off, and I don't want to say something I will regret later, but the more he pushes, the more my walls go up.

"No, you've not been moping because you are too busy playing house with my fucking family!" he roars.

My eyes go wide, my heart thumping almost painfully in my chest, which is dumb because I knew it was coming. The nasty slap that stings with each syllable that penetrates.

"I thought you said you didn't care that I went to Lowerwick? Why are you throwing it in my face now?"

He drops his head, his hands spread wide on the worktop. "I just want to fix this. Let me fix it!"

"I don't need you to fix it, Mase, don't you get it? Whilst you've spent *days* looking for a new studio, I've been here alone dealing with the hurt that comes with losing the one I've built from the ground up. I've been alone when you promised me I wouldn't be again. You. You promised me that. I told myself I was being selfish, and I've tried to put on a brave face, but you don't deserve it."

Tears well in my eyes, but I blink them away. He doesn't deserve them either. "This isn't the Mase I know," My eyes drop down his hunched form. "and you are not the man I thought I was falling for. He wouldn't hurt me like you just have."

"Nina," he warns, his jaw ticcing as he braces himself.

"Get your shit together, Mason."

"Where are you going?" he asks as I walk from the kitchen.

"Anywhere but here."

I hear a bang and glass smashing as I jog up the stairs. I gather up my things and change into my tights, then slip from the penthouse.

I just want my Mase back.

THE GIRLS ARE both asleep when I get to their apartment half an hour later, so I let myself in with my key. I didn't want to call and wake them, but I also didn't want to be alone. I've felt alone for days. As quiet as I can, I start making the coffee, not wanting to wake them but knowing they will be up soon anyway.

"Hello?" Lucy's voice calls out from the lounge.

I spin around, squinting as I try to make her out in the darkened room. "It's me, babe," I call out.

"Oh, thank god." Megan flicks on the main lights, and we all cover our eyes. She stands with a flip-flop in her hand, shrugging when I eye it. "I thought you were a burglar."

"And what was that going to do?" I eye the flip-flop, smiling, even though I feel like shit inside.

"What's going on? How come you are here?" Luce asks, drawing my attention to her.

I take a deep breath in, running my hands over my face and through my hair. "I don't even know." My eyes start to well up and I look between the girls. "He didn't even try to stop me from leaving," I choke out.

Lucy pulls me into a hug. "Come on, everyone in my bed."

The three of us climb into Lucy's double bed, something we haven't done in years.

We lie looking up at the ceiling, not needing to fill the silence that settles over us.

"He wants to buy me a studio," I finally voice.

Lucy smiles sadly over at me. "That explains a lot."

"The money bothers me, but I think it's the fact he's been so cold all week, saying he was busy in the office. I thought I should give him time and the benefit of the doubt with his dad being poorly, but then he said he had spent days looking for a studio. I just really needed him to be here for me, and he hasn't been. Money was the last thing I wanted from him."

"Do you think it's because of Joey? I mean, the guy has had a thing for you forever. Maybe he's pissed about that," Megan asks.

"No. He told me it wasn't, and I believe him."

"Just give him space, babe. He will come around." Lucy smiles, squeezing me tight.

"I don't know if I want to see him at the minute. The things he says when he gets mad. I need space right now, and I will decide when I am ready to go back. Don't go letting him in if he comes knocking."

"You got it," Megan agrees.

"Pancakes?" Lucy asks.

I'M deep in the kitchen cupboard when I hear my phone ringing in the front room. I woke up early and didn't know what to do with myself, and after making myself a cup of coffee and noticing the total disorganisation of the mugs, I decided to rearrange them. It's now late morning, and I haven't been able to stop. The girls reluctantly left me to go to work this morning after a weekend of my tears and moaning. I don't know how they put up with me most days.

Shimmying out of the small space, I dart to the coffee table and check my phone, finding Joey's name lighting up the screen.

The photos.

"Hi, Joey."

"Nina! I'm surprised I caught you. I thought you'd be busy at the studio."

My throat grows tight as I think about the studio. "No, I had some bad news last week. The studio has been sold by the owner."

"What? Can you still use the space, like, rent from the new owners?"

"No. The locks were changed the day it sold."

I still need to get my things.

"Nina, that sucks. Is there anything I can do?"

I smile at his concern. "Not in terms of my studio, but you could show me the bomb ass photos you took. I'd love to see them."

"It's why I was calling. Are you free today?"

I'm about to say yes when I think better of it—eyeing the mess on the kitchen floor and the state of myself in the hallway mirror.

"Not today, but I could probably make tomorrow work?"

"Brilliant, are you okay to come to me? It's easier with the computer."

I have a moment of doubt. I know Mase won't like me meeting Joey, let alone somewhere private, but with the way he has been acting this week—fuck him.

"Yeah, sure, text me your address and I will come to you."

"Will do. Thanks, Nina."

"Bye, Joey."

I throw my phone to the counter and eye the mess on the floor, wondering why I even started in the first place. The girls would give me crap if I left it like this now. Begrudgingly, I finish the cupboards, wiping them down and putting everything away again. I shower and check my phone for any alerts on new premises and then climb back into bed. The thought of doing anything else seems utterly exhausting.

"I SPOKE TO ELLIOT EARLIER. Mason wasn't in the office today, and he asked me if I knew what was up," Lucy tells me as she opens her kitchen cupboards in amazement. "This is incredible. You colour coordinated our tins?"

"I had lots of spare time." I shrug.

"You're acting mopey. Tomorrow you need to get out, go to the gym or something."

"You spoke to Elliot?" I divert the conversation from me, arching a brow at her in question.

"Yes, Elliot. My friend Elliot who is just that, a friend. Is that okay?" She starts to get jerky as her annoyance rises.

"Absolutely." I grin at her from where I'm sitting on the counter.

"You look like a psycho when you smile like that."

I start to giggle. "I feel like a psycho today. Honestly, I don't think I have cried so much in my life. Not even as much as that day Mum left me in that park when I was six." I shake my head at the memory. "This week has been a hyper wave of emotions."

"Have you heard anything from him?"

"Nope. Not even a text." I jab my tongue in the side of my cheek, trying to think about anything else. How did I get him so wrong?

"What is up with him? Why make a fuss of chasing you down to act like a player now. He asked you to move in, not the other way around."

"I don't—"

The doorbell rings, cutting me off. "Hold that thought." Lucy skirts off around the corner, and a few minutes later Mason appears in the doorway. My heart grows heavy in my chest. Lucy stands at his back, and I give her the stink eye as she squeezes past him.

"I'm just going to go take a shower or something," she says, heading down the corridor.

His eyes cut into me. They are full of so many questions, yet neither of us speak.

"Why are you here?" I ask after a beat.

He steps farther into the room, coming to stand in front of me. "I need to speak to you."

"You could have called," I snap, harsher than I intended.

His eyes lock on mine as his hand comes up to smooth my hair. I itch to lean into his touch, but I don't, staring back at him with absolutely nothing in my eyes.

"Maybe I needed to see you," he tells me.

"Yeah? Maybe I needed you too, Mase, and maybe you were nowhere to be found."

"I know." He drops his head, his voice full of remorse. "I am so sorry, Nina, I just needed to fix it. You were so upset about the studio."

"When you get mad you use your words to hurt me. I won't stand for it."

"I know."

"Do you? You keep saying you know Mason, but do you?"

"Yes, would I be here now if I didn't?" He picks up my hand, inching closer. "Come home."

I want to. God, I would give anything for the warmth of his body wrapped around me, but if I let him off now when he can so easily slash me with his words, then I will live a life full of it, and I won't allow that for myself.

"No."

"Nina—"

"I will come home, you don't have to worry about that. Go to work, carry on as normal. When I'm ready, I will be home."

"When will that be?" He frowns.

"I have a studio to find and a showcase to win." I shrug.

I'm not for sale.

"You'll never let me help you, will you?"

"You have no idea what it took for me to allow myself to live with you." I think about how easy it was for him to get me to move in. "But *that* guy. The man who took me to Paris and allowed me to decide for myself. That guy can be pretty damn perfect."

"Come home," he begs.

I shake my head, and his nostrils flare.

"I used to enjoy winding you up. I would tell Vinny how

fun it was, but now? Now I tread the line so careful, afraid of the damage you will do to us with your words."

"Nina, this is ridiculous; just come home. What's the point of waiting a couple of days?"

"Mase, you aren't the man I met six weeks ago. It's been a crazy few weeks. Take some time for yourself, go and see your family." I drop my head to the side, smiling. "I have so much in my own life I need to fix right now, and you should do the same." I bring my hand up and smooth it down his chest. "We can wait."

"You drive me insane," he huffs, capturing my hand in his.

Hope blooms in my chest. "Good, I want your insanity back. You disappeared on me for a few days."

He swallows thickly and takes a deep breath in. "Promise me you will come back to me."

My lips twist up in a smile. "I promise."

26

Mase

I BARELY SLEPT LAST NIGHT—THE NEED TO GO AND GET HER and bring her back to my bed driving me crazy. I wonder how I ever managed before her.

She is the most stubborn woman I know, and I need to sort myself out if I want to get her back.

I run my hand down over my face and lift the phone from the cradle. I dial the number to the estate.

"Hello?"

"Scar, it's me."

"Hello, big brother," she sings down the phone. I can hear the smile in her voice.

"Is Dad there?"

"Uh, yeah, just a minute. Dad," she shouts. "It's Mason."

I get the image of the two of them in the house, and my hand clenches tight around the phone. My intention wasn't ever to abandon them, and it fucks me up inside to think that I have.

"Son?" My dad's gritty voice comes down the line.

"Yeah, I'm here, Dad. How are you?"

"Good. Really good, actually."

"I presume you haven't heard anything yet, from the doctor?" This shouldn't be so awkward.

"No, not yet. But I did have a visitor this week."

I drop my head, my lips turning up just slightly. "Yeah, she said she came out."

"You should come with her next time. I shouldn't be the one showing her the estate."

He's right. As much as I hate being there, I hate the idea of not showing Nina myself more.

Is that why it bothered me so much?

"I carved out some time," I tell him. "you said you had some things to put into place. Do I need to get anyone else in?"

"Emanuel."

"Right." Emanuel is our solicitor, and there's only one reason he would want to meet with him. "I have three weeks today? I will have to see when he is free."

"That will be great. Thank you, Mason."

I roll my lips, unsure if I want what I am asking. "Bring Scarlet, we can go for something to eat after." He is quiet for a moment, and I don't know if he has heard me. "Dad?"

"Three weeks today, I've pencilled you in."

I snicker, knowing he doesn't have fuck all on three weeks from today.

"See you then, son."

"Bye, Dad."

Nina

I'm in awe as I sit flipping through the photos in front of me. Shot after shot of me dancing in the studio. They seem so much more important now—memories I can look back on and cherish.

"Joey, these are beautiful. You have captured it perfectly."

"It's all you; you're a dream to photograph." He bumps me with his shoulder and I chuckle at his excitement.

"I want to buy some of these, is that possible?"

"Yes, although I will only accept lunch as payment." He winks.

"Joey, I can't. Mason—"

"You can't have lunch with a friend?"

"No, I can, I just... I don't want to lead you on."

"You've made it very clear, Nina. Lunch? As friends. You can have a copy of the lot." He pops a thick brow in question.

"Sold." I grin. "I'd be a fool not to."

"Good! I can't do lunch today, but I am free tomorrow?" he tells me.

"As much as I want to, I need to get serious and start looking for a place to rent. I've been putting it off because I miss the studio so much. I know it's only been a few days, but I need to move on."

"I'd say that's normal."

"Can I call you next week? Arrange something for then?"

"Sure, but I am holding the pictures hostage until I get my lunch date."

"Not a date," I remind him.

He holds up his hands. "Not a date."

I'm just pulling on my gym tights when Scarlet calls. I've had a manic morning meeting with Joey and then coffee with Maggie to look at a potential studio. I'm excited to view it tomorrow.

"Hey, Scar."

"Hey girl, what are you up to? I feel like we should be unemployed losers together these days."

I chuckle down the phone. "Speak for yourself. Did you get the forms from the university yet?"

"Yes, I have, actually. But I won't be starting until next September. I want to be here for Dad."

No matter how much I try with Scarlet, she won't pursue going back to uni until she knows her dad's health is better. I just worry about what will happen if Anthony is still waiting for a transplant next year. Will she put it off again?

"I know, sorry. I won't bring it up again—not unless you want to talk about it. I'm just about to go to the gym."

"Ugh, boring. I'm trying to strip wallpaper. I was looking for a willing accomplice."

"I don't think I'd be much help, Scar. I told you I'm horrific at DIY."

"It's stripping wallpaper, you'll do great. I will cook you tea after to say thanks."

"I don't even—"

"Leaving now to pick you up! Are you at Mason's?"

"No." I laugh. "I am staying at the girls' apartment."

"What? Why?"

"I will send you the address," I say, hanging up and rolling my eyes, knowing she will want all the details.

SCARLET HASN'T STOPPED TALKING, from the minute I got in the car to the moment we pulled the final piece of paper from the wall.

It has been the perfect distraction, though.

I can tell she is lonely here. She only has her dad, and from what she has said, he sleeps a lot these days. It makes me sad. I'm excited for her to get back to medical school.

Anthony joined us out on the balcony for the spaghetti Bolognese that Scarlet made. He looks better today, with more colour in his cheeks and a slight spring in his step. I should feel guilty for spending time here after what Mason said, but Scarlet is my friend now, and I want to be here for her.

"How is the search going for a new studio?" Anthony asks.

"Slow, there isn't much around. I am going to look at a space tomorrow which is exciting, but it's expensive."

"I'm sure something will come up, the right place at the right time." He winks, taking a sip of his water.

"I hope so. I have a dance showcase in a few weeks and nowhere to train my girls."

"Why don't you use the gym here? It's quite the space," he suggests.

"That's a great idea!" Scarlet agrees.

I clench my teeth, trying to keep my face neutral. "Thank you. I appreciate it so much, but I have to do this for myself. Also, my girls wouldn't be able to travel out here each day."

"That's rubbish," Scar mutters, stacking the plates and placing them to the side and out of our way.

"Well, if you need a hand with it at all, financially or

otherwise, let us know. We could always set you up with a loan to help cover the costs."

"That's very kind of you."

Although I already know I would never accept it.

"You've brought out a different side of Mason recently. We are thankful to *you*," he says earnestly.

"Different how?"

"He never came here before. Or called, or even texted. The fact I know you is a miracle. I thought he would never come back here," Scarlet expresses.

I smile, glad that they can see that change in him. Sometimes I think me and Mason are pure toxicity, but then I see the parts of him that Anthony and Scarlet are only now finding again, and it gives me hope.

"He is a good man." Anthony sits nodding his head, swirling his water in his glass. "But stubborn. It's the Lowell trait, I'm afraid."

I lift my wine to my lips and take a large gulp. "You're telling me!"

We all chuckle. My thoughts lost to the crazy man who drives me wild with want and need.

"You can't leave now, by the way. Who would I hang with?" Scarlet looks over at me, giving me her best puppy-eyed look.

"Oh, because that's why I'm with your brother."

"No." She shakes her head, sitting up in her seat and resting her arms on the table. "I think you are with him for the Tuesday special."

My eyes go wide, and I stare at her open-mouthed.

She didn't just say that.

"I am going to leave you girls to it," Anthony announces,

standing and making his way towards the door. Thank god he didn't ask what the Tuesday special was.

"'Night, Dad!" Scarlet says sweetly.

"You bitch!" I whisper-shout as Anthony closes the terrace doors.

I chuck a piece of bread at her but miss.

"Leave my brother, and I will go to every newspaper that will listen and tell your anal story." She starts to laugh, and I mimic her sarcastically.

"Yeah, because they will wanna hear that story. Idiot." I giggle.

"You'd be surprised what strings I can pull. I have connections at The Times." She nods but ends up snorting through her nose and breaking out into hysterics. "I can see it now. Dance prodigy QUITS to become Anal Champion."

"STOP IT!" I heave out, trying to control my laughter.

"Heard it here first, folks."

IT'S EIGHT O'CLOCK, and I'm starting to get tipsy. We've only had a bottle of wine between us, but the great outdoors has made it go to my head.

We escape the cold outside and head for the kitchen. "I need to call a taxi," I say, searching for my phone.

"Just stay. I can drop you home in the morning."

"No, Mase would lose his head if he knew I was here."

"Screw him. How would he even know?"

I think on it for a moment. "I should go home."

"Nina, you're more than welcome here," Anthony says, appearing in the doorway.

"It's nice to have the company around here with him sleeping the day away." Scarlet nods to her dad, smirking. "Besides, who is going to help me finish this?" She holds up a bottle of wine.

Rolling my eyes, I give in. "Okay," I drawl.

It's late when we finally make it to bed, and Scarlet leads me to a room at the end of the hallway. She walks me inside with a wide smile on her face.

"What do you think?" she asks.

"It's... nice," I tell her, looking around at the mostly bare room.

My gaze catches a stack of boxes in the corner.

"It's Mason's old room."

"It is?" I start to look around with more interest.

"Uh-huh." Scarlet waggles her brows at me, and I chuckle. She is a little more than tipsy.

"Go to bed, you creeper." I laugh, stepping farther into the room.

"Good night, champ."

"Good night," I call back.

The bedroom is smaller than I expected. It's decorated in creams and navy tones, but nothing really matches. Other than the few boxes it's empty, the walls and surfaces all free of life. I undress and pull on the pyjamas that Scar had already left out for me, then climb into the bed. She must have expected me to stay the whole time.

I scroll through my phone, feeling close to him but not close enough.

"Pix," he answers on the first ring.

"Hey."

"Are you okay?" he asks, his tone laced with concern.

"Yeah, you'll never guess where I am." I bite my lip, unsure as to whether I should have called. I hope he doesn't get mad again.

"I presumed you were at Lucy and Megan's?" he questions.

"Promise me you won't get mad." I toy with a loose thread on the blanket.

"Nina."

"I'm in your bed. At Lowerwick."

"Fucking hell."

I start to giggle.

"Why are you there?" he asks.

"I was helping your sister decorate. And, maybe I feel close to you here."

"You could be close to me, like really really close to me," he groans.

"You were being an ass. I didn't want to actually be with you."

"Thanks," he deadpans, but I can hear the smile hidden in his voice.

"I'm going to look at a studio tomorrow."

"Yeah? Tell me about it."

I start to ramble on about the studio and all that it has going for it, and he sits and listens, only answering when I allow him the chance to ask a question.

I'm midway through talking about the exposed piping when my phone vibrates in my hand. I put Mase on speaker and open the message.

"Oh, wow."

"What?" Mason asks.

410 | JC HAWKE

I stare at the picture Joey has sent me, one I haven't seen yet.

It's my profile, and I'm reaching out to squat him away. It was when he was messing about and took photos of me randomly. The shot looks like I am reaching out to the person on the other side of the camera. It's incredible, and I love it instantly.

I decide to test the waters; he seems to be in a good mood. "So, you know I had those photos taken. Joey, he took them?"

"Yes."

"Well, I went to look at them today. They are incredible, Mase, and he just sent me this photo now, and I think you'd love it. Can I send it to you?"

"You met with Joey today? I thought you said you needed to find a studio?"

"I do, I am. Joey called and asked if I could go over the pictures."

He snickers down the phone, and my eyes close in regret —not for meeting Joey and not for telling him I did, but regret that I ever believed he would be okay about it. "Sure, send the photo. I'd love to see it. I mean, if I can't have the real thing I will take the scraps," he says flippantly.

I run my tongue against the front of my teeth. "Grow up, Mason. You do realise if you weren't such an ass this week, I wouldn't be away from you right now."

"I will add that to the list of endearments, angel."

"Don't call me that," I snap.

"Angel?"

"Yes! You don't get to call me that right now."

"What does *Joey* get to call you?"

I hang up, fuming at the infuriating idiot. My phone starts

to ring instantly, and I decline the call, then I turn it off and drop it onto the bedside table.

Sitting up, I note how empty the room is, and I wonder if he cleared it or Scarlet. Either way, it's as cold as he is right now.

———

I POKE my head around the sitting-room door, finding Anthony sat up in a chair watching a rugby game on television. "'Morning!" I smile, stepping into the room. "I'm off now, but thank you for having me."

"Of course, give me a second." He stands and rounds the sofa.

Leaning down, he pulls me into a hug. "Don't give him too much hell, love. He doesn't mean it." He winks as if he knows his son is a complete asshole.

"Maybe," I mumble, rolling my eyes and giving him a smirk.

"Is Scarlet driving you home?"

"Yes. Thank you again for having me. This place is a dream."

He smiles thoughtfully down at me. "You're always welcome here, love, with or without Mason."

"Well, I promise the next time I come out, I will bring him with me."

"I'd like that." He nods.

———

THE STUDIO IS AWFUL.

It barely looks like the pictures, and the work that needs doing to it to fix it up is colossal. I'd never afford it. Maggie is being her super polite self and entertaining the salesperson. I wish I could be so classy, but I zoned out twenty minutes ago. Disappointment fills me, knowing I will have to keep looking.

I just need a room, close to the city and at a reasonable rate, it doesn't even have to be fancy, but water leaks and broken floorboards? This place is borderline dangerous.

My phone buzzes in my hand, and I look down, noticing a number I don't know.

"Hello?"

"Miss Anderson? Nina?"

"Speaking?"

Please be a potential studio.

Please be a potential studio.

"My name is George. I work for Mr Lowell—Mason."

"Oh, hi." I frown, and then my stomach drops. "What's wrong?"

"Elliot asked that I called. Mason has just left for Lower-wick Estate." I close my eyes, panic making my legs sway. "Mr Lowell, not Mason, Mr Lowell senior. He has been taken unwell."

"Oh, god, which hospital?"

"I don't think they have gone, the doctor was coming to him."

I breathe out a sigh of relief. That's good. If it were serious, they would take him to the hospital.

"Would you like to go? To the estate?" George asks.

"Uh," I pause. *Would Mason want me to be there?* "No, that's fine. I will make my way over later this evening, thank you, though."

"Of course, just call if I can be of any help."

"Thank you." I smile, not missing the fact Mason's receptionist is now in fact, a male.

Once I hang up, I think about Mason at the estate and how much he hated it the last time we went. The image of him at the door, not wanting to even enter past the threshold.

"Maggie!" I interrupt in a panic.

"Yes, darling?" She frowns as she spins around, both her and the estate agent looking at me in wonder.

"I need your car. I have to go."

THE GRAVEL SEEMS to crunch louder than usual under my trainers as I jump from the car. I don't bother closing the door, my feet carrying me subconsciously past the ambulances and multiple vehicles littered around the circular drive. I take the steps two at a time and push open the main doors, propelling myself into their hell.

Soft purple locks lay in a curled mass against Elliot's chest. It's all I can see. And it has tears springing to my eyes and falling to my cheeks within a split second.

"No!" I shake my head, my voice barely above a whisper. "No."

"Nina," Charlie mutters, putting himself in front of me and trying to pull me into an embrace. I look around him: Scarlet, Elliot, his parents, Charlie and Lance.

Everybody but my Mase.

"Where is he?" I ask to anyone and no one, my eyes a blur.

"He needed some air, but I don't know where he went,"

Vinny mutters, stepping out from the kitchen and into the hall.

When did Vinny get back?

"Scar?"

Her sad eyes meet mine, and her head tilts to the side as her body rocks into Elliot's.

More tears start to fall as we look between each other in understanding. "I'm so sorry, Scarlet."

"Go find him." She sniffs, before hiding her face back in Elliot's chest.

I turn and leave through the open doors, taking off on a sprint around the house and across the first field.

He hasn't made it to the meadow when I catch sight of him, still trudging toward the last gate.

I start to run faster, my limbs aching, knowing I need to get to him.

I reach the meadow and climb the gate.

"Mase!" I call, watching as he walks toward the hill.

"Mason!" I cry, my tears falling without restraint. He either can't hear me or he's not listening, too inside his own head. And I know how that feels—wanting to run away and shut the world out.

I continue running for him, knowing I just need to hold him, be with him.

I'm almost to him when he crumbles, falling to his knees onto the damp grass in his immaculate grey suit. "Mase, baby."

I round on him, dropping to my knees in front of him as he lands. "Mase."

Grasping his head in my hands, I try to pull his face down

to mine, but he holds it firm, his body too powerful to control as he stares up at the sky.

"He's gone."

"Baby," I whisper, standing so I can see him, cradling his face in my hands.

His eyes search my face, a lone tear rolling across his temple and into his hairline.

"He's gone, Nina." More tears start to fall, and I wipe them away with my thumbs.

"He hasn't. Mason, he hasn't. Feel him. Let him leave and then breathe him in. He is here, I promise." My own tears stream down my cheeks and drip from my chin.

"He didn't know," he sobs.

I hold him close, leaning down and kissing his forehead as he cries. "I'm so sorry."

"He didn't know." His head falls to my breastbone, and he breaks down in my arms, our tears merging into one as they stream down my chest.

My beautiful, broken man.

27

Mase

IF EVER I WERE TO BREAK, I'D NEVER PICK HER ARMS TO BE THE ones I would fall into. But this wasn't a choice. It was a need, and she showed up.

A feeling I've not felt for many years weighs heavy on me, a feeling I know comes with a loss.

As a child, my mother's passing was hard to take. It didn't make sense, and it impacted me for years. I thought it was my age that made it feel the way it did, but the ache in my chest now tells me I would never have been prepared when it came to losing them.

I thought I was strong.

Walking back to the house with Nina under my arm, I draw from her strength, but I know it won't be enough.

Her head lifts to mine, and she gives me a strained smile. As we near the house, I stop where I stand and pull Nina into me.

"I'm sorry, Pix." I kiss her head.

"Sorry?" she questions as I turn and walk towards my Bentley, leaving her behind. "Hey!" she shouts. "Mason, what about Scar?"

My gaze catches hers, anger brimming behind her deep chocolate pools. "I will see you at home."

Her brows rise in surprise as I shut the door, start the engine and tear off out of the drive.

Nina

MY HEART BURNS as I make my way up the front steps and into the house. I give a small smile to the Montgomerys who sit in the lounge, but I don't stop, moving towards the kitchen where I see Lance leaning in the doorway.

I place my hand on his back. "Excuse me," I whisper.

"Nina," he utters softly, his face solemn.

I swallow down the lump in my throat and avoid eye contact with him. I can't deal with Lance being nice right now. It will send me over the edge.

"Where's Mase?" Elliot asks, tipping his chin.

I look around at the boys, shaking my head, not knowing what to say.

Charlie drops his head, his hands shoving deep in his suit trousers. He knows.

"He hates it here, I don't blame him," Scarlet murmurs from the island.

"He fucking left?" Elliot spits.

Any other day I'd defend him, but that's the last thing she needs to hear right now. Walking to the island, I lean in and hug her shoulders. "What can I do?" I ask.

Her hand encases mine, squeezing tight. "Nothing. Mase is going to need you."

"I know." I just hope he lets me.

"Scarlet, honey." Frey steps into the kitchen with red-rimmed eyes, the only tell that she's upset. "Glen and I think it would be best that you come home with us this evening, or we can come here for a couple of weeks. We don't want you here alone."

"Yeah, that's probably a good idea." She gives her a small smile, and I see the strength behind it. She pulls me tighter to her back and sets her shoulders square, already putting on a front, reminding me of her brother.

"I'm going to go get things straight at the office," Charlie announces, nodding at Elliot then leaning down to kiss Scar on the forehead. "Call me if you need me, okay?"

"I'll come with you," Lance mutters, his hand on the back of his neck as if he is uncomfortable. He gives Scarlet an awkward nod then turns to leave. Charlie following behind.

"Where do you want to stay, Scar? You can come home with us, or we can come here," Elliot asks.

"I can't leave." Her eyes fill with tears, and she bats them away. I look to Elliot, his own eyes shining. "I can't leave them," she adds.

Their sadness seeps into me as their heartache becomes my own. How can someone be here one day and gone the next. Just like that.

"Then we will come here. Give me an hour, yeah." Elliot

looks at me, and my stomach drops. I stand conflicted because that means an hour away from Mase. But Scarlet needs me too.

I nod my head, letting him know he can go.

"You don't have to stay. You can go to him," Scarlet tells me.

"I know, and I will."

We sit in comfortable silence, her head resting on my shoulder as we allow the calmness in the house to settle between us.

AFTER TWISTING my key in the elevator, I stand with my foot tapping, and my hands running through my hair.

Emotions. I know he will be feeling so many of them right now. I expect it. But the unknown scares me because I have no idea what I will be walking into.

The only thing I do know is he will be hurting.

The doors slide open, and my heart sinks as the smell of cigarette smoke fills me, along with a heavy beat. It's so loud I can't make out the words.

Broken shards of a whiskey bottle lie at the bottom of the staircase, the amber liquid that it bathes in telling me he didn't drink much of it.

Taking the steps two at a time, I push through the bedroom door, my shoulders dropping when I hear the shower running.

"Thank god."

Just as I pass the bed, I kick a bottle. An empty bottle.

Picking it up, I walk to the bathroom door and push it open, steam billowing out as I enter.

I can't see anything. "Mase?"

Stepping around the tile wall, I find him lying motionless on the shower floor and completely naked.

I remove my shoes and drop down next to him, my clothes getting soaked through.

"This helps?" I ask, looking at him.

He shrugs, not giving me his eyes, but I can see the bags that sit beneath them. I didn't notice before, but seeing him now, he looks tired.

"You don't need to be here."

"Yes, I do." I take his hand and sit him up, pulling us both out of the spray.

He sways as he rights himself.

Looking up at me, his cold stare slices through me. "You'd be better off without me."

I lick my lips, trying to find the right words. I get why he is lashing out, but it doesn't make it easier to listen to.

Dropping my eyes, ignoring his comment as I grab a towel. "Get up, the water is going cold."

"You should go, Nina. You shouldn't be here," he slurs.

"I want to be here. Now, get up."

He grasps my face, bringing me close. "You wouldn't want to be, not if you knew," he snarls.

I go to grab his hand that holds me, and he yanks it back with a hiss. I grab his wrist, noting the stream of red running down his arm. "You've cut yourself."

"I'm fine." He shrugs me away, getting up in a rush and staggering from the shower as he makes his way into the bedroom.

"Here," I hand him a towel to cover himself, but he doesn't take it from me. "Let me see your hand."

I watch as blood drips to the plush carpet.

"You're perfect; you know that? So. Fucking. Perfect," he sniggers. "You made it so easy for me. Then you left." He swipes the blood from his forearm, and it splatters the bed.

His perfect body ripples as he jerks around the room on unsteady feet, and it only makes my heart hurt more.

"Mason, now isn't the time, please." I plead, holding out the towel to him.

He's talking rubbish, and despite how much his words hurt, I know they're coming from a place of pain.

"I didn't come here to argue with you."

"Why did you come here then? Huh? For this?" He starts to pull at his hardening length, and I turn, disgusted, leaving the room and leaving him. "Off you run." He laughs at my retreating back.

Once I am out of sight, I take a moment, leaning on the bannister and taking in a deep breath.

Don't let him push you away.

I go to the kitchen, find the first aid kit, and then grab the dustpan and brush and some kitchen roll. I clean up the mess at the bottom of the stairs, then make my way back to the bedroom, hoping he will have calmed down a little.

Mason is sitting on the ottoman when I enter the room, his eyes cast down at the ground. He has a pair of boxers on, and a towel is wrapped around his fist, the blood already tainting it a deep red.

I kneel at his feet and take his bloodied hand, not wanting to look into his eyes in case I find the anger that was there before.

The cut isn't overly deep, but the alcohol he has consumed is making it bleed heavier. I try to wrap it the best I can, but I know he will need to get it checked.

Once I'm finished, I sit for a moment and stare at the ground between us.

Silently, he takes hold of my chin in his bandaged hand, lifting my head. Tears line his face, his eyes filled with so much pain it threatens to destroy the both of us.

But it's *my Mase.*

"Promise me when I'm sober."

"Baby." I pull him to me, wanting nothing more than to take it all away.

I want to tell him that everything will be better in the morning, but I can't promise that right now.

IT'S BEEN two weeks since Anthony passed away. The funeral was four days ago, and it's only sent Mason deeper and harder into his grief. He won't let anyone in, me and Scarlet included.

I shouldn't have been surprised that he attended the funeral, but I was, considering I almost left without him when he refused to leave his office that morning. I felt proud when he joined me in the foyer, dressed in his sharp suit, face stoic as he masked the hurt.

Scarlet struggled through the ceremony, but Mason was there to hold her together.

They held each other up.

The boys have visited daily, but with Mason out of the

office, Elliot needed to be in his place. He hates to see Mason hurt like he is, but he knows it's part of the process.

We all want to help, but none of us knows how.

As much as Mason tried to change my mind, I decided to cancel my place in the showcase. I couldn't put in the time it deserved, and with everything else that happened, it didn't seem so important. I knew I couldn't go away and leave him, not when I was afraid he would break at any minute.

I had all the time in the world to pursue my dreams.

Routine fell over us. Every morning I'd wake to an empty bed, the shower running, and the en suite door locked.

He works out, showers, goes to his home office until eleven at night, and then crawls into bed where he wraps me in his arms, neither of us getting any sleep.

Scarlet has been over twice, but I know things are strained between them since she asked Mason to come to the house to go through Anthony's things. It's probably the reason I'm lying alone in bed at two a.m. I know it has been on his mind since she asked.

Climbing from the bed, I make my way to his home gym, finding him running flat out on his treadmill with his earbuds in.

Satisfied he is home and safe, I go to the kitchen and make him a protein shake, then I leave it on the side and go back to bed.

Mase

My ARMS SURROUND HER, sweat dripping from my body and landing on her delicate throat. Her lashes fan out over her cheeks, and I watch as her chest rises and falls, full of life.

"Nina," I whisper.

She stirs slightly, then jolts awake when she sees me hovering over her. I know she hasn't been sleeping long.

"Mase?" Her hands push back my damp hair, her eyes searching my face. "What's wrong?"

"I need you." I drop my mouth to hers, pulling on her bottom lip before sweeping my tongue inside.

"Hmmm," she moans, making my cock grow stiff.

She pulls at my vest, and I adjust my knees on the bed, leaning back to pull it over my head while she whips off her T-shirt.

"Baby," I hum, my mouth wrapping around her nipple. "I have missed this. Us."

Her back arches off the bed as she pushes herself farther into me. "Me too," she whispers.

I pull her pyjama shorts from her legs, chucking them to the floor with our discarded tops.

With the need to feel her, I thrust forward, filling her. A sound rumbles from deep in my chest as her heat sheaths me. She calls out my name, my jaw slack against her neck as I hover over her, unable to move.

I roll my hips. Slowly. "Fuck!"

"Mase," she pants, writhing on the stark white sheets.

She looks like an angel.

Lifting her leg around my waist, I slide in deeper, and we both moan out loud. I drop my head to hers, rocking into her, savouring the feel of her after being deprived so long.

Why did I keep myself from this?

Nina

"Morning, Pix."

The hairs on my neck stand to attention as his arm wraps around my waist. I'm standing at the sink washing up my breakfast dishes, and the feel of his body at my back warms me to my core. I don't know what changed last night, but I woke this morning to find him asleep and next to me in the bed. I thought it was progress, but this right now is a complete one-eighty from yesterday.

"Morning, is everything okay?" I ask, looking down at the hand that rests on my waist, noticing the navy cuff of his dress shirt and his Rolex watch. "You're going to the office?"

I turn in his arms.

"Yeah. It's about time."

Reaching up, I smooth out the deep line that forms on his brow. "That sounds like a great idea." I smile, pleased that he wants to go back. I thought I'd have to push him into it, and I don't think I would have had the heart.

He nods, and I turn, carrying on with the dishes.

"Will you come with me?" he asks me, reaching for the cereal as a small smile tugs at his lips.

I get what feels like a zap of electricity right between my legs.

Shit. I didn't realise how badly I needed *him* back.

"You wish, Bossman." I wink. "If you're going to the office, I will go see your sister. If you don't mind."

He juts out his chin, not answering me with actual words.

"If you don't want me at the house, I won't go, but I know

Scar wants to sort through your father's things, and someone should help her."

I panic the moment the words are out. Why am I bringing up his dad?

Baby steps, Nina!

"I know," he snaps, running his hand through his hair. "Sorry."

"Don't be." I go to him, slipping my arms around his waist. "I won't go today."

"Me neither."

"What? No, Mase, go to the office."

"I don't want to. I just thought maybe I should."

Dropping my head to the side, I smooth a hand down his shirt. He looks so put together in his suit, yet inside he is still so broken.

"You should go to the office," I tell him, placing a kiss on his smooth jaw.

He nods, knowing he needs to. "You'll help Scar? Please."

I wrap my arms around him, needing to get closer than I am, but knowing it's physically impossible. But if it were, I'd follow my soul into the depths of his. "Of course, I will."

―――――――

IT'S NINE A.M., and Mase is still here. He refused to let me shower alone, telling me he needed 'a good luck fuck' for his first day back at work. My man is back, and with that comes his insatiable appetite for *me*. Not that I am complaining.

He hangs from my lips, pulling them between his teeth as he walks us to the elevator. "Come with me," he says between kisses.

"No. Go, now!" I laugh.

He pulls away from me, and his eyes grow hungry, but I see the hesitation lurking in the back of them.

"I spoke to George when you were dressing, told him you were going in today."

He quirks a brow. "Did you now?" He shakes his head, knowing he can't back out. "What would I do without you?" He leans in, giving me one more chaste kiss. "Tell Scar I will see her soon."

I bite my lip, a feeling of contentment settling over me. "Okay."

He winks, stepping away from me and entering the lift. "I love you, my beautiful Pixie."

I AM foolish to spend my time doing anything other than actively looking for a job or studio, but in all honesty, I think I am in denial. I don't want to be working right now, not when I feel like Mase needs me.

Scarlet doesn't answer the door, so I wave Vinny off and let myself in. I find her in the main living room, her hair covered in purple hair dye.

"Hey!" I frown, moving around the sofa to pull her into a hug.

"Thank god you are here! Have I got the back?" She fans a hand around her head. "Dad normally checked—it's the small things!" she tuts.

Spinning around, I check her hairline and see that she has missed a chunk. "Here, give me the brush." I paint the area she missed and hand it back. "How have you been? Are the Montgomerys not here?" I ask, frowning as I eye the blob of dye on the rug beneath my feet.

That isn't coming out.

"No, they left two days ago. Frey is a babe and like a mother to me, but god, she is just too much."

"That's a bad thing?" I smile, happy to see her so upbeat.

"Uh, yeah. She offers me food when I already have food, a coffee when I am sat with a tea. I swear they are waiting for me to break."

"And are you—going to break? 'Cause that would be okay."

"Nina, I'm okay. Honestly."

I eye her sceptically but she only evil eyes me back. "Okay, you sure you want to do this today?" I ask, pointing to the pile of things belonging to her dad that she has gathered on the table.

"Yes, it's got to be done."

"Right, I will put the kettle on."

FOUR HOURS later

We are only halfway through the piles of clothes and boxes. I look to Scar, noticing her beautiful full smile. We have taken our time, pausing when needing to relish in anything that catches her attention. A photo that evokes a memory or a jumper that still smells of Anthony.

I just wish Mase could have been here.

Scarlet powers up the TV as she sits in a sea of boxes. Some will go into the attic and some to charities. Scarlet wants somebody to use the items and not have them sat, but insists the sentimental stuff stays—which is why we're watching their home videos.

"Nina, look at this."

"Is that you?" I laugh, taking in the image on the screen.

A little girl with dark hair is sitting naked in the kitchen sink.

"Yup. Dad always said I was the feral child."

"I can see that."

She eyes me with a scowl. "I can just imagine you with your perfect princess dresses and frilly socks," she mocks.

"God, no. I was lucky if I got a pair of leggings that fit."

"Shit. Sorry, Nina."

"Don't be." I chuckle, reaching into the box at my feet and pulling out a smaller rectangular one.

"Here," she calls. "Ha! Look at how chubby Elliot was."

I carry the box with me, moving to stand behind her at the back of the sofa.

"No! That is not Elliot," I snort out.

"Yep, that's Mase next to him."

"I can see Mase, but that does not look like El. I need to send this to the girls."

I pull my phone out and snap a picture, sending it to Lucy and Megan with the caption 'guess who?'

Sliding my phone back into my pocket, I bring my attention to the next box. Lifting the lid, I find a picture. It's the same photo that Mason has in his home office. A photo of the Lowells before their heartache.

I pass it over Scarlet's shoulder. "Here."

"Oh, Dad told me about this day. Mason was stung by a

bee seconds after this photo was taken." My hand wraps around the notebook in the bottom of the box. It looks like a diary. It's thick, heavy and worn around the edges. Scarlet carries on, "Apparently his face ballooned like it does when he is near a dog." Scarlet laughs as I swipe my hand across the cover, clearing the dust that coats it. "Poor fucker. I hope we find *that* picture. Dad always said there was one, but Mason would hide it."

"What's this?" I ask, my thumb brushing over the initials that mark the bottom right corner.

"What's what?" She asks, still staring at the photo in her hand, reliving memories of the past.

My brain misfires, trying to figure out what I am seeing. Without thought, I flick open the diary and begin to read the first page.

NOVEMBER 16, 1993.

DEAR MASON.

MY DARLING BOY,

Snapping the book closed, I swallow the bile that rises in my throat. "Your mother's name."

"Ellis," Scarlet tells me with a frown.

"Ellis. Marie. Lowell." I remember Mason telling me after I danced for him that night.

"Yes, Ellis Marie. What's wrong, Nina? You look like you've seen a ghost."

"The initials." I trace them like I have many times before. The gilding and font exact. Unique and yet so familiar. "EML."

"What about them?"

"I've seen them before, but on a piano."

"Yeah, Mum's. She was an incredible pianist. Dad said she

would have played for the world someday, but she never wanted to leave this place."

I suck in a breath as I lift my gaze to her. "Where is the piano?"

"Mason has it. Are you okay?"

28

Nina

MASON HAS IT?

I know what those three words mean. They make perfect sense. But my mind is unwilling to connect the dots. Because what the hell does this mean?

"Do you have a picture of it?"

I'm being stupid. There's no way—*is there?*

"Of the piano?" Scarlet frowns, as if I'm crazy.

"Yeah!"

"Probably. It's just a black grand piano."

It's just a black grand piano. There must be hundreds of thousands of them in the world. Maybe I am being crazy.

My eyebrows pinch together.

Were the initials even EML?

The doubt only makes everything a bigger, confusing haze.

"Let me look. I might have a picture." Scarlet starts

digging until she finds more memory boxes that Anthony had made. Each one is labelled with a different occasion.

"Umm... Eclipse, Millennium, Christmas of '89. Oh, this one! Christmas 1990. Mum was pregnant with me at the time. I've seen this one." She beams at me, falling to her knees and connecting the tape to the TV.

A few moments later the screen lights up.

The camera shakes as the person holding it wobbles along the wood floor. A child, I'd suspect. "Mase, he stole the camera. He is so unbelievably cute in this."

Scarlet confirms my thoughts.

"Mason, come here!" a deep but playful voice calls out, making the little boy giggle and run faster, but then two feet come into view, and suddenly he stops. "Mummy. No!" He spins, running in the opposite direction, but as he does, the camera falls perfectly on Anthony's young face. "Gotcha!" his hands come out to catch his son. "Daddy, no, put me down, no tickle, no tickle!" Mason squeals, trying to catch his breath between his hysterics. "Careful, Anthony, you will drop him," a soft voice mutters, the camera now upside down and coming to focus on the woman in the kitchen doorway. *Ellis.* She is wearing a blue floral dress, her stomach a perfectly round shape.

I swipe the tear that forms in my eye.

"Come on, boys." The camera shakes as Ellis leans down to take it, then it spins to Anthony and Mason.

Mason hangs upside down, Anthony's hands locked tightly around his ankles. Moving through the hall, they enter the lounge we are in now. Mason is placed down on the sofa then lifted into his father's arms, his podgy hands wrapping tight around Anthony's neck.

My heart aches for them.

Why couldn't they have had more time?

"Mummy, play! Play!" Mason cries.

I dip my head to the side as my throat burns because I already know I'm right.

Anthony tells Ellis to pass him the camera, the blurred image from before becoming perfectly clear. Mason climbs onto his mother's lap, his hand wrapped lovingly around her baby bump, and his head rested against her chest.

Ellis begins to play, and my eyes drop to the initials on the back of the piano. The very piano that has been sat in my studio for the past year. The piano I have lay on whilst feeling so far from him.

My studio always felt like home to me, and his mother's piano was always a part of that—maybe even the very essence of it.

Ellis looks into the camera, and I feel her eyes on *me* before they flick higher—beyond the camera. A loving smile graces her face that's directed at her husband.

"She was beautiful. You look just like her."

"Yeah," Scarlet sobs. "Sorry, I've seen this a hundred times before."

"Don't apologise," I tell her, moving to sit on the sofa.

I pull her into a tight hug just as the tape cuts off.

VINNY ARRIVES LATE in the afternoon to take me home, and I dread it. I pushed the piano to the back of my mind for the remainder of the afternoon, not allowing my brain to make sense of it. But I know I need to.

Especially before I face Mason.

"Hey, Vin." I smile as I slide into the back of the Audi.

"Good day?" he asks, looking up at the grand house with a thoughtful look.

"Yeah, just draining." I yawn, dropping my head to the seat and closing my eyes. "I will be glad to get in my bed tonight."

We leave the estate behind and head towards the city, which gives me plenty of time to think. And the only thing on my mind is Mason's mother's piano.

Why is it in the studio?

Did Mason know?

I pause at that thought. It's like everything clicks into place. My head calls a ceasefire. The confusion settles as I get the image of Mason in the studio. It was the day Joey took the photos. It was the first time he had been upstairs.

I thought he was mad. I thought it was Joey.

The way his eyes cut through me as if he wasn't looking at me.

He wasn't. It was the piano.

He knows it's there—but how, *why?*

My body flushes ice cold then hot, goosebumps making the hair on the back of my neck stand on end.

He knows it's there.

If the piano is Mason's and he knew where my studio was, why didn't he ever tell me about it? God, that doesn't even make sense. Not with the way he behaved that day. Did he not know? He didn't seem like he knew. He seemed...

"Vinny, do you know anything about Ellis' piano?"

He flinches. It's quick and only slight, but I catch it, and it sets my pulse racing.

"It's just, I think it is in my studio." I shake my head, correcting myself. "My old studio."

He hesitates, and it's obvious he is choosing his words carefully. "Yes, Nina. I've heard about the piano, but you should probably ask Mason about it."

"I'm asking you."

"And I am asking you to speak to Mason about it," he says sternly, and I frown at his tone.

He has been quiet since he got back from his holiday. I put it down to Anthony's passing because I know they were close, but this isn't like Vinny.

Resigning myself to the fact that Vinny isn't going to help me, I try to piece it together myself starting with the day Mason came to the studio.

Joey and the photos. Mason came to me and saw the piano—that much I am sure of.

What was it he said?

Why can't I remember anything, dammit?!

I went for lunch with the girls straight after Mason left. Erin called and told me she had to go home.

Erin!

Why the hell was Ellis's piano in her building?

Nothing makes sense.

I catch Vinny watching me in the rearview mirror, and I know he has the answers to my questions. He disappeared the day after my studio sold. Mase was in a foul mood, and Erin went back to Australia.

Something doesn't add up.

"Your holiday, Vin. Where did you go?"

"Up North. I went to see family." He flicks his eyes

between me in the mirror and the road, and his fists clench against the steering wheel.

"The day after my studio sold, right?"

"Right."

AFTER BEING AT THE ESTATE, I feel like I have lived through Scarlet's nostalgia. So many emotions that are not mine to have, yet I have become so deeply rooted into this family in such a short space of time.

I haven't felt that since becoming a part of Lucy's family, and to think Mason has kept something from me—after everything we have been through—it scares me.

I'm afraid of what my gut tells me.

I find him in the home gym. He's screwing the lid back onto his water bottle, and I watch as his bare chest glistens with a layer of sweat.

His body is phenomenal. His vigorous routine since his father's death is only making him fitter.

"Hi," I say, leaning my hip against the doorframe and making myself known.

"Angel." He makes his way towards me, bending down to kiss me, but my instincts have me pulling away.

He frowns down at me. "What's wrong?"

I swallow thickly, not knowing where to start.

The elevator door pings, and we both bristle. Mason moves past me and out into the foyer.

"Vin, what are you doing here?"

He's here because he knows that I know.

I know what he's done. Or at least, I *think* I do. And it hurts so much.

Mason turns to me as realisation sinks in, his face awash of panic and guilt, only confirming my thoughts. Has his guilt been there this whole time? Because all of a sudden, I feel like I am seeing him in technicolour.

"Nina."

I put my hand up to stop him, my mind racing as I cover my mouth with my other hand.

I don't want it to be true.

His features tighten, and he tilts his head, his anger starting to pull him under. "Say it," he grits out.

My eyes fill with tears. Do I even need to say it? "You promised me—"

"Say it!" his voice booms, cutting me off as he steps toward me.

My nostrils flare, and I hold his eyes, unable to look away. "Did you have a hand in selling my studio?" I ask, my voice strong and clear.

Silence fills the penthouse. My heartbeat the only sound.

"No." He tightens his jaw. Sharp. Deadly. *I don't want to hate him.* "I had the *only* hand. *I* sold it." *But I do.*

"Why?" my voice betrays me, cracking as I utter the word.

Lifting my chin, I don't allow the hurt to show nor my tears to fall. He's already taken too much of me.

I won't give him another inch.

He runs a hand down his face. "You wouldn't understand. I never meant for this—"

"Did you only show interest in me because of the piano?"

"What? No!"

"Why, then?" I snap, my body visibly trembling.

"Nina, please, there's not a simple answer."

"Fucking try me!" I yell, feeling my emotions slipping as I plead with him not to fuck this up any more than he already has.

"I can't."

"What?" I utter, my shoulders dropping.

"Mason, come on, lad." Vinny steps forward, his voice laced with warning.

I'd almost forgotten he was there.

"Fuck off, Vinny!"

"You need to tell her the truth. You can tell her the truth."

"Leave!" Mason growls, his face turning a deep shade of red.

"Don't bother," I tell Vinny, pulling the strap of my bag higher on my shoulder. "*I'm* leaving."

I stare into Mason's eyes, searching for the man I know is in there but continues to shut me out.

I go to move past him, but he grabs my upper arm, pulling me into him. "You're getting good at this. Running."

"And every time I run, you seem to cut me that little bit deeper."

I see the turmoil in his eyes: the fear, the guilt, the anger and pain. I made a decision months ago to be that someone for him.

To stand beside him.

"You're making it impossible for me to love you."

He lowers his eyes to the ground, releasing me. "Just fucking go."

I move on autopilot, entering the lift and letting the doors close behind me.

Mase

"SHE WORKED it out in the car. I don't know how she knew about the piano."

"She needed to know." I shrug Vinny off, pinching the bridge of my nose. "Follow her."

He nods. "What are you going to do?"

"I need to talk to Charlie."

He lingers in the foyer, and I know he wants to say more.

"You could tell her. You know she would understand."

"She isn't the only person I'm trying to protect here, Vinny!" I snap.

His face screws up in disgust. "We don't need protecting! It's about time everyone took responsibility for their actions. You can't keep carrying this so heavily on your shoulders."

"You have no idea what I carry on my shoulders! She is too good!" I roar, pointing my finger at him. "Too good to be tainted with this and too good for the likes of me."

"Maybe you're right. But you need to make a decision, Mason, because if you choose to keep this from her, you will lose her for good."

Then I lose her for good.

Nina

MY FEET EAT up the pavement as I rush down the street and away from the penthouse.

My mum let me down so many times in my life, and every time she did, I'd pull my defences higher, shutting the world out a little more each time.

I let my guard slip momentarily with Mason, and he made promises which I foolishly believed. Now I want to revert back to my safe space, and I don't feel like I have it. This last year my studio became my safety blanket, and I feel stupid to have allowed myself to rely on something that didn't belong to me.

Pulling my phone from my pocket, I try to call Lucy. She doesn't pick up, and I know it will be because she is working. I try Megan instead.

"Hey, babe!" she answers cheerfully.

"Megs, are you free?"

"I'm at work; what's up?"

I look around at my surroundings, noticing I've walked a good distance and I'm close to the city.

"My studio." I shake my head. "Erin's studio—" How the hell did Mason have something to do with selling Erin's studio? "Mason sold it. I don't know how, and I'm so confused." I palm my head and try to digest the words that have just left my mouth.

"What?! What do you mean?"

"I don't even know." I stop short, frowning as I think of something. "Megs, can I call you back?"

"Are you okay?"

"I will call you as soon as I can, I promise. I'm fine. I just need answers."

"Okay, text me, Nina. I'm worried!"

I hang up and scroll through my contacts until I reach Erin's number.

Maybe she can shed some light on the situation.

It rings four times, and I almost give up, but then her confused voice echoes down the line.

"Nina?"

"I know you asked me not to call, but I just found something out, and I needed to talk to you," I rush out, hoping she doesn't hang up.

"No, it's fine. I was hoping you'd call. I'm glad you came to your senses."

The hairs on my arms stand to attention. I need to be smart here. "Yeah, I did."

"Are you safe? He won't leave you alone, Nina. If you are clever you can benefit from this."

Benefit? "How?"

"Money. Money talks, and people will pay a lot to keep those voices quiet."

What on earth?

"Is that what you did?"

She doesn't answer me, and I worry my tone might have given me away. "At first it wasn't a choice. He is a dangerous man, Nina. I did what I had to. You can't give him the control, and you have to use this against him and not let him get the upper hand. I wasn't smart, and now I'm on the other side of the world."

She's in Australia because of Mason?

"How long have you known him?"

"Since... wait. What has he told you?" she asks defensively.

I close my eyes and panic. What do I say to that? "I know about the piano."

"The piano." She laughs, and it's cold and detached. "I will never know how I pulled that off."

"Erin—"

"Will you stop fucking calling me that!" she snaps. "Do you have any idea how much harder you make my life just by calling me? And pretending to know something you don't... that's dumb, Nina. I thought you were smarter. If I were you, I'd get out whilst you can. Don't call me again."

"No! Please, wait!" The line goes dead, and I clench my fists until my nails bite into my palm.

"Why can't anyone tell me the damn truth!" I seethe out loud.

"Nina."

I close my eyes upon hearing Vinny's voice, my head beginning to pound. "Unless you are going to tell me what the hell is going on, leave me alone."

"I always knew you were strong, from that first day I met you."

I glare towards him. "I don't want your voice of reason crap right now, Vinny. You won't win me over today."

"I'm not trying to. I just want you to know that it wouldn't make you weak if you went home. He doesn't see it yet."

"He doesn't see what yet?" I snap.

"Your strength. He thinks he does, but your true strength, deep down inside of you, from the years of hurt at the hands of your mum." He looks at me in knowing, and I'm reminded that Vinny was the one who looked me up for Mason. He probably knows more than anyone. "When he sold your studio I felt disappointed in him—it's why I left. I felt for you, and I tried to stop him, but he was blinded by the need to keep you safe. It was stupid. It didn't protect you at all, and you're not in any danger now. What he did was irrational and impulsive, but he wouldn't change what he's done, and I respect him for that. He is a good man, Nina. His heart is in the right place."

"You didn't go on holiday—you left because he sold the studio?"

"Yes, but don't mistake my cowardliness for anything but that. When the time came, he did what he had to do. I should have stood by him." He drops his head, staring at the pavement.

This is ridiculous. "Please, just tell me what's going on. Erin is acting differently, and I don't know what I'm supposed to do."

"I can't tell you because it's not for me to say, and Mason believes it's not his story to tell either." He grimaces as I step back from him. "Give him your trust and the rest will come."

"You do understand how utterly impossible that is right now?"

He shrugs. "Where are you going, Nina?"

I shake my head, not having a clue but knowing I need the space. From everyone. "I don't know."

"Do you want company?" he calls to my retreating back.

"No."

"But you will call, if you need anything?"

I nod my head. It's impossible to stay mad at Vinny.

29

Mase

CHARLIE SITS ON MY SOFA WITH HIS HEAD CRADLED IN HIS hands while Elliot stands, staring at me in utter disbelief. I lean back against the window with my hands shoved deep in my pockets, giving them the time they need to process what I've just told them.

"When?" Charlie snaps, not lifting his head.

"That redhead I picked up in Melders the start of last year."

"You pick up all the fucking time. You're telling me it has been over twelve months?"

I nod once, and he visibly tenses. "Who the fuck have I been tracking?" he roars, his face hardening.

"I called them off."

"You called them off," he repeats my words, laughing sarcastically. His lip curls in disgust, but it's nothing I didn't expect. "More like you paid them off. Every week, I get that text, and you're telling me it's utter bollocks!"

"Mate, I—"

"Fuck off, Lowell."

"That's fucked," Elliot mutters, running his hand across his mouth.

"I know."

"Why are you telling me this now?"

Charlie's always been smart. He's intuitive and doesn't miss a trick.

"I didn't know how you'd react if it came out. I didn't want you blindsided."

He sniggers under his breath and stands. "So someone has threatened you?"

"Not directly, but the night Lance showed up here, Cara, the redhead from Melders." I run my tongue across my teeth as I spit her name. "She overheard us talking in the office."

"She knows?" His brow furrows and he twists to face me.

I nod.

"And what did you tell her?"

"I panicked; let her make demands." I drop my head, my mind reeling as the memories of that night seep in. "I fixed it, though, took control, found shit from her past and she hasn't been a threat since."

Until now.

"You could go to prison, you stupid fuck!" he sneers, rubbing a hand over his face. "And I wouldn't be able to represent you. The fuck were you thinking?"

"My concern wasn't for me."

"Don't act like you were protecting me," he scoffs. "This is one big power trip to you."

"Bullshit! And fuck you! You know full well what would

have happened if I came to you. You're a fucking lawyer, Aldridge. The fewer people who knew, the better!"

"Calm down, Mason," Elliot warns.

"I get it! I get why, but you should have told me. I'm so fucking pissed with you."

We stand in silence, nobody saying a word for the longest time.

"This redhead." Charlie pulls out his phone. "What does she know?"

Nina

I HAVE no idea how long I have been walking, but when I arrive at my apartment, the sun has set, leaving the street-lights as my only guide.

The apartment is exactly as I left it. It hasn't been touched since the day after we got back from Paris.

Paris.

Looking down at my bangle, I turn it over and thumb the words with a bitter smile on my face. It seems like a lifetime ago now, and the reminder of the weekend we shared makes his betrayal hurt that much deeper.

If there is one thing I do know, it's that the look in his eyes as he watched me leave was one of pure regret. If there is one thing I truly know about Mase–and maybe it makes me a naive fool–it's that he would never intentionally hurt me. But it doesn't make it hurt any less.

If my mother taught me anything, it was the fact she *didn't* care; my hurt didn't penetrate her like it should a mother. She could hurt me in one second then leave me the next—probably to go to *work*.

She never showed me a scrap of remorse.

So the look in Mason's eyes, although I might not be used to it, I sure as hell know what it means. Because when he hurts, I hurt, and I saw that reflected in his eyes today. He cares, he hurts, and he shows remorse.

And I have no idea how to deal with that.

Mase

THE BELT of the treadmill flashes under my feet as it swirls around at a ferocious pace. My chest burns with every kilometre I hit, my body dripping with sweat as I push myself harder than I know I should. But I can't stop. If I stop, I will go to her, and she's not ready for that yet.

Nina left five days ago, and she isn't answering her phone or her door. I've found Lucy and Megan useless. They won't allow me anywhere near her right now. The radio silence was anticipated. I never expected her to stay. I wished she would, just once, but her pride would never allow her to.

I make it into the office early and throw myself into work for the day, knowing it's the distraction I need. I don't get a single interruption for three hours, and I know it's George's doing.

He seems to have picked up on my mood.

"Mason, I have Lance," his voice chirps through the intercom.

"Send him in."

My hand runs over my mouth as I stare down at the photo on my desk. It was taken in Paris. Nina is smiling at the camera, and you can tell she has turned and caught me by the way the dimple pops on her full cheek.

"Lowell."

Lifting my eyes, I nod my head in greeting. "I told Charles and Elliot," I tell him, straight to the point. Standing, I slide my hands into my pockets and round my desk, leaning back against it. "About Marcus."

I knew Lance would be pissed about me telling them, but I also know he will back me. He always has.

"Right, and what now?" Lance asks, rolling his lips.

"Nothing, Charlie wants all we have, but otherwise, nothing changes."

He nods his head. "Does Nina know?"

"No, and I want it to stay that way. I won't have her involved."

"I agree."

"Agree with what?" Elliot asks, walking into the office, Charlie following in behind, both looking sharp in their Armani suits.

"I don't want Nina to know–in fact." Pushing off from the desk, I step closer to them, eyeing them all. "It goes no further than here. I won't have anyone else dragged into this. Understand?"

Lance nods in understanding, and Elliot gives me a wink. "Pixie promise, mate."

"Prick," I tell him, unamused. Charlie stands statue-still, his hands in his pockets not saying a word. "Charles?"

He licks at his bottom lip. "And if she leaves you?"

"Then she leaves me. I'm pretty sure she already has."

I swallow as my chest cracks. At least it feels like it's cracking.

"Nah, Luce said she just needs time," Elliot says, pulling out his phone.

"You've spoken to her?" I snap.

"No, I spoke to Lucy. Put your vagina away, Lowell." He rolls his eyes.

Running my hand through my hair, I blow out a breath. I need to see her.

"Why don't you tell her? I trust her," Charlie tells me.

Lance blows out a low whistle.

"I sold her fucking studio, Charlie! She doesn't even know about the rest of it, and if she did, I can't imagine she would come running to me open-armed. Do you?"

"I don't fucking know." He shrugs, moving to the sofa to sit.

"It's better for everyone if it stays between us," Lance mutters, and I know he's right, even if that means I can't give her an explanation.

"You okay?" I ask Charlie, resting my hand on his shoulder as I lean on the back of the sofa.

"Yeah. Surprisingly, I feel fucking fantastic."

"Good, it's about time."

Nina

MASON HASN'T STOPPED CALLING. He turned up at my apartment late yesterday, but I pretended I wasn't home. Maybe he knew I was in, but I'm not ready to face him yet, and why should I?

I know I need to talk to him. For a start I need answers, but I worry the moment I see him I will relent.

I'm weak for him, and it's pathetic.

Lucy and Megan have been with me every evening, not wanting me to be alone, and Scarlet has phoned almost every day.

"Get in, loser. We're going shopping."

I spin around on the curb, smiling when I spot them all sitting in Scarlet's black convertible. "Shopping?" I frown. "You said lunch. And it's a Monday."

"Lunch, *after* you work up an appetite shopping. Megs started three hours early this morning to make today happen, now get in and stop moaning." Luce winks from the passenger seat as I slide into the back. "Besides, we need some killer outfits for our day sesh!"

"Nuh-uh. I am not going out, don't even say it."

"Okay," Lucy agrees, and I frown again, looking to Megan, who is smiling beside me.

"What?"

"Nina, come on," Megan coos.

"What? I don't want to go out, I feel crappy."

"We haven't been out in weeks. You need a blowout, babe. Monday Mayhem is where it's at!" She grabs my hand, and I notice Lucy's smirk.

"Did you all plan this? You knew I'd say no."

"No!" Scarlet sings, hand on heart. "I suggested Indian at home, but these bitches twisted my arm."

"Cocktails, girls. We need cocktails." Lucy grins, turning up the music.

ADMITTEDLY, it's been a good day. Lucy and Megan haven't stopped running around me while Scarlet has been trying to lift our moods. I adore them for it.

We sit on the terrace at Pons, eating a sharing platter whilst we sink more cocktails than food.

I can think of a hundred reasons why I shouldn't be out spending money right now, but I know I need this, time with my girls chatting shit and getting day drunk.

What could go wrong?

BOUNCING THROUGH THE CROWD, I make my way to the bar and order a round of shots. Downing two, I stack the tiny glasses and pay the barman. I lift the other three shots off the bar and dance my way back to the girls.

"Thanks!" Megan shouts over the music, stepping away from the guys she has been dancing with all night.

She eyes the shot I handed her and frowns. "Where's the rest of it?"

"Sorry." I wince, swaying on my feet.

"You need water!" Lucy chuckles as she appears at my side, grabbing my hand and pulling me in the direction of the bar.

But I don't want water.

"I want to dance!" I pull her back and spin her around, but she trips on her heel and crumbles to the floor. "Oops."

"Nina!" she shouts, laughing as she lies on her back.

"Come on." I pull on her arm. "Let's dance on the tables until they tell us off."

She smiles up at me. "Why you so badass?"

We link arms and dance over to the tables at the back of the room. I pick one and then look down at my heels.

Thankfully, the guy who is sat at said table notices. Smirking, he lifts his pint and gestures to the table as if to tell me it's all mine. He stands and offers me his hand, so I take it and use the chair he just vacated to climb up.

"Thank you!" I shout, pointing at him with a cheesy wink.

"What a babe." Lucy nudges me, taking my hand as she climbs up behind me.

The DJ starts playing "Me & U" by Biscits and puts a shout out to the two hotties in the back, making us both cheer like a pair of teenage girls.

We draw attention from every eye in the club, and before long, all the girls are searching for a table to dance on.

I'm mid slut drop, just about to work my butt back up and into Lucy, when my eyes lock onto Mason.

Oh, Fuck.

30

Nina

HE STEPS UP TO THE EDGE OF THE TABLE, HIS STRONG HANDS finding my waist as he lifts me effortlessly and places me on the ground. My feet hit the floor, and I stare at him through a drunken haze.

Now isn't the time to do this.

"It hurts to look at your face," I tell him.

He nods, his jaw clenching and unclenching as he watches me.

"I need a drink." I leave him at the edge of the dance floor and walk to the bar, trying my best to keep my feet steady.

"Vodka cranberry, please," I ask the barman.

The guy to my left smiles down at me, and I grin wide. "Hi!"

The barman's eyes move past me, and I spin to see Mase shaking his finger 'no' at him.

"Who do you think you are?" I turn back around. "Yes, to the vodka cranberry, thanks," I say, shaking my head.

Does he think he can tell me what to do? He can't.

"You can't!" I mutter when he steps up beside me, and he frowns down at me.

The handsome son of a bitch.

"You and your friend put on quite a show up there," the guy to my right tells me, drawing my attention to him.

"We did, huh!" I chuckle. "I'm Nina."

"Nina," Mason growls at my back.

"Ugh, what? Why are you here? Who phoned you? Was it you?" I evil eye the guy beside me, and he puts his hands up in defence.

"Cause he's an asshole, he sold my studio, and I'm so mad at him I hate him," I slur.

He smirks at me. He's a pretty boy. I give him a wink, but both my eyes squint shut. "I need water," I announce.

I turn to the bar and find a pint of water already waiting for me.

Mason leans in to speak into my ear. "We're leaving. Where is your bag?"

"Get off me." I swat him away. "I'm drunk, not stupid, and I remember everything you know, Mase. Like the night *you* sold my studio, then came home and stuck it in my—"

"Nina—"

"You little prick." I gulp my water, leaning into the guy beside me who clearly finds this conversation fascinating. "Is isn't little," I whisper-shout, then frown as I notice my words slur. "It's isn't little."

He throws his head back, laughing as the glass is taken from me, and I'm thrown over a strong shoulder.

"Oh, how original of you, Mase. You gonna fuck me in your office now?"

"Don't tempt me."

I don't try to fight him as he carries me through the club, but we still manage to draw plenty of attention. Men eye Mason as if to say poor guy, and well, the women? They watch Mason too. I don't blame them, but as if I'd allow him the ego boost right now.

"Don't be fooled, girls; he's completely shit in bed." I hold up my pinkie, wiggling it at the group of ladies seated near the entrance.

Mason's hand shifts, gripping me high on my left leg and dangerously close to my underwear.

He squeezes the smooth skin there, making me gasp and jolt in his hold.

He walks us out of the club and across the street to the Bentley. "You can put me down, you know. I won't run away."

I slide down his body. Every solid, hard inch of it. It has my body thrumming with want. But not need.

I don't need this man.

Swallowing hard, I look up into his tired eyes, and I am instantly filled with worry. Has he been sleeping?

Why do I care?

"It's kind of what you always do. Run."

"That's not fair."

He looks off to the side, his jaw clenching. "Would you have come back? Are you going to come back?"

No.

"You're always so grumpy, Mase. Lighten up. I did, and I feel great!" I go to tap his nose, but it ends up higher than I anticipated, and I catch him in the eye.

"Fuck," he spews.

My face screws up in guilt, and I bare my teeth as I cringe. "I think I just need to go to bed." I shake my head, giggling.

"Me fucking too! In!" He opens the passenger side door, and I slide inside.

Rounding the car, I see him rubbing at his eye, and it sets me off again. I snort through my nose before I start laughing uncontrollably.

"I used to think you were so beautiful when you laughed." He shakes his head, turning the key in the ignition.

"I'm sorry, am I being a bitch?" I try to keep my face straight, but I'm too far gone and can't control it.

"No, I—"

I snort again, cutting him off.

He shakes his head, not at all amused. "Jesus Christ."

"I will st-op."

"And now we have the hiccups," he tuts.

"Oh, no," I say, completely serious. "Not the hi-cups."

I can see Mason's smile, but I can only feel pure panic.

"Lexie Grey's mum died of th-e hiccups."

"Who?"

"Just a friend." I wave him off.

"You're not going to die, Nina," he tells me.

"That's what they told Lexie's mum!"

Closing my eyes, I take a big breath in and hold it. I can feel his eyes on me, but I need to get rid of my hiccups so I don't dare look at him.

"Breathe, Nina, Jesus Christ! You *will* die if you hold your breath for too long." He cups the back of my head, and I snap my eyes open, instantly getting lost in his.

There is so much between us, so much in that one look.

I don't know how we could ever be done. How do you

walk away from someone who impacted you so profoundly and in such a short space of time? A little over two months. It's all it took, and I am head over heels in love with him.

"Why do you have to hurt me, Mase?" I ask, looking at him through my lashes.

"Pix."

"Take me home." I turn my head, pulling from his grip and looking out the window.

I just need my bed.

MY MOUTH IS dry when I wake, and my head pulses as if it has its own heartbeat.

Sitting up, I notice I am in my pyjamas, but I don't remember getting dressed. I don't remember anything after Mason picked me up.

Mason.

He brought me home.

Climbing from the bed, I make the short walk to the kitchen, spotting two socked feet hanging off the end of my sofa. My tiny kidney-shaped sofa. I should feel sorry for him —I don't.

I fill a glass with water as quietly as I can, then peek over the top of the counter.

"Hi," I squeak out when I find him staring up at me.

"You're up early. Considering the state you were in last night." He pops a brow as if I need reminding.

"I needed water. You slept out here?"

He sits himself up, reaching for his T-shirt. It gives me the perfect view of his chiselled abs as they ripple beneath his tan skin. "Yeah, you told me to."

"I did?"

Drunk Nina is smart. I give her an internal high five.

"You don't remember?"

"No," I answer warily, not sure if I want to know.

He snickers, shaking his head. "I'm going to go. Do you need anything?"

"You're leaving?"

My body feels tired, and I have no idea what time it is. This hangover might just be the death of me today.

He frowns, raking his eyes over me. "You want me to stay?"

I shrug. "I have questions."

"I know that," he says with pity in his tone.

"Will you answer them?"

"Will you ever trust me without answers?"

"No." I shake my head vehemently. "I deserve better than that."

He steps forward, cupping my face in his sprawled hand. I lean into the touch. I have missed him so much these last few days.

How would it feel to miss him forever?

His thumb brushes my cheek as he searches my eyes. "Walk away, my beautiful girl. Please." Leaning in, he kisses the space between my brows, his soft lips lingering there for a beat before stepping away.

He slips on his shoes, and then he is gone.

Mase

It' Saturday night and the guys are at my place tonight. Elliot's neighbour is getting married, and he has been asked to be the best man. Ridiculous if you ask me. The only reason they're friends is because they go out picking up women together. That and the fact Elliot is game for pretty much fucking anything. It's why I know the stag he is attempting to plan is going to be an absolute shit show.

They are here to finalise the details, and honestly, if this was my stag, I already know Nina would have my balls.

I let that thought settle. Marriage. I never wanted it before now.

Why would I want a piece of paper that tied me to someone for life? It always seemed like a pointless tradition, but now? Now I would scour the ends of the earth for the last remaining tree if it meant getting that piece of paper. Being with Nina and feeling the contentment she brings, I suppose at some point marriage became inevitable with her. Not an option, just necessary.

"Tits, he loves big tits."

"Find me a man who doesn't." Lance waggles his brows at Elliot over the top of the laptop.

"Lowell, what was the one in Soho called?" Lance asks.

"Vue's," I offer.

Vue's is a high-end strip joint in the West End. It offers some of the best dancers in the city. Again, Nina would have my balls if she heard me say that out loud.

Elliot snaps his finger to Lance. "Write that down. The girls were fucking good in there."

I sit and peel the sticker off my bottle, thinking about Nina and the look on her face when I left the other morning.

I already know I won't stay away, even if she wants me to.

"You spoke to her?" Charlie asks.

He is sprawled out on my sofa, still in his suit. You'll rarely catch him in anything else.

Charlie has known me for years. There used to be nothing he didn't know, but that changed last year. He is probably still pissed at me, but I wouldn't take it back, even if that meant I took the blame and suffered the consequences.

"Yeah, she went to Melders Tuesday night. Jim called me."

He nods his head, his lips pressed into a thin line. "I presume you didn't sort things out?"

Elliot and Lance are hyping each other up about the stag, bouncing ludicrous ideas around and not paying us any attention. I nod my head to the kitchen and stand, Charlie following behind.

"I don't know, Aldridge." I cross my arms over my chest, resting my head back against the fridge. "Nina had a shitty time growing up. She built the studio from nothing to a fully functioning business, and then I came in and fucked it all up. I don't know how she will get over me selling her studio, and to taint her with the truth unnecessarily seems wrong when she already has the twisted shit that she does in her head."

"I get it, I do. But can you see yourself not being with her? Like, if she met someone else and moved on. You could accept that?"

"No," I grit out, ready to brawl with any man who'd dare to look in her direction. "Absolutely fucking not."

"I know," he smiles. "I liked Nina from day one. She isn't like anyone you've dated before. Which is why you can't let my mistakes screw your future. I made the call, Mase, not you. Yeah, you fucked up, but you did what I couldn't. You did what you knew I wanted." He shrugs as if it's simple. "I think you should tell her."

"I already told you I'm not telling her, Charles. The more people who know, the more chance of it coming out."

"You sound like a fucking broken record! What do you think she is going to do? Go to the police?"

"No, but if anyone else does..." I grit my teeth, not wanting to go there. "She can't know."

"Well, then here's to you." He raises his bottle in the air, and I lift mine to his, unsure. "To more stupid fucking mistakes." He bashes my bottle with his and walks out of the kitchen.

Fucking sensitive prick.

Nina

I'VE BEEN MOPEY—WALKING around feeling sorry for myself, and mad at the world when I should be on a mission to find a new studio. Maggie and John have covered the next two months on my rent and I have just about enough to cover my bills, but that's not going to last long.

Today, I am doing something for myself. I have an induction at a new gym that Logan told me about and insisted I check out. I am so ready to get my ass moving again.

After everything with the studio, Mason, and his dad, I feel like I've let myself go. I'm ready to get *me* back—nothing like a girls' weekend to pull me out of my funk.

There's a spring in my step as I exit my apartment, feeling better than I have in weeks.

Sliding my key in the lock, I do a little happy dance, my excitement too much to contain.

I'm actually going to work out!

"Nina."

"Holy fuck!" I scream, my hands grasping my chest as my keys clunk to the ground.

Charlie's broad smile beams at me from his spot against the wall. He must have been waiting for me. "Charlie, you scared the life out of me. Why didn't you knock?"

"Sorry." He chuckles, but his face quickly grows solemn. "I wasn't sure what I wanted to say to be honest."

My eyes are still wide, and my heart pounds. "Is everyone okay?"

"Yeah. But I do have some things to tell you." He scratches his brow. "If you're not busy, of course."

"Sure, come in."

Unlocking the door, I pray I didn't leave anything incriminating out. I don't think I did, but I also wasn't expecting visitors.

I search the room discreetly but don't spot anything out of place.

"Do you want a drink?" I ask, unsure why he is even here.

"No, I'm good." He rubs his hands together, looking anywhere but at me.

My stomach knots, nerves twisting me up inside. "Is everything okay, Charlie?"

He swallows hard, nodding. "There are some things I think you deserve to know, but I want to make sure you understand what knowing the truth means."

We both stand in my tiny apartment, looking at one another. I feel like a deer in headlights, not knowing what to do.

"Do you want to sit down?" he asks.

"Sure. Sorry." I move to sit on the sofa and he follows me.

"Don't apologise. I should have called ahead."

He seems uncomfortable, which makes me feel awkward. Charlie has always been the easiest one for me to talk to out of all the guys. "Does Mason know you are here?"

"No." His brows lift as he thinks on that. "He will be pissed at me, no doubt, but I know he won't tell you." He looks at me and gives me a tight smile. "You seem to be doing good. You look well."

If only he knew.

"I've always been good at blocking out the bad. But I was about to head out to the gym before, and I'm going to find a studio so I can build my business again. Get myself back on track."

"That's fantastic." He smiles at me, but it's forced and I can tell he is anxious.

"What is it, Charlie?" I ask, needing him to spit it out.

"It's about Mason and the studio, and Cara," he mutters, looking down at his feet.

Cara?

"You mean the reason he sold it?" I frown, waiting for him to explain. "Charlie, none of this makes sense to me."

"If I tell you and you choose to leave him for good, that's fine. But what I'm about to tell you doesn't leave this room. You cannot tell anyone, not even Lucy and Meg. I'm very serious about this, Nina. You cannot tell anyone else."

I nod, desperate for him to give me a reason to stay.

He readjusts himself on the sofa, sliding to the edge so he is barely braced against it.

He's so uncomfortable, and it makes me nervous.

"My sister's name was Phoebe. She was six years younger than me. She was sweet and loving, and everything good in the world." His hand shakes as he rubs it over his mouth, and I reach over and take his other hand, sensing he needs the support. "When she was eighteen, she was raped." He turns his head away, composing himself for a moment before looking back down at his hands. "I didn't know. She didn't tell anyone. Not until it was too late."

"Charlie—"

"Mason didn't want to tell you because he didn't think you would be able to handle it, that you have too much from your past to deal with."

He's not wrong.

"I get why he chose not to tell you. It wasn't his truth to tell, and I didn't understand that until now. Mason did what he thought would protect the most people. Even if that meant losing you."

"Protect people from what?"

He nods, then continues. "Phoebe didn't tell me until two years after it happened. She spiralled into depression and cut me and her friends off. It wasn't until I cornered her and demanded she told me one day that she broke down and told me everything—his name included." Charlie's body bristles with anger, his shoulders sharp and his knee bouncing. I squeeze his hand tighter. "I was young and stupid and didn't know what to do. I was in the middle of taking my bar and knew this was the exact scenario I'd want to represent one day. But it was my little sister, so it was different. She wouldn't go to the police."

"But you know who did it?" I state.

"Yeah." He looks at me with so much hurt in his eyes, my own fill with tears. "Phoebe committed suicide three months after I found out. No note, nothing. Just gone."

"God, I'm so sorry, Charlie—"

"I hated him. She was so innocent, never messed around, went to school. She had dreams and he came along and ripped it all out from under her."

I sit silently, knowing there aren't any words that can take Charlie's pain away or bring his sister back.

He is back in the moment, reliving the hurt, and I feel it. I feel it all.

"I asked Mase if he would help me." His voice shakes and then he stands, dropping my hand before walking to the window.

I link my hands in my lap, not liking the loss of connection. I think I needed it just as much as he did.

"I hired a friend of Vinny's. He was ex-special forces like him."

I close my eyes, not wanting to hear the rest of the story.

"I wanted him to be scared. I wanted him to feel every bit of the pain that she did."

"Charlie," I mutter, agonising with him as I look up at him from the sofa.

"I didn't go through with it. We didn't even know where he was at the time, and I knew it wouldn't bring Phoebe back. I hoped one day I could put him away. That I would find him and do it the right way."

My shoulders sag, and I let out a deep sigh of relief.

Charlie stands with his hands on his hips. His bottom lip pulled between his teeth. "I found out three days ago that Mason and Vinny never called it off."

My eyes widen. "What?!"

He nods, then drops his head, eyes on the ground. "It went wrong, Nina. They were supposed to rough him up a bit, but it went to shit."

"What happened to him?" I ask, my voice shaking.

Do I even want to know? This isn't something I can just forget.

"He died."

The air I pull into my lungs doesn't feel filtered. It feels thick and jaded and makes tears burn the backs of my eyes. I swallow the bile that coats my throat, my stomach rolling.

"Mason never told me. He didn't want anyone involved in case it came out. He worried I could lose my job."

I open my mouth to speak, but nothing but air comes out.

"Nina—"

"Why are you telling me this, Charlie?" I finally ask, swiping the stray tear from my face.

His jaw ticks, his mask slipping back into place. "Because the wrong person found out. Someone who saw it as an opportunity."

"What? Who?"

"Cara. The women who owned your studio. She was the only other person who knew besides Mase, Lance and Vinny. Mason thought if you could be linked to Cara through the studio, it would look too convenient. If it came out, you could be seen to have been aware of the situation."

I shake my head, not understanding. "Cara? Do you mean Erin? Erin O'Connor who owns my studio."

Erin knew about this?

"I can't tell you the parts that aren't mine to tell, Nina."

My mind races as I try to digest all that he *has* told me, but all I can think about is the conversation I had with Erin just a few days ago. She thought I knew. She told me to use the situation to my advantage.

If you are clever, you can benefit from this.

"Is she blackmailing him?" I ask, reading between the lines.

"Not anymore," Charlie tells me.

"But she was?" Anger has my tone biting out the words.

He nods, and I stand.

"Where are you going? You can't go to the police," he warns.

"I'm not going to the police, Charlie. I would never." I shake my head. I would be lying if his lack of trust in me didn't sting. "I'm going to Mase."

31

Mase

Locking the Bentley, I round the bonnet and make my way to the elevators, my mind a fucking jumble of thoughts.

I haven't heard from Nina. Not that I expected to, but not knowing where she is and what she's doing drives me wild. Vinny refused to tail her. He has been far less compliant since he came back. It leaves me unable to function. I can't eat, sleep and think about anything other than her.

Pathetic.

Inserting my key into the dial, I press the button to the penthouse, resting my head back against the cool glass mirror.

I need her.

The doors slide open, and I stride out, only making it a foot into the foyer before I stop short. My feet unable to move.

Her chocolate hair is down and flows to her waist. She is wearing a pair of cycling shorts and a pale pink tank, a pair of running shoes adorning her feet. She spins on the spot, facing me with an uncertain look.

"You ran here?" I ask, the last question I want an answer to. I can tell she did by the sheen of sweat that coats her heaving chest.

She nods, looking up at me through her brows. I want to go to her, but something tells me to keep away.

I can't read her right now.

She strides to me confidently, and I instantly regret not going to her first. She shows me her strength in her actions again and again. The fact she is here after I told her to walk away says everything about the woman that she is.

I take her chin as she steps up to me like it's the most natural thing in the world, but she already has it held high. A silent demand to hear the truths I don't want to give her.

"I know about Charlie's sister, and I know what happened to her rapist."

My hand drops along with my stomach, and all the blood inside me drains to my feet, leaving me light-headed.

"Say that again," I rasp out.

"I think it's best we don't repeat it all that often, don't you?"

I frown at her words.

"What are you doing here?" I ask.

"Is that seriously all you have to say right now?"

"Nina—"

"Tell me everything, and so help me God, Mason, if you lie to me."

My skin prickles as I try to trample my emotions.

She is here. She knows the worst of it, and she is here.

With hope in my heart, I search for the right words. "You know about Phoebe?"

"Yes. And about what happened after. Behind Charlie's back," she arches an accusing brow at me, but her eyes don't hold the same conviction. "I want to know what Charlie *won't* tell me. I want to know why your mother's piano was in Erin's studio."

I snigger and look down. "Her name isn't Erin." My eyes burn into the ground at our feet as I take myself back to that night.

Only this time, I drag Nina through it with me.

FOURTEEN MONTHS EARLIER...

Rarely will I pick up at Melders. I try not to mix business with pleasure. But where my father's lack of self-control lies with the bottle, mine seems to lie in the redhead that is currently on her knees, sucking my cock.

The smell of her cheap perfume assaults my senses, giving me a headache. She is hot, though. Damn, she is fucking stunning. She has that natural Jessica Rabbit vibe going on with her bouncy red hair and hourglass figure.

I'm not fooled, though. She is just like the rest of them. Following me with their eyes until I settle on one of them to take home for the night, just to fulfil a need. That's all it is—emotionless sex at its finest.

She starts to moan around me, and I pull out of her mouth, finding her eagerness to please me fucking pathetic.

I just need to fuck.

"Out," I demand, hitting the button to open the elevator doors. My patience has been wearing thin all night.

I haven't heard anything from Vinny yet and I should have by now.

She climbs to her feet as I tuck myself away. The hunger in her eyes only grows when she sees my home, confirming my initial judgement of her.

"Wow. Becks said you had money. This is next level."

She walks into the room, past the sectional sofas and over to the piano. It stands between the lounge and the dining area, the perfect view of the London skyline beyond it.

Using her hands, she pulls herself up to sit on it, crossing her legs and letting her dress slide up her thigh. "Come here," she croons.

Reluctantly I move to her, my fists clenching at my sides as I watch her squirm on the polished wood. I don't like the feeling growing inside me at seeing her on my mother's piano.

Wrapping my hands around her waist, I grasp her tight. She unfolds her legs, lifting them to lock around my waist, and then I lift her from it. "You don't touch this," I warn.

"No? I was hoping you'd fuck me on it." She pops a brow.

Does she think that's going to turn me on? Fucking her on my mother's piano? I've never been so soft in my life.

"You don't fucking touch it. Got it?" I spit out, making her face drop.

Not wanting her anywhere near my personal things or feelings, I take her lips, hoping it will get me going again. I already know I am going to have to work for it. Maybe I'm an asshole, but girls like...

"What's your name again?"

"Cara." She giggles into my neck as I carry her up the stairs.

Girls like Cara are only after one thing. Money. They can smell it from a mile off, and if I didn't take her home tonight, El would have. That's how I sleep at night, knowing she is only after a notch on her millionaire tally. I'm just something to brag about come Monday morning.

Four hours later.

I pace the kitchen as sweat forms on my brow. "Well, where the fuck is he now?"

"I don't know, Mase, you need to calm down. Vin will deal with this." Lance tells me from his spot at my kitchen island.

"Calm down? Fucking murder, Sullivan, that's what this is!"

Everything is fucked.

He screws his face up. "No, it's not. It's a lesson, and he fucking deserved it."

My hands rake through my hair. He deserved it. Fuck. He deserved it.

"How long is he going to be? I can't wait around like this." I snap.

"Give it an hour and we'll call."

"Fuck that—"

Lance lifts a hand to stop me, his face tight. I follow his gaze which is trained on the closed kitchen door. "You hear that?" he mouths.

I walk to the door and rip it open.

The redhead gasps, and I try to remember her name, but my mind is already processing the conversation I had moments ago and how much of it she may have heard. "I was just leaving. I came to say goodbye."

She heard us.

She heard what we said.

Murder.

"*Thank you for this evening, my friend is expecting me home.*"

"*Shut the fuck up,*" I spit.

FUCK.

"*What did you hear?*" Lance asks from behind me.

"*Nothing.*" She says in a panic. "*I'm just going to go change.*"

She spins and runs for the stairs, the sheet clenched white-knuckled in her grip.

"*The fuck, Lowell!*" Lance hisses.

"*She might not have heard everything.*"

"*As if, you saw how quickly she fucking ran from you.*"

My phone starts to ring and I look down to see Scott's number lighting up my screen. Lance takes the phone and steps towards the elevator.

"*Fix that.*" He eyes the stairs. "*Make her keep her mouth shut.*"

I wait for what feels like hours for her to reappear. My hands pulling at my scalp as I fight to find the right words.

How do I explain this?

She scurries from the room and spots me instantly, flinching before she schools her features.

My eyes blaze through her as she pulls her shoulders back, and I watch her put on a front, walking down the stairs, then moving past me and towards the doors.

"*It's not what you think,*" I rush out, and I don't know if it's the panic in my voice, but something makes her pause.

"*How do you know what I am thinking?*" she asks, jutting out her chin.

"*I need your word...*" Shit. What the fuck is her name?

"*Tara,*" she snaps, finishing for me. "*Fucking pig.*"

"*Tara, right. Sorry. What you heard it wasn't what it sounded—*"

"I won't tell anyone," she assures me, and my shoulders drop in relief at the same time her lip curls.

"But not for nothing," she utters.

"Right, you want money." I look her up and down and her face reddens, her fists clenched at her sides.

"You used me tonight, and now I want to fuck you where it will hurt. I want money, and that."

She points over my shoulder, and I turn, my eyes locking on my mother's piano. "No."

Not a chance in hell.

"Oh, you think you have a say here? I could go to the police, you know."

She's brazen. I'll give her that. Most women would be out of here running, but I'm pretty sure I have Satan's spawn standing in front of me.

Lance told me to sort this, to make her go away quietly.

"How much? Name your price."

I see the spark in her eye, and I curse myself.

"I will send a courier, Monday morning at nine. If the door isn't unlocked, I will—and I mean it. I will go to the police."

"You stupid bitch."

She shrugs, smiling sweetly. "Stupid bitch..." She holds up one hand, then the other. "Murderer."

"She took it? The piano?"

I clench my fists as I nod, feeling every bit of the anger I did that night.

"Who is Erin then? And *Tara*? It doesn't make sense." She turns away from me, running her hands through her hair.

"Will you come and sit down?" I ask.

She moves to stand in the space between the lounge and

the dining area, her brows drawn together in question. "Where is it now?"

"In the west wing at Lowerwick."

Her face drops, and I know that hurt her. "You never would have told me, would you? You were just going to hide it away and not tell me."

"I didn't want to." My nostrils flare, not wanting to lay it all out but knowing I have to. "I thought if you knew, I thought you'd never be able to look at me again."

She shakes her head, looking at me in shock. "His actions... that rapist! Mason, he got everything he deserved. I don't condone using your money to play with karma." She walks to me, and my eyes burn. "But I don't *blame* you. You didn't do it for you." She reaches up and palms my cheek. "Mase, you would have lost me. If Charlie didn't tell me." Her brows pull in as she searches my face. "Why do you try and carry it all alone?"

"I don't want my mistakes to burden you, Nina. Despite all you have been through, you are good and pure. I don't want to fuck that up."

"You don't think I'm fucked up? Mase, I dream about the men who took my mother every night. I dream about wrapping my hands around their throats and squeezing until they can't keep their eyes open and on me." She throws her hands out to the side, shocking the shit out of me with her words. "I wanted it all with you. All the ugly parts. All I've ever wanted from you is you."

My eyes close briefly as I absorb her words. The more she gives me, the more I know I don't deserve her.

"I thought you'd run if I told you. I never thought it would bring you back to me."

"I never said I was staying." My chest aches as she utters the words.

I don't know how to be without her anymore.

"I want to know everything," she says. "About Cara, or Erin. Whatever her name is."

I look past her and out the window. "Lance found out about the piano and knew we'd have to do something. I was freaked out about Marcus and hadn't heard from Vinny. I knew I needed to go to work, but Elliot and Charlie would have known something was up, and I couldn't have them finding out. Charlie wouldn't have been able to live with it."

"I think that was your first mistake."

I nod in agreement with her. Maybe if I told him that day things wouldn't have gotten so bad.

"Cara took the piano. She was smart, and she took something she knew I treasured and made sure I couldn't find it."

"The studio. You didn't know it was there."

"No, not until that day I came to you." I give her my eyes, pleading with her to believe me. "Vinny looked into Cara. We found things."

She looks off to the side, shaking her head. "Do you realise how disgustingly toxic it is that you prey into the lives of other people, Mason?"

She takes a deep breath in, and I can see how conflicted she is.

Wetting my lips, I continue, needing to get my side of the story across. "She has multiple, stolen identities. Vinny found a paper trail that allowed us to track her down. She blackmails men. Rich men specifically, using different identities to keep herself covered. Thousands of pounds stolen over the past seven years."

"What?!"

"She would have done it to me, too, if it wasn't for Lance. He threatened to expose her. We had more money between us and more connections. She didn't have a choice but to listen. We sold her businesses, her home." I swallow thickly, knowing how this all sounds. "Then I sent her to Australia and made sure she had nothing to come back to."

"You made her leave?"

"I needed the control, Nina. She was blinded by greed and went willing. She doesn't have a bad life, and I couldn't have her here."

Her face screws up in pain, and I avert my gaze, not being able to stomach that look. "I met her in a café. She told me she had to find a tenant within three weeks. She said her mother was ill."

"Bullshit! Her mother lives here, and she begs to come home for that very reason. I didn't know about the studio, Nina. I swear I didn't. She put it in a different name, Erin O'Connor. It's why I never found the piano before now."

"So, you still pay her? To stay in Australia. Why?"

I don't miss the disgust in her tone. "Lance never set her straight about what happened that night. It was easier to let her believe I was dangerous than risk her wandering around London thinking she had something on me, and I didn't want to give her the advantage of knowing the truth. I took control of the situation when I could. I pay her way, and she keeps quiet. She stays in Australia, and I don't go to every one of the businessmen she is blackmailing and expose her."

"You threw money at it. Always money," she whispers, her expression one of defeat.

"It was the only way. It was on me, and I couldn't let it fall back on Vinny, Scott, and Lance. I didn't have a choice."

"There's always a choice, Mason. And yours somehow always comes down to the same thing. You'd be in prison without your wealth. You let it define you, but you are so much more."

"We did what we thought was best in the moment. I don't know what else to tell you."

She shrugs, throwing her hands out to the side. "I don't even know what to think anymore."

"I can't live without you," I tell her, reaching for her hands.

Her face sours. "Don't be ridiculous; it's been a matter of months."

"And I love you. There's not a doubt in my mind that you're it for me. Don't leave me. I love you, Nina, and I'm sorry. Let me make it right."

"Mason—"

I step forward and slide my hands across either side of her face. "I'll be the man you need me to be, I swear it. Don't leave me again," I beg, unashamed.

Her dainty hands wrap around my forearms with a tentative grip as if she is afraid to touch me. "You sold my studio."

"I couldn't have you involved. If what happened ever came out, and my girlfriend was renting the studio that the woman I blackmailed owned. Can you imagine how it would look?"

"This is ridiculous," she mutters. "all of it."

"I couldn't risk it, Nina. I wasn't willing to put you in that position. Baby, please." I smooth my thumbs across her cheeks, knowing if she leaves now, it's done. She won't come back.

How do you live without the woman you love?

My father couldn't do it, so why would I be any different.

"You have to stay." I wet my lips and my eyes drift closed, feeling completely bared to her. "You're my Pixie."

32

Nina

MY MOTHER NEVER BEGGED ME TO STAY. NOT ONCE. MOST weeks, I'd leave to stay with Maggie and John, and she wouldn't ever put up a fight. She wouldn't tell me to stay or that she would try to be better. She let me go. Every. Single. Time.

I should leave him. I should protect myself and run far away. But I can't. For the first time in my life, I want to plant my feet and throw myself into somebody else's world. I want a home—a forever one.

"I don't want you to help me buy a studio."

"Fine."

"I don't want you buying me anything, period. It's too much, and everything needs to be slower. We are moving a million miles an hour."

"But you will live here?" He means it as a question, but he is telling me, his tone definite.

"I will live here because I chose to, yes. And I will contribute to the bills."

He narrows his eyes at me. He doesn't like that. "I only want to look after you."

"It's too much too soon; give me time. I need to do this my way." I should have done this at the start, made it clear.

I told him I didn't want to be bought, and I know I made that clear, but I should have told him that I needed to move slower. I've done more with Mase than I have with any man ever.

"I know I love you, that part I am certain of."

"Why do I feel like there's a but?" He glares.

"I don't know if I trust you anymore. I feel like we lost it before we even had it."

He closes his eyes, but it's not in sadness. He is annoyed that I feel that way. "You know you can trust me."

"No, I don't. You haven't given me any reason to. The studio, Cara, they're not small things. It's life-changing for me; this is my life!"

"I know that."

"You don't." I pause, fighting against my head, which tells me to hotfoot it out of here, but my heart screams at me to stay, begging me to feed it with the love it craves. The type of love that makes it beat stronger. The type of love only he can give me. "But we can work on it," I force out.

"Yeah?" He questions, taking my face in his hands again.

I have to move forward. I can't run away every time I hit a bump in the road. I have to face it. Overcome it.

"Yeah," I tell him.

"I thought I'd blown it. The studio. I know I fucked up, Nina."

"We have a long way to go, Mason."

We are far from perfect, and we *do* have a long way to go. But today I make a new promise because I *want* to stay.

———

Mase

"Didn't she tell you specifically last month not to buy her shit?" Elliot asks with a smug smile on his face.

"Oh, they never really mean it. This is perfect," George tells me, coming to sit on the edge of my desk.

"If I make it about Lucy, get you to plan it." I look to Elliot, willing him to get on board.

"Fuck off, Lowell, I have enough to deal with."

"Like what?" I frown, calling him out on his bullshit.

"You think they can all just take time off and go on holiday?" Lance asks. "You're fucking gaga over her, mate."

"You pricks going to come or not? Let me deal with the girls."

They all eye each other before looking back at me. "Yeah, I'm in," Charlie says. "I need the break."

I nod, agreeing with him. He seems to be doing alright, but I know this past month has stirred up a lot of shit he had buried. I can imagine getting out of the office is exactly what he needs.

"Count me in." Elliot grins.

"Fuck it." Lance relents, shrugging.

I look up and over my shoulder. "Sorry, George mate, you'll have to man the office this time."

"I'm in charge," he exclaims, hand on his chest.

"Are you fuck!" Elliot laughs, and I smile.

"I will have someone come up from downstairs to check in, but I will call you to make sure things are going okay, and I will work when I can."

"Oh, have a day off, will you," he scolds me. "I'm excited for you! I thought you were all looking a little pale."

"You've gotta get the girls on board first," Lance reminds me.

"It won't take a lot." I smirk, drumming my fingers on the desk. "I have a plan."

Nina

"GIRLS?"

Heaving the suitcase onto the sofa, I take in the utter disarray that is their apartment. Lucy is a clean freak. She can't stand mess. Yet the lounge floor is covered in outfits, some matching and some discarded to the side, clearly not making the cut.

"Girls?!" I shout, frowning. "Where are they?"

Following the music, I go to their shared bathroom, pushing open the door.

And there they are, in all their naked glory. I should be surprised, but nothing surprises me with them anymore.

"Surprise, motherfucker!" Megan shouts, popping off a cork.

"Jesus, Meg, you'll take my damn eye out." I chuckle, shielding my face. "What are you idiots doing?"

Stepping into the room, I take in their glasses of fizz and

skimpy bikinis, both of them covered in shave foam and razors in hand.

"I might have told a little white lie."

"Luce," I warn.

"Girl, we're going to Spain."

"What?!" I frown.

"For my birthday! Girls' trip."

My face drops, and I know I'm about to disappoint her. "I can't go away right now. I have no money."

"I'm paying." She shrugs, turning away from me and cleaning off the razor in the sink.

"Did you win the lottery all of a sudden?" I ask, eyeing her shiny gold bikini. "Love that by the way."

"No! Mum and dad gave me some vouchers, and I thought I would treat your poor ass, but you don't have to come." She grins wide at me.

My lip tips up on one side. God, I need a holiday. Time away with the girls sounds perfect right now.

"What about Jean? I thought you had a fashion thing?"

She looks at me as if I'm stupid. "You think I needed *your* wardrobe to go to Spain with Jean?" She juts her head out, emphasising her point.

"So, I basically just packed my suitcase to go on holiday."

"Yup."

"Shit. I didn't really think about what I was packing." I share everything with the girls, but I'm not about to give up my best clothes. Lucy is a hoarder, and I won't see it for a year.

"Well, thanks!" She laughs.

"We leave tonight. You need to get a move on." Megan grins, handing me a flute.

"Tonight? I can't go tonight."

"Why not?" they both say in unison.

"I... I—"

"Go get ready, bitch!" Luce shouts, waggling her brows at me.

My stomach twists with excitement. It's been so long since we've been away. "We're going to Spain?"

"Yeahhhhh!" Megan bumps her hip with mine as we start to dance around the bathroom to "Post Malone" by Sam Feldt.

TWO HOURS LATER, my skin is as smooth as the day I was born, my hair is washed and set in deep curls, and my nails are a pretty shade of coral.

I feel ready.

I have one more thing I need to do, though, and I know he will hate this. Well, he won't hate the grovelling. I'm sure he will love that part, but the part when I tell him I'm going... Yeah, he will hate that.

The girls told me to call him, but I knew I couldn't leave without seeing him. He would probably have a tantrum and come after me in his fancy plane if I did.

These past few weeks has been our best together. He seems so much more relaxed now and even spoke about his dad a little with me, which came completely out of the blue. And I've been searching relentlessly for a new studio. Nothing is fitting me or my budget. I'm trying my best not to get down about it.

It will happen.

I called Vinny from the taxi to ask if Mason was in the office, and he told me I wouldn't need his ID card. He was right. The lady at the reception smiled when I told her my name, letting me straight up.

Checking myself in the elevator mirror, I fluff my hair and pout my lips, noticing they are a little dry. The door pings open, and I quickly lick my lips to make them look shiny.

"Well, hello," a friendly voice coos.

I spin and find a guy standing behind me at the sofas. He is watering a plant–I'm sure I never noticed plants in here before. His three-piece suit–with bow tie–is immaculate. He is gorgeous and perfectly put together, not a hair out of place.

"Hi," I say warmly.

"You are Nina!" He points at me with complete certainty.

"I am her." I shrug.

His smile is infectious, and I can feel my dimples out in full force. "George?" I question.

"Yes. I am him." He winks. "Oh, you are just as gorgeous in person as in the pictures."

I can feel my cheeks flush red at the compliment, but then I frown, not understanding. "Pictures?"

He drops down the jug of water and comes to stand next to me. "The ones in Mason's office. The ones from Paris."

"Oh, I've not seen them." Mase has my photo in his office?

"Is he expecting you?" He grins, ushering me toward the main desk.

"No, I have an impromptu trip, and I have to break it to him that I'm going away."

"I can imagine that will go down like a lead balloon." He eyes my outfit, a smile tugging at his lips.

"Right." I chuckle.

"You going in? He isn't busy. Well, he pretends he is, but he isn't."

"Yeah, I'm going in. Thank you, George." I lick at my lips again to moisten them.

"Oh, wait." He disappears around the reception desk and dips down behind it. "I have some balm."

I smile like a fool as I wait, imagining how Mason must be with George. I can't even begin to imagine the dynamic.

"Here, it's watermelon. My boyfriend bought it for me. I don't know if that was a hint, but it's not my flavour."

"Thank you." I apply some with my finger noticing it's completely unused. I go to pass it back to him, but he pushes my hand away.

"Oh, no. I don't share." He cringes, making me smile more. "No offence."

"None taken."

"You look good." He gives me a knowing nod—so George knows why I am here.

I throw him a wink over my shoulder as I walk the short distance and push through and into Mason's office.

He sits behind the large desk, his thick, full shoulders momentarily stealing my focus. His jaw has a five o'clock shadow, and his hair is a mussed mess of perfection.

I get the image of him taking me on the kitchen counter only hours ago.

The man is a god.

He looks up when he hears the door, a carnal smile pulling at his lips. How am I supposed to leave him for a week? I already miss him, and I haven't even left yet.

"Hey." I smile, fiddling with my bag.

"Come here, angel," he demands.

I go to him, stepping between his legs when he rolls his chair back to make room for me.

"This is a nice surprise." His hands find the back of my thighs, gently moving up to smooth over my behind.

"I have something I need to tell you."

"Mmmm, and what's that?" He kisses the small slither of skin that's exposed between my skirt and top.

"I'm going on holiday, with the girls—tonight." I cringe, waiting for his tantrum.

"You want to go away?"

I frown down at him. Is he okay? "Well, yeah." I shrug. "I could do with some time with the girls." Maybe the distance between us will be good. It still scares me how much I rely on him and so soon.

"How long will you be gone?"

"A week. Lucy is paying for the majority, and I will pay her back when I can," I explain, even though I know I don't need to.

He nods his head, sitting back in his seat and looking up at me. "You expect me to go a week without you?" He questions, rubbing his pointer finger over his lips.

"You went thirty-two years." I shrug, smiling down at him.

He rolls his lips, clearly pissed off.

Here we go.

"I don't know if I can go that long, Nina." He pouts.

"Well I'm going, whether you like it or not."

His lip twitches before he smiles. "Then why did you come here?" He asks knowingly, rubbing his hands on the armrests.

My eyes drop to his crotch, and I see he is hard, his cock straining against his zipper.

He knows exactly why I'm here.

"Did you know about this?" I ask, my brows drawing in.

"No." He smiles. "I didn't."

"And you don't mind if I go?"

That was too easy.

"Depends." He starts to unzip his trousers and then releases himself. "You're going to have to work for it."

I lick my lips, tasting watermelon, then drop to my knees as I shake my head. "Sex fiend."

"Just you fucking wait, Pix." He drops his head back to his seat as I wrap my lips around him, taking him to the back of my throat. "Fuck!" He hisses out.

I smile around him, loving how I can disarm him so easily. It makes me feel powerful.

Hollowing my cheeks, I draw him in and out of my mouth, flicking my tongue over his slit as I reach the head and driving him wild. His hands soon find my hair, and he starts to guide me, taking the control he can never fully give up.

"You're the hottest fuck, baby." Pushing back the hair that veils me, he uses his thumb to pull on my bottom lip and expose my teeth, grazing his cock in the process as it slides in and out of my mouth.

My eyes lock with his, dark and dilated and completely glazed. He is so hot for this right now.

"I want to remember how you taste," I moan around him, my need just as strong as his. I rub my thighs together, trying to gain some friction—anything to stop this ache.

His hips jut up, and his hands force my head down, his cock hitting the back of my throat with every thrust. I snap my eyes closed as I focus on not retching. My gag reflexes are sharp, but this is deep even for me.

"I need to be deeper," he grits out, and I can tell he is close.

I whimper, knowing I can't take him any more than I am. Instead, I suck him almost violently. Up and down at my own pace, but still as close to the hilt as I can get him.

"Jesus Christ," he pants.

Using my hand, I work him as I suck only on the head, running my tongue up the protruding vein on his underside and then back into my mouth again. Precum coats my tongue, and a growl rips through his chest.

"I'm gonna come," he tells me.

"Hmmm," I groan around him, his eyes locked on mine.

With one hand wrapped around him and my mouth locked on the tip of his cock, I use my other hand to lower my straps, pulling on the material until it slides over my breasts, releasing them.

"Fuck. Yes!" he elates.

Leaning back, his cock slides out of my mouth with a pop, breaking the connection as he reaches down and takes himself in his hand. He pumps himself four times before he is spurting out and onto my chest.

He smirks at me as I slowly rise to my feet and lean back against his desk. Standing, he reaches out his hand and begins smearing himself all over my breasts. Massaging his cum into my skin until my nipples are straining between his fingers and my core is throbbing with need.

"What do you want?" he rasps, looking down his nose at me, completely sated. His neck looks thick and strong.

I want to suck on it.

"I want you to touch me."

He pinches my nipple hard, and I whimper. "I am. Tell me where."

I lean in and rub my lips against his, my nipples scratching against his shirt and causing my flesh to heat.

"I want you to touch me here." Taking his hand, I guide it between my legs, and his palm instantly moulds to me, his middle finger running through my folds and then dipping inside.

His eyes flick to mine. "You came here fucking bare?"

I'm so turned on and wet that I instantly ripple around him, dropping my head to his shoulder on a soft cry.

He dips in and out of me leisurely, taking his time to build me up before adding another finger. Heat flushes through me as his thumb finds my clit, rubbing in circles until my toes curl and I'm clutching his shirt in my hand.

"Fuck." I bite into his pec, trying to keep quiet.

"On the desk. Now," he demands, and I whimper at the loss of his touch.

He makes room for me, the contents of his desk spilling to the floor as he places open-mouthed kisses up the centre of my chest and throat. Once he reaches my mouth, he places a bruising kiss on my lips but then pulls away.

Stepping back, he tugs on his tie, his eyes boring into me as I lie spread out on his desk. He undoes three buttons then pulls his shirt over his shoulders. Revealing his solid chest and chiselled abs to me.

His hands grasp the backs of my knees and pull me to the edge of the desk, and then he is penetrating me.

As always, it's rough and fast and all at once. His head

drops to mine as he squeezes his eyes tight. "You're so fucking wet."

I latch onto his lips as he starts to rock into me, rolling his hips. One hand grips me behind the neck as his tongue ravishes my mouth, whilst his other hand wraps around my back, lifting and guiding me onto his rock-hard cock.

Our pelvises grind together on every roll of his hips, and I know he is close. I'm right there with him.

"I'm going to miss you. This," I tell him, looking into his eyes.

He frowns at first in confusion, but then his face breaks out into the most beautiful smile. "I will miss you, too."

Our eyes hold as he picks up the pace, driving into me faster and harder until we both fall over the edge.

"I love you, Mase," I pant out between ragged breaths as my heart beats fearlessly between us.

"I love you too."

I STAND in front of Mason's bathroom mirror, thanking my lucky stars he even has a bathroom in here.

Who has a shower in their damn office?

My hair is a wild mess, and my skirt is twisted. Mason leans against the doorframe watching as I use a flannel to wipe my chest.

He looks dark and dangerous, and if I weren't in a hurry to get back to the girls, I'd be on him like a leech.

I already know the coming home sex is going to be wild.

He watches as I straighten my skirt, his eyes locked on my legs. "I can see your ass cheeks, Nina." He readjusts himself in his trousers, and I smile, loving that even after two orgasms, I can still get him hard.

His brows draw in. "Is that…"

He steps up behind me as I feel warm liquid dripping from my centre, slowly running down my inner thigh. "Shit." I go to wipe it away, but he is already there, his hand cupping me from behind and sliding over my already sensitive flesh.

"Booossman," I hum, knowing I don't have time.

His teeth sink into my neck, and he sucks, pushing three thick fingers into me, then spreading his cum through my folds and over my clit.

"Yes," I groan, knowing I will come in a matter of seconds with how sensitive I am.

My head drops to his shoulder, and I look down my nose at us in the mirror. His lips lie open against my throat, his eyes trained on the mirror. Specifically between my legs where his hand works me.

I am one lucky, lucky girl.

MY LEGS ARE like jelly as I exit Mason's office thirty minutes later, his hand sat low on my back as he guides me into the reception area. I planned to come here and get him off so I wouldn't feel bad about going away, and I hoped he would be cool about it. I didn't expect anything in return. Well, I knew I would get something out of it, but I feel like I've been well and truly fucked, not the other way around.

My cheeks flush as George looks up at me from behind the desk. I tried to tame my appearance, but I know I look like a hot mess, and I appreciate it when he doesn't say a word, giving me a wink and then carrying on with his typing.

"Don't miss your flight," Mason tells me, tugging the strap of my bag higher on my shoulder for me.

"I won't miss my flight."

He nods his head and looks to the ground. My stomach twists with guilt. Should I be leaving him again so soon? It's not been long since his father passed.

"I don't have to go. If you wanted me to stay?"

His head snaps up. "You would stay? If I asked you to, you would stay?"

"Of course I would."

He frowns before a cheeky smile pulls at his lips. "What have you done with my girlfriend?"

"Shut up!" I push on his shoulder, stepping away from him, but he grabs my hand and pulls me into him, planting his lips on mine as he wraps his arms around my neck.

"Go, Pix. I know you will always come back to me." He cranes his neck back to look down at me. "I love you."

WE ARE LATE. So late that we are those people. The ones that run through the airport with their boarding passes in hand, shouting at people to move.

Classy, I know.

I am out of breath as I lug my suitcase behind me, praying we make it to our gate on time. We would have been here early if Lucy didn't decide to try a new colour. She now has bright pink hair instead of pastel pink. She FaceTimed Scarlet and gave her an earful about how she followed her directions, and it hadn't worked. She was mortified and now has a cap pulled over the bright roots. It will fade in the sun —we hope.

The girls veer off as we pass our gate.

"Girls!" I yell, looking between the gate and then back to the direction they are running. I stand panting and out of breath, a sharp pain shooting through my gut. I haven't had a stitch in years.

Serves me right running on a stomach full of prosecco.

I take off after them, yelling for them to slow down.

"Come on, sugar tits. You don't want to keep them waiting," Megan quips.

"Them? Guys, we've missed the gate."

They chuckle to each other as if that's the funniest thing they have ever heard. It gives me a chance to catch up with them.

The corridor opens up, and we come to a lounge area. It's over-the-top luxury and filled with five faces I was not expecting to see.

Mase approaches me, his hand going to my waist.

His lip twitches. "Happy holiday, Pix."

The cocky bastard.

Lucy stops beside us. "Surprise!"

"Tell me I didn't just give him world-class going away head when he is coming with me?"

33

Nina

THEY WERE ALL IN ON IT: CHARLIE, ELLIOT, LANCE, SCARLET and the girls. Was I the only one who didn't know? I would be lying if I said I wasn't a little disappointed. As much as I want to get away with everyone, what I wanted and needed was a girls' trip.

Mase hasn't stopped smirking at me the entire flight—and it's a long one. Spain turned out to be a decoy and we are currently on our way to Bora Bora on the company's private plane.

He thinks he's hilarious, and he kind of is. He got me on my knees with his sulking, and it didn't take a lot. I give myself a mental slap for being so stupid. As if he would be so chilled with me leaving him for a week.

"You're glaring," Elliot mutters in my ear.

He steps around me and drops into the empty seat next to me.

"Why does he have to look so smug? And why was I the

only one who didn't know? It's Lucy's birthday. She is the one who should have been surprised." I'm moany and ungrateful, but I hate that they didn't tell me.

"You would have come along if he asked?"

"Probably not, but still."

"He's trying to make it up to you; go with it."

"Things would be so much easier if he didn't have money."

Elliot pops a brow at me. "Do you really believe that?"

I shrug, looking towards the girls who are standing at the bar. Lance is making them all cocktails.

"I don't know. I just wish I didn't feel like everything is in aid of something. He throws money at anything that doesn't go his way."

"Wouldn't you? If you had enough money, would you not make sure the people around you were safe and secure?"

Is that how Mason sees it? Is that his only goal? Deep down in my gut I know he is a good person.

It's why I'm still here.

"I suppose it depends who you have to step on to get that security."

"You have to be ruthless in this game, Pix. You'd be surprised how many people only attach themselves to him for his money. I've had it my entire life, my parents, too." His eyes move from Mason to the bar, and there's no doubt in my mind that it's Lucy who has drawn his attention.

She has her head thrown back, laughing freely. Her denim shorts sit high on her hips, and a black bralette scarlessly covers her chest. She looks hot.

"Why pink?" he remarks.

I drop my head back to the seat and laugh lightly. "She's just trying something new. You don't like it?"

He draws his head back to look at me. "It's different."

"I'm watching you, Montgomery." I grin.

"Hey, you know nothing is going to happen there."

"Why not? You'd be like... Barbie and Ken. You're kinda perfect for each other."

"Luce is the girl you marry. She's not the type of girl you pick up on the weekend. I'm too young to get married, and she isn't my type. At all."

"Okay! There is so much wrong with what you just said. Firstly." I hold up one finger. "You're the same age as Mase, right? When is the right time to settle down?" I release a second finger. "Secondly, what is your type? If that's not it." I eye Lucy and her long, tanned legs. "Thirdly." I snap my fingers, bringing his eyes back to me. Yeah, he likes what he sees. "The type of girl you pick up on the weekend? That was *me,* asshole. I was that girl. And because of you and your promise..."

He grins wide. "You're not like the girls Mason used to pick up. Trust me. I didn't even remember that promise until I met you."

"Why did you pick me?" I ask, my fingernails digging into the armrest.

It's not something I've ever thought about before, but now he's mentioned it, I feel almost desperate to know why.

He starts checking off his fingers like I just had. "Hot. Not a psycho." He shrugs, and we both laugh.

I don't know why I expected anything else.

"Move it, Montgomery," Mason demands, looking down at us curiously.

Elliot gives me a wink as he moves past me and over to the bar, where he throws his arm around Megan. I watch as Lucy's eyes follow him. "Something is going on with those two."

"Who?" Mason asks, draping his arm over my shoulder and bringing his lips to rest against my hair.

"Elliot and Luce."

"No," he says, sounding so sure. "Luce isn't Elliot's type."

"Why?"

Elliot said the same thing, which is frustrating. Call it women's intuition, but there's definitely something there.

Mason sits square in his seat, stretching out his legs. "She just isn't."

"Is he gay?"

He seems to choke on air because the next moment, he is bent over trying to clear his airway and control his hysterics. I sit staring at him, unamused, waiting for him to calm himself.

"No, definitely not gay," he tells me.

"Well, I can see it with them. I'm calling it."

He sits up in his seat and pulls me onto his lap so I'm straddling him. "Let's make this interesting." I look around at our friends, but none of them are watching us. "How long?"

"How long what?" All I can think about is how long his cock is right now, pushed up against me.

"Get your head out the gutter. Lucy and Elliot." He rearranges me on his lap, lining himself up perfectly. It's just the right amount of friction.

"Mase," I warn.

"How. Long?" He draws out the words as if he knows what they are doing to me.

"I don't know." I try to form a coherent thought. Luce told

me she isn't interested. It's just a feeling I get with those two. "A year?"

"A year? Shit, I've got this in the bag." He grins. "So, if in one year nothing has happened between them..." He eyes me warily, unsure. "You have to marry me."

"What?" I go statue-still. "Have you lost your mind?"

"Completely." He leans in, kissing my neck.

"No."

"No?" He pulls away, putting distance between us.

"Absolutely not. Christ, I don't even think I want to get married, let alone within the next decade."

His eyes flick around my face, and then he swallows, his hands lingering on my thighs.

"Fuck," he sniggers. "I should set you up with fucking Montgomery." He lifts me and places me back in my seat, then turns to look out the window.

Is he sulking?

"Mase? Sorry, that came out wrong."

"It's fine. Forget I said anything."

"You're mad at me."

He looks back at me, his eyes softening some before his arm lifts for me to slip under. "No, not at you. Forget I said anything, okay?"

I slide into him, wrapping my arms around his waist. If he isn't mad at me, then who?

WE LANDED AN HOUR AGO, and if I wasn't sure before, I'm certain of it now.

Mason is sulking.

We pull up to the villa, and the girls bounce in the seat next to me in excitement. I should feel the same, and I do, but I'm also trying to figure out what to say to Mason to make him understand my reasons. Marriage isn't something I've allowed myself to think about before now. It came out of the blue, and I can't help my gut reaction. I mean, he sold my studio a little over a month ago. At this point in our relationship, marriage doesn't feel like the goal.

Trust. That's *my* goal.

The girls rush through the door and start squealing in excitement. I squint, shielding the sun from my eyes as I smile up at Mason. He has his arm thrown over my shoulder, and I push up onto my toes to give him a dusting kiss.

"Thank you," I tell him.

I leave him with the boys and follow the girls into the house.

The villa is breathtaking. It's set on a private island with only two other homes inhabiting it—one of them being the Montgomerys'. It sits on the edge of the cliff and looks out across the infinite ocean. It's like something from Lucy's Pinterest board, only real.

It's like a shack, but around fifty thousand times bigger and made up of wood and glass panels.

Lucy and Megan are standing in the living room I've just walked into. Their faces are just as awestruck as I imagine my own to be.

Wooden beams line the room, which opens up into a state-of-the-art kitchen. Megan takes my hand and pulls me away just as I head in that direction.

"Let's pick rooms!" she squeals.

"How many are there?" Lucy starts to count the doors as

we walk down the corridor and up the steps. This part of the house is set on two levels, and I spin, looking back down the hall where the ceiling opens up, letting the sun beam through four glass panels. This place is insane.

"Six," Scarlet states, walking up behind us from a different direction with the boys. "Some of us will have to share."

I try to look around her to see where they came from.

"You'll have to bunk with me, princess." Elliot throws his arm over Lucy's shoulder, but she shrugs him off.

"Uh, no." She looks offended, and I scoff at her. No sane women would kick Elliot Montgomery out of bed. "Megs, Scar? Looks like we are rearranging rooms," she tells them, arching a brow and giving them a look that says 'go the fuck along with it'.

"Add 'and drinking cocktails' and I'm down for whatever," Megan says, already in full relaxation mode.

"You got it, girl." Lucy winks.

"What's the plan?" Scar turns, looking at her brother to take charge. "Are we going out tonight or eating here?"

"We can eat here tonight. Get settled, dinner is at eight." His hand snakes around my waist, and I purse my lips as I look to Luce. "If you need anything. Any of you. Don't come knocking."

They all chuckle as he pulls me backwards and through a bedroom door.

"Ma—"

I squeal as he lifts me off my feet and chucks me onto the bed with ease. His top is pulled off over his head, and he is on me in a matter of seconds. "Don't speak," he tells me, hiking my legs up around his waist.

These moments with him are my favourite. We don't need words because they only complicate the easiness that's between us. The way we fit, it's perfect. But the words we utter sometimes have a way of bending the corners, making us jagged pieces of the same puzzle.

I want to iron out the creases and make them fit. I just don't want a marriage proposal, not yet, and maybe not a year from now either.

Mase

No.

That's what she told me. No.

Marriage isn't something I was interested in before Nina. It was never something I contemplated because I had never met someone who I wanted to share my life with.

Now I have, and she doesn't want it.

I've had women throw themselves at me, giving anything for a date. Yet the woman I want to give my world to doesn't want a part of it, or at least not yet.

She lies asleep in my arms, her head on my chest as her breath fans out over my heated skin. It's ten to eight, and I know I need to wake her. I just don't want to. Everything seems better with her locked tight in my arms.

"I'm coming in." The door rattles and then a thud. "Guys, come on!" Megan, I think, shouts from the other side of the door.

Nina jolts awake, looking up at me and then to the door. "Time is it?"

"Almost eight," I tell her, pushing a lock of hair behind her ear.

"Nina! You have my strappy sandals. I want my strappy sandals."

She grins up at me then slides from the bed. I watch as she walks naked around our room, her skin smooth and taut. She is fucking perfect. Dropping down to her knees, she unzips her suitcase, and I pull myself up the bed to watch her, grabbing a pillow and covering my semi.

She opens the door, and a hand reaches in to snatch the shoes. "Thank you. Filthy whore."

She slams the door and spins, leaning back against it with her eyes gently closed.

I love that she doesn't hide from me.

"I need to shower. Do I have time?" she asks.

"No. But I need a shower too, and guess what?"

She cocks her head to the side. "We are having a shower?"

"Come here."

"Nuh-huh." She holds up a finger as I rise to my knees. "We are showering, but separate."

"That's stupid," I protest, dropping the pillow.

"Is it? We know what will happen if we shower together." She eyes my growing length. "We will never make it to dinner."

"Well..." I launch the pillow at her. "Put some damn clothes on then." I stand, my erection only getting harder the more wound up I get.

"Walking around naked expecting me not to want it," I mutter under my breath as I stalk into the bathroom.

Leaning into the shower, I turn on the spray and wait for

it to warm up. She follows in behind me, sliding past and into the heat.

"You're such a child when you don't get your way, you know that?"

I step into her, taking her chin between my thumb and finger. "I always get my way." My free hand finds the back of her knee, and I lift it, wrapping it around my waist and sliding home in one deep thrust. "Always," I whisper against her lips.

She may have told me no, but the look in her eye tells me she knows.

She will marry me.

Even if I have to drag her down the aisle myself.

"Better late than never!" Elliot shouts as we walk across the decking hand in hand.

We cross the small path to the outside seating area. It's spread out on the patio, and the area is littered with lights that Scarlet insisted would set the mood.

Pulling out a chair, I nod for Nina to sit. "So polite, Mr Lowell. Shame you didn't remember your manners a half hour ago." She smirks and my cock twitches. That's the fourth time today. It's either the heat or there is something wrong with me.

I lean down and whisper into her ear. "Careful, Pix. You know what that smile gets you."

"It will fall off if you're not careful, Lowell," Lance shouts, making everyone laugh.

Silly prick isn't wrong; I've been hard on her today.

We settle in and devour our meal. The food is exquisite and I make a mental note to see Hank later this evening. He's been with us since me and Scar were small, and I haven't seen him since last year.

After our food, the girls start working their way through Lance's famous cocktails. They are all light on their feet and giggling loud before long, and I watch them—Nina specifically—as she looks at something on Megan's phone.

They have congregated around her and have their heads smashed together as they laugh at something on the screen.

"Give it back." Nina laughs, leaning in to take the phone.

Lucy grabs it. "Holy shit, Nina."

"Let me see." Scar giggles. "Wow, you look incredible," she tells Nina with wide eyes.

"Guys!" Nina blushes, and I frown.

I want what's on that phone.

I stand. "Pass it to me."

Megan looks at me as if I've grown two heads. "Fuck off, asshole." She laughs and carries on.

"Sit down, Lowell," Lance calls from the other side of the table, a smirk on his face.

"Nina." I jerk my head for her to come to me. She sticks her tongue in her cheek, holding the phone to her chest. "Come here."

She shakes her head, grinning wide. "You come here," she mouths.

I walk to her, needing to see what has caused her to blush. "I want to see," I tell her, stepping up in front of her.

She passes me the phone, and I look down at the screen. My chest constricts as I take in the image. She is breathtaking. It's a photo of her, the one she told me about. She is reaching for the camera, but it feels like she is reaching for me. Her dimple is gracing the side of her cheek, and her eyes are locked on the lens.

I look up at her, that same blush from before colouring her face.

"You're beautiful, angel. You know that, don't you?"

She looks past me at the boys behind. "Give me that." She snatches the phone from my hand as I take her into my arms.

"When do you get the photos?" I ask, knowing they are important to her.

"I was supposed to get them this week. I should probably call Joey."

"Well when you do, I will come with you. I'd like to buy some copies."

She beams at me, and I give her a soft wink.

I will do anything to keep that smile on her face. It will be my life's mission.

"Guys, group photo!" Scarlet calls, passing the camera to Lamona, who is one of our staff.

I lean in and give Nina a deep but short kiss, then pull her over to the group. We always have photos by the rocks. Normally as a family or me and the boys. I've not been out here with Scar for years, not since we were kids. I never asked if she wanted to get away, and I feel shitty for it.

Looking around at the friends we have now, the girls who both fit perfectly with us and include Scar like she has been a friend for life, and then Nina, who I never expected to bring here. She is the most unexpected—the way she makes me feel.

It's like this is how it always should have been.

"Get your hand off my ass, Elliot!" Lucy shouts, making us all chuckle.

"Not me," he says, lifting his hands.

The flash goes off, and the girls all complain. An array of complaints ranging from their eyes being closed, and they weren't ready. We try five more times before me, and the guys get fed up.

We leave it to the professionals and head for the beach.

———

Nina

WE SIT on the smooth sand watching Lance, Elliot, Charlie, and Mase play a variation of volleyball in the sea. I didn't know what to expect when it came to a holiday away with them all, but this wasn't it. It's chilled and relaxing, and I'm having the most amazing time.

"Mase told me he wants to marry me," I tell the girls.

"What?!" Lucy stammers.

All three of them whip their heads to me, completely speechless. "I told him that I thought you and Elliot would get it on, and he said that if nothing happens between the two of you by next year, then I had to marry him."

"Wow. Hit us with it bareback and no lube," Megan exclaims.

I giggle as I lean back on my elbows. They are all still watching me with a surprised look on their face. "I told him no."

"You did?" Scarlet says, sounding dejected.

"I'm not ready for marriage. I'm twenty-eight years old. I pictured myself being a lot older before all that, if at all."

"You haven't been together long, babe. Just think, this time next year you might feel completely different." Lucy shrugs. "It might be exactly what you want."

"Am I a bitch for telling him no?"

"Yes," Megan says at the same time Lucy and Scar say, "No."

"Helpful, girls, thanks."

"Sorry," Lucy mutters. "I think it's lovely that Mason is already so sure. He's a smart bloke." She gives me a wink.

"Hmm, maybe." I hum, silence falling over us as we lie back and watch the guys in the water.

"What's it been like at the house, Scar? You doing okay?" Megan asks.

She shrugs, not giving us her eyes and focusing on the horizon. "It's fine." She pauses. "It's a big old house for just me."

"I can imagine," I muse, hating the idea of her out at the house on her own.

"I won't ever leave, though. It's home, you know."

"I get it," Lucy tells her. "Mum and Dad could easily go out and buy a bigger, better house, but it's *home*. It's where they brought us up, and it's what they've made it now."

The way she says 'us' makes my chest warm.

"Yeah, exactly that." Scarlet smiles sadly, burying her feet deeper into the sand.

"Right, who's coming for a dip?" Megan jumps up, clearly trying to lighten the mood. Scarlet is rarely anything other than happy and excitable. It's hard to see her anything less than her vibrant self.

"Heck, yes!" she says, pulling her lavender hair up into a bun as she stands, then jogs off with Megan to the sea.

I sit with Lucy as we watch them in the water together.

"Easy view, huh?" She nudges my arm, smiling out at the gods before us. "I don't think I've ever seen four men so physically fit—playing with their balls out in the ocean. Didn't know I needed it." She waggles her brows at me.

"I'm just watching the sunset." I defend myself, and she giggles.

We fall quiet again as we watch Megan trying to climb onto Scarlet's shoulders. They stumble, almost making it, but then fall, splashing back into the water with a screech.

"I wasn't surprised, you know," Lucy mutters.

I turn my head and catch her frown, her eyes still on the water. "You think that you're a certain way. That you always leave."

"Well, I have run out on Mase at every opportunity so far," I remind her.

"And you always go back. Like how you'd come to mine when your mum was working. You'd have no trouble leaving, getting the space you needed because it was what felt right for *you*. But you always went back, willing and hopeful for it to be better when you got home." She looks at me, her lip turning up on one side. "It's why I knew you'd go back to him. You shouldn't feel bad about it. And you shouldn't let it hold you back. Marrying Mason Lowell would be..." I raise an arched brow at her. "Scary. Hot as hell, but petrifying. I mean, he isn't your typical husband." She laughs. "But you have to make shitty mistakes to learn. We both know that. And for the record, I don't think marriage would be a mistake. No matter what he did, you decided to put it in the past."

I haven't told the girls about the studio and why Mason sold it. They know he did and that Erin isn't who she says she is, but I agreed that no one else should be involved beyond that, and the girls never asked questions once I explained it was all I could say.

I run my fingers through the sand beneath me. "It's the trust thing. It will come in time I'm sure. Or I hope it will. But right now. it's not there—not fully."

"Because he sold the studio?" I look at her. "Because of the things that he kept from you, that you have to keep from me?"

"Exactly that." I chuckle.

"It will come, Nina. I think he's a really special guy. It's obvious he adores you."

I drop my head back and look up at the sky. Soft pink hues painting it a mesmerising shade as the night draws in. The air is warm, and I feel completely relaxed.

"Twenty-nine tomorrow, Luce." I grin, feeling her lie down next to me.

"Ugh, don't. I'm getting old."

"You are not old! You're in your prime. Embrace it."

"Remember when we were young, and twenty-eight-year-olds seemed so mature and put together."

"Uh-huh." I nod, reminiscing.

"Well, I don't feel like that. Put together or mature. In my head, I am twenty-one still. I consider going back to uni on the daily, yet I love my job. I can't hold down a relationship because what I want isn't real." She blows out a harsh breath. "I applied for an internship in New York."

"What? When?"

"Three months ago, I got it. They gave me four months to respond."

I sit up in a rush, turning to look down at her. "Luce! That's huge."

"I turned it down."

"What?!"

I see her throat bob as she swallows the lump there.

She regrets it.

"I didn't think I could do it on my own. I'm twenty-nine tomorrow," she sniggers. "and I don't feel independent. I don't feel like I'm my own person."

"What makes you think you aren't independent? You're one of the most grounded people I know, Luce."

She shrugs, looking for the right words. "I guess it's me holding myself back, and I feel like I should be loyal to Jean. I don't know what she'd do without me."

"The fact you worry about being loyal says everything about your loyalty. Jean wouldn't let you stay if she knew. You know that."

"I know, which is why it's a rubbish excuse."

"You don't want to go," I state.

She shrugs, smiling softly. "My gut told me no."

"Then you did the right thing," I affirm. "Don't ever think you need to be more than you are right now, Luce. You may be feeling a little lost, but I know exactly who you are. So do you, deep down."

"Thanks, Nina."

"Always." I stand and take her hands, urging her to get up. "And don't worry, there's always Botox."

"Piss off, you cheeky bitch." She laughs, standing and slipping her arm in mine as we head for the shoreline.

IT'S LATE AFTERNOON, and the girls are all holed up in Mason's and my room. The boys are sat below us on the patio, their chatter drifting up and into the room.

We have been here for four days and have to go home soon, and I don't want to leave. Mason is happy here, and I mean really happy, which is remarkable given what he and Scar have endured recently.

I wish we could hide away here forever.

Me and my Mase. The happy version, where there isn't work and money and responsibility.

I pull open the shower door and frown. Megan is in the bathroom pulling on a floral two-piece.

"I'm pretty sure that's mine," I tell her.

"But look how good it looks on me." She pouts.

"I know, it's super cute. That's why I bought it." I smile, checking her out as I slip on my underwear. "It does wonders for your tits mind."

"Right!" She sulks as she starts taking it off. Lucy and Scarlet are already dressed and are lying on the bed, looking at something on Lucy's phone. I drop my towel and start to dress.

I can feel Megan watching me as I pull on the shorts. "Fuck off. It's my outfit; get your own." I chuckle.

"I wasn't looking at that." She nods to my stomach and frowns.

I look down, running my hand across my belly defensively. "What?"

"Turn to the side."

I spin and look down in the mirror, noticing Lucy and

Scarlet's eyes now on me also. "I'm really bloated," I say in annoyance, slumping my shoulders and pulling the shorts higher over my hips. "I'm due on, I think."

"That's quite the bloat."

"Alright! I haven't been dancing as much. I'm back to it now, though. It won't take long to lose the few pounds I've put on."

"Oh, please! You look phenomenal. That's not what I meant, silly." Megan tries to assure me, but I feel crappy. "You have... a... a little... bump." Her brows shoot up as she says it.

"Nina?" Lucy questions.

"I'm due on, and I'm bloated. Stop being a dick, Megs!" I tut. "I'm on the pill."

"Nobody actually said that word," Megan says.

"But you implied. With your judgey eyes." I glare, pulling the top over my head.

"Nina." Megan steps up to me. She isn't a serious person, but the look she gives me fills me with worry, and my gut twists. "Babe, it doesn't look like bloat. I'm not being mean. When are you due on?"

Panic fills me as I run my hand over my stomach, trying to think.

Fuck, when am I due on?

"I can't think."

"Don't panic," Lucy coos, jumping up from the bed and coming to me.

"Do you track your periods?" Scarlet asks.

"Yes, always." I run my hand through my hair and notice I'm shaking.

I'm on the pill. This is ridiculous. I've not been dancing, and they are working me up over nothing. I've been in a bikini the whole holiday, if it were anything other than bloat they would have noticed before. I would have noticed.

"Where is your phone?" Lucy starts moving around the room in search of it.

I rack my brain, thinking back to the last time I had a period.

And then it comes to me. "The day I crashed Mase's car. I came on that night. He almost called an ambulance."

"When was that?" Megan snaps.

I stare at her. "I don't know." Fuck! "I can't think."

Lucy takes my hand, her face panicked. "Nina, are you pregnant?"

34

Nina

"KEEP YOUR FUCKING VOICE DOWN!" I HISS, MOVING TO THE double doors and pulling them closed. I do not need the boys hearing this. "Scarlet, when was the accident?"

"Must have been a good couple months ago? I think," she tells me, and my body heats instantly, a cold sweat breaking out across my skin.

"Fucking hell." Lucy fans her face, her eyes wild.

"Calm down. I'm not fucking pregnant." My eyes flick between them all, my stomach in knots. "Cocktails. I need a cocktail. You're all a bunch of drama queens."

I move to the bathroom and close the door. Needing the space from them. I'm not easily influenced, but the way the girls were looking at me has panic clawing its way up my chest.

I look in the mirror and eye the slight swell that sits below my belly button.

Lowering my hand, I stretch the skin, noticing how the

bulge only protrudes farther.

I'm due on. I know I am. And I always bloat. That with the bread we had last night and all the alcohol, it's given me bad bloat.

The door knocks open against my back, and I move to let the girls in. None of them say a word, and their silence pisses me off more than their probing.

Lucy pulls back my hair and starts braiding it while Megan drops sandals at my feet. Scarlet follows their lead, blotting at my cheeks before covering my face with a ton of makeup.

I hadn't realised I was crying.

Mase

NINA HAS BEEN quiet all night, and I don't know why. I just know something is wrong.

Maybe it's because I brought up marriage. I know it was too soon, but she has seemed okay since I told her not to worry about it.

It's something else.

Everyone has gone to bed, but I'm still up, sitting on the terrace and watching as the waves crash against the rocks in the distance. It's been an incredible week with everyone, but I know I have things to deal with when I get home. Dad didn't get around to managing his affairs, and if we don't handle it right, then the properties he owned could end up in the wrong hands.

We need to be smart.

I just don't want to deal with it yet. With any of it.

"Mase?" Scarlet's soft voice pulls me from my thoughts as she drops to the seat next to me. "Can't sleep?" I ask.

She shakes her head, and I pull her into my side. We used to do this when we were young. Only Mum and Dad would be cuddled up on the other sofa.

"Do you think about them?" she asks after a while, so quietly I almost don't catch it.

"All the time," I tell her honestly.

"Me too. I like being here. We should've come out together sooner."

"I know, and I'm sorry, Scar," I say against her head. "I've been shit, and it isn't fair on you."

"Everyone deals with grief differently, Mason. It's how you move forward that will show me you're not a complete ass."

My chest vibrates with a light chuckle.

"There is something I need to tell you," she says, leaning her head back against my arm so she can see my face. "I spoke to Dad's doctor at the house that day."

My heart jolts in my chest. How can she talk about it so frankly?

Why is my baby sister stronger than I am?

"He never received any treatment offered."

"What?" I snap, my face screwing up as I look down at her. "What do you mean?"

"He rejected the option of having a transplant. He didn't think he deserved one."

"He knew he was going to die?"

"Yeah, maybe not as soon as he did. But Dr Sarnmer told me he was aware the end was near. Nearer than *we* thought anyway."

"Why didn't he tell us? Tell you?"

He wouldn't have told me. He probably thought I didn't care.

"Because he knew we would never have allowed it."

"Fucking hell."

"Sorry, I just thought you should know," she whispers.

I wish I didn't. He spent months at the house knowing he would die and didn't do a thing about it.

"He met Nina." She smiles. "I know having you come to the house was important to him. He saw the shift, Mason."

"Yeah."

She smiles up at me knowingly, and I glare back, unsure of what is about to leave her mouth. "Nina told me about the proposal."

"It wasn't a proposal!" I drop my head back. Why did I ever say that? I should have kept my mouth closed.

She laughs. "She isn't as freaked out as you think. She just wasn't expecting it."

I shake my head, thinking about my stubborn Pixie. She drives me crazy in the best possible way.

"She's special. You did good," Scarlet tells me.

"I only mentioned it because I felt like I could see it. You know, marriage, kids, a place out of the city. I know how desperately she craves a home—something more than she had."

"Kids? Did you just say kids?"

"Not yet." I shake my head, smiling. "But in the future, with Nina? Absolutely."

"Interesting."

"Yeah." Real fucking interesting since she point blank told me no.

Nina

THE LAST FEW days have passed in a blur. The girls haven't mentioned what happened, and I'm grateful. I've still not had my period, and although I've tried to bury my head in the sand about it, my conscience has been working overtime.

I've barely drunk, and I have faked two migraines to get out of the evening drinking sessions. No one suspected a thing, and I didn't make a big deal out of it, but the girls know me. They can tell I'm rattled.

It's our final day on the island, and we are supposed to be going out for the day. The boys told us to be ready for ten a.m. but wouldn't tell us what we are doing.

Slinging my towel over my shoulder, I leave our room and go in search of the girls. Mase was already up and gone when I woke this morning.

I have no idea what they have planned, but the secrecy is exciting. Lucy thinks it's a boat trip around the island, and I hope she is right.

The girls are already out on the patio when I round the corner, and it's the first time I've gotten the chance to have them all alone without prying ears, so I use it to my advantage.

"Hey!" I step up to them. "When we get home, we need to meet up. I'm going to buy a test. Put my mind at ease." I say nonchalantly, pulling my hair into a high pony.

I can see the surprised looks on their faces, but none of them question me.

Lucy finds her tongue first. "We will come to you. Maybe

before Mase finishes work one day?"

"He has a stag do on Saturday night, Elliot's friend. You can come over then."

"Good idea. I'll bring wine." Megan winks, trying to lighten the mood.

"I can't wait that long." Lucy panics.

"Well I'm not doing it when he is around!" I hiss.

"When who is around?" Mason's arms wrap around my stomach, pulling me back into his hard chest.

I twist and look up at him, plastering a fake smile on my face.

"Hey, you." I relax into him, the warmth of his large body soothing my inner turmoil.

He gives me a look, and I know he is up to something. "You girls ready for today?"

"What exactly are we doing?" I ask, nerves fluttering in my stomach.

"No fucking way."

Lucy stands on the edge of the clifftop, her eyes wild as they flick towards the boys as if they have gone mad.

As much as I find her dramatics funny, I can't help but agree with her. There is no way I am jumping off the edge of this thing.

"God, it's been years. It never seemed so high as a child." Scarlet smiles, chucking her towel to the side and rocking on her heels.

"You've done this before?" I ask her, just as she steps up to the ledge.

"Yeah! Come on." She steps forward, and I hold my breath, watching as she jumps off and falls to the water.

"Yes, Scar!" Elliot yells.

The boys all shout and holla, Charlie and Lance taking a run-up and following Scarlet's lead.

"No fucking way," Lucy snorts, moving three steps back.

"I'm game." Megan smiles, hands on hips as she bounces with excitement.

Elliot steps up next to her and points to the water. "Make sure you step out far enough to avoid the rocks. We checked it this morning, and it's plenty deep enough. Aim for the others, and you'll be fine."

"Megs!" Lucy warns, panic in her voice.

"Shut up, princess," Elliot tells her. "You're next."

Megan steps up to the edge, her hands curled into fists. Looking back at us, she screams. "Shit! Fucker! Fuck! Ahhhh."

We all laugh as she lurches forward and jumps off. I count to five in my head before she hits the water.

It's *so* high up.

"Coming, baby?" Mason takes my waist and pulls me to him.

He knows I'm nervous. Should I jump? What if...

"Nina, I don't think you should be doing that. This is so dangerous." Lucy stands and moves to the edge. "Jesus, it makes me feel sick just looking that far—" Elliot's hand shoots out, pushing her from the edge. She screams, her arms and legs flailing ungracefully as she flies through the air.

He turns, grinning at us then dives in after her.

"Motherfucker!" Lucy shouts as she surfaces.

She starts to splash water at Elliot, but he only laughs

524 | JC HAWKE

harder than he already was as he tries to grasp her wrists.

"Your turn," Mase whispers into my neck, his hands braced on my back.

Bollocks. How am I going to do this?

Is there a safe way to jump off a cliff when you know you're not pregnant, but you might be?

"I've got you," he tells me, probably sensing my hesitation.

Lifting me, he wraps my legs around his waist, locking them together behind his back.

"No frolicking on the rocks, thank you," Lance shouts in a stupid voice.

I smile down at them all as they look up at us. Lucy looks pissed as hell, and it makes me chuckle.

"Ready?" I can feel Mason's muscles tense as he steps up to the edge. His shoulders are strained from my weight, his muscles popping in all the right places.

"No. But do it anyway." I screw up my face and hide my head in his chest. He turns, putting his back to the sea, and then we are free-falling. I hear the slap on his back, and then I am submerged in cold water.

The temperature shocks me, and I fight to reach the surface.

Mason grabs onto me, and I cling to him, wrapping myself around him like a koala. "Oh my god! That was incredible!"

He beams at me with his megawatt smile, and it's the most honest smile I've seen from him in weeks.

I lean in to kiss him, grinning back against his lips.

"What?" he asks in wonder.

"Seeing you happy makes me happy," I tell him, not being

able to take my eyes off him.

He shakes his head, fanning his hair across his face and spraying me with the water droplets and making me giggle.

"I am so fucking happy, angel."

I'M SITTING on my suitcase trying to get it closed when my phone starts ringing. Looking over at the screen I see that it's my mum. She hasn't called in weeks, and I can imagine the only reason she is calling now is for more money.

A smart person wouldn't answer. I ignored it last time, and she eventually gave up, but in the time that she didn't call, I found myself a little lost. It was as if she had given up. I'm not sure what on exactly because she only ever called for more money, but it hurt nonetheless. She is my mum, so to see her name flash on the screen now—even if it is for more money—it has hope blooming in my chest.

"Hi, Mum."

"Nina. I haven't heard from you in so long."

My shoulders sag, and I slide from the bed. I never call her. My crappy childhood is on her—she wasn't there for me, but maybe the way we treat each other now that I'm older is on me too. It's a two-way street and right now it's a ghost town.

"Yeah, I have been busy. I have had issues with the studio."

"Oh, but you are still managing?" she queries.

Do you actually care, though, Mum? "Yeah. Maggie and John have covered a couple of bills this month, and the bank gave me a payment holiday on my loan."

"I see. Well, I was calling 'cause I'm a little short this month—" I close my eyes and zone out.

She doesn't give a crap. I don't know why I expect anything more from her.

"I'm sure you or your new man can help me out," she sniggers.

What did she just say? "Excuse me?"

"I heard you have a rich new boyfriend."

"From who?"

"Can you help me or not?" She sounds so uninterested, bored and calm, too calm.

She sounds high.

I see red.

"Sure, Mum, I will just wire across a couple grand from Mason's account. He won't even notice," I say deadpan, ending the call and tossing my phone.

Why can't she just be a mother? She doesn't even have to be a really good one. But right now, she isn't a bad mum. She is nonexistent. I look down at my stomach as bile rises in my throat.

Oh god.

I rub my hands down my face as I try to calm myself. I could yell at her until I am blue in the face, but it's just not worth it.

Dropping my hands, I see Lance standing in the doorway, his brows pulled in as he hangs off the frame. "We are leaving in half an hour. Lowell is looking for you."

"Yeah, I will be down in a minute," I tell him, composing myself and returning to my suitcase. I don't want Lance to see my hurt. I need the girls. Or my Mase.

35

Nina

I'M IN THE KITCHEN WASHING UP WHEN THE GIRLS ARRIVE. THEY are later than I expected, and because of that, I've not been able to stop pottering around the penthouse—the need to get the test over and done with too much.

Mason texted me half an hour ago to check in, but I didn't reply. He is out on a stag do and I don't want to lie to him. He has had enough trauma this year. He doesn't need to know that I am stressing over this.

Especially when I don't know what *this* is.

"Sorry we are late," Lucy sings as she dumps the bags of shopping on the counter. "We stopped in at Tesco's, but I knew the cashier so I had to bail and go to the pharmacy instead."

"What's all this?" I open the bags she placed on the counter.

They are filled with junk.

"The stuff from Tesco's. I couldn't just buy a test, and I

528 | JC HAWKE

wedged it in the magazines when I spotted Annie on the checkout and just brought this. She totally knew I was being sketchy."

"For goodness' sake. Only you." I smile, shaking my head at her.

"We got the test. Four actually," Megan tells me as she walks into the kitchen.

"Four?"

"We read up on false negatives and faulty pee."

"Faulty pee? That's not a thing." I laugh out loud awkwardly, and they both turn to look at me.

"Well, no, I'm sure it's not, but time of day and shit," Megan says with a shrug. "It's something to do with your hormones."

"Right. Give it here." I hold my hand out.

"You're going to do it now?" Lucy asks.

"Yeah, pass it over. I want to get this over with, then sink a bottle of wine."

I take the test Megan holds out to me and walk into the lounge and towards the stairs. I pause when I spot Scarlet sitting on the sofa.

"Scar? You okay?"

She spins, her phone clutched tight in her hand. "Uh, yeah. Sorry, just on the phone."

I cringe. "Sorry!"

Spinning on my heel, I leave her to it and head for the bedroom with all four of my tests, hoping that I don't have 'faulty pee'.

Mase

THE NIGHT HAS GONE AS EXPECTED. It's trashy. Top shelf trashy, but still trashy. The music is blaring, the club alive with the thrumming atmosphere.

Greg has his arm thrown around a blonde as he sips his scotch, a cigar in his hand. He is a great bloke—as a friend. But I can't help but feel sorry for his soon-to-be wife.

Pulling out my phone, I check my screen for the one hundredth time, noticing that Nina still hasn't replied to my message. I know she is with the girls, so I don't worry, but I hope she isn't ignoring me because she's pissed I'm not home yet. She doesn't seem like that kind of girl, but I did say I wouldn't be late.

"Hey, my man," I greet Charlie as he approaches me.

"You good?" he asks, not waiting for an answer before he says. "Greg's a piece of shit."

I take a swig of my drink, smiling at him over my glass. "I have some things I need clearing up with Dad's properties. Can you carve out some time?" I turn and rest my arm on the bar.

"Course. Send me the dates, and Kelsey will sort it."

"Thanks mate. You all good now?" I ask, referring to everything that unfolded before the holiday.

"Yeah," he answers quickly, dropping his head. "I think it needed to come to a head. I've been..."

"Fucking hard work." I knock his shoulder with my own.

"Prick." He laughs.

Charlie hasn't been hard work at all, but his inability to sleep with a woman unless he is in an established relation-ship? That's new. He changed his ways after Phoebe died, and

I think it has a lot to do with the reasons behind that. Specifically, consent. It made him softer, more aware, and sensitive. It's a tough pill for him to swallow, being the notorious hard-faced lawyer he is.

"Honestly, though, thank you. I can never repay you for what you did for me, for Phoebe."

"You don't need to. Prick got what he deserved."

He nods his head, smiling. "You think El will ever change?" I follow his line of sight to Elliot, who has a curvy brunette writhing on his lap.

It's been a while for him, and I know he will go hard tonight.

"Nope." I laugh, turning back to the bar.

"You have, though. You and Nina seem pretty serious."

A wide smile breaks out across my face, and I do nothing to hide it. "It happened fast. And fucking hard." I smirk. "But we've been through so much already. I suppose we just always snap back to one another when shit hits the fan. I'm fucking obsessed, Charles."

He chuckles, clapping me on the back. "So romantic, mate."

"You know it." I wink, lifting my hand and ordering another round of drinks.

Nina

Is there a protocol for how I should be feeling?

A wife would be excited, right? She would be elated that she even needs to do a test. But the girlfriend? How is she supposed to feel as she pees on the little white stick?

They don't put that on the box.

I feel stupid for feeling the way I do. A small ball of energy in my gut rears its head and tells me everything will be okay, and we have got this.

The wife in me, the woman I want to be in ten years, once I have achieved my dreams, she is excited. But the girlfriend who will be seen as a money-hungry whore to anyone who doesn't know me, she is shitting it. She wants to run and not do a test at all.

Taking all four tests, I put them into the packet and wash my shaking hands. I go to the landing and take a deep breath before taking the stairs one step at a time.

"We have to wait for Meg. Our takeout is here." Lucy bounces on her toes, her excitement evident.

"Calm down, you're stressing me out."

I wipe my forehead, feeling hot.

This is torture. I need the alarm to sound. I won't be able to wait for Meg.

"Come sit down, Nina." Scarlet smiles warmly.

"I can't." I fiddle with the end of the white stick, flip it over in the packet.

I don't look, but I know if I pull it out, I will see the result.

My heart starts to pound, and my chest grows warm. Adrenaline is pumping through me.

I try to control my breathing. "Shit!"

"Stop panicking." Lucy catches hold of my wrist and squeezes it tight.

I nod my head and close my eyes, counting to ten.

One, two, three, four, five, six—

The elevator doors ping. Meg steps out, the takeout in one hand and an envelope in the other.

"Hurry up, will you!" Lucy hisses, letting my arm go.

"Sorry, there was this with the food at reception."

She starts to pull open the envelope, and my timer chimes. I swallow thickly and pull out the test, looking down at the two lines that sit perfectly clear in the small square box.

"Oh my god," Megan and I say in disbelief.

"No way!" Lucy jumps up and takes the test. "Fuck. Yes! Nina, oh my god, you're pregnant!" She covers her face with her hands.

My gaze is fixed on Megan, though. Her face is pale, and her hands shake, the envelope clutched tight in her hand, and our takeout is spilling out of the bag at her feet.

I wonder when she dropped it. I never noticed.

"Megs?"

"I... I don't know what to say."

I step down from the last stair and walk to her, the test momentarily forgotten. "What's the matter?"

"Nina, I'm so sorry."

Reaching out, I take the glossy pieces of card from her, flipping them so I can see.

What I'm met with destroys me. My legs give out from under me, and I feel Megan reach for me, trying to take my weight, but I collapse to the floor despite her hold on me.

Please, no.

"Nina? Oh god, Nina?!" I hear Lucy shout. "What is it? Nina? Megs, she is pregnant."

"Scarlet, call an ambulance," Megan calls out.

"Nina?" I can hear their cries. I can feel tears on my face. But inside, I feel nothing.

Mase

MY HEAD SPINS, the room flashing.

My head feels foggy, heavy.

Fuck, I don't feel right.

"Mason."

My head connects with something hard, liquid rolling down my temple.

What's wrong with my hands?

A rush of cold surges through my chest and spreads through my torso.

"I don't fucking feel right."

Darkness takes me.

36

——————

Nina

I'M FOUR MONTHS PREGNANT.

Four months.

I stare at the image in my hand, stare at the perfect life that is preparing itself for what? A perfect mother? A family? This isn't how I wanted it to go.

The nurse told me the bleeding I experienced after the crash was most likely from the trauma and stress of the accident, but assured me the baby is healthy and that there was no need to be concerned.

Guilt fills me. The guilt that I missed it. The guilt for what I have put my body through these past few months. And the guilt to the life that I now have to guide when I have no clear path for us to go down.

The nurse told me they want to monitor me for the next forty-eight hours after I fainted, but I don't want to leave. If I leave, I have to go to Lucy and Megan's, and they are already fussing. Lucy is asleep in the corner, refusing to leave my side for a second, and I know the rest of them are in the corridor. I heard Elliot's voice booming in the early hours, demanding he be let in. They eventually settled down, but it didn't matter anyway because I haven't slept a wink.

Mason isn't here.

He hasn't been here all night.

I hear a loud bang and then shouting outside the door, and I look across at Lucy as I jump but she doesn't flinch. I close my eyes.

I don't want to see him.

Gripping the sheet spread over me, I pull it tight, my throat burning as I prepare myself.

How do I do this?

The door flies open, and he falls through the door, the nurse and Megan at his back. "Nina."

"You cannot be in here; she needs to rest," the nurse tells him sternly.

I catch his frown, but as he brings his eyes back to me, I dip my head. It hurts too much to look at him.

He doesn't deserve anything from me, but he needs to know about the baby. It's not my reality to withhold.

"He can stay," I tell the nurse, surprising myself when my voice doesn't waver.

The nurse moves toward me, checking my blood pressure.

Lucy stirs, lifting her head from her shoulder. She sits up and spots Mason. Her posture stiffens. "You!" She is on her feet and over to him before I can speak. Her hand connects with his cheek with a solid whack.

"What the fuck!" he roars.

"Out! All of you. How dare you," the nurse scolds, authority lacing her tone, but still she keeps a levelled voice.

"You will never! Never! Hurt her again," Lucy grinds out, wiping her tears and stepping in front of me.

"What the hell is going on?" he spits, trying to look past Lucy.

I have to face him. Tell him I'm pregnant. I have to.

"Can you give us a minute? I promise I will keep calm," I tell the nurse and nod at Lucy.

She dips her head to the side, her eyes shining.

"You have a minute," the nurse tells Mason. "If I can hear you from out there, you are out. The lot of you. Never in my forty-four years have I seen anything like it!"

She leaves the room, and Lucy follows her, shutting the door slowly behind her.

Mason rushes me. "What happened? Scar wouldn't tell me, she said she couldn't." He goes to grasp my hand, but I pull it away. "Baby, I'm sorry. I woke up in a hotel. I cut my head. I think I fell. I don't know what happened last night."

I pull the photos from under me, placing them between us. Not being able to look at him, I turn my head to look out the window.

My teeth are clenched so hard they hurt, and it does nothing to hold back the pain that threatens to bring me down.

"You're pregnant?" he asks. "I... fuck. I'm the dad? We are pregnant?"

The ache in my heart becomes too much, and the first tear rolls down my face.

"No, I am pregnant. And of course, it's yours." My voice cracks as I utter the words.

I need to keep calm. I have to.

"Oh my god." I can hear the smile in his voice. "And you're okay?" He takes my hand again, and I pull away. "The baby?"

"Healthy."

Leaning over, I pull my bag from the end of the bed, reaching in and pulling out the envelope. I thrust the images into his chest. "Here. Congratulations."

My chest starts to rise and fall as he stands motionless at my bedside, the photos held tight in his hands as he observes them.

"What? I don't understand. This isn't me."

"Don't!" I scream, making him jump. "Don't you fucking dare lie to me!"

"I'm not. Nina, this isn't me."

"Get out," I say, deathly quiet.

His face hardens, panic flaring in his eyes. "No!"

"Get out! Get out of my life and stay the hell away from me. I hate you! I hate you so much it hurts because you have me now, you have me trapped for life, and I can't leave. I hate you, Mason Lowell, with everything inside me."

"Don't say that. Let me fix this. This isn't real." He screws up the picture in his hand.

"Yes, it fucking is, Mason! It's real. She is real. That *is* you."

"I don't understand. Give me a chance to figure this out, and I can explain."

"Explain what? How you fucked a prostitute? Because if the picture wasn't clear enough, the fact you never came home last night is explanation enough. Done! I am done!" I yell, my tears falling uncontrollably. "A stripper? You might as well have fucked my mother."

"No, I didn't sleep with anyone. I woke alone." He tries to

hold me, but I shove him off. "Stop! Please, I don't want to upset you. Nina. You can't leave me again."

I lift my eyes to his face as his voice wavers. Tears stream down his face, dried blood lining his forehead and cheek, mingling with his tears.

He looks utterly broken.

"Nina, we are having a baby. Let me figure this out," he pleads.

"No." I hold his eyes, defiant, with tears spilling down my cheeks and matching his. "Believe me when I tell you, this is it. I can't do this anymore." I look away from him, tearing off the last two scan photos and pushing them into his chest. "Get out."

"I didn't do this. I didn't do anything."

"Leave!" A sob breaks through and my body quakes.

"Walk away from me now, Nina, without giving me a chance to explain, and I won't ever forgive you for it. I won't keep begging on my knees to keep you." His voice is laced with anger, and I believe his every word.

For the first time in our relationship, his words hold the conviction they should.

"You think this is me leaving you? You ended this." I gesture between us, wiping at my tears. "The minute her lips touched yours. Now, leave. Please, just go."

"That's it. We're done?" He wipes his face and looks down at the scan photo in his hand.

"Yes."

His chest visibly shakes as more tears fall down his face.

I can't bear to look at him.

His lips meet my forehead, and I don't move. I don't breathe.

"You were everything I wanted and more. I promise you were enough."

My tears fall heavy as the other half of my soul walks out of the hospital room, and it hurts more than anything ever has before because I know I won't ever let him in again.

To be continued...

GRAND LIES CONTINUES IN...

GRAND LOVE

Pre Order Now!
https://amzn.to/3zarlFk

AFTERWORD

Thank you so much for reading my debut novel.
If you enjoyed Grand Lies, please consider leaving a review
on Amazon!

Want to be notified about future book releases of mine?
Sign up to my Newsletter via my website
www.jchawkeauthor.com

Come join my Facebook reader group for a first look at sneak
peeks and teasers. This is a PRIVATE group and only people
in the group can see posts and comments!
Hawkes Hangout - JC Hawke's Reader Group

ACKNOWLEDGEMENTS

To my betas, D, Jo, Lindsay, Annie, Lauren & Jessica. Thank you all so much for your time and love for these characters. D, Jo, Lindsay & Annie, you have been with me since day one and I couldn't have written this book without your constant cheerleading. Know that you are never allowed to leave me.

To The Fourway, my team! I probably ask more questions than any of us and I'm only ever met with love, eyerolls, and a wealth of knowledge. Katie you are next level wonderful *salute* Really, though, thank you. For being supportive, bad ass, and inspiring every day. I appreciate you all.

To my sisters, Gem, Rach, and Dani. My safety blanket. I couldn't do this without you. Simple. The fear that you squash daily, and the confidence that you instil in me as you place me on a pedestal knows no bounds. What we have is different and special and I know we are incredibly lucky. There's no one else I'd want to discuss book boyfriends, or dance on tabletops with. I love you all.

To Mum and Dad, thank you for raising me to be the anxious introvert I am today. Somehow it led me here. Seriously though, thank you. For everything. I'd be truly lost without you.

To Shelley, thank you for always pushing me to be better, for loving Nina and Mason as much as I do, and for rooting for me in not just my achievements but failures too. You've been there through it all and I couldn't be without you.

To my Jessica Jones, I've said it once and I'll say it again. If I never sell a single copy of this book, it would be okay. Why? Because I met you. I never knew I needed your friendship, but you seemed to show up in my life at a time I needed you the most. You're so much more than just my friend. You know it all—the good, the bad, and the ugly, and you still believe in me every day. Your friendship is invaluable, and I hope you know how grateful I am to have you as my soulsie! Thank you. Thank you. Thank you. For chasing Rhiannon. For teaching me to be better. For your friendship. I could go on, but I'd be here all day and you're currently pinging off in my DM's being all needy. There's no one else I'd want to author with.

To Chalk, well... I should probably start with an apology. I know I got a little lost along the way, with late nights, early mornings, and day sessions that seemed to steal our weekends. But I did it! I did it, babe. And it wouldn't have happened without your constant support and love for my craziness.

Three years ago, you bought me a pad and pen for Christmas, and I frowned up at you wondering why. You told me it was to write my book.
Somehow, you knew. Long before I did.
Thank you. I love you.

To my girls. You won't get to read this for a little while, but I want you to know that—today, tomorrow, and forever—I am proud of you. Your love for life and everything in it inspires me every day.

And of course, YOU, my reader. Thank you for reading Nina and Mase. It means the world to me that you've picked up my story out of millions of others. You make this possible for me and I am forever indebted to you.

Stay wonderful xo

ABOUT THE AUTHOR

JC Hawke is an author of contemporary romance. She lives in the South-West of the United Kingdom with her husband, two curly haired daughters, and beagle woofer.

CPSIA information can be obtained
at www.ICGtesting.com
Printed in the USA
BVHW031035071121
621014BV00012B/53